## PRAISE FOR *IN THE CARDS*

"Infused with . . . fresh detail. Between the sweetness of the relationship and the summery beach setting, romance fans will find this a warming winter read."

—*Publishers Weekly*

"Fans will love the frank honesty of her characters. [Beck's] scenery is richly detailed and the story engaging."

—*RT Book Reviews*

"[A] realistic and heartwarming story of redemption and love . . . Beck's understanding of interpersonal relationships and her flawless prose make for a believable romance and an entertaining read."

—*Booklist*

## PRAISE FOR *WORTH THE WAIT*

"[A] poignant and heartwarming story of young love and redemption and will literally make your heart ache . . . Jamie Beck has a real talent for making the reader feel the sorrow, regret, and yearning of this young character."

—*Fresh Fiction*

## PRAISE FOR *WORTH THE TROUBLE*

"Beck takes readers on a journey of self-reinvention and risky investments, in love and in life . . . With strong family ties, loyalty, playful banter, and sexual tension, Beck has crafted a beautiful second-chances story."

—Starred review, *Publishers Weekly*

# Worth
## *the* Risk

# ALSO BY JAMIE BECK

*In the Cards*

## The St. James Novels

*Worth the Wait*

*Worth the Trouble*

## The Sterling Canyon Novels

*Accidentally Hers*

*Secretly Hers*

# Worth
## *the* Risk

A St. James Novel

# Jamie Beck

Montlake
Romance

Published by Montlake Romance, Seattle

www.apub.com

Amazon, the Amazon logo, and Montlake Romance are trademarks of Amazon.com, Inc., or its affiliates.

ISBN-13: 9781503938816

ISBN-10: 1503938816

Cover design by Eileen Carey

Printed in the United States of America

*For Christie.*
*Thank you for a lifetime of friendship and love, and for the endless hours you've spent talking with me about my stories. I finally forgive you for leaving me to find my own way home after my first day of kindergarten at a new school.*

# CHAPTER ONE

Jackson St. James hadn't prayed for anything since he'd sprinkled dirt on his mother's casket almost three years ago. At that moment, he'd decided God didn't give a shit about him or his prayers. Everything that had happened to him since then had only confirmed his hunch. But just now, when another crack of thunder shook his SUV, he considered sending up a Hail Mary.

A coal-colored sky spewed torrential rain onto the mountain road winding its way toward Winhall, Vermont. Autumnal leaves blew about, pasting themselves on his windshield. Trees bowed—bent to the point of breaking—as they fought to hold their ground while straining against unrelenting winds. Only their deep roots kept them from toppling.

A superstitious person might take the weather as a sign of an ill-conceived journey and reconsider. Fortunately, Jackson wasn't superstitious. And while he didn't much appreciate God's twisted sense of humor today, he wouldn't give him the satisfaction of that Hail Mary, either.

Irritated by the satellite radio cutting out for the umpteenth time in twenty minutes, Jackson punched it off. Only the rapid thumping of his wipers—sounding oddly like a sturdy heartbeat—offered a distraction from his gloomy thoughts.

If the berm of the road were wider, he'd pull over and wait out the heaviest part of the storm. Instead, he flicked on his hazard lights, eased up his speed, and squinted at the few feet of centerline still visible.

He hugged close to those double yellows—the lifeline leading him through the dark to safety. Had he not been so far to the left of his lane, he'd have crashed into the idiot who not only failed to park a massive Chevy pickup truck away from the road's edge, but who also leapt out and ran to its rear.

Was help needed?

For a split second, Jackson thought to keep going. He had his own problems to sort out, after all.

Of course his conscience kicked in, reminding him that he'd never ignored a person in need, not even a stranger. Apparently not even a stupid one who just might get them both killed.

He steered his Jeep as far to the right side of the shoulder as possible while avoiding the drop-off to the river on its other side. Twisting to the right, he considered reaching for his umbrella. Then the howling wind shifted and rain began to pummel the car sideways. Cursing, he left the umbrella under the passenger seat and stepped out of his car.

Within three seconds, his clothes were as soaked through as if he'd been tossed into the swollen river ten yards away.

Muttering to himself, he jogged back to where the pickup remained precariously parked, trying to ignore the way his jeans had transformed into some kind of Chinese finger trap, tightening with each step.

Just then a small figure circled around from behind the truck bed. A woman—a young woman—stopped in her tracks, wide-eyed, teeth chattering. "Oh!"

Like him, her soggy clothes dripped. Long brown hair adhered to her cheeks, neck, and shoulders. Raindrops bounced off the thick lashes framing her impossibly round, pale eyes.

Unlike him, however, she didn't look particularly miserable. In fact, she looked kind of cute in her oversize barn coat, with the skirt of her multicolored, floral-print dress clinging to her legs, which were slim and long despite her short stature. Like a rookie schoolboy with a first crush, he felt a grin tug at the corner of his mouth.

"Looks like you need help," he shouted above the din of another peal of thunder. "Flat tire?"

"Yes." The young woman stepped back slowly. She flashed a brave yet tight smile and took another step away from him. "But don't trouble yourself. I'll be okay, thanks."

The rain made it difficult to see her face clearly now that she'd put distance between them, yet the spark of attraction charged through him. Attraction he hadn't felt in a long time. Attraction he had no business indulging for many reasons, not the least of which being the fact that she looked like a college coed.

Too young and innocent for a guy like him.

"Your jack probably weighs more than you do." He took a cautious step toward the back of the car so she wouldn't be alarmed. "Have you ever changed a tire?"

"Please don't bother." She held up one hand. "You can't help, anyway. There's no spare."

Jackson frowned, noticing the flat front tire. He stooped to take a closer look at the gash. No sealant would fix that tear, and his compact spare wouldn't fit this huge wheel rim. He glanced at the decal on the side door: Gabby's Gardens.

*Gabby.* Cute name, too.

"Did you call for help?" He stood, his hands tucked under his armpits, water sluicing off every inch of his body.

"No service." She shivered.

Oddly, the chilly rain hadn't cooled him off. In fact, his body temperature had only increased since he first set eyes on her, despite the gusty weather.

A truck honked as it zoomed by, simultaneously hurling a gritty spray at them and causing Gabby's pickup to quake. Jackson swiped his bangs from his eyes, slinging a handful of water from his face.

"Why don't we get off the side of the road before we both end up dead?" He gestured over his shoulder. "Hop in my car and I'll drive you to the nearest dry spot with cell service."

Presuming common sense would force her to agree, he started back toward his car. When she didn't catch up to him, he glanced back at her. "Aren't you coming?"

"I don't think so, but thank you." She darted for the door of her vehicle. "If you wouldn't mind calling a tow truck when you reach an area with service, I'd appreciate it."

"Miss, you're parked right at the edge of the road. I'm afraid you'll get hit." When that failed to persuade her, he added, "If *I* were going to hurt you, I could've done so already."

"All the same, I'll take my chances here. Not much traffic at this time of day." She waved before ducking into her truck with a quick "Bye!"

He heard her car doors lock. For three seconds, Jackson stood there, dumbfounded . . . and a little insulted. No one had ever refused his help or considered him a danger. Then again, a small woman like her probably shouldn't take chances with any stranger.

Another heavy rumble overhead forced him to shrug and return to his Jeep. He knew, from dozens of ski trips to the area, that the Stratton resort area wasn't too far ahead, so he flicked the hazards back on and drove away.

Leaving her alone didn't sit well with him, but it made no sense for both of them to indefinitely park there, wedged between the road and the engorged river. He couldn't very well have tossed her over his shoulder and thrown her in his car.

That idea, however, looped a thick curl of desire through his gut.

Obviously it had been too long since he'd been with a woman. Shaking his head to erase the image, he refocused on the road. Of course, it only took seconds before his mind began racing ahead of his car, mulling over why he was even on this road in the first place.

He hadn't come to Vermont for pleasure, and he sure shouldn't become sidetracked by a woman. Not even an adorably drenched kitten of a girl like Gabby—no matter how bright her eyes or sweet her dimples.

He'd allotted himself six weeks to get his shit together. His business demanded it—his family, too. Hell, according to them, his very life depended on it.

Following the surprise intervention his older brother, David, had sprung on him, he'd remained completely sober these past several weeks while making arrangements for this hiatus.

Of course, the stress of temporarily handing over the reins of his construction projects to his friend, Hank, had made it difficult. Made him crave the slow burn of whiskey sliding down his throat. Made him yearn for numbness to wind its way through his limbs and mind.

He'd resisted the impulse—barely.

Pride had kept him from surrendering to the siren call of Glenfiddich. He remained determined to prove to everyone that he could stop whenever he wanted.

Neither David nor his sister, Cat, understood him. They took after their reserved father, keeping their emotions locked down all the time. Jackson, on the other hand, had always reverberated feeling, temper, passion. He'd merely hidden it in recent years, after getting burned too many times.

Concealing pain, however, didn't mean insults no longer hurt or that slights merely skimmed the surface. No. Those things buried themselves deep inside, like a bullet in bone. Even if plucked out, there would always be a scar.

Whiskey had helped him soften the jagged edges of bitterness. The fact that he hankered for the smell and taste of it didn't mean a damned thing. Everyone drank, some even more than him.

Now that he'd arrived in Vermont, it'd be easier. The extended vacation—with abundant outdoor activities and unscheduled days—would give him time to unwind, to think, and to figure out how to move forward. He'd picked this area because it was close enough to return home quickly in an emergency, but distant enough to escape the family microscope.

He'd refused to consider rehab. That was for addicts, not guys who'd just fallen into bad habits. But he'd promised to check out counseling, so he'd called a local doctor to set up some appointments, for whatever that would be worth.

If only that damn lawsuit wasn't hanging over his head.

Somehow he'd missed pegging Doug as a bad guy when he'd hired him. Huge mistake. How that guy convinced some lawyer to file a bullshit suit for wrongful termination and a bunch of other bogus claims boggled Jackson's mind.

At least he could rely on his brother, David's, law firm to secure him the best defense possible. Jackson's only real regret about the whole incident involved Hank's accidental wrist injury. He prayed he hadn't permanently sidelined Hank from being able to build furniture or work as a carpenter. If Jackson didn't find some way to compensate his friend, his sister would make damn sure he did.

Cat and Hank—a couple more unlikely than David and Vivi, which had been about as big of a surprise as he could've envisioned at the time.

Never in a gazillion years would Jackson have thought *he'd* be the lone St. James, still single in his thirties. Hell, *he'd* been the most romantic of his siblings. He'd flung himself into every relationship, no holds barred. At a time when most guys had run away from commitment, he'd run straight at it, like a lacrosse attackman racing downfield toward the goal.

Until Alison bodychecked him with her decision.

Her name might as well have been a hunting knife for the way hearing it still carved his heart into ribbons. Without whiskey to blunt the pain, he'd need to find some other way to forget her betrayal. Forget the loss. Moving on might've been easier if she'd been the only one who'd let him down.

His text message chime jerked him to the present and brought to mind the girl he'd left stranded a few miles back.

He yanked the steering wheel and drove into a nearby empty lot, then searched Google for a local tow service. After he ended the call, he made a U-turn and returned to Gabby and her truck.

Gabby's Gardens.

A gardener. Landscaping or vegetables, he wondered? Then he frowned. Gabby and her gardens weren't the answer to his problems. If anything, she'd only unleash new ones.

When he passed by her truck this time around, she appeared to be reading in the front seat. He pulled up behind her, flicked on the hazards, and killed the engine. Through her rear window, he watched her twist around to look at him. She was too far away for him to tell whether his return caused alarm or relief.

He got out of the car, thankful the rain had slowed to a steady drizzle. He popped open the rear hatch, dug around his emergency kit, and retrieved two reflective emergency road triangles. Jogging about two car lengths, he placed one in the berm and then, about halfway back to his car, he placed the other slightly inside the roadway. Satisfied with his handiwork, he returned to his Jeep.

Wet jeans on a damp seat—damned uncomfortable. Cold denim, clinging to him like an awkward second skin. Still, he'd sit and wait until the tow truck arrived and he could be sure she was safe.

His stomach gurgled, reminding him it had been several hours since he'd eaten. He noticed Gabby turn around another time or two, either in discomfort or confusion. Had she really thought he'd leave her stranded and defenseless in the middle of nowhere?

When her truck door opened, he straightened up, curious about what she'd do next. Clearly, she no longer feared him. She dangled one of her tempting trim legs from the cab, like she was still deciding what to do. As he waited for her next move, something deep inside whispered in his ear, *"You're the one in trouble."*

～

Reckless. That's what she'd always been—plain old reckless when it came to men. She'd thought having Luc would wise her up, but apparently her toddler hadn't yet knocked common sense into her brain. Boundless love, enormous responsibility, and a long spate of chastity: yes. Wisdom? Not so much.

Nothing else could explain why she'd risk her safety to go trade words with the crazy man playing white knight in a thunderstorm. Then again, recent weeks of meditation—her last-ditch effort to cope with the demands of parenting—were teaching her to experience everything openly and without judgment. To be present. Mindful. And right now, curious.

She jumped down from the cab and began her approach. That's when she saw Connecticut plates on the front of his car. A tourist. Hopefully not a rapist or murderer, too. To her knowledge, murderers didn't usually draw attention to themselves with reflective roadside emergency gear. Then again, she'd never known any violent criminals.

Whether habit or nerves took over, she didn't know, but one of those two caused her to smooth her wet hair. Like that would help.

Resolved, more or less, she trotted to the passenger side of his car and motioned for him to roll down his window. He donned a pleasant expression but remained seated, making no attempt to approach her or the passenger door. She guessed he froze in place to keep her from getting jumpy.

When she stepped close enough to peer through the open window, she noticed the spotless interior. No wadded-up wrappers or napkins, no stray sippy cups, no scuff marks on the seats. Either this guy was a neat freak or he didn't have kids. "I don't mean to be rude, but what are you doing?"

"Making sure you don't end up as roadkill." He grinned. A heart-stopping, full grin surrounding stark white teeth contrasted against his olive-toned complexion.

Growing up in this rural, tiny town of eight hundred residents, she hadn't seen men who looked like him except in magazines. Around here, clean-shaven was a bonus, let alone this guy's level of H-O-T. She'd been right to think him deadly, just wrong about the why of it.

"Oh." Her heart began pumping as hard as it might during a hike up Mount Equinox. "Thanks, but I'm sure the tow truck will be here soon. I told you, not many cars pass this way on Tuesday afternoons. You really don't need to stay. I'm fine."

She swiped her palm across her face to wipe away the water. Darn rain. Surely she had mascara streaks down her cheeks.

"I'm fine, too." His gaze strayed to the raindrops coming in through the open window. Tilting his head, he said, "You're welcome to take a seat if you'd rather continue your interrogation someplace dry."

Gabby stepped back and shook her head. "No, thanks."

He rolled his eyes. "Do I look like some kind of murderer?"

"Frankly, I've got no idea. I've never met a murderer." His wide-eyed reaction spurred her to tease him. "But Ted Bundy was good-looking, so for all I know, you're a serial killer."

Instead of arguing, his devilish smile emerged, which set free a thousand butterflies in her stomach. A magical, brightening sensation she hadn't felt in years and now wished she could capture in a box to take home to experience again and again and again.

His smile expanded. "You think I'm good-looking?"

As if he didn't already know. Every woman on the planet would consider him handsome . . . and sexy. She could only imagine how fine his dark, curly hair would look when it dried. Fistfuls of it, she knew that much. Broad shoulders—very broad—and a square jaw. Amber-colored eyes set deeply beneath dark, heavy brows, although those eyes looked quite melancholy for someone wearing that smile.

She crossed her arms and chuckled. "That's all you heard?"

"I've got a talent for homing in on the most important point." Then his playful expression swiftly shifted, as if he'd scolded himself for flirting. Perhaps he had a girlfriend, or a wife. It would be a stretch to think that a guy his age—who was also beautiful and considerate—would still be single.

"Go on back to your car and get out of the rain before you get sick." He jerked his chin toward her truck. "Don't worry, I'm not a stalker. As soon as the tow truck comes, I'll grab my stuff and go. Gotta eat."

If she'd had good sense, she'd have nodded and scooted back to her car. Naturally, she didn't. He might be a million miles out of her league, but for now they were stuck together. She couldn't force herself to walk away while those butterfly wings still tickled.

"I see you're from out of town. Do you like French food, because there's plenty of it around here, or are you hungry for a burger and fries?" She wiped more rain from her face in a futile attempt at poise.

"Burger."

Of course. He didn't look like the type who'd order duck and wine at lunch. He had too much testosterone, too much swagger. Even though he was sitting still, she could feel the masculinity rippling off his body like heat radiating off asphalt. Just staring at him warmed her from the inside out.

This kind of rock-my-world chemical reaction should've made her wary. Last time it had struck, she'd gotten Luc out of the deal, along with a side dish of heartbreak. She loved her son to pieces, but didn't need to risk another life-altering consequence merely to satisfy a healthy dose of lust. The mere thought of Noah, the cocky local cop who'd knocked her up and left her hanging, shot heated shame straight to her cheeks.

"If you're heading toward Manchester Center, you'll pass by Bob's Diner on Route 11," she said. "Or you could go a little farther to a tavern called The Perfect Wife."

"Diner's fine, thanks."

A heartbeat passed before she realized there was nothing more to say. She should return to the car, not stand in the rain ogling a man she didn't know. The blasted man was a stranger. A very attractive stranger who, sadly, hadn't once asked for her name.

The fact that thought even crossed her mind proved how pathetic her personal life had become. Honestly, didn't she have any self-respect? He hadn't said or done a single thing since the Ted Bundy conversation to suggest he found her the least bit appealing. "Thanks for looking out for me. Enjoy our little corner of the world while you're here."

His eyes clouded over with something that looked a lot like regret—an emotion she knew well thanks to teenage rebellion and other mistakes. "Thanks."

She waved good-bye and then jogged back to her truck. For the next ten minutes she pretended to read her *People* magazine. Knowing he continued to watch over her swept a prickling sensation over her scalp.

A pleasant kind of prickling. The long-forgotten kind.

She deemed it a blessing that he didn't live around here because that way she'd never be disappointed to learn he wasn't as good as he appeared. She could pretend heroes weren't only in movies and romance novels. She'd simply enjoy their brief encounter for what it was, nothing more or less.

Yep, just as well she never got his name.

Luc needed a mother who'd put him first, unlike her own pill-popping mom, who'd walked out on her and her dad almost seven years ago. Gabby would be a mom her son could rely upon to care for him, protect him, teach him right from wrong. Not the madcap girl she'd been before her unplanned pregnancy. A girl prone to impulsive behavior. One whose head had been too easily turned by a handsome face.

Mr. White Knight from Connecticut would forever remain nothing more than a nameless fantasy. A fantasy she might have to satisfy in private later that night.

Although thoroughly convinced of how much better off she was that she'd never see him again, a little piece of her heart sank when Manchester Towing arrived.

"Hey, Paul. That didn't take too long." She smiled through her window.

"Gabby, didn't realize I'd find *you* here." He glanced at Mr. White Knight, who was picking up his emergency gear from the road. "Who's that guy?"

"A Good Samaritan." Gabby smiled, although her chest tightened a tiny bit when he climbed into his car and drove away without any kind of good-bye.

"Let's get you off the road." Paul slapped his hand on the sill. "Go jump in my truck while I get this baby hooked up."

"Sounds great."

The inside of Paul's tow truck left a lot to be desired. Two crushed soda cans, an empty Doritos bag, and crumpled receipts lay scattered on the seat. Nothing like the spick-and-span inside of her white knight's Jeep. Sighing, she set the trash on the floor, then closed her eyes and rested her head against the back of the seat.

Before she could stop it, an image of her Good Samaritan's smile flickered like a favorite scene in an old movie. For once she'd made the smart choice by being wary of the stranger from out of state. Still, her reckless side—the trait she worked hard to bury—beat against her conscience, telling her she might have just missed out on something special.

# Chapter Two

Jackson shrugged out of his wet jacket and tossed it on the passenger seat before heading into the diner. If the sharp edge of hunger weren't gnawing on his stomach, he would've first stopped to pick up the keys to his apartment and changed into dry clothes.

He pushed through the door and stepped into the old diner. Like a lot of other places in this part of Vermont, it probably hadn't been renovated since it was built. He stood surrounded by small black-and-white mosaic-tiled flooring, round vinyl stools at the counter, and no shortage of aluminum. The greasy aroma of the griddle invaded his nostrils, too, whetting his appetite.

He sat at the counter.

"Looks like you've been through the wringer." The bottle-redheaded young waitress smiled. She cocked her hip when handing him a menu. A tattoo of blood-red roses on a vine climbed up her forearm. Multiple piercings dotted her ears, and she'd painted her nails dark gray. "How about a beer while you decide what you want? A Bud, or maybe you'd like my favorite, Switchback?"

Ice-cold beer sounded perfect. He looked around, knowing no one here would think twice about a guy ordering a beer with lunch. After the storm he braved today, he deserved one, too. His family would never know. Just one cold beer to take the edge off.

His mouth began watering, but he stopped himself. He'd never been a liar, and he didn't want to start today. Something sweet always curbed the craving, so he ordered a chocolate milkshake.

The waitress's heavily lined eyes slightly widened with surprise. "You got it, handsome."

Some guys envied the regular attention women gave Jackson. Most of the time, he wished to be more invisible. Especially in this case, because he had no interest in hanging out with an obvious party girl. Besides, meaningless flirtations usually made him feel lonelier—emptier—than ever. They made him yearn for the kind of love and family he'd always assumed he'd have by his thirties.

"Thanks." He scanned the menu, then set it aside and glanced around the diner. An elderly couple sat in a corner booth, two middle-aged moms with toddlers in another. And at the end of the counter sat a scraggly-looking guy about Jackson's age, drinking the beer Jackson would've liked to order.

Someday. Once he'd shown himself and others how they'd overreacted to his drinking.

The waitress pushed a tall, frosty shake in front of him. "Ready to order?"

"Cheddar burger with onion and tomato, and fries." He smiled and handed her the menu, then returned his brother's earlier text with a phone call.

"Jackson, how's the apartment?" David asked.

"Don't know. Stopped for lunch first."

"Oh? Did you hit a lot of traffic?"

"Storm slowed me down, and then some girl with a flat needed help."

A brief pause ensued. Jackson figured David was weighing whether or not to ask more about the girl. "Are you feeling optimistic about this trip? I still wish you'd stuck closer to home or checked into a formal program."

Jackson suspected his family wanted him where they, or someone else, could keep a close eye on him. He, however, needed privacy to figure out how to finally deal with the fact that both his siblings, among others, had betrayed his trust in one way or another. The thought roughened his voice.

"I need space. Hank and I have a plan to address any business issues he can't handle. I've got my first therapy session tomorrow. I just ordered a milkshake instead of a beer. Any other concerns?"

He heard David exhale. "I know you're still upset with me about Hong Kong, and the intervention. When you return, I want to resolve everything."

"How about you let me take one step at a time?"

"Of course," came David's quick reply.

For years, Jackson's friends had confessed to being glad they'd never had to live in the shadow of an older brother like David. David, the star pupil and athlete—a perfect rule follower, adored by teachers, girls, and other parents. But Jackson hadn't minded that part. He and David had never been in competition. If anything, he'd admired his brother as much as anyone else, and he'd believed David would always have his back.

Then, when their mom died, David had moved halfway around the world, cutting everyone out of his life for eighteen months. Offered no comfort while Jackson mourned their mom—a time when he really needed his big brother's company. After that, Alison ripped what remained of Jackson's heart in half by terminating her pregnancy, and all the while David remained blissfully unaware.

By the time David had returned to the family, the gulf between them might as well have been the damned Grand Canyon. Jackson didn't know how to bridge it, so he'd been polite yet continued to emotionally withdraw. He no longer trusted that David—or anyone—would be there for him through ups and downs, thick and thin. How *does* one rebuild broken trust?

Hopefully he'd figure that out here in Vermont.

"Before we hang up," David began, "I spoke with Oliver and he wants you to consider settling Doug's claim."

Oliver Nichols, his lawyer for this case and one of his brother's law partners, was a white-shoe, pencil-pushing pussy who never gave Jackson a straight answer. He wished David were handling the matter, but David's specialty was mergers and acquisitions, not litigation.

"Settle?" Jackson slurped the shake through the thick straw. *No way.* Doug had never done a great job, and his big mouth had caused problems within the crew. The guy sure had balls, though. First he dissed Jackson in front of other employees, then he threatened to spread exaggerated rumors about Jackson's drinking to clients and competitors. When Jackson fired him on the spot and kicked him off the site, Doug shoved him. Hell, Jackson hadn't done a thing wrong, and never even hit Doug. "I didn't do anything wrong. Doug was insubordinate, slanderous, and *he* made the first move."

Honestly, what kind of dumbass thinks he's entitled to keep his job after that kind of behavior?

"Even if that's true, protracted litigation only serves us lawyers." David sighed. "You don't need extra stress or mounting legal fees in your life now. Litigation could stretch for two years and hurt your reputation. Better to settle quickly and get a confidentiality agreement in place. You don't have to admit anything, just offer a number to make it go away."

"No." Jackson's calm tone belied his outrage. "No way in hell" was what Jackson wanted to shout into the phone.

"You won't even consider it?"

"Nope." He tossed the straw and guzzled some of the shake straight from the glass.

"Oliver doesn't get the sense Doug's going to back off. He's got less at stake than you."

"That's what he thinks. But if he intends to trash my reputation, I can do equal if not more damage to his. I'm the one with a good history and tons of friends in the business. I'm the one with a string of satisfied homeowners to vouch for my character and reputation. He's a young punk with jack shit for a track record, and if he pushes me harder, I'm going to make it impossible for him to work in Connecticut."

"Don't say that to anyone but me, Jackson." Following another pause, he added, "Maybe it's best that you've left town for a while."

"Seems so."

David huffed and Jackson could picture him closing his eyes and counting to three, like he always did when Cat or Jackson exasperated him. "You're clearly spoiling for an argument, so let's cut this short. I'll let everyone know you've arrived and will check back in with you in a few days."

"Fine." As an afterthought, Jackson added, "Thanks."

"Jackson, all I want is for everything to get better, for you and for us." David's quiet, sincere tone hit its mark.

"So do I." That much was true. Beneath the recent disappointments and distance, he knew David loved him and missed the closeness they'd once shared as much as Jackson did. "My lunch arrived. I'll touch base in a couple of days."

He wedged his phone into his pocket and then shoved a handful of fries into his mouth. Salty, hot fries. Tasted damn near perfect.

While he gorged on the most fattening lunch he'd eaten in weeks, two cops came into the diner. One had a paunchy gut and salt-and-pepper hair, the other looked extremely fit and young. Midtwenties, if Jackson had to guess. Sandy-colored hair, ice-blue eyes.

The older officer slapped the scraggly customer on the shoulder and started a conversation.

When the younger cop sauntered to the counter and smiled flirtatiously at the waitress, Jackson got a better look at him. Something about the guy made Jackson uneasy. He didn't look malevolent so much as phony. Slick. Untrustworthy. A smidge of arrogance. Just like that asswipe Doug. Not exactly the qualities one seeks in a policeman.

"Noah, what can I do you for and Lou?" The hot-to-trot waitress sashayed closer to the good-looking cop, eating up his attention.

"Two sodas and an order of fries for the road, Missy." The young cop's answering smile caused her to bat her lashes and giggle. He then glanced at Jackson, and his gaze narrowed. "Lose a battle with a hose?" He chuckled, like he was Stephen Colbert or something.

Jackson's skin itched from the way the man homed in on him—focused, curious, assessing. "Feels like it."

He took another bite of his burger, hoping to signal polite disinterest in further conversation.

No such luck. Apparently Jackson's odd appearance piqued this officer's interest, because he showed no sign of backing off.

"I'm Noah." The young cop stuck out his hand then nodded toward his partner. "That's Lou."

"Jackson," he replied as he shook the man's hand.

"You don't look familiar." He tipped his head, giving Jackson a closer inspection. "Where're you from?"

"Connecticut." Jackson wiped his mouth and met the cop's even gaze. "Came up here for a little r-and-r."

After a slight hesitation, Noah nodded. "Fly-fishing should do the trick. Orvis runs some programs down in Manchester Center."

Thankfully, Missy returned with a bag of fries and two sodas. She handed them to Noah and stuck her chest out a bit. "Here you go, boys. Stop back for coffee later."

"Wouldn't miss it." Noah winked at her and then he tilted his head and mock saluted Jackson. "See you 'round, Jackson."

Maybe Jackson had become overly paranoid this year, but something about Noah's tone sounded a little bit like a warning. Missy's gaze followed Noah until he left the diner, then she leaned her hip against the counter and brazenly checked Jackson out. "So, you here alone?"

Jackson managed a friendly smile, although he wanted to escape before she said something that would make them both uncomfortable.

"Yes, and I'm looking forward to a little solitude." Jackson opted for a quick exit, so he stood and threw twenty bucks on the counter. "Keep the change, Missy."

His damp clothes chafed his skin with each step. So far nothing about this day had gone smoothly. As soon as he picked up his keys, he'd take a hot shower and change. He fired up the engine and headed back to Winhall to find his landlord, Jon Bouchard, and check out the carriage house apartment he'd rented above the man's garage.

~

Three hundred dollars later, Gabby finally pulled her truck in behind the home she and her son shared with her father. At least the rain had finally stopped and her dress had dried from sopping to damp.

She gathered her notebook from the front seat and strode toward the back door, passing by her pumpkin patch. Pumpkins weren't easy to grow in Vermont, but she'd promised Luc she'd grow some for Halloween. A quick perusal indicated she'd have not only one for him, but also a dozen or so to sell in a couple of weeks.

The little garden reminded her of her summer visits with her grandmother in Burlington, when they'd spent endless hours together gardening. Under her tutelage, her preteen self had taken pride in her first crops of cucumbers and lettuce, tomatoes and carrots. Her grandmother had also taught her about horticulture, and the two of them had worked together around her grandmother's house, planning and planting flowerbeds. Gabby had taken those lessons and tested things here at her own house, as if making it look pretty on the outside could somehow fix what had been broken inside. Epic fail there.

Still, gardening gave Gabby a much-needed sense of control and peace at a time when her life had been in constant upheaval. In high school, she'd joined the local gardening club and learned even more about design. She'd spent some of her summer days working with her dad in the yards of the homes he maintained. His clients always praised her ingenuity and creativity. If she hadn't gotten pregnant, she'd have gone to college and studied to become a landscape architect. But she wouldn't dwell on that old dream. Now she made do just fine with the skills and resources she already had.

When she entered the house through the kitchen door, she heard her father, Jon, call out, "Gabby, that you?"

"Yeah, it's me. Sorry I'm late. Flat tire." She plucked a banana from the fruit bowl and meandered to the living room. Luc sat on the floor playing with old Tonka trucks she'd bought at a yard sale. She bent over and kissed his head before doing the same to her dad. "Luc give you any trouble?"

Silly question. What toddler didn't fuss and throw tantrums? He might've just turned three, but his "terrible twos" behavior lingered. Her dad's helpless shrug told her everything she'd already guessed.

"At least he took a short nap." When he rose from his chair his knees cracked, evidencing his age. At only fifty-three, he looked fit and trim, but his sandy hair also had hints of gray. She'd always thought him handsome, and felt guilty that he'd never met anyone new to love, probably because of her and Luc. She and her dad had both ended up in a situation that made finding love tricky, if not impossible. "Good gracious, girl. You got drenched."

"I know." Gabby picked at her dress, thinking back on her highway interlude with the handsome stranger. "I've got to change."

"What's got you smiling?" He cocked his head, crow's feet crinkling at the corners of his bright blue eyes.

"Was I smiling?" How embarrassing. She and her dad were close, but she wouldn't confess the little daydream she'd just had about the Good Samaritan. After three years filled with obligations and an utter lack of romance, the idea of a little fling with someone like him held a lot of appeal. Sadly, daydreams were all she'd have. Then again, unlike reality, daydreams never disappointed.

Her dad didn't seem to notice her evasive answer, because he prattled on. "Our tenant should arrive any minute. You remembered to clean the garage apartment this morning, didn't you?"

"Of course." Her dad still hadn't noticed how responsible she'd become, apparently intent on viewing her as the hapless screwup who got pregnant. Couldn't really blame him, though. Responsibility hadn't factored into most of her choices before Luc came along. At least Dad never rubbed that in her face. So until she could stand on her own two feet with Luc, she'd have to tolerate being treated like a child herself.

"Good." He folded his arms and fixed the "father knows best" expression on his face. "The extra couple grand will come in handy with the cost of Luc's nursery school."

"Too bad I need some of the rent to pay for the new tire I just bought." Gabby broke off part of her banana and handed it to her son. Would she always view Luc as a child, she wondered absently. "On the upside, the Clarks emailed asking me to redo their backyard in the spring."

"That's terrific!" His proud smile took the sting out of his earlier parental condescension.

The doorbell rang, interrupting their conversation. Gabby wrinkled her nose, knowing her warm shower and change of clothing would need to wait a few minutes longer.

"I'll get it." Gabby hastened through the front hall and opened the door, then she almost fainted. Her heart lodged itself smack in the middle of her throat, so it took a second for her to force any words. "You?"

Her Good Samaritan's eyes widened before he frowned. He stepped back to glance at the address on the porch and then at his phone.

Finally, he held up his hands, half stunned, half laughing. "I swear, I'm *not* stalking you."

Her lips quirked before she could stop herself. "So you say."

"Seriously. I'm looking for Jon Bouchard. Is this the wrong address?"

*He's our tenant?* She wished the thunderstorm would return so he couldn't hear her heart galloping right out of her chest.

"Dad," she called out as she opened the screen door to let the handsome man inside. "Your tenant's here."

She glanced back at her white knight. His hair had dried. Messy, sexy hair, like she'd suspected. He was a bit shorter than six feet tall, which meant he still stood several inches taller than her five foot two. The heat of him seemed to brush against her skin when he stepped beside her.

Pressing her lips together, Gabby forced a burst of giddy pleasure back into her lungs to avoid humiliating herself. A second later, she rushed to fill the awkward silence. "So, this is kind of serendipitous."

"Lucky coincidence?" He grimaced. "Doubtful."

"Aren't you the flatterer?"

He grinned then, the same playful grin she'd witnessed earlier that day. The one that turned her knees to jelly. "Nothin' to do with you. It's just that Lady Luck hasn't paid me a visit in a long time."

The sorrow she'd noticed earlier flickered in his eyes once more. Before she could respond, her father arrived.

"Jackson St. James?" Her father extended his hand.

"Yes, sir." Jackson's gaze darted from her dad to her and back before they shook hands. "Excuse my appearance. I got caught in the storm."

"Actually, Dad, he got caught while trying to help me with my flat tire." Gabby smiled at Jackson. Jackson St. James. She liked his name—a lot. Masculine yet refined. It suited him, or what she knew of him so far. "*Jackson* was quite the gentleman. Waited with me until the tow truck came."

"Thanks for looking out for my little girl." Her father wrapped his arm around her shoulder and squeezed, smiling. Heat washed through her cheeks at being called a "little girl" in front of Jackson, who looked at least half a dozen years older than her, possibly more. "You're probably eager to change into something dry. Let me go fetch the key, then Gabby can take you over and show you whatever you need to know."

Her dad disappeared down the hallway, presumably to go to the junk drawer in the kitchen.

She looked up at Jackson again, her lungs expanding with irrational happiness. The lighter-than-air feeling sharpened her senses. The old hallway seemed to shrink around her. The floorboards beneath her creaked when she shifted her weight to one leg. Even the dining room behind Jackson brightened, as if the sun were fighting hard to illuminate the cloud-covered sky outside. It was as if Jackson's presence had transformed a mundane moment into one brimming with excited anticipation. "By the way, thanks for today. Once I realized you weren't a threat, I was glad you were nearby."

"My pleasure." Again he smiled, and again it didn't quite reach his eyes.

Luc appeared in the hall and then trotted toward her, arms raised. "Up, Mama."

Before she leaned down to lift him onto her hip, she noticed Jackson's brows rise before his eyes softened as they settled on her son.

"Luc, say hi to Jackson. He's going to live over the garage for several weeks."

Her shy son laid his head against her shoulder and peered at the stranger with one eye.

Jackson stepped forward and gently tapped Luc's nose. "Hey, buddy. It's nice to meet you." Then his expression tightened. He didn't look angry, just distant. The air around him turned so heavy its weight pressed on her shoulders.

The sadness she'd seen earlier that day intensified. Had Luc somehow triggered it, or was that her imagination?

When her dad returned with the keys, she tried to hand off Luc. "Stay with Pappy while Mommy takes Jackson to the apartment. I'll be back soon."

"No!" Luc clutched her, his fingers digging into her like cat claws.

"Listen to Mommy, Luc." She pried him off her body and handed him to her dad, at which point he burst into manipulative tears. If she hadn't been embarrassed by his behavior, she'd have been annoyed. "Come on, peanut, you know crying won't get you your way."

"Go on, I'll deal with him." Her father shook his head and turned toward the kitchen, speaking to a despondent Luc. "How about we get a snack?"

After flashing an apologetic grin at Jackson, she gestured toward the front door. "Let's go."

Jackson's gaze darted from her to her father's retreating form and back again, then he opened the screen door and held it for her before following outside. If he had questions about her son, he kept them to himself.

"Let me grab my bag," he said, dashing toward his Jeep.

Seconds later, he hefted a giant duffle bag over his shoulder and then shadowed her across the driveway to the detached garage.

Gabby had a truckload of questions. Where was he from? Why did he choose Winhall, of all places, to visit? Why was he staying for six weeks? And why did he look so downhearted? Of course, she asked none of them. He didn't strike her as the kind of guy who'd open up easily, if at all. And certainly not to a nosy landlord.

Still, his comment about being unlucky stuck out. Jackson St. James presented a puzzle, and an alluring one at that. Her humdrum life would be a little more interesting this fall thanks to him, and she intended to take full advantage of a break in the monotony. First she'd need to observe him longer so she could find her way around the heavy curtain he hid behind.

She led him up the outside stairwell and then unlocked the door. Thankfully she'd done a good job cleaning this morning. Still, a guy who kept his car so tidy and could afford to take off for six weeks probably had money and a pretty nice home of his own.

"Hope this will do." She swung the door open.

Once inside, he dropped his duffle by the door.

As he glanced around the well-worn space, she tried to envision it through his eyes. A queen-size bed with a patchwork quilt peeking out from behind a trifold furniture screen, a fake-leather loveseat and recliner clustered around a vintage coffee table in front of an old television, and a kitchenette along the far wall with a table for two.

Suddenly feeling self-conscious about the apartment's lack of style, she blurted, "It's a little dated, but it's clean and dry. Two things you can't say about lots of places in Winhall. The bathroom is around that way," she said, pointing toward the bedroom area, "and everything else is pretty much right here. Vermont's strict about recycling, so use clear bags for recyclables, and there are special bags for regular trash under the sink. You can toss it all in the bins outside the garage and we'll take them to the dump on our runs."

"It's great, thanks." He looked at her expectantly, and when she didn't speak, he asked, "Your dad had promised Wi-Fi. Is there a password?"

"Yes. GGguest. GG for Gabby's Gardens, in case that helps you remember it." She held out the keys. "I'm Gabby, by the way."

His hand grazed hers when he took them, sending a shock of heat up her arm.

"I know your name. It's all over your truck." When he winked, that heat raced straight to her face.

"Oh, I guess you're right." Their gazes locked for a second or two longer than expected, which shot another warm rush through her limbs, making her insides gooier than the center of a roasted marshmallow.

The golden streaks in his amber eyes now lit with something other than sorrow. She hoped she'd put that flicker there and provided a temporary break from whatever had him troubled.

Tongue-tied again, she practically stammered, "I should probably let you get settled, and I'm dying to get out of these wet clothes."

As soon as the words left her mouth, she wished she'd chosen a phrase that didn't sound like a come-on. Her reckless subconscious had probably taken over and said it on purpose.

His gaze smoldered again and she almost compounded her mistake by suggesting his luck was about to change, but then he glanced away. "Good plan. I'm sure I'll see you around later."

And that was that. She'd leave without answers to any of her questions. Berating herself for caring one little iota, she nodded. "Have a good rest of your day."

She let herself out and trotted down the metal staircase. As she crossed the driveway, she turned to look back at the windows above the garage. They'd had short-term renters before. People who'd come and gone without attracting her notice. Clearly, Jackson was different.

Who *was* he, and why did it matter? The haunted look in his eyes should be enough of a warning. Life with her mom had introduced her to that kind of empty gaze, a look she supposed everyone who ever lived in a small rural town knew in one form or another.

Still, fate had thrown her and Jackson together twice. And despite the hint of unhappiness simmering behind his eyes, she couldn't escape the sort of momentous feeling he inspired. Anticipation bloomed in her fallow heart like the fragile shoots of winter aconite breaking through freshly thawed soil.

Then, laughing to—or at—herself, she turned and went inside, back to reality. Whatever did or didn't happen between her and Jackson, six weeks from now he'd leave, like everyone else, and never look back.

# CHAPTER THREE

Listening to the rhythmic crunch beneath his feet as he ran along the tree-lined road, Jackson pushed aside the cramps that reminded him how long it had been since he'd actually exercised. Building and remodeling jobs kept him trim. But aerobically, he had some serious catching up to do.

At first he'd lumbered, unable to move at anything faster than a slow jog, until old habits had kicked in and his body responded with its reliable agility and strength.

His sweat-coated skin didn't reek of whiskey—a change he reluctantly acknowledged. With each breath he inhaled invigorating, earthy aromas like tree molds, loamy soil, pine. The recent sunrise hadn't yet burned off the fog that pillowed around him as he ran back toward his temporary home.

No traffic, no cell phone. Only the sounds of his steady footfall and the sparrows' early-morning whistling, punctured occasionally by the drumming of a woodpecker. At his current pace, he'd enjoy another twenty minutes or so of peace and solitude as little clouds of breath puffed from his mouth like smoke rings.

Although he wrestled to pin his thoughts on the beauty around him, they kept wandering to the appointment he'd scheduled at eight o'clock.

He could cancel.

It's not like he'd promised his family he'd talk to a shrink while he chillaxed in Vermont. He'd agreed to address their concerns, but he hadn't forfeited the right to make decisions for himself about how to do that. Still, he'd mentioned it to David yesterday, and he didn't want this journey to be wasted.

Whatever mistakes he made, whatever promises he broke, he needed to own.

The final minutes of his run consisted of a quarter-mile uphill climb. His breathing had grown heavy, lungs burning, as he rounded the corner where the Bouchards' wooded driveway came into view.

Yesterday he'd been too tired and waterlogged to pay much attention to the house. This morning, however, the early-morning sun—diffused by remnants of fog—bathed the aging, farmhouse-style home in a dreamy light. A good thing considering the fact that, when one looked closely, everything about the place was worn.

He slowed to a walk and studied the scene. Vermont's dank weather demanded a ton of maintenance if a homeowner wanted to prevent disrepair. Patches of rotted wood marred the beauty of the front porch. Both the house and garage needed a new coat of stain, too. Yet the aging home had the potential to be a knockout, especially if the Bouchards would upgrade to modern farmhouse windows and choose a deep green stain instead of the more traditional red.

The idea of transforming the home got Jackson's creative juices flowing.

His gaze swept across the yard. The landscaping had been better maintained. Interesting groupings of small boulders, shrubbery, and mums carpeted the area surrounding the house. A fieldstone-and-grass walkway led from the gravel driveway to the front steps, enhancing the storybook setting.

He visualized what other flowering plants must bloom in spring and summer, but were now pruned and protected. Then he imagined

Gabby kneeling at the edge of the bed, digging her hands into the soil, her cute little rear end hovering a foot or so above her heels.

That image got his juices flowing, too, albeit in a completely improper way.

On his way to the garage, activity in the side yard caught his attention. Luc's little squeal of delight penetrated the air as he dashed around on wobbly legs. Gabby had set a mug of coffee up on a fence post while she bent over to inspect something in her vegetable garden. Nearly a perfect replica of his little fantasy.

Luc stopped and noticed Jackson watching them.

"Mama!" He clutched a little toy close to his chest with one hand and pointed at Jackson with the other.

She glanced over her shoulder. Smiling at him as if he were a friend rather than a new acquaintance, she called out, "Good morning."

Busted, with no clean getaway.

Not that he minded talking to her, exactly. She seemed agreeable and outgoing . . . and too damned cute. Therein lay the problem.

Women were a complication he didn't need, especially this woman, with her smile that tipped him off his axis, and her toddler in tow.

"Morning." He waved and found himself crossing the yard to get to her, like his body had flipped the finger at his brain and gone after what it wanted.

She looked so young, but here she stood, raising her child and running her own business. A lot for anyone to accomplish, let alone someone at her tender age. She deserved respect, not lust.

Gabby rose and brushed off her hands before reaching for her coffee mug. Meanwhile, Luc stared at him, wide-eyed and cautious.

To distract himself from ogling Gabby, Jackson crouched down by Luc. "Who's this?" he asked, pointing toward the brown-and-white stuffed animal currently held hostage in a white-knuckled death grip.

"Bingo." Luc twisted his torso to keep his dog out of Jackson's reach.

"Bingo's a great name. Did you pick it?" Jackson smiled at Luc, whose round, baby-blue eyes resembled his mother's.

He nodded. Apparently Luc had already learned some economy with words—a male trait Jackson could appreciate. Had Luc's father taught him? Jackson hadn't seen a guy other than Jon around the property since he arrived yesterday, but perhaps the man traveled for work.

Then again, Gabby didn't wear a wedding ring, so maybe she was divorced, or widowed. The thought of her suffering either of those losses slid uncomfortably through his gut, but he shook off the feeling. Maybe she didn't wear a ring because her hands were always working with dirt and stone. The fact that she lived with her dad, however, suggested Luc's father wasn't part of her life.

*Enough about Gabby.* Jackson returned his attention to Luc.

"Looks like you take good care of Bingo. He's a lucky dog." The awkwardness of carrying on a conversation about a pretend dog with a kid he barely knew took hold. Jackson stood and risked a quick glance at Gabby.

She grinned, head tilted, both hands holding her mug, clearly caring not one whit that her hair blew about in a tangled mess of soft brown curls, or that her sweatshirt had some kind of jelly stain on it, or that he'd caught her in her fuzzy pajama pants.

"You're up and at 'em early." Faint dimples dented her cheeks. "Getting a healthy start on your day?"

"Trying something new." His tone sounded teasing, but he knew the words to be a sad truth. He remembered, then, how *he* must look. Sweaty, grimy, tired.

She fingered her son's hair once he walked over to clutch her leg.

"Mama has punkins." Luc's chin remained tucked despite his direct address to Jackson.

"For Halloween?" Jackson saw at least a dozen orange gourds behind her. "Looks like you have extra for pumpkin pie."

Luc's eyes opened wide, clearly having not realized the better use of pumpkins. He pinned Gabby with a pleading gaze. "Pie, too, Mama!"

She chuckled. "Pie with plenty of spice."

Jackson took advantage of the opportunity to study her little vegetable garden. The vines, heavy with nearly ripe pumpkins, laid on top of a bed of straw. "What's with the straw?"

"Helps keep weed growth to a minimum, and cuts down on mold and other rot that can happen when pumpkins are on the ground."

"So Gabby's Gardens are fruits and veggies?" Good God, was this really the best conversation he could invent when he was trying hard *not* to flirt? Had he really disengaged so much from anything real that he couldn't remember how to converse like a normal person?

"No, this here is for personal pleasure." She flushed then, as those last two words hung suspended between them.

He realized then their mutual attraction. Not good—yet *so* good. It'd been too long since he'd been genuinely attracted to a woman for more than her looks. Figures it'd happen at the least opportune point of his life. Seemed like the only luck he could ever count on lately was bad luck.

"My business is landscaping. I'd like to be a landscape architect, but that takes a lot of school. I got a bit sidetracked." She grinned while nodding toward her son. "I piggybacked off my dad's business and now design and install small residential landscape projects for locals and some of his out-of-town clients."

Enterprising, determined, outdoorsy. Damn if she didn't push all his trigger points. He should get away from her and go shower, but his stubborn feet remained rooted to the spot where he stood. "He's a caretaker, right? Vacation homes?"

"Yes. Between the two of us, we somehow pull off running the two small businesses and raising Luc."

Jackson stopped himself from asking about Luc's dad. That question crossed all kinds of personal lines. Instead he pointed to the far end of the garden, where a path cut through the yard and disappeared into the woods. "Where does that lead?"

"To the prettiest pond, complete with lily pads and loons." She drew another sip of coffee. "It's probably less than a quarter mile down that path. Too cold to swim now, but you could fish or kayak."

Luc must've mistaken Gabby's pointing as an invitation, because he tore off toward the path yelling, "I go fish!"

"Luc, get your butt back here now!" She schooled her features in an attempt to look stern.

Jackson stifled a chuckle at how unthreatening her lilting voice sounded when trying to yell, and how ineffectively her baby-doll eyes conveyed irritation. Her whole approach reminded him of Snow White managing Grumpy.

Unsurprisingly, Luc scowled and defiantly took another few steps toward the path. As Jackson predicted, the boy didn't fear his mom's temper.

"I mean it, Luc. No fishing today."

Jackson couldn't help but contrast her quiet yet firm reprimand to the way he'd recently started chewing out his crew when they screwed up. That thought reminded him of Doug's lawsuit, which in turn cast a long shadow over his otherwise pleasant morning.

Luc dropped his bottom to the ground and whined his displeasure. Gabby closed her eyes and began counting to herself, her lips silently mouthing one, two, three.

Jackson suspected she had to do that pretty often. Must be exhausting to chase after a toddler, especially doing it more or less on her own. He doubted he had the patience to be a good father these days.

"Maybe you ought to get around to building that fence so he can't wander off," Jackson said, nodding toward the pile of lumber lying beside the garage.

"That's actually a swing set we bought for Luc back in May. My dad planned to build it, but none of the wood came labeled, so he set it aside to puzzle over later." Gabby shrugged with a pleasant sigh, clearly unperturbed by her father's failure. "One of these days."

Luc finally scampered back around the garden and tugged on her sweat-shirt, leaving a dirty smudge to go with the jelly stain. "I hungwee, Mama."

"Okay." She bent down to kiss his head. "Let's go make some oatmeal with raisins." Then she turned to Jackson. "Would you like some, too?"

*Very much.*

"No, thanks. Actually, I need to run to an appointment." He saluted Luc, who'd begun to stack a pile of small stones. "Have a good day, buddy."

Then he turned and beelined to the garage before he changed his mind. He jogged up the metal stairs, sneaking a final glance at the twosome as they ducked around the back of the tired little farmhouse.

Jackson sighed. It'd been weeks since he'd had a drink, and longer since he'd had sex. Now he knew six weeks here would test a lot more than his ability to control his impulses with alcohol.

~

By eight-thirty in the morning, Jackson had shifted his position on the doctor's sofa for the fourth time. Avocado-green carpeting spanned the floor of the tiny office. A wall of bookshelves cluttered with books and knickknacks added to Jackson's sense of claustrophobia. The old-fashioned clock ticking off each second didn't help matters. If not for the abundant light streaming through the large plate glass window to Jackson's left, he might have lost his mind.

Doctor Joseph Millard, or Doc, as he'd asked to be called, sat opposite him in an Eames-style lounge chair, with pen and paper in hand. The man's salt-and-pepper hair matched his closely cropped beard. His eyes and mouth were bracketed with the deep lines one would expect to see on a person who spent a fair amount of time outdoors in harsh climates. His eyes, green and alert, twinkled with what appeared to be good humor. He wore a long-sleeve Polo pullover, khakis cuffed at the ankle, and Birkenstocks that looked twice as old as the furnishings.

Despite Doc's friendly and relaxed demeanor, Jackson had been perspiring as if he'd been handcuffed to a chair beneath a single, bright spotlight. Torture. Cruel and unusual punishment. Either term would apply to the experience of being forced to talk about personal things with anyone these days, let alone a stranger.

"I'm not going to shoot you, you know." Doc chuckled, set aside his notepad, and leaned forward. "I don't have every answer, but I can tell you this. We could meet every day for the next six weeks, but if you don't talk, we won't make much progress."

Jackson scrubbed his hands over his face. "Sorry."

"Don't apologize. I'm just trying to tell you that this is a safe space. Nothing you say goes beyond these walls. No judgment, either."

"That's a neat trick." Jackson slid his hands along his thighs without looking directly at Doc. "Teach me to be nonjudgmental and I'll be your slave for life."

"That's hard for you, then?"

"Me and most of the world." When Doc watched Jackson without comment, he continued. "We're raised to know right from wrong, live by the 'Golden Rule,' and all that shit. So when people do wrong or screw you over, it's pretty hard not to judge, isn't it?"

"What's the payoff from casting judgment?"

Jackson scowled, crossing his arms. "I feel better."

"Do you?" As he uttered the words, sunlight split through the prism of the crystal pendant hanging in the office window, scattering tidbits of rainbows across the walls. Like opposing perspectives, the rays of light looked entirely different depending on which side of the prism you stood, or sat.

"Yeah, I do."

Doc's skeptical gaze caused Jackson to make yet another judgment. One having to do with his general sense that New Age juju wouldn't help him find answers. If Doc started chanting, he was outta here.

"Listen, Doc, I'm on a short timeline here, which means it's probably best if we don't waste a lot of time with hypotheticals and what ifs. Just tell me, straight up, what I need to do and let's get it done."

Doc grinned and slouched back into his seat, crossing one sandal-clad foot over his knee. "Sorry to tell you, it doesn't work that way. You have to be willing to examine your thoughts and behaviors, to identify your triggers, and then, ultimately, begin to modify the stuff that gets you into trouble."

Jackson practically flung his head back against the sofa cushions. "Shit."

"Don't lose hope. Today wasn't fruitless. I know your mom's death was the first major setback in your life. You've alluded to some things with your siblings and ex-girlfriend, and I can see you're a man who prefers action to discussion. We can build on this, as long as you're willing to challenge yourself. To get real honest and stop pretending that you have no role in your own problems."

Jackson cracked his knuckles while keeping his gaze on the floor. Doc was no dummy, as evidenced by the way he framed this as a challenge. Apparently he managed to pick up on Jackson's pride and competitive spirit during this first forty-five-minute appointment. Maybe the guy had something to offer after all.

After another moment, Jackson raised his head and met Doc's inquiring gaze. "Friday morning, same time?"

"Friday morning."

Jackson rose and shook the man's hand before bolting to his car. On the drive back to his apartment, he realized he had an entire day to kill. He'd already exercised and eaten, and he didn't want to waste time watching TV, especially considering the ancient model in the apartment.

No work. No distractions. No booze.

Scratching his head, he wondered what had convinced him downtime would be a good thing.

He pulled his Jeep up to the garage. None of the Bouchards were in the yard, and Gabby's truck was gone. He started for the apartment stairwell when he noticed the play set lumber stacked there waiting for someone's attention.

A project would be a productive use of his time and talent, and it had been a long time since he'd been anyone's hero. What better than to be one for a little tyke whose dad seemed to be MIA? Besides, few things provided a more satisfying way to release tension than the contents of his tool kit.

He reversed course and went to fetch it from the back of the Jeep. A man in his business never traveled far without a basic set of tools at the ready. He scanned the yard, wondering where Gabby would prefer to locate the swings. He only saw two viable options in terms of sizable plots of flat ground, and one seemed too close to the garden.

Although it might be better to wait and clear it with her or her father first, having a purpose for his day seemed critical. Plus, the surprise element of his plan excited him. Worst-case scenario, he'd disassemble the swing set and reassemble it elsewhere if Gabby didn't approve of his choice. Not like he didn't have time.

∽

Gabby unbuckled Luc from his car seat and plopped him in the grocery cart seat before slamming the door shut. Once they entered the store, she fumbled through her purse, searching for the grocery list.

Naturally, Luc began reaching for every bright-colored, plastic gizmo within what he considered to be his reach.

"No, Luc. Mommy's in a hurry. We have to go home and cook dinner." *And clean dishes, bathe you, read you a story, tuck you into bed, and then maybe, if I'm lucky, I'll get ten minutes to myself before I collapse into bed.*

They passed by an end-cap display unit filled with Halloween Oreos. Luc's little legs began kicking, catching her once in the gut. "Mama, cookies. I want cookies."

His cherub face turned bright red with the strain of his yearning, making her feel guilty for saying, "No, buddy. Not today."

"Aw, come on, Gabs. Give my boy some cookies." Noah's smooth-talking voice took her by surprise, which she covered before turning around to face him. How like Noah to turn up when least expected, or wanted, and undermine her authority.

"Hello." Beneath a polite smile, she buried the hurt, anger, and flat-out irritation seeing him inspired. *I wouldn't have Luc without him.* She reminded herself of that blessing each and every time she saw Noah, which had kept her from punching him square in the face that first year after he'd left her.

It must work well, because he seemed fairly oblivious to the fact that she had any negative personal feelings about him whatsoever. He still tried to charm her at every opportunity. Like now, she thought, as he leaned in and kissed her cheek.

"Dada!" Luc reached toward Noah.

"Hey, Luc." He high-fived his son, but didn't kiss or hug him despite having not seen him for fifteen days—not that she was counting. Then again, Noah's affection had always been reserved for the ladies.

"Why can't Luc have any cookies?" Noah asked.

"Because they're loaded with artificial food coloring that isn't good for him or his brain." Then she frowned. "You'd see the effect it has on him if you paid better attention."

Noah shot her a sharp look of disapproval. "Don't start, Gabs. I know I was pretty shitty that first year, but I'm getting better. He knows I'm his daddy."

"Barely," she mumbled. She could go on for hours about the many ways that Noah had failed both her and Luc, as a man and a father. But she wouldn't. Not now, and certainly not here in the middle of the grocery store.

"That'll change." Noah spoke with certainty, like always, but she didn't believe him. She'd learned the hard way not to count on him in any way that mattered.

She looked at him, standing there in his police uniform with his hands on his hips. Dashing. Still as handsome as he was that summer they'd spent making love as often as and wherever they could. *Two fools.*

When she'd told him about the pregnancy, he suggested an abortion. She'd refused but, afraid of losing him, she'd countered with the compromise of giving the baby up for adoption.

Noah had stuck around until her belly started growing. Then things got too real. Or maybe granny panties and a baby bump didn't turn him on. All she knew for sure was that he gave her the heave-ho and moved on to Linda Wallace for a few months, and then others after that.

By the time Luc was born, she'd gotten over Noah and fallen in love with someone worthy—her son. With her dad's help, she'd kept Luc and never once regretted the decision.

Eventually Noah did begin to take some interest in their son, although it often seemed as unreliable as his interest in any one woman. Luckily, Noah had never once demanded any kind of shared custody, most likely because he didn't want to be responsible for paying child support. Gabby never asked for a dime because she didn't want to share custody. Honestly, she couldn't think of anything she'd like less than having to deal with Noah on a more regular basis.

So now she and Noah did a polite dance in front of their son. She'd never keep Luc from knowing his father, but she worried about her son forming an attachment. Noah didn't do commitment with anyone, so it would only be a matter of time before Luc's heart would get trashed by his father just like hers had been stomped on by her mother.

Some people simply aren't meant to be parents. Woe to the children of those folks, because that kind of rejection reverberates over and over, like an echo in a canyon. Gabby planned to protect her son from ever experiencing the pain of being crushed by someone he trusted.

"Hey, pal, whatcha gonna be for Halloween?" Noah asked Luc as he lifted a bag of Oreos from the display and tossed it in her cart, eliciting a rapturous clap from their son.

Luc raised both hands overhead and spread his little fingers wide. "Cookie Monstore!"

"Huh?" Noah's dissatisfied expression deflated Luc's enthusiasm. "How about a cop, or football player, or a superhero?"

"Silly Daddy." Gabby elbowed Noah out of the way. "Cookie Monster is an awesome costume." And then under her breath, she added to him, "And a warm one."

"Sooner or later he's got to give up stuffed animals and learn to be a man, Gabs," Noah said quietly. At least he hadn't made that pronouncement loud enough to inflict further damage on his son's little ego.

She bit back a quip about Noah needing to learn that lesson himself. "Maybe next year *you'd* prefer to buy his costume and take him around town for candy?"

He flushed, which she knew he would, just as she knew he'd be evasive and never commit to that plan—certainly not this far in advance, at any rate.

As predicted, he quirked his killer smile. "I still miss that pointed tongue of yours, Gabs . . . and all the things it used to do to me."

Now it was her turn to flush. Noah had never made secret his interest in the two of them revisiting their former sexual relationship, but she'd never trust him again with her heart, or Luc's.

As far as she could tell, he hadn't changed at all in three years, but she sure had. "Now I'm using it to say good-bye. I've got things to do, Noah. See you 'round."

"Brush me off now, but sooner or later you and I *will* kiss and make up. After all, we," he circled his finger amid himself, Luc, and her, "are a family."

The possessive tone in his voice caught her so off guard, her mind blanked. Apparently mistaking her silence as some kind of consent, Noah winked and walked toward the registers.

When his back was turned, she returned the Oreos to the display and braced for Luc's disgruntled wail. Her son let one rip, but she pushed the cart down the aisle before Noah turned around to see the cause of the commotion.

Twenty minutes—and, to her chagrin, one bag of orange-and-black Oreos—later, Gabby pulled into the driveway. The day, the run-in with Noah, and the battle she'd valiantly fought and lost with her son had all exhausted her, making her feel much older, if not wiser, than twenty-two.

Dusk had gobbled up the sky, but the shadows of the yard looked different. She blinked several times. In the side yard, beneath a maple tree, she watched Jackson putting away tools beside a swing set.

Luc's swing set.

Gratitude bubbled up faster than frothy soda in a shaken bottle. Who *was* this man? She turned off the truck and set her hand to the base of her throat to try to calm her throbbing pulse.

Jackson looked up and waved.

Gabby jumped down from the truck and unfastened Luc from his seat. She held his hand and walked him around the front of the cab. Kneeling down, she pointed toward Jackson. "Hey, Luc, look at what Jackson built."

Luc's eyes widened over a giant smile before he took off toward the slide, his little legs nearly tripping over themselves along the way.

"Whoa, buddy. Take your time so you don't fall." Jackson chuckled while watching Luc dive-bomb the base of the slide and attempt to scale its surface. With lightning-quick reflexes, Jackson leapt to Luc's side. "Maybe you should use the steps, Luc."

Jackson's grin broadened as Luc scrambled around the swing set while happiness shot out of her son in high-pitched squeals.

Anyone who said Tom Cruise had the world's greatest smile had never seen Jackson St. James smile. Even his eyes crinkled with joy this time. Positively breathtaking.

Gabby had never had anyone do something so generous for her or her son without expecting payment of one kind or another. Somehow, without asking, she knew Jackson's gift came without strings.

Such a rare and unexpected thing, like snow in Florida, or finding a four-leaf clover. Lightness stole through her, fizzy and warm, and happy tears welled in her eyes. Without a thought in her head, she walked right over to Jackson and wrapped her arms around his waist.

"Thank you!" She pressed her cheek to his chest for a second—long enough to hear his heart stutter—then released him and stepped back, somewhat disoriented.

Even in the dim light, she saw Jackson's cheeks turn crimson. He rubbed the back of his neck, which revealed his modesty. "My pleasure."

It occurred to her then that he had no idea how incredible he was—how extraordinary his gift.

"This is honestly the nicest thing anyone has ever done for Luc and me." She felt her eyes mist again. "How can I repay you?"

"I like to keep busy." He waved dismissively. "This gave me something to do today."

Gabby rolled her eyes, laughing. "As if you couldn't find anything better to do than build this swing set."

Luc's sudden cry of pain made them both swivel in his direction. He'd reached the bottom of the slide with too much speed and done a face-plant.

In an instant, Gabby knelt by his side, brushed a blade or two of grass from his forehead, and kissed his boo-boo. "You're okay, buddy. Now, what do you say to Jackson for this awesome job he did today?"

Luc grasped her shirt and stared up at Jackson through wet eyelashes. "Fank you."

"Anytime. Maybe tomorrow we can show your mom how high you can go on this swing." He gave the empty swing a little push and raised his hand about chest high. "Maybe this high?"

Luc nodded. "Higher!"

"Oh, yeah! I knew you were tough." Jackson then introduced Luc to the fist bump.

Gabby knew she was gaping at Jackson, but how could she help it? Not long ago, Luc's own father thought himself "the man" because he'd handed him a bag of cookies. Meanwhile, Jackson had built the swing set and seemed comfortable talking to Luc, too.

If she were cynical, Jackson's grand gesture might raise all kinds of red flags. Thankfully, she wasn't particularly cynical. At her core, she believed most people were fundamentally good and sincere. In twenty-four hours, Jackson had already proven himself to be both, if not much more.

"If your mom says it's okay, we'll see how high you can fly." He winked at Luc and then hefted his toolbox off the ground. Glancing at Gabby, he said, "Time for a much-needed shower."

"Jackson." She reached out to grasp his forearm. "At least join us for dinner. Pork roast, carrots, and homemade applesauce."

His gaze rested on her hand, which remained on his arm. Apprehension seemed to seize control of his body, tensing his muscles. When their eyes met again, she held her breath until he let loose a sigh and grinned. "That sounds delicious, thanks."

"See you in an hour. Come right through the kitchen door."

He nodded without further comment, and then wandered off to his apartment. She watched him go and, when he was out of view, spun around and allowed the satisfied grin she'd been repressing to spread. Though utterly pointless, she held fast to her mad crush. It had been too long since her heart had sung this particular song, and she had no wish to silence it.

Luc had sprawled his belly across a swing with his arms and legs out, pretending to be some kind of airplane.

"Come on, Luc. Let's go see if Pappy's home." When she took his hand, she remembered the groceries she'd abandoned in the truck.

She should probably worry about the fact that Jackson's presence stirred up the restlessness she'd buried three years ago. Sitting on her impulses had kept life sane these past few years. Sane and boring.

On second thought, how much harm could come from chasing a little short-term thrill?

# CHAPTER FOUR

Jackson crossed the yard unsettled about why, exactly, he'd accepted Gabby's dinner invitation. Could be that he hadn't enjoyed a home-cooked meal in months. Or that Gabby and Luc's gratitude had restored a fraction of his rusty sense of well-being. Or it could be that he simply didn't know what else to do with himself for the next several hours.

Admitting that last part made him cringe and wonder when he'd become *that* aimless guy. Swallowed pride tasted more caustic than cheap Scotch, which he'd still settle for right about now. His mouth watered in response to the easy option of lying on his sofa with a neat glass—or more—of whiskey to chase away stress, resentment, loneliness, and pretty much every other discomfort.

Contrary to others' opinions, he didn't disapprove of numbness as a coping mechanism. What was so wrong with dulling the bruising ache of life's sucker punches? Numbness helped a man heal. He'd just been slow to mend.

No matter what his family or others thought, booze had merely been his *choice*, not his vice. Besides, it seemed pretty hypocritical for society to pop Xanax and Oxy like Smarties while sanctimoniously looking down on a man who appreciated the benefits of bourbon.

The chilly bite of a crisp fall breeze sank its teeth into Jackson's shoulders. Some of the trees retained a handful of leaves, which rustled overhead. Twilight transformed dull gray tree bark into silver coats of armor, creating an army of soldiers to protect the Bouchards' home.

Funny how vivid everything now looked, sounded, tasted.

During recent weeks his senses had reawakened somewhat painfully, like the prickling, itchy twinges freezing hands suffer when plunged into warm water. Maybe that explained why the hairs on his body stood, uncomfortably, in a state of constant awareness. Why he kept questioning every small decision. Why anxiety tickled its way up his neck like a centipede.

Jackson trotted up the two steps to the back door. He blew a warm breath on his knuckles before knocking.

Jon greeted him with a pleasant smile. "Come on in."

"Thank you, sir." A sweet-and-savory aroma wafted toward him when he entered the kitchen, which had been slightly overheated by the ancient-looking oven. The scent invaded his nostrils, its homey essence gliding through his body like a gentle caress, loosening his bunched muscles. "Smells awesome."

Jon closed the door. "Gabby cooked up her maple-mustard glazed pork. You're in for a treat."

"I appreciate the hospitality."

"I ought to be thanking *you*." Jon slapped Jackson's shoulder. "One look at all that unmarked lumber made me run in the opposite direction. How'd you build it so fast?"

"Experience." Jackson unzipped his fleece. He looked toward the hallway when he heard footsteps approaching. Gabby appeared in the doorway with Luc in tow.

She'd cleaned up a bit since he'd last seen her. Old jeans exchanged for leggings and a cozy sweater, mussed hair combed into long, loose curls, gloss smeared on petal-pink lips.

Doubtful she dressed like that just for dinner with her dad. Jackson covered a surge of pure male satisfaction with a modest grin.

"Hey, Jackson." She lifted Luc into his booster seat. "Hope you brought your appetite."

Her cheery face shone like an evening sun, tinting her cheeks with peaches and pinks. He needed to stop thinking about her fresh-faced prettiness, yet his mind couldn't think of much else whenever he looked at her.

Jackson forced his thoughts back to the conversation and patted his stomach. "Always."

"Have a seat," Jon said, gesturing toward one of the wooden chairs gathered around a small oak table.

While the Bouchards went about setting out a pitcher of lemonade and ladling fresh applesauce into a communal bowl, Jackson took advantage of the opportunity to study the kitchen, which hadn't been updated since the 1970s. Dark wood-laminate cabinetry, mustard-colored Formica, vinyl flooring. The bones of the roughly two hundred square feet of space were good, though, needing only cosmetic upgrades.

The substitution of a large picture window above the sink and a French door to the backyard would immediately brighten the room. His mind immediately envisioned the walls outfitted with reclaimed wood cabinetry, accent beams on the ceiling, a slate floor, and stainless steel appliances.

"So where'd you get experience with swing sets?" Jon asked while taking the seat to Jackson's left. "Do you have kids?"

"No kids, although in about six or so months I'll be an uncle for the first time." Jackson grinned at the image of a pregnant Vivi, which made him happy despite also being a reminder of the chance at fatherhood that had been taken from him. He pushed that anger aside and looked at Jon. "I'm a general contractor—focusing on residential projects. That play set was no big deal, I promise. But I'll still cash in on this dinner."

The bleating of the house phone interrupted their conversation. Gabby set the pork roast on a cutting board before answering.

"It's for you, Dad." She handed her father the phone and then quickly sliced the roast and spooned roasted carrots into another bowl while her father spoke to whomever had called. Jackson caught himself admiring her multitasking efficiency.

Jon hung up the phone and sighed. "The burglar alarm went off at one of the vacation homes I manage. Got to meet up with the cops to check it out."

"I'll set your plate in the oven." Gabby removed his plate from the table.

"Thanks." Jon looked at Jackson, shrugging. "Guess we'll finish our conversation some other time." Then he snatched his car keys off a hook by the door and disappeared into the darkness.

"Pappy!" Luc bellowed as he banged a tiny, rubber-handled fork against the table.

"Settle down, Luc." Gabby hastened to shut the door, rubbing her arms with her hands for warmth. "It's already so cold this early in October. We could see frost soon."

"Probably," Jackson replied, watching her cross back to the stove. She moved fluidly but with purpose, unruffled by disruptions. Made her appear more mature than he suspected was true. "Need help?"

"No, this is all set. You relax." She then went about setting all the food on the table while humming, which drew on memories of his mother in the kitchen.

He'd made peace with her passing, or so he'd thought until that specific remembrance rolled into the present like a bowling ball, crashing into his thoughts and sending them spinning.

Like Gabby, his mom's name began with a *G*, Graciela. Like Gabby, she met the world with a combo of candor and good humor. Like Gabby's, her mere presence had comforted.

He'd thought he could manage a little crush on a girl he barely knew, but he could *not* afford to start to see her as someone or something . . . more. More intriguing, more layered, more appealing. Thinking her to be more of anything only proved him to be moronic, given how many of the people he'd believed in had ultimately disappointed him.

If it weren't for the fact that Gabby looked happy for his company tonight, he'd have bolted to escape his disconcerting feelings. Like a reflex, his discomfort summoned a craving for whiskey.

He glared at the pitcher of lemonade, which wouldn't numb one damn thing. Nor would it help him come up with something to say to make the whole situation less awkward. Not that she looked the least bit self-conscious. He braced against a wave of envy at her apparent peace of mind.

Collecting himself, he smiled at Gabby when she finally took her seat at the table. After she piled applesauce and carrots onto Luc's plate, she began meticulously cutting his pork into bite-size pieces. Her fingernails were short and unpolished, but her hands were nonetheless graceful in motion. Jackson found himself oddly captivated watching her with her son. Despite her youth, Gabby had obviously taken to motherhood quite naturally.

She glanced at him, so he masked his thoughts before she took notice. Waving toward the steaming serving dishes, she said, "Don't wait for me. Help yourself while it's still hot. I'm used to cold dinners."

Her offhand complaint held no note of resentment. She must be used to making dozens of such sacrifices for her son each week. Had he honestly been as prepared to be a father as he'd believed back when Alison stole the choice from him?

Niggling questions aside, any remembrance of that loss—and lack of vote—flared like fanned coal embers. Jackson loaded his plate, praying the heavenly scented glaze Gabby had smothered over the roast would divert his thoughts.

The mustard-maple medley did not disappoint.

"Holy he—" he began until he remembered Luc. "*Heck*, Gabby, this is delicious."

The compliment earned him one of her half-dimple grins. "Thanks."

A man could grow dependent on the high from those grins.

Jackson stole a few glimpses of her while she cut her own food and wiped up one of Luc's applesauce puddles without criticism. Watching her raised a dozen questions, but he kept quiet, apparently still incapable of conversing with a woman he wanted but *would not* seduce, even if she had dressed up for him.

He suspected she was forming questions of her own as an awkward silence descended.

Luc fixed the problem by kicking his feet and reaching toward the giant bowl of applesauce in the center of the table. "More!"

Gabby slid him a cockeyed stare. "No seconds until you eat your meat, buster."

Ignoring her, Luc groped, with both hands, in a desperate effort to reach the serving spoon while whining, "More, Mama!"

"I should've warned you it wouldn't be a relaxing meal." Gabby glanced at Jackson apologetically. Then she speared a bite of pork and engaged Luc in the airplane game. "Zoom zoom. Open wide for Mommy."

Did any real kid ever fall for that ploy? Luc sure didn't, but it forced him to stop whining long enough to seal his lips. Jackson couldn't help but chuckle. Taking pity on Gabby, Jackson leaned toward Luc. "If you don't want that pork, I'll take it."

Without a warning, Jackson swiped a piece from Luc's plate and popped it in his mouth, licking his fingers for good measure. Both Gabby's and Luc's eyes widened. Jackson raised his left arm and made a muscle while looking at Gabby with grave seriousness. "Is it working? I mean, I'm going to win the swinging contest tomorrow, right?"

Gabby caught on quickly. "I think so. If you eat all that pork, you'll be really strong."

"That's what I thought." Jackson swiped another bite of Luc's dinner.

Luc scowled and batted his hand down a touch too slowly. "Dat's mine."

"Oh, you want it now? 'Cause I really like it." Jackson slowly reached toward Luc's plate one last time, but Luc tugged his plastic dish away. Then, with some amount of bravado, his grubby little fingers stuffed a piece of pork into his mouth.

Jackson's little victory brought a smile to Gabby's face, which in turn breathed new life into his own lungs. Funny how such a simple moment could do that for him. He winked at her and then met Luc's wary gaze with an exaggerated look of defeat. "Okay, you win. Guess I'll have to find some other way to grow big muscles."

Luc didn't take his eyes off Jackson as he chewed a second bite of pork while wearing a look of challenge. It took every ounce of control at Jackson's disposal to suppress the laughter and lightness pushing out from within—a welcome relief from the snug band normally cinching his chest.

"You'll be a great uncle, Jackson." Gabby's quiet declaration shook him as much as it pleased him. Of course, she had no way of knowing his history with Alison, or his reasons for being here in Vermont.

When Vivi and David had questioned whether his drinking might someday hurt their child, even inadvertently, it had taken the fight right out of him. Made him feel about two inches tall, in fact. It was the single most compelling reason why he'd caved to his family's demands that he "reevaluate" his habits.

Each time he recalled the ambush—er, intervention—it set him on his heels. While he still didn't believe he'd ever been a drunk, he did recoil each time he remembered the helpless, despondent look in Vivi's eyes, or the steel audible in her promise to protect her child. The fact that she worried Jackson would turn into a man like her dad had stung.

"Why'd that make you frown?" Gabby stared at him, head tipped in question.

"Was I frowning?" Jackson ate his last scoop of applesauce and decided to turn the tables on being the center of attention. While he hoped one day to recapture the open spirit that used to be second nature, it seemed too fraught with consequence right now. "Have you lived here your whole life?"

"Pretty much. I was born in Burlington. My great-grandparents immigrated there from Montreal, but my parents and I moved here when I was about Luc's age."

At the mention of parents, it occurred to him he hadn't seen or heard anything about Mrs. Bouchard. He sat back and stretched his legs, assuming Gabby, like him, had lost her mother too young. "My mom died a few years ago, so I know how tough it is to lose a mother, especially when yours could've helped you with Luc, too."

"Oh, I'm sorry for your loss, Jackson. But my mom's not dead." She scrunched her nose. "Not literally, anyway."

Before he could ask a follow-up question, Luc interrupted, his cheeks glistening with applesauce. "All done, Mama. All done!"

She rewarded his empty plate with applause and kissed his sloppy cheeks. When her tongue licked her lips to test the sweetness, she might as well have been licking Jackson's neck for the way his entire body hummed in response. "Good boy, Luc. You're going to be big and strong, like Jackson."

"Like Dada," he said, blissfully unaware of the way his mother winced at the mention of the man.

"Mm hmm." She helped Luc down from his booster, then shot Jackson a quick glance. "Hang on a sec. I'll get him settled in with a video so he doesn't destroy the house while we have coffee."

Once Gabby left the kitchen, Jackson wondered what kind of man would walk away from her—or worse, from his own son. A moron, that's who. Why'd such a cute, capable girl fall for a moron? Then again, Luc's dad had probably been young, scared, and unprepared. Jackson knew firsthand that unplanned pregnancies were the quickest way to have the rose-colored glasses stripped away from a relationship.

He stood to make himself useful rather than sit around getting irritated about a guy he didn't even know. Gathering the dishes, he rinsed everything and had begun to load the dishwasher by the time Gabby returned.

"Oh, please stop! You're our guest." She hurried toward him, shooing him away. "You don't need to do dishes."

"Surely you know the main rule in the kitchen: the cook doesn't clean." Jackson nodded toward the roasting pan. "Gimme that pot. I work magic with a Brillo pad."

She cracked a smile and then followed his orders.

"I bet you do." She picked up a clean dish towel. "I'll dry."

Gabby leaned her hip against the counter and, with a grin on her face, waited in companionable silence. Rather than shake off the sense of comfort she inspired, he decided to enjoy it.

He plunged the pot into hot water, picturing her standing in this kitchen night after night, feeding and cleaning up after her son and father. Must be exhausting and, at times, lonely. Again he couldn't help but wonder about Luc's dad, and whether or not Gabby missed the man, or resented him.

Realizing that he'd only be in town a short while, he decided to pry.

"So, I have to ask, but you don't have to answer. Is Luc's dad in the picture?" Jackson kept his eyes on the pan in the sink as he scrubbed, allowing her some privacy despite the probing question.

"He's around." A long sigh preceded the tumble of words that spilled out next. "I was only eighteen when I got pregnant. He was twenty-one and wanted no part of fatherhood. When Luc turned one, he started taking an interest, but he's not what anyone would call an 'involved' father." She shrugged. "Suits me fine, though. The only thing I need from him is his promise not to meddle in how I raise my son. That would make my life harder, and frankly, worry me. For the most part, our informal deal seems to work for him, too, so all's well that ends well, right?"

Her gentle snicker didn't fully conceal what Jackson guessed was a deep-rooted sense of disappointment, if not for herself, then for Luc.

He handed Gabby the pot to dry. Although he wouldn't say he exactly applauded her glee in limiting Luc's father's role, he also couldn't help but respect her fortitude. "I give you a ton of credit. Lots of women in your shoes would've made different choices."

Women like Alison. Once again the frosty memory of her chilling text—the one notifying him she'd aborted their child despite his pleas—traveled so icily through his veins it seared.

Why hadn't Alison been more like Gabby instead of like Luc's deadbeat dad? At moments like this, Jackson couldn't remember why the hell he'd ever thought himself in love with that woman. Maybe Gabby felt the same way about Luc's dad. Either way, his mood began to wither.

"I thought about giving him up for adoption, but by the end of the pregnancy there really was no other choice for me." Gabby's feminine sigh yanked him back from his morbid flashback. "God forbid I be like my mom."

Having already invaded her privacy about Luc's dad, he decided not to press her about the "not literally dead" mom, opting instead to wait and watch.

For the briefest moment, her guard went down and the light in her eyes dimmed. He recognized that bleak sense of betrayal, but could think of nothing to do or say to soothe her. After all, his default method of choice—a bottle and a tall glass—hadn't worked out so well for him.

She set the dry pan on the counter and faced him, head-on, like she seemed to do most everything else. In a moment of sheer envy, he discovered her grit to be more than a little breathtaking.

"She left my dad and me right before my sixteenth birthday. It all started when she got a severe case of shingles, of all things. She had complications—postherpetic neuralgia—and suffered intense nerve pain for months, so her doctor gave her heavy painkillers to help. She got hooked on them, though. When the disease went into remission and the prescription ran out, she found other ways to get the pills in town. Eventually those dealers led her to heroin, which is cheaper. When my dad finally drew a line in the sand, she chose that life over rehab and us. It stinks because a part of me will always wonder why, wonder where she is, wonder if there'll ever be a day when we might meet again under better circumstances."

"What would you do if she reached out?" Jackson knew his question had as much to do with his own situation as it did with hers.

"I'm not sure." Then a frown wrinkled her forehead. "I have good memories from before she got sick. But those last few years were ugly, so when she actually left, I mostly felt relief." Gabby grimaced. "Am I awful for feeling that way? 'Cause relief was at least equal to grief. I miss what was, but I don't miss the daily worry. After the shock and sorrow passed, we found peace at home—except for the times *I* acted out now and then." She shrugged apologetically.

Jackson worked to maintain an unruffled expression in the wake of her emotional outpouring, but inside his stomach twisted like a screw. Had David, Vivi, Cat, and Hank all felt a sense of relief in *his* absence?

Had he gotten so absorbed in his own pain that he really hadn't recognized he might be causing theirs? "So you don't want to see her?"

After a pronounced pause, Gabby sighed, gazing off at some distant point while she spoke. "Normally I believe in second chances, but in this case, I'm not sure. It's not worth considering, since it'll never happen." A note of sadness rang in that last remark. "The most important thing the whole experience taught me is that I have to be a mom Luc can always be proud of. One he can count on. I won't let him be hurt by someone he should be able to trust. Not even if that person's his own father."

Gabby's gaze returned to him. "You're pale. Have I horrified you with my seedy family history?"

Pale? That was better than blood red, which was what he would've guessed given his spike in body temperature. A beat of misplaced anger surfaced thanks to the unwanted mirror she'd thrust at him. But she had no idea of his life or his secrets, so she hadn't known how her feelings about her mother's behavior would affect him.

Gabby's baby blues filled with concern, which chased away his irritation. God, he admired her strength and sincerity. So resilient, which reminded him a bit of Vivi. Well, minus the quirks and the fact that he didn't—in any way—think of Gabby like a sister.

Somehow the fierce little warrior in front of him remained chipper and compassionate despite being abandoned, getting pregnant by a dickhead, and living her whole life in this tiny town. Tar-thick shame stiffened him as he contrasted his relative weakness against the strength of this wisp of a woman.

"No. It's not you." He cleared his throat. "It's me."

"Oh?" Her brows furrowed. "So someone close to you battles addiction, too?"

"In a manner of speaking." He twisted his neck, scanning everything in the room but her, unable to remember why he'd thought for one second opening this door had been a brave move. His shirt clung to his skin thanks to a sudden trickle of perspiration.

"Cryptic." A resigned grin flickered, but she didn't press.

Suddenly infuriated with himself for being comparatively spineless and dishonest, he met her gaze in an endeavor to deserve her respect. Too bad the truth would probably shatter her opinion of him.

"According to my family, I'm the screwup. I'm on this 'hiatus' because they ambushed me—told me to change my drinking habits if I wanted to be part of my niece or nephew's life." He watched her jaw drop open and then, with some chagrin, said, "Told ya you wouldn't think our meeting 'serendipitous' for long."

Gabby's mind blanked upon hearing his unexpected confession. A confession that explained the occasional melancholy she'd witnessed behind his smiles.

She floundered for the right words while reconciling this news with the man who'd kept her safe in the storm, who'd kindly built Luc's play set, who'd burst into her mundane existence and unknowingly stirred hope for something more from life—something better—that she'd previously all but surrendered.

How could *this* man be anything like her mother?

The unwelcome insight cast him in smoky light, making her distrust her instincts. For a day he'd shimmered like an oasis in the desert, and apparently that had been exactly what he was. A fantasy—the swift, sudden loss of which hit her hard.

Of course, unlike her mother, Jackson had chosen his family over addiction. He'd chosen to try to change for their sakes. And he'd been honest with her despite knowing how she might view him in light of her own past.

Sensing he didn't often open himself up that way, she shouldn't take it lightly.

"For what it's worth, you seem to be handling it very well." She stood uncharacteristically still, hearing nothing but the low murmur coming from the television in the other room.

"I've only been here twenty-four hours—or three strong cravings, depending on how I keep track." He shoved his hands in his pockets. "Time will tell."

Little by little the warm, playful Jackson who'd tricked her son into eating pork withdrew behind a hard shell. Head slightly bowed, gaze darting around the room to avoid hers, a frown wrestling for control of his face.

She knew exactly how sickening it felt to expose an unflattering self-truth. How he must feel standing before her now—vulnerable—braced for judgment and disappointment. Precisely how she'd felt when forced to announce her accidental pregnancy.

So while she couldn't pretend enthusiasm or nonchalance, she would take care not to treat it, or him, with scorn. "And in that twenty-four hours, you've twice proven yourself to be a caring, generous guy. A guy who also, obviously, loves his family enough to make changes. All in all, I'd bet on you."

She noticed the corners of his mouth twitch upward for an instant, but then they settled back into a grim line.

"Listen, if it's okay with you, I'm going to skip coffee tonight." He let his arms fall to his sides.

Just then her father bustled through the kitchen door. "Wind's picking up out there. Think a storm is coming."

"Then it's a good thing I'm heading out before it starts." Jackson nodded at her father, a polite smile replacing his formerly serious mien. "Hopefully your 'emergency' was a nonevent."

"Nothing was missing, but the back slider was unlocked. I'm thinking some local kids know the house is empty and tried to sneak inside to drink or whatnot, then took off when the alarm went off." Jon shook his head. "Guess I shouldn't be surprised. People are forever making bad choices when it comes to booze and sex."

Gabby glanced at the floor, knowing her father had spoken without thinking. He hadn't meant to insult her. But given her own history, and everything she and Jackson had just discussed, the comment sucked the air out of the room.

Her dad seemed oblivious to the layers of tension as he crossed to the oven to retrieve his plate. He dipped his finger in the glaze and licked it, then slid an enthusiastic look at Jackson. "Good stuff, right?"

"Excellent, sir." Jackson grinned. "Enjoy your dinner."

Gabby followed behind Jackson and stood in the doorway as he made his way down the steps. The moon played hide-and-seek behind quick-moving gray clouds, but its light occasionally glinted off the dark strands of his hair. "Jackson!"

He glanced over his shoulder. "Yeah?"

"Thank you for trusting me . . ." She didn't know quite how to finish the sentence.

He merely nodded before turning and striding off to the garage.

"Close the door! It's cold in here," her father called from the table.

She doubted the warm kitchen would thaw the chilled hope still lodged in her heart, but she closed the door and went to sit with her dad while he ate.

Jackson's revelation didn't erase all the kindness he'd shown her, but it did shatter her illusions of him as a dependable sort of man.

She knew an addict wasn't reliable. Shouldn't be trusted. Could hurt her, and more importantly, Luc. Yet she wanted to believe otherwise about Jackson. Wanted to hold on to the bubbly feeling he inspired. To prove him to be unlike her mother and Noah, whom had both let her down.

"Everything okay?" Her dad's narrowed gaze demanded an answer.

"Yes, why?"

"You look troubled." He set down his fork. "Jackson didn't do anything disrespectful, did he?"

"No, Dad! He was a perfect gentleman. Got Luc to eat *and* did the dishes."

One of her dad's brows cocked, skeptically. "Don't go setting your sights on that man. He's going back to his real life next month."

She huffed to signal that *of course* she hadn't forgotten, which in fact she sort of had. Perhaps not forgotten so much as shoved aside. Willingly ignored in order to convince herself a brief flirtation would satisfy her well enough.

That kind of foolishness only proved the truth of her dad's belief about booze and sex. The clattering of hundreds of Legos being dumped onto the floor underscored the point, as if that were necessary.

# CHAPTER FIVE

Jackson heard the buzzing whir of a leaf blower start up. He glanced out his apartment window and saw Gabby blowing leaves from the driveway onto the lawn. Why would she do that?

He could help her but he hesitated, thinking it best to keep his distance. Ever since their conversation in the kitchen two nights ago, he'd been uneasy. Uneasy about what he'd divulged. Uneasy about his attraction to her. Uneasy about everything, including whatever the hell it was he thought he'd accomplish here in Vermont.

Aside from keeping his promise to play with Luc on the swings yesterday, he'd more or less kept his contact with Gabby to a minimum. Turning away from the window, he poured himself another cup of coffee and read through a lengthy update from Hank on two of their bigger renovation projects.

Growing increasingly antsy, he grabbed the old hiking boots he'd brought. A brisk climb up the nearby portion of the Appalachian Trail would be a healthy way to work off extra tension. At the very least, it would eat up another two or three hours of the day, which also meant that much less time to dwell on his troubles or to break down and chug a cold beer.

He was tying a double knot when he heard a loud clatter from outside. Rising from the kitchen chair, he strode to the window in time to see Gabby gingerly climbing up an extension ladder while carrying two buckets. For crissakes, a faint wind would blow her over. *So much for my hike.*

He dashed out the door and down the stairs. "Hey! Hold up."

She stilled, brows raised, and looked down. "What's wrong?"

Jackson grabbed hold of the ladder to steady it. "You shouldn't climb up there. It's dangerous."

"I know what I'm doing." She shot a patronizing smile his way before taking another step up. While he might otherwise like to stand there and admire this particular view of her rounded behind, he didn't want her to climb any higher.

"Gabby."

She huffed. "What?"

He scrubbed one hand over his face. "Maybe you do know what you're doing, but it's making me nervous."

"Then don't watch, but I've got to clean the gutters. Today's a perfect day—barely any wind, sunny."

"Okay." He could see reason. "Then come down and finish the leaves. I'll handle the gutters."

Her mouth opened and closed, then she scowled. "Don't tell me you're a chauvinist."

"I'm sure what you meant to say is 'Thank you for being so *chivalrous.*'" He grinned, not wanting to continue to argue while she dangled on a ladder rung several feet above him.

At least she laughed. "You're serious. I'm really making you nervous?"

"Yes, you really are. Please, I climb ladders and hang off rafters on a near-daily basis. Let me do this."

"Fine." She climbed down the ladder. Setting the buckets on the ground, she removed her gloves. "I doubt these will fit you, but you need something if you're going to clean out the muck."

"I've got work gloves in my car, thanks."

"Looks like you've got it all covered, then."

Gabby appeared miffed, which confused him. He scratched his head. "I sense that you're mad, although *my* typical response when someone offers help is to say 'thank you.'"

"Sorry." She glanced away. "Obviously I'm out of practice."

For some reason, that fact bothered him. And *that* reaction bothered him even more. He didn't want to care that her life seemed difficult and lonely. He had his own shit to sort out. Yet, she seemed like a girl who deserved a whole lot more than she was getting out of life.

When he'd been her age, he'd been freshly out of college, collecting his paychecks, and living the carefree life of a single guy. He'd never lacked for friends or amusement. In the few days that he'd been around here, he'd seen no evidence of either of those things in her life. He wondered if she even remembered how to have fun. Then the devil on his shoulder whispered that he could show her a good time.

"Forgiven." He excused himself to go grab his gloves before he did something stupid, then made his way up the ladder and started the unpleasant process of clearing the gutters.

While he worked, Gabby resumed leaf blowing. They didn't speak for the next several minutes. When she disappeared, he wondered where she'd gone until he heard a lawn mower engine sputter to life.

He glanced over his shoulder and saw her pushing a mulching mower straight toward the house. He froze on the top of the ladder, praying she didn't knock it out from under him.

She began mowing the leaves systematically, in neat rows, stopping occasionally to loosely rake a mowed area and remulch any remaining leaves. Then she attacked one large pile of leaves with that mower and shoveled the remains into a wheelbarrow, which she rolled over to her garden to spread.

Once again he had the chance to observe her industriousness. He could've sworn he saw her smiling at one point. He doubted Alison, or any woman he'd ever dated, would be smiling while mulching . . . if they'd ever mulched in the first place. The whole absurdity of the afternoon caused *him* to smile, and he realized he'd smiled more in the past couple of days than he had in longer than he could remember.

When he finished the gutters, he retracted the ladder and put everything away in the garage. Before he finished, she rolled the empty wheelbarrow into the garage.

"You don't like bark mulch?" he asked as he removed his gloves.

"Leaves are free." She shrugged. "Every penny counts."

He nodded, although truthfully he hadn't ever had financial worries. At least, he hadn't until this damn lawsuit.

"Listen, Jackson, I'm sorry if I came across as ungrateful earlier. Your help made such a difference. Now I have time to call Trax Farms about delivering the hay bales I want for our little Halloween party later this month *before* I get Luc from preschool."

He heard most of what she'd said, but his mind had stuck on, "Hay bales?"

Her eyes glinted with mischief. "I want to build a little maze for the kids over there. We'll do the traditional apple bobbing and such. You should come! Costume required, though."

"Sounds like a lot of work for you."

"Payoff is worth it." She smiled. "Anyhow, I've got to go start dinner and throw some laundry in the washer, so I'll see you later."

Work, work, work. Didn't she ever get tired, or resentful?

"Like I said before, I've got lots of spare time. When you need an extra hand, just ask."

"Thanks, but . . ." She fell silent, looking uncharacteristically shy.

"But?"

"I'm afraid accepting your help over and over will only make it harder when you go. You know, like how they say you don't miss something you never had? Kind of like money, I suppose. I suspect it's a lot easier to always be poor than it would be to suddenly lose money and go without what one used to take for granted." Her voice drifted off, presumably to the same distant spot reflected in her pretty eyes.

It took him an extra second or two to follow her logic, but he did get her point, even if it bugged him. He didn't want to make anything harder for her, so he relented. "Is that your polite way of asking me to keep my *chivalry* to myself?"

She smiled, and her cute little dimples popped into place. "Exactly."

Screw that, actually. She needed someone to shake her up and remind her that there were things equally as important as her damn responsibilities.

He hesitated before saying, "This may be out of line, but I hate that you seem so willing to settle for being alone, with no one to help you."

"I'm not alone." She seemed so earnestly satisfied. "I have Luc, and my dad helps a ton by giving us a safe, free place to live."

"You're so young. What about spontaneity? What about flirting and dancing and going to the movies? What about friends who pitch in and lighten the load? Make Luc's dad take more responsibility so you can enjoy life!"

He stopped, sensing that his tone had come out terser than he'd intended. He shook his head, unsettled. One look at her reddening face told him he'd gone too far.

"I don't *want* Luc's dad to be more involved, thank you. Besides, I thought you were here in Vermont to sort out your *own* stuff." She cocked her eyebrow. "Or is this one of those 'misery loves company' things, where your crappy situation seems better if you focus on what you think are my problems?"

"Hey, I don't deserve that." Maybe he'd spoken out of turn, but he hadn't meant to offend her.

"And *I* don't need to be analyzed by you, a guy I barely know, who apparently let 'fun' overtake his life to the point that his family gave him an ultimatum." As soon as she'd finished, her eyes widened as if she'd regretted the scolding. "Jackson, I'm sorry. I didn't—"

"Never mind." He waved her off. "I think I'll get on with the hike I'd been planning before I saw you hanging from the ladder."

Before she could say more, he stalked out of the garage. Mad at her, but madder at himself. What the hell had possessed him to start that conversation anyway?

Damn, he needed a drink.

~

Gabby sat near the living room window, watching Jackson's Jeep pull into the driveway. She wished she hadn't been taking so much notice of his comings and goings since their confrontation last week. After she'd thrown his drinking in his face, she'd wished she could've bitten off her tongue. Had her ugly words set him back? Had she somehow jeopardized his recovery?

The ever-present tendrils of uneasiness she'd known as a teen—those long hours spent studying her mom's moods and behavior to predict when she'd be high or pass out—had returned with a vengeance.

Resentment toward Jackson festered for bringing that burden back into her life, although perhaps that was unfair of her, given that he'd neither asked for her concern nor owed her anything. Still, she worried that he'd been drinking, and she prayed he had not. Most troubling, and despite having no business involving herself in his drama, she wanted to help him avoid temptation.

Her mind wandered back to that pleasant day Jackson had played with Luc on the swing set. Gabby had watched him from afar, listening to her son's delighted squeals. She'd remained in her garden, harvesting some pumpkins and attending her fall vegetable crop, although her thoughts had been tangled up with a dose of hopeless attraction and some serious curiosity about whether Jackson could conquer his addiction.

Watching Luc come alive under Jackson's undivided attention had planted a bittersweet knot of emotion inside Gabby's chest.

Naturally she'd loved hearing laughter mixing with birdsong. Luc had vibrated with joy beneath a brilliant October sun. Jackson had even raked a pile of leaves around the bottom of the slide, which Luc had then cheerily slid into over and over and over, screaming "Try again," as if each time had been a wholly new experience.

Even the memory of her son's giddy, windburned face still made Gabby smile.

Yet the fact that it had been Jackson instead of Noah playing with Luc picked at the scabs of her own wounds. Forced her to acknowledge that, despite her abundant love, Luc would grow up like her, able to rely only on one parent. That nothing she could do would ever completely fill the little hole in his heart that would always wonder why his father never loved him enough.

Worse, it made her realize that, despite the many and persuasive lies she'd used to convince herself otherwise, Luc needed a father. A devoted man, as opposed to a biological dad who *sometimes* stopped by to take his son for ice cream.

And abundant good looks and hints of humor aside, Jackson would never be that man. He didn't live here, he had a drinking problem, and—oh yeah—he'd never indicated any interest in the role.

Since that argument, he'd restricted their encounters to discussions about the best hiking trails or local restaurants. Occasionally Luc would rope him into a brief game of chase, but then Jackson would excuse himself before any discussion turned more personal.

Perhaps she'd scared him off, or perhaps he merely regretted sharing his personal struggle with her. Either way, he'd left her with a chaotic blend of anxiety and yearning.

"Whatcha doing?" Her dad's quizzical gaze flooded her with embarrassment.

"Nothing. Jackson's car pulling in caught my attention, that's all."

Her dad grunted knowingly, so she avoided meeting his gaze. "He stopped me yesterday and offered to fix the patches of rotted wood on the house."

"Oh?" Gabby sat up straighter and fought to keep her brows from gathering. "Can we afford it? I thought we'd earmarked his rent to offset Luc's preschool."

Her dad waved his hands. "He said he'd do the work for free. I'd only have to pay for the supplies, which he can buy wholesale."

"He did?" She pushed some Lincoln Logs aside with her toe, frowning. Could he honestly be that generous, or did he pity them and their blue-collar budget? Pity her and her sad little life?

"He says he likes to keep busy." Her dad picked up the remote and turned on the television. "Seems to me he's got a lot on his mind. Some men like to sit and think through their troubles, others need to keep moving."

Gabby hadn't told her father about Jackson's confession, mostly because she could tell Jackson needed privacy. He posed no threat to her dad, so there'd been no reason to share the revelation.

"Should we take advantage like that?" She clicked her fingernails while thinking.

"It's not like I asked him for help. He offered. He *wants* to do it." He pulled the lever on the old recliner, picked up the remote, and leaned back. "Patriots versus Giants in forty minutes."

Normally she'd settle in with him and watch the game. Maybe make some popcorn and crack a beer. Now restlessness stole through her. Jackson's rant came rushing back, causing her to think about the socializing she rarely enjoyed. Maybe he had a point. She did spend entirely too much time in this living room for someone her age. While she wouldn't trade Luc for a party life, she did miss the spontaneity of her life before motherhood.

"If I can get Luc down for a nap, would you mind if I went to Mulligan's to watch the first half of the game with Tess?" She stood, sending her dad a hopeful look. "I'll be back by the time Luc wakes up."

"Could you make me a sandwich first?" His sly smile always made her chuckle. Her dad was her rock, and she never took for granted how his love and acceptance enabled her to keep a roof over Luc's head and food in his stomach.

"Deal." She touched his forearm when she passed him on her way to the kitchen. "Thanks, Dad."

~

Gabby arrived at the sports bar right before kickoff, decked out in her favorite Pats sweatshirt and faded jeans. A surge of energy pulsed through her from the prospect of watching the game with a crowd. Plus, her friend Tess always offered to bartend on game days because of the big tips. Drunk people also tended to talk a lot, and loudly, so Tess usually had the most colorful gossip. That meant today Gabby would learn the latest scoops, too.

When she entered the bar, the blaring sound of sports broadcasters talking over the background din of a crowded stadium roared in her ears. Picking her way through the decent-size crowd already gathered, she waved at Tess as she approached the bar.

Mulligan's interior sort of mimicked the Applebee's chain, with its big windows, tables skirting the outside of a square bar in the center of the room, and multiple TVs playing at once. Clean, friendly, consistent; pretty much all you needed in a local pub.

"Didn't expect to see you today." Tess smiled at her while filling a mug of beer from the tap. "What can I get you?"

The customers' sudden uproar about a bad ref call startled both women.

"Bud Light, loaded potato skins, and the best juicy tidbit you've got." Gabby set a precious fifteen dollars on the bar and slid into one of the last stools. They both watched the Pats gain five yards.

"Actually, it's been boring lately. But I did hear that Jan is cheating on Tim *again*. With some golf pro at Stratton."

"Why does he stay with her?"

Tess shrugged. "Some guys love those bitchy girls."

"Tim's sweet. He deserves better."

"Maybe I should make a play for him." Tess wiped up the bar in front of Gabby. "It's been a while, if you get my drift."

"You and Tim? I can't see that. He's too laid-back for you."

"Look around, Gabs. Not really a lot of other options. Better to accept what's available than wish for what will never be." She chuckled. "Let me put your order in."

Gabby rejected the idea of settling for the status quo, even as she sat in the middle of a bar filled with the same people she'd known her whole life. This town might not be bustling with options, but men like Jackson were out there. Maybe she should sign up for an online dating service and expand her dating pool by thirty miles. Of course, what guy her age would want to date a single mom who still lived with her dad?

Sighing, she gazed at the closest TV screen. Giants had the ball now, having prevented a Pats first down.

While she waited for her food, she scanned the bar looking for suitable company, but no one in particular made her want to move from her seat. Most were huddled around pitchers of beer at the tables. Some old men were scattered around the bar, and one group of couples hugged a prime corner, beneath one of the bigger TVs.

In her peripheral vision, she noticed a dark-haired man in a New York Giants cap enter the bar. Holy moly, that guy was asking for trouble. Then he glanced up and froze in his tracks. Amazingly, she didn't fall off the stool when Jackson's caramel-colored eyes widened upon recognition.

He'd come to a bar!

# CHAPTER SIX

Darkness settled around her like midnight under a new moon. Jackson halted, his gaze darting around as if he might miraculously see someone else he knew to sit with. Once resigned, he grinned and sidled up to the stool on her left.

"Looks like you got a hall pass," he said. He must've noticed her eyes glance at the Giants logo. "Can I count on you to defend me here in enemy territory?"

"I'll do my best, though I can't make promises." She sipped her beer. "I have to say, *this* is the last place I'd expect to see you."

He shot her a quelling look. One that warned not to lecture or throw his confession in his face again. She couldn't help herself. Having watched her mom lose the dance with addiction had made her unable to trust recovery.

Eventually, he sighed. "I started to watch the game on that old TV in the apartment, but missed the high def. Plus, it's no fun watching the game alone. Sooner or later I need to be able to come to a bar without gritting my teeth or getting drunk, so it might as well be today."

*Oh.* Gabby allowed the sweet flow of relief to rush through her veins. So he hadn't come here for a drink. Made sense, really. If he wanted to drink, he could've bought a case and holed up in the apartment. That's like what her mom had always done—used in private.

"Sorry." She scrunched her nose. Fortunately, he smiled, apparently happy to allay her suspicions. "Can we start over? Pretend we just met, or at least pretend you didn't see my ugly side last week?"

"What ugly side?" He cracked a smile, and she relaxed until Tess delivered the potato skins.

Her self-proclaimed horny friend then proceeded to lean over the bar to get closer to Jackson, her D-cups practically busting out of her snug T-shirt. Tess pointedly stared at his baseball cap. "You got a death wish, mister?"

"Maybe." He smiled, but not with his eyes. Those settled on her name tag for a second longer than necessary. "Tess, is it?"

Gabby picked up a potato skin, hoping it would stop the churning in her stomach. She couldn't even blame Jackson if he wanted to flirt with Tess. Tess, with her straight blond hair. Tess, with her long legs and short skirt. Tess, with her throaty voice. And let's not forget, Tess, the kid-free girl in the bar.

Never before had she hated the sound of Tess's name. Then she hated herself for being petty.

"And you are?" Tess flipped her hair over her shoulder.

"Jackson."

"Well, Jackson," Tess cooed, "I hope you're a good sport, 'cause your team is about to get crushed."

"Oh, really?" Jackson turned to Gabby. "You agree, Gabby?"

Gabby shrugged and, to distract herself from being jealous, conjured up the image of her longtime fantasy lover. "Tom Brady's the man, in more ways than one."

Jackson rolled his eyes. "He's an ass."

"Jealous much?" Surely every guy envied the handsome, athletic god that was Tom Brady.

"Of an accused ball-deflating pretty boy who also ditched his pregnant girlfriend for a supermodel?" Jackson chuckled. "Nope, not even a little bit jealous."

Before Gabby could recover from that slam of her beloved sports hero, Tess asked, "You two know each other?"

"Jackson's our tenant for the next few weeks." Gabby sipped her beer again, uncomfortable with Tess's scrutiny.

"Lucky you." Tess cocked her hip, clearly eager to welcome the newcomer to town, and apparently now unwilling to settle for Tim. "Hey, Jackson, let's make a bet. If the Pats lose, I'll pick up your tab. If the Pats win, you owe me a dinner."

Gabby almost choked on her potato skin. She and Tess had never competed for the same guy before, so she'd never been bothered by Tess's aggressive flirting. Not that Gabby had any intention of getting together with Jackson now, but still.

"Can't do the dinner," he began, "but if the Pats win, I'll give you a one hundred percent tip."

Another sigh of relief flowed through Gabby after Jackson turned down Tess's unsubtle invitation.

Tess wrinkled her nose, but didn't push. "Cold hard cash isn't exactly what I was after, but it's a fair bet. You're on."

Jackson nodded and quickly scanned the menu. "I'll start with the 'Next Size Up' Nachos and," his gaze darted toward the bottles behind the bar as his hand balled into a fist, "a root beer."

"Root beer?" Tess's eyes widened.

Gabby noticed Jackson's shoulders pull back a touch. "Sweet tooth."

Tess nodded then spared Gabby a quick glance. "You need anything else, Gabs?"

"I'm good, thanks. Looks like those guys over there want another pitcher." Gabby nodded across the bar, thankful for a legitimate excuse to send Tess away.

Gabby turned to Jackson and bit back a smart-aleck remark about blondes. "My dad says you offered to repair our rotted clapboard. First the swing set, now this. I wonder what you must think of us and all of our shortcomings."

Her question drew a sharp glance. He swiveled in his stool and leaned close enough so that she, but only she, could hear him. "Far as I can tell, you don't have any flaws, Gabby."

Her gaze dipped to his mouth, but then he pulled away.

Drumming his thumbs on the bar, he said, "Frankly, given what you know about me, I'm surprised you'd care what I think, let alone feel awkward about *your* faults, if there are any."

Once again he'd set her adrift. Her thoughts spun like a whirlpool, while she groped helplessly for something, some comeback, to stay afloat.

Why *did* she care, really? Allowing herself to feel anything for him, to actively invite him into her thoughts or heart, would cause misery when he left, if not sooner. If it were only *her* feelings involved, she'd probably take the risk. But Luc's tender heart didn't deserve the special hell of a wasted attachment.

Luckily, the football game gave Jackson and her an excuse to exit the awkward conversation. Jackson let out a little whoop when his team gained forty-three yards on a single play.

Tess reappeared with Jackson's root beer. "Nachos should be up in a second. You two okay?"

"Given the Giants field position after that punt return, I'd say I'm more than okay." Jackson's easy smile may as well have been some kind of laser beam for the way Tess positively melted in its presence. "In fact, maybe I should order up a feast, since it looks like it's gonna be on the house."

Gabby cleared her throat. "If you're hungry, you can have one of these skins."

"Thanks." He grabbed one and took a big bite, licking the sour cream from his lip as he chewed. He hadn't done it with the intention of making her thighs clamp together in a hot rush of lust, but it happened anyway. *Shoot.*

"I'll be back with your nachos soon." Tess winked at Jackson then sashayed to the next customer. At least two other men at the bar followed her ass with their eyes. No wonder she made buckets of money on game days.

"You're one of the few guys I've ever seen turn Tess away." As soon as the words left her mouth, she pressed her lips together. Jeez, she really needed to think before she spoke.

"Why does it sound like that makes you happy? You don't like Tess?" He leaned closer, grinning.

"Of course I like Tess. She's my friend."

"Yet you don't want to see her with me?" He wore a subtle grin that suggested he had a good suspicion about the reason.

Embarrassed, she blurted, "Why would I care if you're with Tess, or anyone else for that matter?"

"You tell me." He turned toward her now so that his knees touched her thighs. The temperature in the bar soared. His flirtatious grin—at least, if her memory served her well, that's what it looked like—sent tingles fanning through her core. He touched her arm. "I'm glad to see you get out of that house and relax a bit."

"Me too."

He seemed to be holding his breath as if weighing his next words, but then he merely turned back toward the TV.

She missed the feel of his knees against her leg, and caught herself staring at the space between them when she said, "You weren't one hundred percent wrong last week."

"I was wrong." He glanced at her. "Wrong to badger or judge you. You've got your shit together, which is more than I can say. Doesn't say much for me, seeing that I'm almost a decade older, but no wiser."

"Maybe instead of beating yourself up for mistakes, you should take pride in the effort to change. I mean, it's kind of a big deal, right? It's not easy to change. God knows I wish I could change some things about myself." She bit into a potato skin to avoid looking at him.

"Like what?" His gaze narrowed.

"For starters, I don't often look before I leap, as my dad likes to remind me." She shrugged. "Luc's living proof of how that kind of impulsiveness can end."

"Something tells me you've grown up a lot since becoming a mom."

"I like to think so, but then I do or blurt something stupid before I take a second to consider the consequences."

"I wouldn't worry. Your tendency to say exactly what you think is attractive. At least, I think so."

"You do?" Her body involuntarily tilted toward his.

He stared right in her eyes, his gaze warm and reassuring. "I do."

Over Jackson's shoulder, Gabby then saw the last person in town she wanted to talk to. "Noah."

"Gabs." He rounded Jackson and wedged himself between them before planting a kiss on her cheek. Then he eyeballed Jackson, clearly engaged in some kind of manly squaring off. Not that Jackson would've been aware of it. Gabby just knew Noah.

"Hey, I think we met the other week at the diner." Noah's hand remained on the back of Gabby's chair. "You were soaked through, right?"

"I was." Jackson's demeanor turned guarded.

Noah's gaze darted from Jackson's cap to Gabby.

"Why are you sitting here feeding the enemy?" Noah's joking tone didn't quite camouflage the edge in his question. "Surely that's illegal."

He chuckled at his stupid cop joke.

"Jackson's our tenant for the next few weeks," Gabby replied.

"Is that right?" Noah pasted a smile on his face. The one she used to find winsome, but now knew to be calculating. "Did you get around to fly-fishing yet?"

"Not yet. I've been busy." Jackson flicked a quick glance at Noah and then forced his eyes back on the game. All traces of his warmth had vanished.

"Hiking?" Noah pressed.

"A bit." Jackson gave Noah a sidelong look before casually chomping down a huge bite of the nachos Tess had just delivered.

"Noah, quit quizzing the guy. He's on vacation." Gabby wished she could close her eyes and make Noah disappear.

"Sorry." Noah raised his hands in surrender. Then he casually brushed his hand across her shoulder and let it linger, as if it belonged there. "So, how's our boy? I was thinking maybe I'd swing by and take Luc out for ice cream."

Jackson flinched. Not noticeably enough to catch Noah's attention. In fact, to the rest of the room, Jackson probably appeared riveted to the screen. But Gabby, with her heightened awareness of everything he did, had detected it.

She shrugged Noah's hand off her shoulder. "Luc would love to see you." And then, because she couldn't help herself or stop her stupid impulses any more than she could breathe underwater, she added, "You could play with him on the swing set Jackson built."

For a millisecond, Noah's eyes widened. Gabby had never before seen him thunderstruck, so she savored the little win before her inevitable regret wiped it away. She should know better than to bait Noah. It usually didn't end well.

"Well, ain't that kind of you, Jackson." Noah's gaze narrowed a touch. "I see now what's got you so . . . busy."

Gabby held her breath.

Jackson flitted a quick glance at Noah. "Happy to help." Then the bar erupted in a cheer and Jackson's face contorted thanks to a fumble recovery by the Pats. "Dammit!"

Although only at the end of the first half, Gabby's appetite had fled. For a precious few minutes, she'd felt like a single girl again, flirting with a handsome boy. But between Noah's uninvited company and watching Tess flirt with Jackson, she'd had her fill of the bar. Perhaps the comfort and security of her living room suited her after all.

"Guys, this has been a blast, but Luc will be waking up soon. Don't want to take advantage of my dad." She scooted off her stool. "See you all later."

Jackson nonchalantly waved good-bye and then cheered when his team blocked a long pass. When Noah slid onto her seat and called out to Tess, Gabby watched Jackson's eyes close like he'd sent up a silent prayer for patience.

*Amen, brother.*

On the way home, she sent up her own prayer. *Please don't let Jackson believe one word that comes out of Noah's mouth.*

Excepting the frequent interruptions from Noah and Tess, Jackson divided his attention between the television and his nachos. By the end of the third quarter, however, his hopes for a good time watching the game had all but evaporated.

He barely remembered the days when having fun had been easy. When he could enjoy a bar, a game, a meal, without a care. When he'd lived moment to moment, worry-free, because he'd believed himself invincible. Because he'd believed the future to be full of promise. Because he'd trusted others as well as himself.

*Ha.* Because he'd been stupid.

"Looks like Tess is hot for you." Noah tossed back a handful of mixed nuts. "Been there, done that. But *you* might want to go for it."

Noah wasn't the first guy Jackson had met who bragged about his conquests, but considering the fact they barely knew each other, well, he couldn't believe this asswipe was Luc's dad. Did Noah talk about Gabby that way, too?

"In fact, she'd be perfect for a guy like you." Noah gulped down more of his beer and turned toward Jackson.

Jackson didn't want to take the bait but—his nerves no longer subdued by booze—he couldn't let it pass. With contrived composure, he crunched down another nacho before replying, "A guy like me?"

"Yeah." Noah slapped Jackson's arm as if they'd been buddies for years. "A vacationer looking for a good time, not a good girl."

If any guy ever talked about Jackson's sister that way, he'd end up with a black eye in two seconds flat. Tess wasn't a relative or even a friend, but he'd defend her anyway. "I doubt Tess would appreciate *that* particular praise."

"Oh, I don't know." Noah smirked. "The way she's been watching you, I think she just might."

Jackson hadn't quite figured out Noah's real agenda, but he doubted the guy wanted to be pals. And Jackson wasn't looking for friends—definitely not one like Noah.

"Either way, I'm not interested." He ate another nacho, wishing Noah would take the hint and wander off.

"In her, or in women?" Noah chuckled. The guy had a bad habit of laughing at his own jokes. Why'd Gabby's ex have to be Noah, of all people? A small-town cop he couldn't risk antagonizing. On that thought, he let that last jibe go.

"What I *am* interested in is watching the rest of this game." Jackson faced the screen again, hoping Noah would lose interest and wander off.

Noah tossed another handful of nuts back before he leaned close. "Guess I don't have to worry about you going after Gabby, then. Cute as hell, that one, though not as much fun as she used to be. She's lost all her humor since becoming a mom."

Jackson wasn't born yesterday. He recognized Noah's ploy—first urging Jackson toward Tess, now undermining Gabby's appeal in an attempt to turn Jackson off. Only a true dick would talk about the mother of his kid that way to mark his territory. Gabby deserved so much better.

Perhaps Jackson should've stopped to think about how what he said next could affect her, but Noah had pushed one too many buttons. "Probably 'cause being a single mom *isn't* too funny."

"She won't be single forever." Noah finished his beer in one long gulp, then studied the bottleneck while picking at its label. "We were too young to know what the hell we were doing when she got pregnant. But I've had my fun these past few years. Now I'm ready to settle down."

Jackson bit back a curse. "You think she's been waiting around for you?"

"Not exactly. I know I hurt her. We were great together before Luc, so I just need to remind her of all that. And after all, I *am* Luc's dad." Noah turned to Jackson and, for the first time, Jackson considered maybe Noah wasn't only jerking him around. Despite being an utter jackass, this guy actually did want Gabby. That much was written across his face, plain as the sun in the sky.

"Let's face it, I don't have much competition in this town. Besides, coming from a broken home," Noah continued, "Gabby's always wanted a secure family. I can convince her to give Luc what she never had, even if she still has some doubts about me."

The candid admission of rather manipulative plans caused Jackson to accidentally bite down on his tongue while chewing his nachos.

After an initial "over my dead body" reaction, Jackson couldn't help but wonder if Noah's claims were true.

Jackson didn't know Gabby well enough to know whether she'd honestly gotten over Noah, or if her harsh opinions about him the other night were simply pride covering hurt feelings. And at the end of the day, this lame excuse for a man *was* Luc's dad. If the guy was ready to commit to his son and Gabby, what right did Jackson have to interfere or cast judgment?

He'd be out of this town in a month, anyway. The fact that Gabby deserved someone ten billion times better than Noah shouldn't matter to him a bit. But it did. Damn if, in twelve days, her happiness hadn't become important to him.

"I'm not overly worried about losing my girl. One way or another, I'll make sure we end up together."

Like the first time they'd met, Jackson's spine tingled from the chill in Noah's tone. He wouldn't call the dude evil, but determined and potentially dangerous fit the bill.

"Well, pal," Noah sighed, "enjoy the rest of the game. I'll make sure no one here harasses you too much when the Pats win."

Noah threw twenty dollars on the bar and strode over to the tables where three other men were drinking. Apparently the sole purpose of Noah's little visit had been to investigate Gabby's "new friend" and then warn him off.

Jackson ogled the whiskey bottles behind the bar like a teenager looking at tits on the Internet. The sound of the crowd blurred and dimmed as his mouth watered and his throat yearned for the smooth burn just within reach. No one would blink at his ordering a drink.

"Sure you don't want something stronger than root beer?" Tess teased. "It'll take the sting out of Butler's interception."

Wait—Pats were up by three *and* intercepted? How'd that happen?

Between Gabby, Tess, and Noah, he'd hardly been able to watch the game. Coming here today had proved to be one of his shittier ideas. In fact, this whole getaway was probably a waste of time.

Instead of making headway on solving his old problems, he'd fallen headlong into new ones. That outcome seemed to be par for the course these days.

He eyeballed the Jameson bottle again: his *choice*, after all.

# CHAPTER SEVEN

If he'd known the Giants would lose, Jackson might've had that drink after all. Stone-cold sober amid a crowd of elated, buzzed Pats fans, he now did his best to take the good-humored ribbing in stride. His team had lost, but he had won another battle against the urge to drink.

Tess sauntered over to him as he stood to go.

"Don't worry. I don't welch." Jackson winked and tossed sixty bucks on the bar to cover his tab and his bet. "Congrats."

Before Tess tucked the prize money in her pocket, she asked, "Sure you don't want to take me up on my original offer?"

"No, thanks. I'm not available." That was the truth, even if she misinterpreted it to mean he already had a girlfriend.

He *wasn't* available, or good for any woman, until he figured out how to be happy again. How to believe in the goodness of people—another thing Alison had stolen from him. How to resolve the lawsuit, convince his family he wasn't a drunk, reclaim the sense of purpose he used to feel. Until he accomplished these goals, it'd be selfish to drag another soul into his personal hell.

Whether or not this jaunt to Vermont had been the best plan was unclear, but he liked Doc, he loved the area, and he didn't have a better idea.

During the drive back to his apartment, Hank called. "Hey, Hank. You see the game?"

"Brutal."

"Tell me about it. I watched it surrounded by Pats fans."

"Ouch." A brief pause lingered and Jackson could practically feel apprehension coming through the phone. "How'd that happen?"

"The TV in the apartment sucks, so I went to a local sports bar. Wore my Giants cap, too." Jackson whipped his cap off and scrubbed one hand through his hair.

"Oh." Hank fell silent, not asking what Jackson knew he would be wondering.

"Don't worry, I haven't had a drop since the intervention. I'm fine, just like I keep telling you all." The fact that Jackson thought about drinking at least once each day didn't bear mention. That admission would only fuel their concern. They needn't worry, because he'd be damned before he'd lose his grip on one of the few things he *could* control. "So, did you call for something other than to gripe about the shitty game?"

"Actually, yeah." Hank hesitated. "Have you talked with your lawyer or David recently?"

"Not since I arrived. Why? What's up?"

Hank paused before answering. "According to the grapevine, Doug's lawyers are planning to question Ray, Jim, and me about what happened that day."

"And?"

"And I was hoping you might settle all this so we don't have to be involved. I don't want a bunch of lawyers up my ass with questions that could hurt you and your business. Plus, it'd be better to end this before it gets around to your clients."

Jackson counted to three, fully aware that Hank only wanted to help, yet still irked. "I'm not settling. Tell the truth and I'll be fine."

"It's not as clear-cut as you think. Depending on how far-reaching the questions are, I'm afraid it could hurt you."

Jackson's ego shot a heat wave through his body. How could anyone believe *Doug* could hurt him?

Jackson had a perfect track record for bringing in projects on time and on budget. That's all clients cared about. "Has any client ever complained about my—our—work product?"

"No." Hank sighed.

"Aside from that one day, did I ever do anything questionable on-site?"

"Not that directly affected a project, no."

Jackson huffed triumphantly. "So what's the problem?"

"You were hungover on-site more than once this past year, and your moods affected the crew. They noticed."

Big fuckin' deal, Jackson thought but didn't say. "Did I ever mistreat anyone or unfairly judge their work, even in one of my hungover 'moods'?"

"Not exactly."

"Then I still don't see the problem. As long as my behavior didn't hurt anyone but me, it's nobody's damn business."

"Except it did eventually hurt me, even if accidentally. And it worries everyone who cares about you." Hank's quiet admonishment fell on him like a hammer.

A lack of an easy comeback made him suddenly queasy.

Jackson turned down the private road that led to the Bouchards' home, his mind recalling the look on Hank's face right after his wrist took the full brunt of his fall. It wouldn't have happened if he hadn't been trying to break up the fistfight brewing between Doug and Jackson.

"I'm sorry about your injury, Hank, and I don't expect you to lie about anything. But I stand by my actions. Doug started everything with his big mouth, and then he shoved me."

"After you grabbed him by the shirt."

"What?" Jackson had been hungover, not drunk, so his memory had to be right.

"He shoved you *after* you grabbed his shirt."

"That's not what happened." Jackson's grip tightened around the steering wheel, his mind straining to replay the incident.

"Yes, it is. You fired him and dumped his tools on the floor. He made another smart-ass threat and you grabbed his shirt, *then* he shoved you. I stepped in because I saw your hand balling into a fist."

Jackson's entire being rejected Hank's version of the story, yet he knew Hank had no motive to lie. *Had* he grabbed Doug first?

He had been outraged upon overhearing Doug trash-talking him to the others and threatening to destroy his reputation. Jackson had never been a violent guy until that day, but, in truth, he'd never been a lot of the things he'd become lately.

"You still there?" Hank asked.

"Yeah." His thoughts were still racing when he pulled into the driveway. He noticed Luc dashing around the play set, right past Jon, who seemed to be dragging his left foot while grasping for the slide. The man didn't look right. "Hank, I gotta go. I think my landlord needs help."

Jackson bounded from his Jeep before giving Hank a chance to say good-bye, calling out, "Jon, you okay?"

Jon didn't respond. Jackson hustled across the yard and helped him sit at the bottom of the slide. The man's eyelids fluttered and he appeared confused.

Jackson knelt in front of him. "Jon, does your chest or arm hurt?"

Jon numbly shook his head, mumbling, "No."

"Okay, that's good." *Thank God.* Jackson composed himself. He spoke slowly and smoothly to help Jon remain calm, too, while he ran through the quick stroke symptom test he remembered learning from someone sometime. "Can you smile for me?"

Jon's brows pinched together, and only the right side of his mouth quirked.

JAMIE BECK

*Right-side movement only. Remember that.* "How about trying to raise both arms, high as you can."

Again, only Jon's right arm went up, and then he mumbled what sounded like, "Tingles."

Damn. Stroke.

Jackson remembered Luc, who'd gotten distracted by a pile of rocks. He darted a glance at Jon. "Is Gabby home?"

As soon as Jon nodded, Jackson hauled him up and supported him as they walked toward the house. Then he glanced over his shoulder. "Luc, come on, let's get your mommy."

Luc ran ahead yelling, "Mama, mama!"

Jackson burst through the front door, calling out, "Gabby, get some aspirin and call 9-1-1."

He heard her running up the basement steps. "What's all the racket?" Then she took in the scene and dropped her laundry basket. "What's wrong, Dad?"

"I think he's having a stroke." Jackson settled Jon in his recliner. "Get him an aspirin and call 9-1-1, unless it'd be faster to drive him to the hospital."

Gabby stood, frozen in place, growing paler by the second.

"Gabby, aspirin, 9-1-1," Jackson urged. "Now!"

Tears sprang from her eyes and then she forced herself into action. Within seconds she was back with aspirin and water, and very shaky hands.

"I'll call 9-1-1." Jackson turned and stepped away from her and her father so he could talk to the emergency operator.

Tremors shook Gabby's small frame, probably from adrenaline. "Luc, baby, come. We're going on an adventure."

Considering the way Gabby already had become unglued, Jackson knew having to manage Luc while dealing with her dad's stroke would send her over the edge.

He crouched before her, grabbed hold of her hands, and squeezed them reassuringly. "Gabby, let me watch Luc so you can focus on your dad."

"No, I couldn't. He can't . . . Luc doesn't know you well enough," she said, her tone thinned from strain, her eyes darting from her dad to Luc and then to Jackson. "Do you even know how to deal with kids?"

"It's already four fifteen. I think I can handle a couple of hours until he goes to sleep."

Gabby looked straight at him, her desperation almost as clear as her demanding eyes. "Did you drink anything after I left the bar?"

Their gazes locked while he suppressed his immediate "what the fuck" response. He released her hands and stood. When did *he* become a guy that couldn't be trusted? *He* didn't let people down; it was the other way around.

"No." He couldn't fault her mothering instinct to protect Luc, but it didn't make the blow any easier to take. "You can trust me. I swear on the memory of my mother."

She glanced at her father, who seemed to be slipping into a deeper state of confusion. Luckily an ambulance siren wailed outside the house.

"Thank God they got here so fast." Gabby bolted off her chair and swung the door open. Luc started crying, likely panicked by the loud noise and his mother's frenzied behavior.

The EMTs questioned Gabby, but she hadn't been outside with her father when it happened.

"Gabby, take Luc for a sec while I talk to these guys."

She looked relieved to have Jackson take over.

After getting Jackson's explanation of the precipitating events and timeline, the EMTs did a quick neuro exam and tested Jon's vital signs, confirming Jackson's suspicions. They began loading Jon onto a stretcher, which made Luc cry louder.

Gabby had Luc on her hip, shushing him and kissing his head. "It's okay. Pappy's going to be okay. He's just exhausted, Luc. He needs a good rest."

She tried to put Luc down, but he molded his entire body against hers, crying louder and harder. "Please, buster, I can't take you with me. Stay here with Jackson. I'll be back later. I promise."

"No, Mama." Luc climbed over her body like a monkey in a tree. "No!"

Jackson had no frickin' clue how to help, but he ventured in with the first thing that came to mind. "Hey, Luc. I hoped you'd show me where you go fishing. Maybe we could catch a frog or something."

Luc continued crying, warily peering at Jackson.

"There's still some daylight left if we hurry. Maybe we could even take some cookies with us." Jackson shrugged. "Or maybe you don't like cookies."

"I *do* like cookies," Luc said over a hiccup.

"Oh, good. I like cookies, too. Do you know where your mom keeps them?"

Luc nodded, his grip on Gabby softening a bit.

Jackson raised his hand to shield his mouth as if he was letting Luc in on a secret. "You know, once your mom's gone, you'll be the boss, 'cause I don't know where anything is. Maybe we'll have cookies for dinner."

Gabby must've felt Luc's resolve wavering, because she managed to slide him off her body.

"You okay to drive?" Jackson asked her.

"Mmm hmm." She kissed Luc's head and said, "Mommy will be back later."

He wailed again, but she made a run for her purse and then for her car, ignoring his cries so she could get to her father. Jackson scooped Luc up and let him watch through the window. The toddler strained toward the windowpane, but Jackson kept a tight hold on him.

Once the ambulance and Gabby's taillights disappeared, Luc's meltdown took a spectacular turn. He twisted and screamed like a banshee. Naturally the little guy was terrified. The only permanent male figure in his life had just been strapped to a gurney and swept away, and his mom had left him.

Jackson knew these kinds of moments taught a person something about trust and faith, and even though he seriously doubted the goodness of mankind these days, he'd be damned if he wouldn't do his best to ensure this little boy's faith wasn't compromised so early in life.

Taking care to make sure Luc didn't hurt himself, Jackson fastened him to his side and started toward the kitchen as if Luc weren't having a fit. It proved a challenge because, despite his pint-size body, the boy's hysteria gave him the strength of the Incredible Hulk. "Let's find the cookies first. Your mom says the pond's got lily pads, so there should be frogs."

Luc finally stopped wriggling, but the crying persisted, so Jackson started opening cabinet doors until he spotted Halloween Oreos. "Ah ha!"

He held the package in his free hand, which got Luc's attention. Luc stopped crying long enough to reach for the cookies.

"Oh no. Not until we get to the pond. So, if I put you down, are you going to stop crying and take me to catch frogs?"

Luc strained toward the cookies, which Jackson then held far outside his reach.

"Luc, answer me or I'm gonna put the cookies back." He donned a solemn expression. "What's it going to be, buddy—cookies and frogs, or crying?"

Jackson shook his head at how idiotic he sounded. Luc's churlish expression caused Jackson to suppress a smile. He could tell he'd won the battle because Luc's eyes remained focused on the Oreos.

"Cookies," Luc whined.

"And frogs?" When Luc nodded, Jackson set him down. "Awesome. Take me to the pond, little man."

Jackson opened the kitchen door, waiting for Luc to lead the way. Luc raced toward the edge of the yard to the head of the wooded trail.

Watching him dash on unstable legs made Jackson smile, which felt inappropriate under the circumstances.

Still, seeing Luc's in-the-moment mindset sparked a memory of running through the woods near his childhood home with David when they were young kids. Playing with army men in the dirt and tree roots until their fingernails and knees were caked with grime. Even back then, David had been the cautious caretaker while Jackson had impulsively barreled through each day.

They'd been good friends, and Jackson wouldn't pretend he didn't want that back. But David still kept secrets, which meant he could still close Jackson out again at any time.

The crunch of tiny feet on dry leaves pulled Jackson from his reverie. Luc had gained several yards on him, so Jackson picked up his pace.

Remnants of daylight filtered through the canopy of gold and red leaves and crickets hummed in the background. The peaceful scene stood at odds with what was really happening in this little boy's life.

The wooded path opened up to an idyllic mountain lake, exactly as Gabby had promised. Any kid would deem this a haven, as would Jackson. Kayaking in the early-morning mist, skating on its frozen surface, hiking around its edges. A peaceful place one wouldn't want to leave.

A collection of lily pads floated along a marshy-looking edge to the left. "Let's go over there. That's where the frogs will be hanging out."

"Cookies, peese?" Luc came to a dead stop, his gaze resting on the Oreos.

With each interaction, Jackson became more certain that Luc would never be anyone's doormat.

"All right, buddy. Let's have two now. After dinner, we can have a couple more."

Luc's hands shot out, awaiting their prize. Before Jackson took a cookie for himself, Luc had already shoved one of his into his mouth.

"Jeez, Luc. Small bites. You're gonna choke."

Luc bit his second cookie in half—a tiny victory for Jackson.

"Come on, now. Let's find a frog." He ruffled Luc's hair and guided him to the marshy edge of the lake. "Have you caught frogs before?"

Cookie crumbles stuffed Luc's mouth, but he managed to shake his head.

Jackson smiled, delighted to be the first to do this with Luc, though *why* that mattered, he couldn't say. Setting the cookies aside, he crouched on the bank of the water. "Frogging is a slimy mess. Does that sound fun?"

"Uh-huh." Luc crouched beside him, waiting.

"First we have to be quiet and watch for a frog. It'd be easier if we had a net, but we've got superfast hands, right?"

Luc imitated Jackson, who'd rested his hands on his knees and craned his neck to and fro in search of anything interesting. Jackson smothered a smile at the mimicry and pretended to be serious about the search, doing whatever he could to keep Luc's mind off his grandfather.

Luc quickly grew restless. Jackson whispered, "Shhh. I think I see something right there."

He didn't, but it got Luc's attention and bought him another minute or two.

"No fwogs, Jackson."

The funny mispronunciations always caused a smile to form deep within Jackson's gut. "Be patient." And then, miracle of miracles, Jackson spotted a wee little frog on one of the lily pads. Holding one finger to his lip to shush Luc, he pointed with his other.

Luc's eyes alighted and he stood. "Dere!"

Jackson yanked him back down into a crouching position and then the pair waddled closer to where the little frog sat. "Do you want to spring for it, or should I?"

Luc's little blond brows knit together in tight concentration while he decided. "You go."

"Okay. Watch closely so next time you can try." Jackson slowly held out his hands, preparing to pounce. He edged nearer, hoping he'd be close enough to have a shot at reaching the damn thing. Just as he sprang forth, Luc called out, "Catch it, Jackson!"

Naturally, the commotion caused the frog to jump out of harm's way, and Jackson ended up knee-deep in mud and reeds. He'd have been miserable about the icy water if he hadn't heard bubbling laughter from the edge of the lake.

"Are you laughing at me?" Jackson asked before standing.

"You're funny." Luc giggled again and then noticed the unattended Oreo package.

"Don't you do it!" Jackson stood, water now dripping from his arms. He decided a surprise attack was his best bet to stop Luc from making off with those cookies, so he splashed a bit of water onshore. "If I catch you, I'm going to tickle you."

Luc yelped and then turned and ran toward the path, laughing that terrified yet playful laughter unique to small children.

Jackson snatched the Oreo package and then chased after Luc, pretending to growl. "I'm gonna get you."

Another squeal ripped through the air before Luc disappeared down the path. Jackson let him have the lead until they got to the yard, then he dropped the cookies, caught Luc, and turned him upside down by the ankles.

"I've got you now." He shook him a little to make the kid giggle. Ten seconds later, he righted Luc and set him down, careful to make sure he wasn't too dizzy. He grabbed the cookies and looked at Luc.

"Okay. Come with me so I can change into dry clothes, then we'll make dinner." Jackson reached out his hand.

Nothing could've prepared him for the swell of pride warming his heart as Luc took hold of him. Everything else faded away and Luc's pudgy soft hand, so miniscule compared with his own callous palm, became Jackson's sole focus.

Then a ripple of sorrow disrupted his satisfaction.

No one had placed any faith in Jackson for quite some time. He'd been too busy disengaging from everything and everyone real to notice, until Luc reminded him of how good it felt to be counted on. To make someone feel safe.

Maybe Hank had been right. All this time Jackson had believed he hadn't hurt anyone with his withdrawal, with his barely repressed anguish. He'd considered himself to be the only person who *could* be trusted or counted on for anything, when, in fact, perhaps he'd become the opposite of dependable.

Luc reached for the stairwell railing, his stumpy legs straining to climb the steps. After Jackson changed into old sweatpants and a long-sleeve pullover, he decided to carry Luc and the Oreos back to the main house. "So, what do you want for dinner, buddy?"

"Hanga-buggers." Luc raised a hand over his head as if making a toast.

Jackson chuckled and hoped he'd find ground beef in the Bouchard refrigerator. And then, for the first time in a while, he remembered why he was babysitting Luc, and wondered how Gabby was holding up. Even if Jon only suffered moderate stroke effects, she'd lost her sole support system for a while, and their little business would be in trouble, too.

Although Gabby had warned him she didn't want to rely on him, Jackson would have to convince her she had nothing to lose by accepting his help until he returned to his life in Connecticut next month.

# CHAPTER EIGHT

Gabby's brain—jammed full of medical jargon, endless questions, and a heaping dose of anxiety—had hit a wall. The last thing she needed on her list of worries was wondering why her house looked so dark when she pulled into the driveway.

Jackson's Jeep sat parked by the garage. She'd checked in with him a couple of hours ago and he hadn't raised any concerns or complaints. Still, the eerie stillness raised the hairs on the back of her neck.

Of course, it was after ten. Maybe he'd fallen asleep in front of the TV—not that she saw it flickering through the living room window.

When she entered the kitchen, which was illuminated only by the light above the stove, she saw her first hint of how Jackson's evening had gone. Despite him being a neatnik, he'd left a half-eaten carton of Oreos on the table. A frying pan lay soaking in the sink, but crumbs and ketchup globs surrounded Luc's booster seat.

As she wandered into the shadowy bowels of the house, she managed to sidestep the discarded laundry basket and toys scattered across the living room floor. Quietly, she made her way upstairs.

The hall bathroom's light remained aglow. Inside, bath paints and toothpaste decorated the sink bowl.

She crept toward Luc's room, still dimly lit by his nightlight, and pushed the door open. Jackson's body swallowed Luc's toddler bed, where the two of them were fast asleep. Several Curious George books lay sprawled on the bed and floor. Luc had his stuffed lovie tucked under one arm and his head peacefully nestled against Jackson's chest.

*Lucky Luc.* Unlike her, he'd found someone to make him feel secure.

She crossed to the edge of the bed and studied their sleeping faces, swallowing the lump in her throat. Luc looked happy, if such a thing was possible in one's sleep. He'd probably quickly forgotten about the drama and savored every minute of his time with a young, playful man.

Once again she was reminded that, despite her efforts to be the world's best mom, she and her dad really weren't enough for Luc. That, fervent wishes to the contrary, a man *would* complete her family. And even though Luc would survive not having a loving father, looking at her son peacefully snuggled up to Jackson made her heart ache anew. After the evening she'd had, that was all it took to wring her dry.

Selfishly, she took advantage of the opportunity to study Jackson's beautiful features at rest. He looked deliciously cuddly . . . and completely uncomfortable. If he slept in his current position, he'd end up with a crook in his neck. She adjusted the blanket around Luc and leaned in to kiss his cheek. Jackson must've sensed her presence, because he woke with a slight start, looking confused.

She pressed her finger to her lips to remind him to be quiet. He glanced down and, as if having just remembered where he was, grinned.

Jackson twisted to slide his body free, while Luc slumbered on in that near-dead stage of sleep adults can only envy. Gabby backed away quietly and then made her way downstairs. She heard Jackson's footsteps following, but didn't slow down until she reached the kitchen.

"Thank you so much for watching Luc." She dared a glance at him, hoping he wouldn't notice how seeing Luc curled up with him had affected her. "You were right; it would've been a nightmare to have taken him with me."

"Glad to help. We had a good time." A warm glow shone through his eyes.

Gabby cocked an eyebrow. "Judging by the trail of stuff around the house, I guess he kept you busy."

"Very." Jackson grinned and crossed his arms. "Once he stopped crying, he pretty much wanted to show me every single thing in the yard and in the house."

"So he wasn't defiant or troublesome?" She did, after all, know her willful little boy.

"Not once I laid down the law." Jackson donned that unintentionally smug look of a sitter who had no idea what day-to-day parenting entailed. She wouldn't rob him of his win, although she'd bet the house that Luc would wear him down if given enough time.

"I'm happy it went well. I owe you, for everything."

"What'd the doctors say?" Jackson yawned, stretching his arms above his head. He looked rumpled and sleepy and totally sexy in the faint lighting, which flustered her. The spark of desire made her feel guilty, too, considering what was happening with her father.

"He had a stroke, but it isn't as bad as it could've been, thanks, in large part, to you. The fact he got medical attention right away made a difference." Suddenly the long hours and anxiety caught up to her. She crossed to the sink to clean the pot, hoping the task would keep her knees from buckling. "He's able to talk okay, but still has some left-side weakness. He'll be in the hospital for a couple of days to complete a whole bunch of neuro and cardio tests. Once he's released he'll need occupational therapy for a while."

She set the clean pan in the drying rack. Gazing out the window, her worries poured out. "I don't know how we'll afford all the medical co-pays, not to mention how I'll manage our two businesses and Luc until my dad can drive again."

The panic she'd been repressing since first seeing her dad on Jackson's arm mushroomed, the rush of adrenaline making her body tremble. Tears pricked her eyes and, despite her embarrassment about crying in front of Jackson, a tight, exhausted sob erupted from her throat.

She felt Jackson approach her from behind, but he didn't touch her. She whirled to face him, tears now streaming down her face. "I'm scared. I'm so scared about how I'll keep everything going. And what if it had been worse, or *the worst*? I've got no one but my dad. No one."

Jackson encircled her with his arms, placing one of his steady, large hands on her back while the other stroked her hair. "Shhh, shhh. Everything will be all right. I promise, you're going to be fine."

Burrowing against his chest, she could almost believe him. His body and husky voice offered much-needed comfort and a certain security. She relished every second of the embrace—the brush of his silky cotton shirt against her cheek, the stroke of his hand across her head, the soft hum of his voice, his clean, masculine scent.

As she stood there, suspended in the unguarded moment with him, her recent years of living without any man's touch, affection, desire compressed into one simple, urgent need.

Without further thought, she slid her hands up his chest and hooked them over his shoulders while tipping her head until her lips reached his neck.

His body stiffened, although he didn't release her—at least, not immediately.

"Gabby."

A whisper, a prayer, a pleading refusal?

She couldn't tell, but she didn't want to give him the chance to clarify, either. She parted her lips and kissed his jaw.

He sucked in a breath before lowering his head. His hands tightened around her briefly as their lips brushed together, but then he touched his forehead to hers. "Stop."

Her body, so hot and needy of comfort, refused to listen. She raked her fingers through the hair at his neckline. "Jackson."

Their gazes locked, breaths mingling, hearts pulsing. When his amber eyes blazed with longing, she smiled.

Then he cursed under his breath and stepped back. His gaze held hers, searching and conflicted. She heard his uneven breathing and saw evidence of his arousal thanks to his thin sweatpants.

Still, he insisted, "No."

Embarrassed heat rose to her cheeks and new tears—humiliated ones—spilled over. "Sorry."

"Don't apologize." He reached out and wiped her cheek. "It's been an upsetting day, but we both know this isn't the answer."

"I just, I . . ." She hesitated, looking away. "Why not?"

"Because I'm not a guy who takes advantage of an emotionally overwrought woman, for starters." He slung his hands on his hips.

"It's not taking advantage if I'm the one asking." Feeling strangely emboldened and determined, she added, "And, as you know, I'm no virgin."

His lips quirked into a quick smile, but then fell flat again. "Nothing good can come of this. I'll be returning to my real life in a few weeks."

As if she needed a reminder of that sad fact.

His *real* life. The one with his *real* friends and family. The murky yet potent attachment between them was purely temporary on his end. She did know that, but right now she didn't care.

"I don't expect anything. Only one night to be held. To escape. To *feel* again. To be a woman instead of someone's mom or a frightened daughter."

"You deserve a helluva lot more than being my one-night stand, Gabby."

"But I'd settle for that tonight." Honestly, she could barely believe the words bursting from her lips on a whisper. Something about the calamity of the day must've unhinged her. Made her believe that the most she stood to lose was pride. Given what she stood to gain, she willingly let her ego take the hit. "One kiss?"

He shook his head. "It wouldn't stop there."

"Why not?"

"Because apparently stopping at one of anything isn't my strong suit. That's what landed me here in the first place."

She frowned, feeling exactly how Luc must feel when denied a hot-from-the-oven batch of cookies.

"Let me be a good guy, okay?" Jackson folded his arms across his chest. "Earlier tonight it struck me how long it'd been since I'd been completely unselfish. Earning Luc's trust made *me* feel something that *I* needed. If I take you to bed right now—which would be my plea-sure, believe me—we'd both regret it tomorrow. I like and admire you enough not to want to be remembered as a mistake you made in a moment of weakness."

It took a second or two for the sublime compliment to register. That, coupled with her knowing the demons he fought, made his plea irrefutable. She wouldn't jeopardize any step of his recovery. And although his remark helped soften the blow, she now wanted to be alone as soon as possible.

"Then I guess that's that." She pressed her palm to her forehead. "I'm worn out, so I should get some rest. Thank you, again, for helping my dad, and handling Luc."

"Like I said, it was my pleasure. And other than an eight o'clock appointment in the morning, I can watch him tomorrow, too."

"Thanks, but now that my dad's out of immediate danger, I think seeing Luc might lift his spirits. It might be good for Luc, too."

"Okay. Just remember, as long as I'm here, you're not alone. I can help, but I won't intrude unless you ask."

She smiled then, even though she didn't feel particularly happy about the way the night was ending. "I see how it is. You want to make me beg."

Jackson barked a quick laugh, easing the tension. "Good night, Gabby."

He crossed toward the kitchen door. As he passed her, he brushed the back of his hand along her arm. One tender caress and then he was gone, her heart trailing behind him like a duckling.

Not that he knew it.

~

Jackson's knee bounced while he toyed with the magnetized sculpture balls on the end table in Doc's office. He could feel the weight of Doc's patient gaze resting on his shoulders, but took his time looking up. "It's been several weeks since the intervention and I haven't had a drop to drink, so no, I don't think I've got a serious problem."

"Then why did it get so out of control?" Doc leaned back, crossing one foot over his other knee.

"Who says it did?"

"You."

"I never said that!" Jackson leaned forward, defiance seizing every fiber of his body.

"Not in so many words." Doc's matter-of-fact delivery and passive expression only irritated Jackson, who sat on the razor's edge of exhaustion thanks to a restless night fantasizing about Gabby's plump lips, loopy curls of hair, and tight little body. About the way she looked at him like he was some kind of savior—unlike anyone else in his life did these days.

"How 'bout you say whatever it is you want to say," Jackson huffed.

"You don't strike me as a guy who's easily led, so I'm thinking you wouldn't have gone through the trouble of arranging this sojourn, or these sessions, if *you* didn't think you needed help."

Jackson balled his fists twice before pushing his body deep into the sofa cushions and sighing. "I admit I could use a little help getting past some things that have been weighing me down. But taking time to think about what's next isn't an admission of being a drunk."

"Huh. Tell me then, what *is* next for you?"

"I don't know, because nothing's really changed. When I go home, I'll take back the reins of my business and then I don't know."

"Nothing's changed? If I recall," Doc began, glancing over his notes, "your sister's getting serious with your friend, and your brother's wife is pregnant. Those are two important changes in your family. Most people would be excited for them, yet when you mention them, I hear latent animosity."

"I'm not jealous, if that's what you think." He wasn't, not really. He was truly happy for them all.

"I didn't say you were. But it's interesting that *you* used that word."

Jackson threw his arms up. "You know I don't like this indirect way you talk to me. If you've got an opinion, just out with it."

Doc chuckled. "My opinions aren't the point in here, though. It's your opinions, your thoughts, *your* feelings that matter."

"Fine. Fine, then. Yes, it's a little ironic that my brother and sister are both in healthy relationships when, for most of our lives, I was the one who related best to others. I was the fun one who always went the extra mile for a friend. *I* was the one who wanted love and a family."

"So why don't you have them?" Doc shifted his notepad from his thighs to the table on his left.

"Because I can't fucking trust anyone!" Jackson blinked, stunned by the words that had exploded from him before he'd taken their measure.

Doc's brows rose in a knowing manner. "Finally."

Jackson tipped his head. "What's that supposed to mean?"

"Finally we're getting to the root of it."

"Like hell we are, Doc." If he didn't know better, he'd have sworn the room shrunk in half. A quiet rage braced against the pressure squeezing in on him. "I didn't drink because I'm *lonely*," he spat with disgust.

"So you say."

"Damn straight, so I say. Booze just helped me relax. Took the edge off some of my troubles."

"You could've turned to your dad, siblings, or your friend Hank."

"David had moved halfway around the world when he and my dad weren't speaking. Made things a little awkward for everyone, and the fact that neither will tell me why they fought makes it hard to trust them much now. Meanwhile, Cat was wrapped up with her ex, which ended in disaster. Hank had his own problems to deal with. So I coped on my own."

"But your brother returned to the States more than a year ago, and your sister and her ex split at about that same time. Both of them seem to have found a way to move on and form attachments without Scotch, unlike you."

*Fuck off.* The words bunched up, ready to spring from the tip of his tongue. Instead of hollering, his tone turned acerbic.

"David and Vivi's 'attachment' goes back fourteen years, so that doesn't really count. As for Hank and Cat," Jackson stalled, scratching the back of his neck, "I'm still getting used to that one, but I hate the way she stole him from my payroll."

It burned to remember how, after years of him being a loyal brother, employer, and friend, Cat and Hank had teamed up to go into the furniture-making business together, cutting him out in the process. Of course, their venture stood on wobbly legs at best, and Hank had since stepped up and helped him out this fall, so maybe it was time to let that hurt feeling go.

"Are you trying to argue that alcohol is a better coping mechanism than friendship and love?" Doc raised one brow. "Trying to persuade me that you haven't met a single person in two years that you could confide in, turn to, or trust?"

The image of Gabby's smile arrested him. He'd confided more in her recently than he had in anyone other than Doc. That probably signified something, but he shooed the thought away like a stray cat.

Gabby lived in Vermont, with her son, whose bio-daddy wanted back in that picture. Although she was attracted to him on some level, he doubted she wanted a man with a drinking issue in her life . . . or Luc's. Besides, his life was in Connecticut.

"One minute you say I'm an alcoholic, the next you're encouraging me to find love. I thought recovering addicts weren't supposed to get involved."

"First of all, I never once used the words 'alcoholic' or 'love.' In recent years, the paradigm on alcoholism has shifted. Alcoholism, alcohol abuse, 'almost alcoholic' . . . some now believe these things sit on a spectrum. Alcoholism is linked with dependency. Accepting what you've told me as the whole truth, you've kind of butted up against that line, but maybe not crossed it. You restricted your drinking to evenings, which casts doubt on physical dependence. You quit at will and, so far, without relapse, which weakens a claim of mental *dependence*. But you're probably craving it in times of stress, and you've definitely abused alcohol based on volume alone."

"That's even a stretch. A few drinks a night isn't abuse."

"Jackson, sixty percent of Americans drink less than one drink per week. Thirty percent drink between one and fourteen drinks per week. Only ten percent of adults drink more, with some extremists clocking in at about four bottles of whiskey per week."

Holy hell, a few weeks ago he'd been in that top ten percent. He shifted uncomfortably on the sofa, avoiding eye contact while he processed that information. David had mentioned something similar during the intervention, but Jackson had dismissed it as being, well, David.

"Bottom line, if you're self-medicating with alcohol, you've got a drinking problem. So you shouldn't drink until you've found healthier ways of dealing with stress and disappointment. I'd recommend going at least a year without it and see how you feel, and then, if you think you can have a social drink without it turning into three or four, maybe it'd be okay." Doc leaned forward, resting his elbows on his thighs. "Prior to the year of your mom's death and the fallout with David and Alison, it sounds like you didn't abuse alcohol. I'm thinking we need to dig into the root of your pain in order to get back to a place where you were able to rely on sports, friends, and hobbies to cope."

Jackson rubbed his left palm with his right thumb, remembering the feel of Luc's hand and the surge of happiness it had wrought. Then a shiver shot through him from remembering Gabby's warm kiss on his neck. Maybe . . . "So you're saying I could start a relationship with someone now if I wanted to?"

"Not a romantic relationship. I think it's a little soon because if it failed, you might not be ready to handle the disappointment without turning back to alcohol."

Like bellows, Doc's opinion cinched, forcing hope from Jackson's chest with a whoosh.

"You're talking out of both sides of your mouth, Doc. First you tell me to connect with people, then you tell me I'm too damn fragile to handle it. Which is it?"

"When I said to invest in relationships, I was speaking of your family and friends. Clear the air with your siblings and your dad. Rebuild the trust and love that once sustained you. Then, assuming you manage that alcohol-free, you can probably safely venture into a new romantic attachment."

Rebuild the trust. *No shit, Sherlock.*

Jackson inhaled and counted to three. Sarcasm and denial weren't going to do a damn thing to change his outlook. And despite his protests, yesterday had made him realize he wanted to experience happiness again without it being remarkable or taking effort.

Swallowing his pride, which went down a little like swallowing an apple whole, he asked, "Here's the thing. How do you rebuild trust, especially when people keep secrets?"

Doc inhaled slowly, nodding pensively. "Perhaps we start by inviting your family to a group session."

Jackson leaned forward, grinning. "Doc, getting that group to open up is like trying to shuck an oyster with your teeth."

Doc clasped his hands behind his head and sat back in his chair. "I like a challenge, don't you?"

# Chapter Nine

While pushing Luc on the swing, Gabby's thoughts strayed back to her earlier hospital visit with her dad. She supposed she couldn't blame him for being grumpy today. Noisy hospitals allowed for little sleep and served lousy food. That, coupled with a month-long ban on his driving, had overshadowed the gratitude he should've shown for the fact that the doctors also predicted a full recovery.

The crunchy sound of tires grinding gravel caused her to look up.

"Dada!" Luc yelped from the swing as Noah's patrol car came into view.

*Oh, great.* She steadied the swing in case Luc wanted to jump down and hug his dad. Luc sat there, swinging his legs, apparently satisfied to stay put.

Noah strode toward them, dressed in his uniform, looking handsome as usual. It'd be so much easier on her if he'd have a bad case of adult acne, or start losing his hair, or something—anything—that might put a chink in his cocksure attitude.

"Hey, Gabs, real sorry to hear about your dad." Noah then crouched down and pinched Luc's feet. "You swinging, Luc?"

Luc nodded enthusiastically.

"Watch me, Dada." And then he looked up at her and ordered, "Push me high, Mama!"

Gabby complied before returning her attention to Noah. "Thanks. He's lucky, though. The doctors say he'll be feeling more like his old self by Christmas."

"That's great." Noah's gaze traveled around the swing set, then he slapped his hand against one of the swing set beams. He narrowed his eyes and spoke in a flat tone edged with a hint of envy. "Guess Jackson did a good job here."

"He's a builder, so he said it was easy." She pushed Luc again while a grin curled the corners of her mouth. That seemed to happen whenever she recalled any image of Jackson, especially the one of him watching Luc's reaction to this particular gift. "Refused to take a penny, too."

Noah cocked his head, then glanced away for a moment, looking almost tormented.

"Maybe he's got another form of payment in mind." Noah issued an arch look, lest she missed the warning in his accusation.

*I wish.*

"That's *your* speed, not his." She flashed her best sarcastic smile. Jackson had his own problems, to be sure, but she could tell he didn't use women. Not even women who threw themselves at him, apparently.

"Higher, Mama!" Luc's command rang out. Then, as he rose higher into the air, he shouted, "Look, Dada!"

"Good job." Noah offered his son a brief smile and then mocked Gabby. "And FYI, that's *every* guy's speed. Trust me."

She snorted, wondering how she hadn't seen this side of Noah long before she got pregnant. "It's sad that you believe that, but I'm not going to argue with you."

"Good." He removed his hat and fidgeted with its rim, looking uncharacteristically awkward as he reverted back to his normal, flirtatious mode. "So, I stopped by to check on you and Luc. If you need anything, you let me know."

For a split second, Noah appeared almost vulnerable and sincere. If prior experience hadn't taught her that he couldn't be trusted, she'd have thought him quite an angel then, with the sun creating a halo effect around his blond hair. No doubt, however, he'd fail even the simplest test of sincerity.

"Actually, could you watch Luc tomorrow while I visit my dad?"

"Oh, uh, well, what time?" He tapped his hat against his thigh. "I've got to work, you know."

Hedging—how predictable. With the exception of putting his personal safety at risk at his work, Noah rarely went out of his way for other people. Any nice thing he did, he did at his convenience, and usually with his own agenda in mind. She couldn't imagine why he'd even bothered with his unenthusiastic offer, nor did she much care.

"I'd planned to go around lunchtime so I could bring him a better meal." Gabby stopped pushing Luc, letting him struggle a bit to keep it going on his own.

"Sorry, Gabs." The look of relief on Noah's face almost made her laugh aloud. "I'm working the day shift tomorrow. Can't babysit during lunch."

Gabby rolled her eyes and settled a fist against her hip. "It's not 'babysitting' when a father spends time with his son."

Noah sighed, shaking his head. "Never a break with you. And you wonder why I wasn't racing down the aisle."

"No, Noah. I don't wonder at all."

At eighteen she'd wanted a commitment more than anything. Looking back, she guessed part of that need had been driven by fear of being a teenaged single mom. Another part had come from wanting to start her own family after her mother had blown hers apart. Teenage lust and hormones must've accounted for most of the rest of what she'd thought had been love.

By the time Luc was born, she'd figured out some hard truths about herself and Noah. It seemed, however, Noah still wanted something from her despite her obvious lack of interest.

Just then, Jackson's Jeep pulled into the driveway. Noah's shoulders straightened and he put his hat back on, tipping the brim down to look more threatening, she guessed.

As for her, she hadn't seen Jackson since she'd made a fool of herself last night. Good God, she'd rather be caught naked in public than face him now, in front of Noah. Hopefully she could keep her chin up and her expression relaxed. Act as if nothing happened last night, which, of course, was basically—and very regrettably—true.

When Jackson got out of his car, Luc tumbled off the swing in an attempt to hurl himself across the yard. "Jackson!" He pushed off the ground and tore across the driveway, arms held high. "I want to play monstore!"

After a quick nod toward Gabby and Noah, Jackson turned his killer smile on Luc and caught him, raising him overhead and shaking him in the air like he weighed little more than a sack of sugar. "You know what happens if I catch you, right?"

"Tickles!" Luc's giggle lightened Gabby's heart, but Noah's expression turned dark.

Jackson set Luc on the ground and started counting. "One, two, three . . ."

Luc ran back to Gabby, screeching in joyful terror. Jackson growled and lumbered toward him, arms outstretched. "I'm comin'!"

Luc dashed between Gabby's legs, trembling, his arms stretched up to her for protection. "Mama, Mama!"

Gabby scooped him up onto her hip and then mock-yelled at Jackson. "Stay away, monster, or I'll lock you in the basement and feed you spiders for dinner."

"Okay, okay!" Jackson stopped on a dime, feigning horror and raising his arms in surrender. "Spiders taste gross."

He winked at Gabby then extended his hand to Noah. "Noah. Nice to see you again."

*Liar.* Gabby covered her thoughts with a pleasant grin.

"Looks like my son's taken a shine to you." Noah's voice, tight yet polite, sliced through the air.

"He's a great kid." Jackson's grin faded. "You're a lucky guy."

"Let's catch fwogs." Luc's gaze homed in on Jackson.

"No, no." Jackson shook his head, wagging one finger. "You just want to see me get muddy again, don't you?"

Luc giggled, nodding excitedly.

"Looky there. Seems you don't need my help after all, Gabs." Noah gestured toward Jackson. "You've already got a built-in babysitter with this here man of leisure."

The antagonism in Noah's voice set off a tiny quiver of alarm, but she dismissed it as pure macho BS. She knew Noah's ego, not his heart, was the only thing bruised by the fact his son had bonded with another man.

"A good one, too," she replied, not exactly proud of her taunt, especially after Jackson's reaction evidenced his disappointment in her.

"No sitter's as good as a father." Jackson gave Noah a meaningful look, but Gabby didn't think it appeased him.

Noah decided, suddenly, to be affectionate with Luc. If Gabby hadn't been leaning against one of the swing set poles, she might've fallen over.

"Give Daddy a hug good-bye." Noah lifted Luc from Gabby's hip and hugged him.

"Bye-bye, Dada." Luc's hugs always came with a fair amount of dirt and slobber, so Gabby wasn't surprised to see Noah dust himself off after handing Luc back to her.

"Don't forget to let me know how I can help . . . when I'm not *working*," Noah instructed Gabby before strutting toward his car. "See you later."

As soon as he pulled out of the driveway, Gabby sighed, hard and long, shaking her head.

"How's your father today?" Jackson's beautiful eyes bored into hers with genuine concern.

"He'll be home in two days, but no driving for several weeks. With therapy he should be in pretty good shape by Christmas."

"I'm glad to hear it."

Luc squirmed, so she put him down and he went directly to the slide. With her security blanket now otherwise occupied, she'd have to address Jackson, and the memory of his gentle rejection, head-on.

Right before she launched into an apology, he said, "I've been thinking."

Hope filled her lungs like helium, raising her spirits. She teased, "Careful, there."

The little joke earned her an amused grin.

"Seriously, here's the deal. Instead of replacing the rotted wood, how 'bout I help pick up the slack with your dad's business? I'm guessing he has a weekly schedule of tasks for the homes he oversees. I'm here another four or so weeks, so that will get you partway through his recovery period."

Although the offer wasn't what she'd hoped he'd been considering, she wouldn't turn it down. Pride had never stood in the way of her accepting help. "If I weren't desperate, I'd refuse your help. You're supposed to be wrestling your *own* problems, not getting distracted by mine. But, lucky for you, I *am* desperate, so yes, feel free to use me as a diversion."

Wait, that sounded different than she'd intended. No way to hide the fact that she had a one-track mind where Jackson St. James was concerned. Thankfully, aside from a quick grin, he didn't make a deal out of the sexual connotation.

"Okay, then. Maybe once Luc's asleep you can give me a rundown of what's what. Then I'll start up tomorrow. But first," he raised his voice and whipped around to look for Luc, then reverted to his growly monster voice, "I've got a little boy to eat."

Luc's eyes widened with glee. Peals of nervous laughter accompanied him as he dashed toward her garden gate.

Jackson stomped off, chasing him down, making all kinds of scary grunts and other noises. And although nothing made Gabby happier than to hear her son laughing, this time a thin layer of melancholy settled over her mood like fine ash.

Some kids enjoyed this kind of exchange every day of their lives, but not her son. Some women came home to a man like this—well, maybe not *quite* like Jackson—every day, but not her.

Her mind chewed on that thought while she meandered down the driveway to grab the bundle of mail that had been shoved into the mailbox. She tucked it under her arm and strode back toward the house, still preoccupied with chastising herself for her choices.

Yes, Noah had bailed on her, but she'd bailed on herself, too. She'd let three years pass without making any attempt to date. In doing so, she'd failed herself and her son. That couldn't continue.

She wanted a father figure for Luc. She wanted a man to love. She wanted to be loved.

Luc's happy screech drew her back to the present. Jackson tossed Luc in the air, all traces of his troubles temporarily erased from those gorgeous eyes.

Unfortunately, Gabby realized then that she wanted the impossible, because right now she just wanted Jackson.

Standing there feeling foolish, she removed the rubber band from the bundle and sifted through the mail. Bills, ads, a catalogue of stuff she could never afford, and a letter. A letter addressed to her?

The handwriting . . .

She stopped in her tracks, not even flinching when an insect buzzed past her ear. Her mouth turned pasty as her eyes homed in on the return address—Hammill, 15 Mills Avenue, Burlington, VT.

Hammill.

Her heart had somehow climbed into her throat, where it throbbed. Could it be? Why now? Why would her mother contact her after all this time?

"Gabby?" Jackson called from the garden. "I've got some things to take care of now, but I'll see you later. Luc's checking the pumpkins."

Gabby swallowed and nodded as he waved and went to the apartment.

"Luc, let's go inside." She crossed to the house on shaky legs and opened the back door. "Come on, bud."

Setting the bills on the kitchen table, she then tossed the junk mail and her mom's unopened letter into the trash.

Twenty torturous minutes later, Gabby forced herself to return to the kitchen. She stood, staring at the trash can, debating.

～

Jackson chowed down on the remnants of the leftover chili he'd brought back from lunch. A quick glance at the microwave clock told him he could probably go to the main house now, because Luc should be tucked into bed.

Seeing Gabby and Noah in the yard today had been a practical reminder of one of many reasons why he shouldn't act on his attraction. In a few weeks, he'd be back in Connecticut. If he allowed Gabby and Luc to get attached to him, they could get hurt—and like Doc suggested, so might he. Plus, he didn't need an angry cop breathing down his neck, either.

Noah's ice-blue eyes had flared earlier, despite his civil behavior. If Jackson had been thinking, he wouldn't have horsed around with Luc in front of Noah. But how could Jackson resist such a welcome greeting from the kid? It'd made him feel like a superhero.

At least Noah's presence had prevented any awkward discussion between Gabby and him about their near kiss. Halfway across the yard last night, he'd considered going back and giving her what she'd wanted. He'd even stopped in his tracks and looked over his shoulder. Thankfully, he'd hesitated long enough for her to turn off the lights and go upstairs without him.

Score one for team responsible, zero for team horny—which he was. Not that he should be thinking about that right now. No. He'd promised to help see her through this crisis with her father, and that's *all* he was going to do, even if it meant spending a lot of time with Rosy Palm and her five sisters.

He set the clean bowl on the counter and turned off the lights. As soon as he opened the door, he smelled smoke. Not enough to be concerned, but he was curious because he didn't see anything puffing from the Bouchards' chimney.

Once the backyard came into full view, he glimpsed Gabby on the patio, adding more kindling to a fire pit that was springing to life. Unlike most of the time, her expression looked serious—somber, even—making him wonder if her father's recovery had taken a bad turn.

When she saw him, she waved without smiling. "Mind sitting outside to talk? Sky's so clear. An hour from now it'll be lit with stars. Might even see some satellites cross the sky."

Jackson glanced up and saw faint stars appearing against the ever-darkening expanse. It'd been forever since he'd relaxed in front of an open fire, surrounded by the scent of dry leaves. "Sounds great."

"I made cocoa." She gestured toward a thermos and empty cup. "Want some?"

Cocoa? A mom thing to do, he supposed. Very cute. Too damn cute. And in lieu of something stronger, cocoa sounded like a great substitute. "Don't mind if I do."

He poured himself a mugful, and then sat in one of the Adirondack chairs gathered near the round copper pit.

"Thanks, again, for offering your help. I don't know how I'll ever repay you."

Her uncharacteristic lack of animation struck Jackson hard. Something had happened. He could pry, but maybe she'd tell him in her own time. Or not.

He frowned at that last thought. "Don't even think about it."

"If you end up changing your mind at any point, just say so." Gabby sat in a chair that had a notebook perched on its arm. She slid it onto her lap, opened it, and without further preamble, launched into an explanation. "So basically my dad oversees thirty homes. Luckily, the snow hasn't started yet, so I won't need you to get up at four o'clock to start plowing people's private lanes and driveways." She shot him a wry grin. "But it could happen by early November. If that isn't something you're up for—which I totally get—I can subcontract out or something."

"I said I'd help, so whatever that means, you can count on me. These days I'm not finding it too difficult to get up early." He sipped his cocoa, abashed by how much better he'd been feeling in the mornings. No headaches, no dry mouth, no stomach pain. He'd even dropped a few pounds.

Gabby looked like she bit back a comment or question. If he had to guess, she'd probably been about to probe him about his drinking. He couldn't blame her for her heightened sensitivity. Instead of being irked, he felt grateful she cared at all, considering their short-lived acquaintance. Still, he didn't want to discuss that tonight, so he kept his mouth shut.

"Hopefully we won't see heavy snowfall before my dad can drive." She sighed and flipped one page. "October is typically a month of rodent issues. Temperatures are dropping, so mice and snakes and stuff seek shelter indoors. My dad has a rotating schedule where he checks each house for pests, leaks, furnace and appliance issues, etc. Monday is garbage day, so he takes the pickup and makes a few dump runs for people who've come to their homes for the weekend. In November, we'll start checking propane levels and add an extra day per house to check electrical and heat issues. We make special runs on Fridays to turn up the heat and turn on a light for owners who will be arriving in the evening. Stuff like that."

"Sounds pretty straightforward." He tipped his head.

"Only gets interesting when something goes wrong, which we never hope for, of course." She wrapped her hands around her mug and sipped. "I thought maybe this week we'd do it together, then once you're familiar with the routine, we can split the work or something. I've still got to do my landscape work—leaf removal and cold-season prep—and on top of all that, I need to get Luc back and forth from day care."

"I heard Noah offer to help." Jackson watched Gabby's gaze drop to her lap. "Maybe he could do the drop-off or pickup, whichever best works in his schedule? I'm guessing Luc would like to ride in that patrol car."

Gabby looked up, chagrined. "Luc probably would *love* that. Unlike you, however, Noah hasn't proven to be too reliable. I could totally see him forgetting to pick up Luc one day."

Jackson nodded, not knowing exactly why he'd encouraged her to involve Noah when Noah didn't seem to be a great guy. Must be the part of him that had been denied fatherhood hated to see any guy denied the opportunity. "You might be underestimating him. Maybe if you give him some responsibility, he'll take it seriously. Luc *is* his son. That must mean *something* to him."

Fifteen seconds passed in silence. Apparently he'd crossed a line. Funny, 'cause Gabby hadn't struck him as a girl with many boundaries. It was one of the traits he liked best about her—that willingness to open herself up, come what may.

"Let's not talk about Noah, okay?" She closed the notebook. "He's not a bad guy, but he's not a good one, either. Cocky, selfish, and he left me high and dry. I don't trust him not to break Luc's heart like . . ." Then she stopped suddenly. Jackson guessed the end of that sentence might've been "like he broke mine." The fact that she ran her own little business, this household, and her son's life like a champ some-times made him forget how young she was. But just now, her bravado reminded him.

"Deal." Jackson offered an apologetic smile and sipped his cocoa. "This is great, by the way. Is there peppermint in here?"

"Yep." Gabby breathed a relieved sigh. "Let's plan to get moving at eight. I can drop Luc off beforehand and then meet you here. We'll go around to half the houses tomorrow, and the other half the next day. Takes about ten to fifteen minutes per house plus travel time, so that'll take us into mid to late afternoon."

Jackson stretched his legs toward the fire. "Guess I'll get to know all the back roads of Winhall by the time I go home."

Home.

He'd been treating his time away from home like a vacation, if one ignored the therapy sessions and lack of partying. Doc's suggestion that he invite the family up for a group session replayed, causing him to shift uncomfortably in his chair.

"Do you miss it yet?" Gabby asked.

"Hmm?" He met her gaze, confused from being lost in his own thoughts. "Miss what?"

"Home." She set the notebook on the ground and pulled her legs up to her chest. Curled in a ball that way made her look even more sweet than usual. The unjaded air of innocence appealed to him so damn much.

Jackson shrugged one shoulder. "I miss my own bed."

As soon as that word left his mouth, he pictured Gabby in his bed. The flush creeping up his neck had nothing to do with the fact he sat before a crackling fire. Maybe Gabby envisioned something similar, because she looked away for a second before clearing her throat.

"What about your family or friends?" She hugged her knees tighter, and all he could think about was how he'd like to snuggle up with her on his lap. "Are you eager to return to them?"

Normally he wouldn't answer that question honestly, but something about the crisp fall night and cocoa and his growing infatuation urged him to open up. Or maybe pulling information from him was a special gift of Gabby's.

"Not exactly." He shifted again.

Gabby didn't ask him why. He suspected she'd become preoccupied with her own thoughts again. She held her mug beneath her chin, as if using it for additional warmth. Her gaze remained fixed on the flames, which popped occasionally, shooting glowing embers upward like tiny fireworks.

He watched her as if he could will her to share her thoughts. Odd, considering how long it had been since he'd cared to know someone else's thoughts about anything. What he guessed he really wanted was to find a way to make her dimples reappear.

A canopy of stars now hung over them, vivid and dense like in a planetarium. He'd experienced this wonder in the Rockies, too. Spectacular, really. The enormity of the galaxy—of the universe—could make a man feel miniscule, or just damn lucky to be alive.

Depended on his mood.

"Satellite!" Gabby pointed at the westward horizon and then traced her finger eastwardly, following the dim white dot steadily drifting across the sky.

Jackson grinned because she looked almost childlike then, her face awash in the golden glow of firelight, excitedly watching something he suspected would bore most of the women he'd spent time with this past year.

Gabby glanced at him and then her brows knitted together. "Maybe I should keep my mouth shut, but I need to apologize about last night. I'm sorry I made you uncomfortable. I just . . . I want to clear the air so we can start fresh. As friends."

"I already told you, no apologies needed. No explanations, either." Then, because once again her courage oddly empowered him, he confessed, "One thing I could really use these days is a friend."

Not that, under other circumstances, she wouldn't tempt him to want more. Much more. Wrap her in his arms and don't let go kind of more.

"Me too." Her melancholy aside ruffled him like the cold gust of air that swept over the yard. A resilient, caring girl like Gabby ought to have a long list of friends instead of settling for a transient one like him.

Her uncharacteristic attitude all night convinced him that something weighed heavily on her mind. Although it went against everything in his St. James nature, he jumped headlong into personal territory. "You seem preoccupied tonight. Did something happen with your dad since I saw you earlier?"

"No." She pressed her lips together while staring at the fire. Then she rested her cheek on her knees and met his gaze. "I got a letter from my mom."

"Really?" He leaned forward, uncertain of what to say. "That must've been a shock."

"Apparently she'd written to me a few times years ago, but it turns out my dad kept those letters from me." Gabby hung her head for a second. "She's living in Burlington now, working at a B and B. Last weekend was parents' weekend at the University of Vermont and she ran into our neighbors, the Dresslers. They mentioned Luc. Of course, my mom had no idea she was a grandmother. She wrote to ask if she could come see Luc and me."

A bunch of thoughts crowded Jackson's brain at once, not the least of which being that he'd stepped in way over his head with this conversation. He sucked at giving advice, so he decided to take a page from Doc's playbook and listen, validate her feelings, and let her come to her own conclusion. "That's a lot to think about."

"Is it?" The hostile edge in her voice caught him unawares. "I mean, honestly, why should I even care about her or what she wants? Why should I *ever* let her near my son after the choice she made?"

Validate and let her decide, he reminded himself.

"Fair points." Then he paused. "But it seems the real question isn't why you should care; it's *do* you care?"

He couldn't see her eyes too clearly in the dark, but he thought he heard a sniffle. *Shit.* He'd made her cry. "Gabby?"

"I'm fine. Or maybe I'm not. Maybe I'm mad, and not just at my mom. My dad kept those old letters from me like I'm some kind of baby. Like I didn't have the right to have contact with my mom. And I'm mad at my mom for being so weak. For walking away instead of fighting for our family, for me."

Her normally melodious voice had become strangled with emotion.

"I'm sorry you're upset." He sat back in his chair. "Your feelings are totally justified."

Discomfort squirmed through his body from the venom in her voice when she spoke of her mom's addiction. Did Gabby consider him weak because of his alleged drinking problem? Worse, did that kind of anger lie beneath the concern Cat and David were showing him lately?

"Justified, but not helpful. They don't change anything or make it easier." She looked at the fire again, clearly delving deeper into her own thoughts. "The thing is, I'm being a hypocrite. If I want to be seen as something more than my mistakes, don't I owe my mom the chance to make up for hers?" She whipped her head back toward him. "Look at you. You're beating your problem. Maybe my mom is finally beating hers, too. She said she's been clean for twenty-two months. That sounds like a long stretch, right?"

"I don't know." He crossed his ankles and avoided her gaze.

Out of nowhere, she turned the discussion on him. "How long have you been sober?"

"Hold on." He frowned. "First of all, my drinking's not the issue. Secondly, you can't compare your mom to me. Maybe I drank more than my family approved of, but I'm not an alcoholic or a drug addict. I never abandoned my responsibilities or the people who loved me."

He drew a deep breath to slow his heart rate, which had started racing. Did she honestly think him comparable to her mother? Meanwhile, Gabby seemed calm as she dismissively waved one hand.

"Semantics, really. I mean, your family *did* kind of force your hand. You *did* take time off to come here and regroup. So you know more than I do about fighting habit-forming impulses."

"Considering your low regard for your mom, I really don't like the comparison. And I'm not going to tell you what choices you should make regarding her or your dad."

"No?" For the first time since their only other argument, she scowled at him. "So this friendship doesn't include honesty and advice?"

He had two choices. He could get pissed at her for poking him so hard, or he could consider that her mom's letter had thrown her into a tizzy, and she had no one else to take it out on but him. It wasn't personal. She needed to vent, and he needed to take it. But he didn't need to encourage her anger or let it escalate.

"Gabby . . ." Not knowing how to steer the conversation, he joked to lighten the mood. "God, are we as pathetic as we sound?"

But Gabby's tone remained decidedly serious. "Maybe."

He frowned while gulping the majority of his drink, which had turned lukewarm.

"That bothers you, huh?" Gabby cocked her head. "Is it because you care what others think, or because you weren't always 'pathetic'?"

Hell, maybe she should go apprentice with Doc. Her forthrightness kept him in a constant state of suspense. Before he had time to think, he blurted, "Both."

She cocked one brow. "That's what I thought."

"Oh, really." He leaned forward, half teasing, and fully glad to have moved away from the hot topic of her mom. "You think you've got me all figured out?"

"Not *all* figured out, but I've got good intuition." Gabby sat back and straightened her shoulders.

Morbidly fascinated by what she might say next, Jackson couldn't break away from her gaze.

She pressed her lips together tightly, as if telling herself not to speak, but then did. "Someone really hurt you. Made you doubt yourself."

*Direct hit.*

Jackson's entire body flashed hot. He liked Gabby, and even trusted her, but he wouldn't spill *all* his guts. Not now, not here. Especially not right after she'd struck a bull's-eye.

His mind jumped from thought to thought as he set his mug on the chair's arm. Leaning forward, he said, "I think I should probably go to bed soon if we're going to get an early start tomorrow. Thanks for the hot chocolate."

"Jackson." She remained seated when he stood, but set her feet back on the ground. "Whoever she was must be an idiot."

He huffed an amused chuckle. "*They*—plural. So it seems more likely that *I'm* the idiot."

Gabby's eyes widened, but he lost focus on her expression when a slideshow of images—Alison, David, Cat—shuffled through his mind, causing him to frown. Tugging on his earlobe, he finally managed to settle his thoughts. "Just so you know I can be a friend who offers advice, if I were you, I'd see my mom—alone, not with Luc. Otherwise the not knowing might eat away at you." He blew out a breath. "See you in the morning."

He crossed the yard in silence, thankful that Gabby seemed caught up in her own thoughts again, content to sit in front of the fire and consider her options. He needed to retreat and regroup. Clamp down on all the emotions she'd once again whipped into a mild frenzy.

Yet, when he climbed the stairs to the apartment, he could see the wavering light from the fire pit casting about the edges of the yard, like hopeful fingers extending through the darkness, offering the promise of comfort.

# CHAPTER TEN

The following several days passed in a blur of chores during which Gabby's mood blew about like the mass of fallen leaves she'd failed to rake. Between dealing with her dad, Luc, Jackson, and Cami—her dad's militant occupational therapist—she'd rarely found a moment's peace.

"Thanks, Cami. See you on Friday." Gabby waved good-bye at the door and then quickly closed it against the blustery weather.

Standing with her forehead resting against the wall, she drew a deep breath. Most days her father's therapy sessions left him ornery. No reason to suspect today would be any different. Might not be so bad if the lingering tension from their fight about his hiding her mother's old letters weren't adding to the friction.

The shrill whirr of a drill sounded from the upstairs bathroom where, after a lengthy debate with her stubborn dad, Jackson had finally gotten permission to install a grab rail in the shower.

One would think Jackson would steer clear of the Bouchard home to avoid being roped into performing task after task. Gabby had learned to expect the unexpected when it came to that man, who also didn't seem to mind having Luc plastered to his side whenever he stopped by. No doubt Luc was in the bathroom this very minute "helping" Jackson with the project.

The image of her son eagerly watching Jackson work prompted a grin, even though it shouldn't. As a "friend," she also shouldn't make cow eyes whenever Jackson came around, but she feared that was exactly what she did. In fact, lately she'd been doing and thinking a lot of things she shouldn't—like daydreaming—instead of focusing on what mattered, like her real-life problems. Like making a decision about her mom.

On her way back to the kitchen to check on the beef stew she'd been cooking, she stopped by her father, who sat in his recliner. "Cami says you've made good progress this past week."

"Not enough." He kept his gaze on his left hand while he stretched his fingers. "I'm hungry. When's dinner?"

"It should be ready now." She knew how much he hated being sidelined. Hopefully he'd start making the best of his situation instead of fighting her every step of the way. "Need help getting up?"

He waved her off, brows snapped together. "No, I can manage. Don't mother me or I'll never get back to normal."

"Sorry!" Gabby scowled, exhibiting her frayed patience. Turning on her heel, she muttered, "See you in the kitchen."

Her dad moved slowly these days, so she'd already begun to ladle stew into each bowl by the time he arrived at the table.

"*Four* bowls?" He lowered himself into a chair. "I suppose this means Jackson's joining us for dinner again."

Gabby set a steaming bowl of stew in front of him. "It's only polite, considering how much he's been helping with your business, Luc, and even pitching in around here."

Her dad shot her an annoyed look. "I may be a little weakened, but I'm not blind. You're getting attached to him. Worse, Luc is, too."

"Now I'm not allowed to make new friends?" Gabby returned to the stove, glad for an excuse to hide her face. Good grief, how obvious her feelings must be if her dad had noticed despite his preoccupation with therapy. Still, it was her life, not his. He had to stop treating her like a child. "Don't interfere with Jackson like you did with Mom's letters."

"Like I could ever stop you from doing whatever you wanted. And don't start up with that nonsense about me treating you like a baby. You *are* my baby. I did what I did to protect us both from your mom's highs and lows." He laid his napkin across his lap. "Honestly, I'd think you'd know better than to let Luc grow close to someone who is going to leave, not to mention a man with Jackson's particular problem."

Gabby whirled around. "What's *that* mean?"

Her father's eyes locked on hers. "You know exactly what that means. I'm surprised you'd risk the same kind of disappointment you had with your mom."

"How do you . . ." Gabby's voice trailed off because she didn't want to betray Jackson's confidence.

Her father's dismissive wave of the hand rankled. "The day of my stroke, I overheard the way you asked Jackson if he'd been drinking. That, plus how the folks around this small town talk about the handsome stranger who keeps to himself and never has a drink—not even in a bar during a football game. Life with your mom taught me how to read the signs."

"Why is the fact he *isn't* drinking a problem for you?" Gabby's harsh tone caused her father to raise his brows again.

"Don't get me wrong." Her dad set both hands on the table. "I like him and I'm grateful for his help. But I also loved your mom, and you and I both learned, firsthand, short stretches of clean behavior don't mean the problem is gone. Who says she's even telling the truth about her situation? Don't be gullible, Gabby, with her *or* Jackson."

His expression had shifted from critical to mournful, and she knew he'd really been thinking, *Don't be as stupid as I was.*

She supposed he had a small point. Her mom had been a beautiful young woman. Lively and witty. Her dad had never stood a chance against such beauty and charisma.

And when she got sick and things turned bad, he thought he could save her. Took four years before he gave up. Gabby couldn't really blame him for wanting to protect her from the same fate. But unlike her dad, Gabby knew going in that there'd be no happy ending with Jackson.

Her little fantasies were harmless, really. After all, they'd agreed to be friends. Period. End of story. No heartbreak involved.

"I haven't decided what to do about Mom. But it's not fair to assume Jackson's like her. Shouldn't he get the benefit of the doubt until he proves himself unreliable?" She set Luc's and Jackson's bowls on the table, thankful she could speak the truth—more or less. "And anyway, Jackson and I are friends. Nothing more."

Out of nowhere, Luc interrupted the conversation by climbing onto his booster seat. Gabby's head snapped up in time to notice Jackson hovering in the hallway right outside the kitchen.

*Smile and pretend he heard nothing.* Hard to do when her heart hit the floor.

"Come sit!" She waved Jackson into the kitchen just as she heard Luc exclaim, "Yuck!"

Luc wrinkled his tiny nose as he peered at the beef stew.

*Oh, joy.* Another night of cooking only to end up arguing about the dinner. She really ought to give in and make chicken fingers every night. Unfortunately, she poured the frustration her father's pessimism prompted onto Luc. "Oh, come on, Luc. Don't you want to be strong like Pappy and Jackson? I bet they're going to lick the bowl clean."

Jackson stepped into the kitchen holding his toolbox. "Actually, I'm on my way out. I don't want to impose on another family dinner."

*Shoot.* He'd heard something. Hopefully not everything.

"It's not an imposition. Please, you just did us another favor. Stay and have some dinner." Gabby pointed at one of the empty chairs. "Despite Luc's opinion, it's pretty good stuff."

"Sit dere, Jackson." Luc pointed at the seat to his left while kicking his feet.

"Not tonight, buddy. But your mom's right. You need to eat a good dinner." He approached Luc's seat and sniffed. "Smells delicious." Then, turning to Gabby, he said, "Maybe I could take a little home and return the bowl in the morning?"

She hated the way her entire body deflated at that request. Hated that her dad had embarrassed her and probably offended Jackson. Hated, most of all, that her father's warnings couldn't be wholly ignored. "Okay, sure. Let me wrap it in foil for you."

A minute later she handed him the warm bowl, wishing he would change his mind. Why would he? Poor guy had put up with a lot these past few weeks. First she'd begged him for sex, then she'd dumped all her personal problems in his lap, and now her dad had essentially labeled him an unreliable drunk. Come to think of it, Jackson's leaving right now would spare her having to hide her humiliation yet again.

If she had any pride, she'd shove him out the door. "Thanks for installing that railing."

"You're welcome." He turned to her dad, polite smile in place. "Jon, enjoy your dinner." Then he winked at Luc. "I'm going to ask your mom if you ate all that beef. If not, then I can't let you help me with my next project."

Luc picked up his spoon and pushed the food around the bowl.

Then Jackson left through the back door, letting a frigid blast of air into the kitchen. As if she weren't already cold to the bone.

"Big storm's coming," her dad mumbled through a bite of stew. "Expect trees down and other problems on tomorrow's house checks."

Gabby slumped into her chair, appetite gone, caring very little about the impending storm or damage it might do, which paled in comparison to the silent uproar in her chest.

Jackson opened his eyes and saw his breath. That wouldn't be too remarkable if it weren't for the fact he was still lying in bed, covers tucked up under his chin.

The old refrigerator's rattling hum had fallen silent at some point in the night. That, combined with the chilly temperature, suggested the storm had knocked over trees and taken down power lines. One peek at the blank face of the digital alarm clock confirmed his suspicions.

Across the room gray skies clouded the window, but at least the rain had stopped. From the gentle sway of the treetops, he surmised the worst of the storm had passed in the night.

He didn't feel eager to get moving today. The memory of Jon's unflattering assumptions still singed his pride. He couldn't blame the guy for looking out for his daughter, but he couldn't stand the idea of her trust in him wavering, either. The whole situation with her mom had complicated things well enough without her dad piling on.

*Shouldn't he get the benefit of the doubt until he proves himself unworthy?* Her words had hurt. Not because there wasn't some truth in them, but because he knew that's how his family and friends at home must feel about him, too. From now on, they'd be watching and wondering. Questioning and testing.

The idea of being scrutinized had festered all night like a bad dream he couldn't escape. Maybe he'd close his eyes for another fifteen minutes. If he curled into a ball, he might even manage a little warmth.

Bang-bang-bang.

The rapid knock at the door startled him.

"Jackson?" Gabby's voice rang out. "You awake?"

"Hang on." Forcing himself out of bed, he cursed when his bare feet hit the icy floor. Wrapped in the old quilt, he shuffled across the room and whipped open the door. "Everything okay?"

"Yes, but we need to get an early start." Her smile faded when she noticed his patchwork cloak. "Oh, shoot. I forgot the apartment doesn't have a generator to keep the heat running. Grab some things and come get showered and dressed in our house. Then we need to roll out. There will be tons of cleanup today with all the fallen branches and trees. We need to check every single house for damage to roofs and other areas."

Her alert eyes bored into his, energy and a little tension crackling around her like static electricity.

"I see you've already had your morning coffee." He yawned and then raked one hand through his hair. "I'll change here. If there's still no heat at the end of the day, I'll take you up on the hot shower. Go on back home. I'll be there in a few."

After closing the door, he searched for clean sweats and a fleece. His phone rang, which told him it had charged before the power died. He put it on speakerphone mode so he could get dressed at the same time.

"Hey, Cat." He hopped on one foot while jamming his other leg into his pants. "You're up early."

"I haven't heard boo out of you in weeks, so I wanted to catch you before your day started."

"Too late. I'm actually in a bit of a rush." He shoved his arms through his old Michigan Wolverines sweatshirt, thankful for the warmth it provided.

"Rush to do what? I thought you were taking time off to destress and . . . recover."

Jackson rolled his eyes. "I'm relaxing. Just keeping busy while I do it."

"How very like you." Cat chuckled. "What's got you busy, or maybe it's a who?"

"Don't fish, Cat. You stink at it." Jackson grinned, although the fact she wasn't far off the mark should've made him nervous.

"Fine." Cat paused. "So, have you talked to anyone, like a therapist?"

"Nosy question for someone who doesn't like to share." Jackson thought about his last few sessions with Doc, and how he'd been stalling inviting his family to join in the fun. "Actually, my doctor suggested a family session."

"Oh?" Cat fell silent. "Why? I mean, what do I have to do with your drinking?"

His heart pinched a little. "Does that mean you wouldn't come?"

"Of course I'll come," she responded immediately. "It's just . . . you know I'm uncomfortable sharing personal stuff. Look at how I squirmed at the intervention. Can't imagine being quizzed by a doctor."

"He's actually not so bad. Kind of laid-back. Besides, he's more interested in digging to the root of my issues than he is in your box of secrets. But you can relax, because I haven't agreed to involve everyone."

"If he thinks it's important, then you need to involve us. David and I will be there for you. You know that, right?"

"But not Dad?"

"I don't know. You know he's not a big believer in therapy. And he and David together with a doctor who's probing our family dynamic? Well, that could backfire."

"Maybe we'll finally get the truth about what's going on with them." This possibility in and of itself might be the main reason he'd even been considering the idea.

"Maybe we're better off in the dark. David has repeatedly said we are. He must mean what he's saying. David doesn't lie."

True enough. David had mentioned, on more than one occasion, that Jackson and Cat were better off not knowing. However, like Gabby, Jackson didn't appreciate people "protecting" him by keeping secrets, as if he were still a kid who couldn't handle the truth. Besides, the truth had to be easier than wondering about the rift because, at times, his imagination could wander into dark territory. "You think he's told Vivi the truth?"

"Actually, I do."

"To hell with that, Cat. I can handle whatever Vivi can handle. It's my damn family. I deserve to know at least as much as she does."

"First, let's face facts. Vivi's stronger than you and me. I mean, look at how she handled her sucky childhood with a smile and a side dish of optimism. Plus, the fact Vivi *isn't* one of Dad's kids gives her a certain distance from whatever it is." Cat hesitated before speaking again. This time her voice held a note of sorrow. "What if knowing the truth only drives you further away?"

*What if?* He supposed it could happen. The thought made him reconsider the advice he'd given Gabby. Would facing her mother backfire or give Gabby closure? Who knew? Not him, that's for sure. Right now the only thing he could help soothe was his sister's melancholy.

"Sounds like you miss me," he teased. "Don't worry. I'll be back in a few weeks. Besides, you've got Hank keeping you company, right?"

"Yes. He's been great, but that doesn't mean I don't want you back here, too. It's been so long since we've all been happy." She heaved a sigh. "That's what I want most, Jackson. I want us all to be happy again."

So did Jackson, which was why he'd decided to come up to Vermont in the first place. Yet, he couldn't make promises when he still felt mistrustful.

Then again, each hour he spent with Gabby passed without reliving old hurts and bitterness. A growing sense of peace had planted itself in his mind, and he didn't want to disturb it before the roots took hold. Maybe being a gardener really was Gabby's calling, he thought with a smile.

"Look, I appreciate the call. Sorry if you've been worried. I'm fine. I'm keeping busy. My landlord had a stroke, so I'm pitching in to help his daughter while she manages their business during his recovery."

"His daughter?" His sister's smile could be heard through the phone. "Now it's all becoming clear. Maybe I ought to pop up to Vermont for a visit and check her out. I've always loved the Equinox Hotel in the fall."

"It's a free country." Jackson didn't know why he'd resorted to sarcasm. He'd enjoy seeing Cat, but he didn't want her judging him, or Gabby. Come to think of it, he'd probably not yet invited his family up precisely to avoid being trapped under the microscope.

"Thanks for the enthusiastic welcome." Cat laughed. "Now you know I'm coming, if only to taunt you."

He knew she'd never come without an express invitation, so he brushed off her remark as a joke.

"That's why I love ya, sis. Now I've really got to run. Bye." Jackson hit the End button and shoved the phone into his pocket.

~

By late afternoon, Jackson's lower back had tightened from overuse. Axes and chainsaws weren't tools he handled often, and it showed. He couldn't help but marvel at the fact that Jon and Gabby did this work on a semiregular basis, considering how often smaller trees would be felled by stormy mountain weather.

He and Gabby hiked up a steep dirt road to a private lane to check on the final home, because the town municipal services hadn't yet cleared a massive tree from the public road just below.

Branches—large and small—lay everywhere. This entire ridge suffered the worst wind damage he'd seen all day. He couldn't be happier that the roof of the ranch-style home remained intact.

He noticed the For Sale sign in the front yard. The 1940s home appeared long neglected, but it was surrounded on two sides by National Forest land, and the neighbor to the left was a couple of acres away on the other side of a thick stand of trees.

"I need to use the restroom, then I'll clear some of these branches from the shrubs while you check the house," Gabby said, focused on the task at hand instead of being caught up in the romance of the possibilities of this property.

Once inside, Jackson found himself surveying the structure—not for the reasons he should be, but with an eye toward remodeling. In no time at all, Gabby reappeared.

"Find any leaks?" she asked.

"Oh, no. I'm just admiring the property. This place is awesome."

She looked at him like he'd sprouted another head. "*This* place?"

"Hell, yeah. It's solidly built, so imagine if I tore out the ceiling and took it up to the rafters. Throw in some beams up there for a cool look, and take out this ugly old window and make the whole back of this house glass to take advantage of those long-range views. I'd rip out that brick mantel and replace it with a twelve-foot-high dry-stack stone one. Redo the kitchen with knotty alder cabinetry and stainless steel appliances. Fix that stone patio and add a built-in fire pit." He stopped and glanced at Gabby to find her smiling, deep dimples on full display. "What?"

"You. You were in another world now. When you describe everything you want to do, I wish I could afford to buy this place and pay you to remodel it."

"Me, too." For one wistful moment, he envisioned sitting on the rebuilt terrace, having coffee and scanning the paper, eating some great breakfast Gabby—er, *he* cooked. He shook his head and walked away from the window. "I'm going to the basement to check for water damage."

"I'll meet you outside." She walked away, but he caught her glancing around now with a critical eye, as if she, too, were thinking about the house differently.

When he exited the garage ten minutes later, he glanced around and spotted Gabby working near the front of the home.

It'd been a long day of clearing debris. Hard, dirty work. Not without a fair amount of bugs or an occasional snake, either. Yet instead of complaining, Gabby'd spent the better part of the afternoon humming to herself, pausing only long enough to wipe her brow, seemingly unaware of his notice.

Nothing about her fit the stereotype of what one might expect from a girl who accidentally got pregnant in her late teens. He liked her all the more for her grit, determination, and good humor. She was one of a kind, no doubt about that, and he'd miss her when he left. He knew that, and he knew he'd probably think about her and her family for some time to come.

He wondered, now, if she'd come to a decision about her mom, but didn't want to pry. Wasn't really his business, was it? Still, the thought replayed like a skip in the groove of one of his Dad's prized old albums.

"Watch it, Gabby!" Jackson called as she caught her foot on one fallen branch while trying to rescue some shrubs from the clutches of another.

"Oof!" She landed on her side, ankle twisted. "Ow."

He jogged to her and threw aside the branch she'd been moving. She winced while freeing her wedged foot. After watching how tough she'd been all day, he knew her ankle had to hurt pretty bad for her to grimace.

"Can you stand?" He set one hand on her shoulder.

"We'll see." She held her hands up like a child. "Help me up, please."

"Let's not dislocate your shoulders, too." He went behind her and placed his forearms under her armpits. "One, two, three, up you go."

He held her until she seemed stable. Gingerly, she tested the bad ankle and immediately yelped, then hopped around on the good leg.

"Whoa! Stop before you fall again and hurt something else." He curled his arm around her waist, wishing he didn't like the tingle of awareness fanning along the whole left side of his body. Privately, he loved the excuse to hold her. To let her soft hair brush against his neck. To be physically connected in any way, really.

Just friends, he'd told her. But each day they'd worked together, that mismatched characterization of his feelings became more and more apparent. "Let's see if we can get you back to the truck in one piece."

He kept one arm around her and they took three steps before he realized she'd never make it back down the mountain to where they'd parked her truck. Stopping in his tracks, he said, "I think our best bet is if I carry you piggyback."

"It's a long way, though." She tested her bad ankle again and winced.

"Exactly. Too far to hop. The only sure way down without another stumble is if you're on my back."

Gabby shrugged. "Works for me."

Jackson squatted a bit and hefted her onto his back.

"Don't go fast! It's muddy. If you fall, we're both in trouble." She rested her chin on his shoulder.

He turned his head slightly and gave her a sidelong glance. "You think I'm some uncoordinated oaf?"

"No, but it's steep and slick. You're not used to these roads." She adjusted her position, gripping him more tightly around the waist with her legs.

Carrying her down the mountainside required concentration and blood pumping through his limbs, but her movement set his oversexed imagination off and pooled all the blood in his groin.

"Stop wriggling or we *are* going to fall." He sidestepped down the road to reduce the risk of losing his footing.

"Sorry." Gabby sighed and then rested her cheek on his shoulder. "Thanks. You're a good friend. A good guy."

"Sometimes, anyway." He wondered if she was thinking about her father's warnings. He kept his eyes on the road ahead, but could feel her gaze roving his hair, profile, even his ear. "Stop."

"Stop what? I'm not doing anything."

"You're staring at me." He stepped over a large crack in the road where running water had eroded the surface.

"Sorry. I was just wondering."

*Uh-oh.*

When he didn't pry, she spoke with a manly sounding voice. "Oh? What were you wondering, Gabby?" Then she went back to her own voice. "Well, seeing that we're friends and all, and seeing how friends care about each other's feelings, I was wondering how much of my dad's lecture you overheard last night."

This? Now?

"Enough to know he's concerned about you and Luc."

"I was afraid of that. Don't take it personally. My mom hurt him so much, he can't be objective."

"And you can?" Jackson deliberately kept his eyes ahead. "Your mom hurt you, too, otherwise her letter wouldn't have upset you."

"True, but it's different from my dad. Unlike me, he *chose* her. I think he feels guilty about that, like his bad choice screwed up my life." Gabby shrugged. "The truth is, my life's not all that screwed up. I could waste time wishing my mom had never gotten sick, gripe about how her drug habit embarrassed me, how her leaving hurt, and even blame her for my teen rebellion and pregnancy, but what good would any of that do anyone? Besides, I love Luc so much, how can I regret him? Heck, in a twisted way, maybe I even owe her. Ultimately, what happened in my family forced me to grow up and get my priorities right. Sometimes life feels hard and lonely—and I envy my friends, like Tess, who have freedom and options I no longer do—but then nice surprises happen, too. Like you. You've been a great surprise."

He couldn't help but smile at the compliment. More importantly, he admired the way she could turn pain on its head and embrace the silver linings. If anything, *she'd* been the great surprise, not the other way around.

"As have you." And then, because she'd somehow unlocked the closed-off part of his heart, he added, "Meeting you has been the best thing that's happened to me in quite some time."

Instead of saying anything, she readjusted her arms, keeping one slung over his right shoulder while the other now snaked beneath his left armpit. Clasping her hands together in front of his chest, she hugged him. The whole maneuver fitted her body even more snugly against his back. "Better?"

Not really. Well, yes, actually. It did feel better.

Safer. Warmer.

So warm, he started feeling flush from it.

Thank God her feet weren't locked at the ankles, or they'd have butted up against the bulge growing in the front of his sweats.

He couldn't close his eyes and think of anything else without losing his balance, so he shifted his focus to the stones on the road, counting his steps in his head, something—anything—to take his mind off how much he wanted to twist her around and kiss her.

"You know so much about me, but you haven't told me anything about your family except that your mom died and you'll be an uncle soon. How many brothers and sisters do you have?" Gabby's breath brushed over his skin, as enticing as the soft scratch of a woman's fingernails.

Of course, thinking about his family helped douse his libido a bit, so he seized on it. "Older brother, David, and a younger sister, Cat."

"Ha, Cat St. James, like the model."

Jackson chuckled. "Exactly."

Gabby gulped. "Exactly? You mean your sister *is* the model?"

Jackson nodded, finding it amusing to hear Gabby's reaction to learning about Cat. He knew his sister left some—mostly men—starstruck, but he'd always seen her as the hedgehog—his nickname for her—who could be his best friend or a pest, depending on her mood.

"Wow . . . I guess I can see how she looks a little like you, but a lot prettier." Gabby snickered. "Only kidding. You're pretty, too."

"Pretty?" Jackson scoffed, and she snickered again.

He stepped over a fallen branch, thinking about his family now. He glanced over his shoulder at Gabby, who'd fallen silent. Finally, she sighed. "It's nice that you have them. I've always hated being an only child. Are you close?"

"Yes," he said, then elaborated. "We were closer, but after my mom died, things got a little weird. David moved to Hong Kong for a while, and Cat got herself involved in a bad relationship. So did I. Everything kind of went to hell for a while, but somehow David and Cat landed on their feet. I'm still finding my footing, I guess."

"Sounds like you don't like the fact that it's taken you longer to recover. You know what I think, though? I think the more deeply you care, the more deeply you hurt, so of course it takes longer to heal. If I were you, I'd be proud of the fact that I could be *that* hurt. A caring heart is a good thing, Jackson."

He might've stopped breathing for a minute. She'd voiced the exact thing he'd wanted to believe about himself. Somehow Gabby really saw him—or at least the "him" he wanted to be. Whether they both were right or just crazy didn't matter as much as the fact that they were in sync. Suddenly neither her age, the geographical distance, nor Doc's warnings mattered.

When they arrived at the truck, Jackson opened the passenger door and turned so she could scoot off his back. As soon as her butt hit the seat he whirled around, cupped her face, and kissed her.

# CHAPTER ELEVEN

Heat flared throughout Gabby's body as Jackson's gentle kiss turned rough and hungry. One of his callused hands settled behind the base of her neck, and the other quickly groped her hip, yanking her forward so he could nestle himself between her legs. The throbbing in her ankle disappeared only to reappear higher up inside her thigh.

He nipped at her lip with his teeth before kissing her again. She threaded her fingers through Jackson's silky waves of hair, sealing herself to him in a passionate tangle of tongues and lips and warmth and moisture. A sensual, gentle, giving kiss, just like the man she'd known him to be. It outperformed every fantasy she'd had about it and him.

A satisfied moan rattled in his chest, shooting a burst of tingles straight to her core.

"Jackson," she whispered when his mouth began exploring the contours of her jaw and neck.

But somehow speaking had been a mistake—a terrible, spell-breaking mistake—because he pulled back, blinking as if shaking himself free from a haze. He then hugged her against his chest and kissed the top of her head. "Sorry. I got selfish and greedy and didn't stop to think. We shouldn't cross this line, but damn if you don't have a way of saying things that make me feel so . . . so much. Honest to Christ, I don't know how you do that."

She tipped up her chin so her lips pressed against his neck again. "Don't stop."

He held her tight once more before kissing her forehead and then backing away. Chilly October wind rushed into the now-empty space between them, making her shiver.

"Gabby, you know this isn't smart." He crossed his arms, stuffing his hands beneath his armpits.

Probably true. He'd be here only long enough for her to get crushed. And then there was the not-insignificant issue of his drinking, or rather her aversion to inviting that kind of worry back into her life.

Yet, to have experienced—even briefly—his intense brand of lust and tenderness only to have it ripped away felt like a cruel slap across the cheek. The other day they'd agreed to be friends. She'd heard the sincerity in his voice when he'd admitted to needing a friend. Yet none of the complications stopped her from wanting to explore this powerful affection.

"Maybe we should seize the moment. Look at it like a breezy, short-term vacation fling?"

His eyes widened in response to her proposition, then he frowned. "No."

"Why not?"

He looked right in her eyes. "Because flings are what you have with people you can't see yourself caring about, and that's not the way I feel about you."

His flattery, so unpracticed and sincere, swaddled her heart with hope.

"If that's true, then maybe this," she gestured between them, "is worth the risk."

He hesitated before responding, as if searching for a reason that could convince them both.

"My life's in Connecticut, and yours is here, in Vermont, with your dad and your son. Then there's Noah. And even if you are mature for your age, you are still young and don't need to be saddled with all my shit." He looked off for a moment. "A happy ending here seems damn

JAMIE BECK

near impossible, so we'd be stupid to start something that could only hurt us both to lose."

"Jackson—" she began, until he interrupted, making it clear the discussion had ended.

Staring at her foot, he asked, "How's the ankle?"

She glared at him, irrationally angry. "Fine."

"Don't be like that, Gabby." Jackson sighed. "I'm trying to do the right thing."

Maybe he was, but she didn't have to like it or make it easy. Yanking her legs inside the cab of the pickup, she muttered, "We should get back. Luc is probably getting dropped off soon."

Jackson closed the door and walked around the front of the truck, his expression shuttered. He climbed behind the steering wheel and started the engine without another word.

Awkward tension thickened the air inside the cab. Both kept their gazes on the road ahead for the duration of the ten-minute drive back to her house. When he finally killed the engine, he said, "Let me help you inside."

"No, thanks." She knew moping wasn't attractive, but in the heat of the moment she didn't care.

"Come on, your ankle's still a little swollen."

She turned on him. "Contrary to what you and my dad think, I'm actually a grown-up, capable of asking for help if I need it, or making decisions about what I can handle. So thanks, but I can manage without you."

For a second, she felt rather self-satisfied. Then he reached across the seat and gripped her arm. "Stop it, Gabby."

"Stop what?" Her petulant tone rang out.

"Pouting like a baby because you don't want to face the truth about us. Refusing my help now because you're pissed at me for not giving in."

She shrugged out of his grip, chastised and embarrassed.

Jackson continued speaking, although with a tempered tone. "Grown-ups think things through instead of acting on impulse. They have the perspective to forego short-term fun to avoid long-term pain. They appreciate a compliment instead of sulking."

He watched her until she met his gaze. Like always, his caramel-colored eyes affected her like black magic, bathing her in a frustrating wash of desire, intimacy, and wistfulness.

"In my opinion, a grown-up recognizes how rare this kind of connection is, and doesn't give it up without a fight. But maybe that's what got you stuck here in Vermont in the first place. Maybe sticking around to fight for someone isn't in your DNA after all."

The golden flecks in his eyes flashed with disbelief and a little anger. Gabby decided not to hang around for whatever he might say next.

She practically leapt from the car, thankful to land on her good ankle. She scrambled, as fast as she could hop, to the front door without looking back. As she entered her house, she heard the truck door slam shut. Once inside, she closed her front door and rested her forehead against it until her heart rate slowed.

"That you, Gabby?" her father called from the living room.

The man had been her hero for so long, but ever since she got her mom's letter, the sound of his voice hurt like a bruise being bumped. Like Jackson, he didn't think she was strong enough to handle disappointment, or to make decisions about her own flippin' life.

The days of being seen as a child should've ended when she'd birthed her own.

"Yeah, Dad. I'm home." She limped into the living room and glanced at the clock. "Didn't Noah bring Luc home yet?"

"I'm sure they'll be here any minute." He waved dismissively, then narrowed his gaze. "How was the damage? Any major problems?"

*Not with the homes.*

"Surprisingly, no. Basic stuff . . . limbs to clear and so forth. Signal Hill was blocked, so we hiked up to get to the Harris home. I suspect that road will be cleared tonight. Only a few places lost power, but all backup generators were running. I'll check them again tomorrow and confirm that power is restored."

His taut expression loosened in obvious relief. "Thanks for picking up the slack. I hate being sidelined for another few weeks."

As if she didn't know. Her father's desperation for recovery showed in everything he did. Even Cami had warned him to lighten up a bit, which hadn't gone over well. Sighing, Gabby hobbled to the nearest chair and sank into the cushions.

"What happened to you?" Her father frowned.

"Twisted my ankle while clearing some heavy branches." Gabby set her foot on the coffee table to keep it elevated. "It'll be fine in another hour or two. Was Cami here today for therapy?"

"Yes." He tugged at his ear, scowling. "Slow going, but at least it's going. I know I got lucky with the so-called moderate aftereffects, but I hate being stuck here like an invalid. Worse, though, is thinking about what could've happened to you and Luc if my stroke had caused more damage."

"If Jackson weren't here, I'd have had to hire extra help. Probably would've had to pull Luc out of nursery school to pay for it." Gabby shot him a rueful smirk. "Let's be grateful for your recovery, and for Jackson's help."

Her father nodded. "We should refund what's left of his rent, actually. I don't like being a charity case, or feeling indebted."

Although her dad had the right idea, she suspected Jackson would be offended by the gesture. "I'm not sure he'd appreciate the offer. It might even offend him."

"Oh?" He snorted. "You've really got him up on a pedestal, don't you?"

"Hardly." Naturally he'd reduce her concern to something silly and naïve instead of considering its merit. "But helping us is making him feel good about himself. I think it's been a while since he felt that way, so I don't want to take it away from him, that's all."

"My business, my call."

Great. *Father knows best* should be stamped across his forehead. Fine. Maybe he could control that decision, but he couldn't control her. "Speaking of calls, I've decided to talk to Mom."

"Why?" Her dad huffed and raised his hands toward the ceiling. "Why would you let that woman back into your life?"

"Because 'that woman' is my *mom*. I'm curious, Dad, and I want some answers." Then she wrinkled her nose. "And, honestly, probably a little bit because you took the choice away from me before."

"Not that again." He shook his head. "While you're busy judging me, think about what you'd do to protect Luc from an unbalanced, unhealthy person." His features softened. "In case you've forgotten, your mother's leaving sent you into a tailspin. You shoved your hurt down deep—covered it with a smile and some teenage rebellion—but it killed me to know you got a raw deal because I'd waited too long to draw that line with your mother. Think back and remember living through years of her highs and lows, of her lies. I didn't trust her when she first wrote, and I don't trust her now. That's not bitterness talking, it's concern and experience, plain and simple. Please don't open yourself up to pain and aggravation. And don't expose Luc to her kind of poison."

Seeing her father's remorse and genuine sorrow deflated Gabby's animosity.

"Maybe that's all true, but I can't live with the unanswered questions now that she's reached out. I have to see her, but I won't take Luc." She offered a compassionate smile. "I'm sorry if this upsets you, but it's my choice. I know all the awful things she did, and how much she hurt us both, Dad. But, she's my mom. Somewhere under all those drugs is that woman who loved me. The woman we both loved.

"The fact she's reached out before proves that she didn't coldly walk away and never look back. That she had regrets. I can't pretend I don't care at all if I ever see her again. And you always taught me to give people a second chance. What if Mom's been working hard at being clean? Maybe she deserves a chance to prove she's changed."

Her father shook his head in resignation. "If I had a dime for every chance I gave her, I could retire."

Gabby's shoulders slumped in response to his fatalistic opinion. Luckily, the doorbell put an end to the discussion. "That'll be Noah and Luc. I'll get it."

A quick glance at her dad's unfocused gaze suggested he'd already vacated the room even though his body remained in his chair.

When she opened the door, she found Noah holding Luc in his arms. The uncommon sight made her breath catch, and forced her to acknowledge the similarity in the shape of their faces. She reached for her son. "Thanks, Noah. I had a long day today, so this really helped."

Noah smiled the old familiar smile that used to turn her insides to jelly. Although hesitant to give Noah credit for much, she did have to admit that he had been trying a little harder recently with Luc, and with her. If she were willing to hand out second chances to her mom, maybe she could also dial back her sarcasm and be friends with her son's father.

She kissed Luc's cheek. "Did you have fun in Daddy's car?"

"Dada put on the wed-and-blue lights!"

Gabby widened her eyes in feigned excitement. "Oh, my! That sounds like fun." She set Luc down and he galloped down the hallway calling for his pappy.

"Gabby, can we talk for a second?" Noah had removed his hat and was holding it in front of his body. He jerked his head to the left. "Out here?"

"What's up?" She stepped onto the porch and cast a furtive glance toward the garage, wondering if Jackson could see her and Noah.

Noah fidgeted with his holster and flashed an awkward grin. For the first time in ages, he wasn't acting like the cock of the walk. "Guess I'll just— Aw, hell, Gabs. I've made mistakes, and I could've been—could be—a better dad. A better guy for you. We both know I wasn't ready before, but now, well, now I feel like I could be." He must've read the utter dismay in her eyes, because he cleared his throat before bumbling toward the finish line. "I guess what I'm trying to say is—what I'm hoping is—since you're not involved with anyone, and since I *am* Luc's dad, maybe you'll let me try to put our family back together. Try to make it work this time."

Gabby would've sworn her jaw had dropped to the ground, but a quick touch with her hand proved it hadn't. Although she'd just argued the virtues of giving him a second chance of sorts, the walls of her heart hardened against Noah's suggestion. "Noah, I . . . you've surprised me. Forgive me if I'm a little skeptical."

"Are you really? You know you've always been my favorite girl. This really can't be a complete shock."

"If I've always been your favorite, then why'd you need Linda, Jessie, Annie—"

"Okay, okay. Stop!" Noah interrupted and chewed on his lip. "I was twenty-one when you got pregnant, and scared shitless, by the way. Nowhere close to being what you and Luc needed. I thought I could outrun the responsibility and all my mixed feelings. But no one else came close to you, Gabs. Not ever. Once I messed up, I was too proud to admit it. Then time passed, and you were so mad and hurt—as you should've been. I suppose I'm hoping now maybe enough time has passed that your anger has faded and we can talk."

"So you've had this sudden epiphany?" Gabby shook her head, guessing that Jackson's arrival on the scene had as much to do with this little show as any genuine change of heart. "Noah, whatever feelings I had for you are gone. Maybe a couple of years ago I could've found some leftover love in my heart, but now it's too late."

"Won't you even give me a chance to prove I've changed?" He reached out to touch her arm. "Let me try to be a better guy for you, a better dad for Luc."

"God help you if you use Luc to try to win me over. Right now he's fine with the *loose* relationship you two have. Don't you cozy up to him to try to convince me to give you another chance, and then go back to your casual regard when your ploy doesn't work."

"Wow." Noah's brows rose. "I see I've got a lot of work to do before you'll take me seriously. This isn't a ploy. I'm trying to be honest with you for the first time in years."

Was he? Gabby couldn't tell, and that was the problem. Even if she could erase the heartache he'd caused her and wanted to take him back, could she really trust him? At the end of the day, she didn't believe he'd ever love anyone as much as he loved himself.

"Please, let this go. You'll always be in our lives because you *are* Luc's dad. We are a family, dysfunctional as we may be. Let's let that be enough."

"I won you over once." Noah put his hat back on and rested his hands on his hips. "You can't stop me from trying to do it again."

"Then how about a word of advice." She raised her brows. "Disregarding my feelings isn't a great place to start."

"That's one of the things I love about you, Gabs. You always throw a straight punch." He winked as if his charm would melt her defenses, then strode toward his car while gazing at the garage apartment window. He turned to her as he opened his car door. "I'm going to change your mind about me."

Before she could beg him not to try, he slid into the front seat, closed the door, and fired up the engine.

Gabby sagged against the door, exhausted from the hard day's work, the sore ankle, and the three arguments she'd had within the past forty-five minutes.

~

Jackson watched Noah's patrol car pull away from the house. He hadn't been able to see Gabby because she'd remained mostly hidden by the roofline of the front porch.

The nettling final words of his and Gabby's earlier argument drifted back to him. *Maybe sticking around to fight for someone isn't in your DNA after all.*

*Bullshit,* he thought. He fought for everyone. He'd fought for his mom when she'd been sick, he'd fought for his brother in those early months after David had run off to Hong Kong. He'd fought for his son or daughter until Alison hauled off to the clinic and disposed of their "mistake." That still cut the deepest, as did the wondering about whether he might've had a son or a daughter.

Didn't matter now, he supposed. The point was that he fought for people he loved. Right now he fought to protect himself and Gabby from pain. Too bad she didn't understand that often in life the best offense is a good defense.

Jackson checked the time and then called David for the conference call with him and Oliver, the useless lawyer. While he waited for them to assemble, he wished to hell this suit with Doug would disappear. He had enough on his mind without having to kowtow to that son of a bitch.

"Jackson?" David's voice came through the line.

"I'm here." Jackson sat at the little table where he'd had a notebook and pen ready.

"Oliver will be another minute."

"So I'm not getting billed for this part of the call," Jackson joked, needing to lighten his mood.

"Not unless you piss me off." David didn't tease much, but Jackson could hear the affection in his tone. He'd wallowed in his hurt by David for so long, he'd forgotten about his brother's good side. "Cat told me she spoke to you this morning."

He'd suspected David and Cat were checking up on him and then checking in with each other. Gabby's wistful remark about wishing for siblings replayed, forcing him to admit how lucky he was that they cared enough to do so.

"Yep." Jackson stretched his legs out. "Now's not the time for that discussion, though, if it's okay with you."

"Of course. Just know I'm here, whatever you need."

"Thanks." He twirled the pen in his fingers, unwilling to let his mind wander to thoughts of family therapy when he had so little emotional energy left in his tank.

"Ah, here's Oliver," David announced.

"Jackson, sorry for the delay." Oliver's deep staccato made Jackson edgy. He wished David specialized in litigation instead of corporate transactions, but at least he knew David would be looking over Oliver's shoulder, too.

"No worries." Jackson drew a breath. "I'm hoping you've got good news."

"Unfortunately, not at this time. I've received interrogatories, and anticipate deposition notices soon."

"In English, please." Jackson rolled his eyes.

"Sorry. Basically, we're now in the discovery phase of the suit. I've received pages of questions intended to provide them with evidence the plaintiff—er, Doug—can use to build his case. The depositions are basically interviews, most likely of the witnesses to the incident, but also potentially of some of your clients."

Jackson bolted upright. "Why can he get to my clients? They weren't on-site, nor do they have any say over my hiring and firing practices."

"The problem is that the wrongful termination element of the suit, based on a skewed interpretation of retaliation, is Doug's weakest claim, so the assault, infliction of emotional distress, and defamation claims will be the ones they push harder."

"Defamation? He's the one spreading tales about me and my work ethic, not the other way around." Jackson's palm slammed the table. "Why can't I sue *him*?"

"If you recall, we did file counterclaims, but either way, there will be depositions unless we settle this before things escalate."

"So he pops off his mouth to my crew, sues me, and then *I'm* the one stuck paying? No offense, guys, but the legal system sucks." The silence from the other end of the line didn't help Jackson's mood.

David decided to chime in. "Jackson, you need to approach this with your head, not your heart. Fair and unfair don't matter as much as your reputation, your business interests, everything you've built here. That's all best served if you make a decisive move to end this nonsense before Doug gets the evidence he needs to improve his chances in court."

"Dammit, there is no evidence." But then Jackson recalled how Hank's recollection of the incident differed from his own.

"I don't think you should rely solely on your own testimony and memory to make that decision." David hesitated. "Based on my off-book conversations with Hank, at the very least, Doug's civil assault claim has legs."

"You two want me to tuck tail?"

"No," Oliver answered. "If you want to fight, we'll fight. But what we're telling you is that you should strongly consider what's in your own best interest, and the interest of your other employees. My advice is to make a settlement offer, conditioned on Doug's silence, of course."

"Like we could ever enforce that!" Jackson scoffed.

"Admittedly, it isn't perfect, but yours is a closed community. If you got wind of Doug talking, he'd have to return the money plus other costs." Oliver then fell silent.

"But if he breaks his end of the deal, all the damage I'm seeking to avoid by paying him now would happen anyway." Jackson rubbed his hand over his face.

"In all likelihood, he'll take his money and abide by the terms," Oliver said.

"So what, now I pick a number out of the air and pay the fucker?" Jackson doodled cash symbols across the notepad, then crossed them out.

David piped up. "What's it worth to you to have this go away? To get this one item off your list of concerns and move forward?"

He wanted to shout *"Nothing!"* But he thought about Hank, Jim, Ray, and the new crew members. He thought about the years he'd already spent building the company and its reputation. He thought about the fact that recently he'd finally begun to feel better in his own skin, and better about the future. Maybe David was right. Maybe locking horns with that asshole wasn't worth it.

"Jackson?" David asked again.

"You think a month's salary is fair?"

"What's the number?" Oliver asked.

"Four grand."

Jackson could hear them whispering. "I can hear you two conferring even if I can't see you."

Oliver cleared his throat. "Sorry. I was telling David I doubt that will be enough. Even if Doug were willing to accept it, which I doubt, his lawyer probably will aim higher because his compensation is a percentage of whatever he gets for his client."

"That's fucked up."

"I don't disagree, but I'm giving you my best counsel. Would you be willing to offer twenty-five grand to end this now? It's well below your insurance limits."

*Twenty-five grand?* Oliver must be a lunatic. It wasn't only about the number, either. It was principle.

"Oliver, can I speak with my brother alone for a minute?" Jackson impatiently tapped his toes.

"Sure. I'll step outside his office," Oliver said.

"Thank you." Jackson could hear papers shuffle and movement.

"He's gone now. What's up?" David asked.

"Do you agree with him?" Jackson snapped.

"About settling?"

"About the amount. I mean, that's six months' salary. Seems like a lot for a guy who got fired for trash-talking the boss."

"I think the key is expediency. There's a cost associated with getting this handled quickly. If you roll the dice and get hit with any kind of punitive damages on the assault charges, those won't be covered by insurance and you could be in a tough spot. So while I get that you're looking at this from the standpoint of 'justice,' now is the time for pragmatism, not idealism."

Suddenly an overwhelming sense of defeat cascaded over Jackson. The darkness that had consumed him the past two years swelled up inside, squeezing his lungs. His mouth felt dry, and for the first time in days, he really wanted a drink. "Offer twelve grand. Not *one* penny more. That's three months' pay."

"I'll tell Oliver." David paused. "I hate to say this now, but you should brace for a counteroffer."

"Hell, David. Can't Oliver make the other lawyer see reason? For crissakes, this is extortion."

"You know enough about negotiation to know the game." David paused and Jackson closed his eyes, frustrated. "While I've still got you on the line, can we talk about this family counseling session Cat mentioned now?"

"Actually, I've had a helluva day. I'm not trying to put you off." Jackson leaned forward and rested his chin on his fist. "Okay, yeah, I am, but not because I'm not willing to talk about it. I'm just not up for it right now."

"All right. Like I said, I'll be there if and when you want me. Vivi sends her love."

"Thanks, David. Tell V hi. And thanks for staying involved in this mess, too. I know you're not charging me for your time."

"Don't mention it."

"Okay. Talk soon." Jackson hung up and tossed the phone on the table.

After a minute, he stood and crossed to the fridge. Dinner options were limited: grilled cheese, canned soup, or an egg sandwich. He looked across the driveway to the Bouchard home. Gabby had probably cooked something hearty and savory. The girl had mad skills in the kitchen.

And elsewhere. Remembering their kiss sent a sizzle of electricity through him. Was she right? Was he a coward instead of a wise, self-sacrificing guy?

It seemed beyond ridiculous to think anything good could come of getting more involved with her, and yet, she was the first—the only—person in more than twenty-four months who had sparked hope in his chest. Who understood his heart. Who was willing to risk something to be closer to him.

Intelligence wrestled instinct, desperate to shine a floodlight on the insanity of them being together. Yet, instead of the stark rays throwing the flaws into sharp relief, it merely made the intangible, compelling facets of their relationship sparkle to life.

His confidence that he'd be strong enough to resist her for another few weeks flagged. Hell, even one more day would be tough.

# CHAPTER TWELVE

At ten o'clock, Gabby turned off the television after realizing she'd done nothing but channel surf for the past half hour. Her father had gone to bed early. And unlike her thoughts, Luc hadn't stirred for hours.

She meandered through the first floor, picking up a toy Luc had left in the kitchen, loading her dirty cup in the dishwasher, and then straightening the throw over the back of the sofa. Until Jackson had arrived, she'd accepted this series of mundane activities and small joys as a good life. Now her peek into a world shimmering with the possibility of something like love made her normal life feel incomplete.

Glancing outside, she noticed the pale golden light shining through the garage apartment window.

She wondered if Jackson had spent the evening replaying their argument. Or reliving that all-consuming kiss. Or caring one way or another about what Noah had wanted from her this afternoon.

*Noah.* Gabby rubbed her forehead, puzzling about how long he might pursue his crazy idea of reconciling. Honestly, had he lost his mind? Only a man so caught up in his own life would think the girl-friend he'd dumped when she was pregnant with their child would be waiting around for him to come back—for her *or* their son.

In a matter of weeks, Jackson had managed to be more of a male role model for Luc than Noah had ever been. Certainly Jackson oozed more warmth and natural comfort with children than Noah.

Her head pounded from all the day's events. Yet despite hours of mental gymnastics, she knew only one thing with certainty. She would get no sleep if she didn't smooth things over with Jackson first.

She spied out the window again. Just twenty yards away. A one-minute walk. All she needed was a little courage, something that had always come pretty easily to her. Decision made, she shoved her feet into her sneakers and slipped out the back door.

Maybe he was right . . . she was young and impulsive. But maybe that's exactly what Jackson needed—someone who took action instead of overthinking everything until all the joy and excitement got sapped from the situation.

When she reached the top step, she listened at the door but no ambient sounds came from inside. No television. No radio. Nothing.

Drawing a deep breath, she knocked three times. She heard his footsteps before he opened the door.

"What's wrong?" His brows were drawn and he looked past her shoulder to the house. "Another problem with your dad?"

"No. At least, not in the way you're thinking. I came to talk. Can I come in, or are you busy?"

Without a word, he stepped back and waved her in. When he closed the door, she noticed him clutch the doorknob and hang his head for a beat or two before he faced her.

"I'm just reading." He faced her and leaned against the door, hands behind his butt, shifting his weight from one leg to the other.

Tilting his head, he waited for her to speak. She supposed it made sense, considering she'd initiated the visit. Problem was, she'd rushed over without a plan.

"Can we sit for a few minutes?" She gestured toward the sofa.

"Sure." He pushed off the door and followed her, but sat in the chair instead of beside her on the sofa.

She scooted along the cushion to get closer to him, and he visibly tensed.

Not a good start.

Did he anticipate some kind of rehashing of their kiss-and-fight moment? She decided to start from a different direction. "I'm going to meet with my mom."

"You are?" Jackson leaned forward, more engaged now that the conversation had nothing to do with him or them. "How'd your dad take it?"

"We argued again." She shrugged. "Not shocking, is it?"

"He's only looking out for you, you know." He narrowed his eyes. "What drove your decision?"

"You."

He sat back, palm to his chest. "Me?"

"That night by the fire, you suggested if I didn't go, I'd probably have questions my whole life. I think you're right. Like I told you once before, she's messed up, but she's still my mom. Maybe I'm naïve, but the little girl in me still wants some kind of connection to her mother." She didn't mention the fact that she also wanted to see if her mom had beaten her addiction. At this point, she'd given up lying to herself about one reason why that part mattered. The answer sat beside her now, looking antsy. But surely if her mom could beat addiction, Jackson could, too.

Jackson bit his lower lip, which drew her immediate attention. As if she could ever forget the shape or taste of his mouth—or want to forget, for that matter.

She watched conflict go to war in his eyes.

"I hope you don't end up resenting me if things don't go well." He tapped his fingers against the arm of his chair. "From what little I know, it seems a fifty-fifty chance it goes south. Are you prepared for that?"

"Probably not." She scooted to the edge of the cushion until her knee touched his. His eyes immediately veered to the point of contact and lingered. "Jackson, would you come with me? For support."

The hum of the refrigerator reverberated through the silence. Jackson leaned forward, elbows on his knees, and tapped his fingers together while thinking. "Why me?"

The words filled her mouth before she could stop them. "Because unlike Tess or my dad, you won't judge."

Embarrassment took hold, causing her nose to tingle.

Jackson reached out and clasped her hand. "Judge you?"

"Yeah, for being dumb enough to give her another chance. And judge her for her drug problem." Gabby looked away when she said that last part, but not soon enough to miss seeing him cock one brow. "Before she left, people whispered about her all the time. Other moms looked down on me, like I might be a bad influence on their kids. Then she left, and people had opinions about that, too. I guess I don't want anyone else to know that, after everything she did to my dad and me, I still care enough to want to see her. Does that make me a coward?"

He gripped her hand tighter.

"You are the furthest thing from a coward that I've ever met. But I have to be honest. I wouldn't judge her for struggling with drugs, or judge you for wanting to make peace with her. But I can't pretend I don't judge her for walking away from you." He leaned closer and wiped a stray tear from the corner of her eye. In hushed tones, he said, "Then again, it was her loss, not yours."

She raised her hand to touch his while he held her cheek. "Thanks."

When he tried to withdraw his hand, she gripped it firmly. "Jackson, I also want to talk about our argument."

"I'm sorry if I hurt your feelings with that baby remark. I was mostly upset at myself for the kiss." He wrested his hand free, because he needed space if she intended to talk about that kiss while sitting there in her pajamas and no bra. "Let's put it behind us and move on."

"Move on?" She smiled at him, and he could read the hope in her eyes. "How do you mean?"

"Move on as friends. So there's no need to talk it to death—I'll be gone in a few weeks."

"I know." She held his gaze.

"Okay, then. I'm glad we agree." When the relief he expected to feel didn't come, sorrow whooshed in to fill the void.

"I wouldn't say that, exactly." She licked her lips. "If it were up to me, I'd see where all these feelings might lead."

No doubt she would barrel ahead, but could he be so reckless with both their hearts? "Why would you invite me and my real problems into your life? And I'm not just talking about the drinking."

"What other problems are there?"

"Does it matter?" He stood, hands on his hips, and began pacing. "You're young, and you've got a son to care for, and your mom might be coming back into your life. You've got enough on your plate without a hefty serving of my bullshit, too. And then, poof, I'll be gone. What's the point?"

"Quit doing that." She crossed her arms, which resulted in giving him a perfect view of her cleavage.

He stopped pacing and dragged his eyes up to her face. "Doing what?"

"Saying things pretending like you're protecting me, when actually you're creating distance to protect yourself."

Her ability to read him so well had a downside—he couldn't easily hide. "If I'm such a coward, that's another reason for you to walk away."

"There you go again, deflecting." She refused to look away.

He threw his hands out to his sides. "There *you* go again with an answer to everything."

"Trust me, I have way more questions than answers. But our kiss was more than some one-off. Deny it, fight it, shove it away, whatever, but the truth is that there are feelings here." She gestured between them.

"Real feelings that go beyond friendship. I don't know about life in Connecticut, but around here, that doesn't happen all the time."

He scrubbed both hands through his hair, frustrated and unsure of what to say. No, these kinds of feelings didn't happen every day . . . or week or month or year. Naturally it would be his dumb luck to have them happen at the most inappropriate time and place imaginable, with a completely inappropriate woman.

Gabby's shoulders slumped and she looked at her feet. "I only want a chance to know you better. Why is that so wrong?"

His throat squeezed, making it hard to swallow. She looked frail and young, vulnerable. As exposed as he felt every time she tried to peel another layer away and dive inside his heart. Once again, her openness called to mind his younger self. A man who'd been comfortable in his own skin, comfortable expressing affection through words and actions.

He'd like to think that better part of him still existed despite his cynicism, like water circulating beneath the frozen surface of a pond.

"It's not wrong." Still, he didn't want to infect Gabby with his pessimistic poison. "Just unwise."

She looked up, her baby blues filled with unhappiness. "You don't trust me."

"It's hard for me to trust anyone." He saw the force of his words set her back.

She straightened and watched him, but her mind appeared to be off someplace else. Finally she said, "Before, you said a lot of people hurt you. Is that why you won't give me a chance? You assume I'll let you down, too."

He couldn't help but grin at her unabashed manner. "I'm learning not to make any assumptions where you're concerned."

She flashed a saucy smile. "Good."

Gabby stood and started toward him.

Restlessness wriggled through his limbs, and he fought the urge to rip off his sweatshirt in search of cooler air. The walls of the apartment closed in around him.

"You look uncomfortable." She stopped inches in front of him.

"I'm damn uncomfortable. I don't know what you want from me."

She laid her hands on his chest. "Yes, you do."

His pulse raced, and despite knowing better, he gripped her waist. Five seconds passed, each of them watching the other, breaths and limbs growing heavy with want. "This is a mistake."

"Maybe." Gabby's eyes—now calm and clear—held no sign of doubt. Then she rose onto her toes and kissed him.

Any ability to resist fled as he gave over to her coaxing mouth and tongue. Unlike with the good-time girls of the past two years, Gabby's kiss reverberated all the way inside and gripped his heart like a vise. That kind of terrifying, awesome, upside-down-and-inside-out sensation he'd forgotten existed rushed in and consumed him.

He dug his fingers through the loose, loopy brown curls that had captured his attention weeks earlier, then slid his hands down her back to cup her ass and tug her snugly against his body.

Without breaking their heated kisses, she wound her arms around his neck and held on tight. "Take me to bed, Jackson."

Hearing his name on her lips tipped him headlong into a tumble of erotic sensation. Between kisses, he muttered, "Are you sure?"

"Yes," she replied without hesitation.

He swept one hand under her thigh and hauled her up his body. Reflexively, she wrapped her legs around his hips. Right where he wanted her. Where he wanted to bury himself again and again and again until neither of them had anything left to give.

He tottered toward the bed in their passionate embrace—mouths seeking pleasure, hands exploring, pelvises desperately grinding—until they fell onto the mattress together.

Gabby proved to be as forward in seeking pleasure as she'd been in every other aspect of her life. While Jackson remained off-balance, almost dazed by the rush of lust coursing through his veins, she'd begun loosening his clothing and stroking his back.

He didn't want to rush, but he couldn't slow down either. Madness—the only explanation. They'd both lost their minds to something he couldn't identify, and maybe didn't want to. Not when letting go of the fear and doubt felt this damn good.

All over his body, his skin broke into goose bumps—subtle ones that trailed behind her fingers wherever they brushed against him, like ripples across a lake.

He tossed his sweatshirt on the floor and then pinned Gabby's arms over her head to regain control of the pace. Otherwise, it'd be over before it got started.

She strained toward him, panting hard. "Come back."

"I'm not going anywhere," he murmured against her ear. "But this isn't a race. If we're courting the devil, let's take our time."

That earned him a broad smile. He kissed her then, because he could. Because he'd wanted to for weeks. Because this girl made him want to reconnect to parts of himself he'd thought out of reach.

He ran his tongue along her neck until his mouth found the sensitive spot behind her ear. Her body writhed in response. He liked that . . . a lot.

He nibbled her lips and kissed her again, then began raising her shirt with one hand while his other kept hers at bay.

No bra, as he'd suspected. He kissed her stomach and slowly made his way up her torso until he closed his mouth around her left nipple. She moaned and arched into him while he circled his tongue around and around before moving on to the other side.

Her blemish-free skin—silky yet taut—smelled fresh yet sweet, like a ripe pear. He pulled back to look at her face, her flushed cheeks, swollen lips, tangled hair fanned around her head. "You're so damn pretty."

Before she responded he kissed her again, deep and possessive. Needing to feel her touch, he released her hands, which immediately went to his waistband and began to yank his pants off his hips.

He was so hard it hurt. Within a minute, they'd stripped off each other's clothes. He stroked her inner thigh until his hand found the center of her, wet and ready for him.

"Oh," she moaned when his fingers entered her body. She writhed against his palm in a steady rhythm and then her hand gripped his erection, pulling a groan from his lungs.

At that point, their bodies intertwined and moved in harmony, like cogs that knew exactly how to maximize pleasure. Heady, warm, tender sensations crashed and rolled through him in waves, surprising him and drawing him under deeper and deeper.

When neither could wait any longer, he slipped on a condom and then seated himself deep inside her body. He hovered above her, braced on his forearms, hands cupping her face. Kissing her, he probed her mouth slowly, his hips moving in unison with his tongue, and then gradually increased the pace of his thrusts until they were both strung tight to the point of snapping.

"Yes!" Gabby cried out as she tightened around him, milking him as his own orgasm exploded. "Oh, yes."

He'd buried his face into the crook of her neck. Rather than withdraw, he kept himself lodged inside her. A smile formed as he brushed aside some of her sweaty curls, which were plastered to her face.

As the frenzied whirlpool of desire ebbed, a new emotion fought its way through the formerly hardened muscle of his heart: peace. He couldn't think of a better word, although it seemed too pale for the perfect state of grace consuming his very soul.

Gabby craned her neck to kiss him, and stroked her fingers lightly along his back. Her gentle touch made him smile because it seemed out of character for the girl who came straight at him with her questions and feelings.

Then she glanced at the clock and sighed. "I wish I could stay all night, but I'd better go home in case my dad or Luc wakes up and needs me."

For the first time in years, Jackson wasn't happy for an excuse to uncouple and sleep alone. He almost resented the other men in her life, but he kicked the feeling aside and nipped at her lower lip. "Leaving me wanting more, are you?"

"Am I?" Her dimples deepened beneath twinkling blue eyes.

"You are." He forced himself to release her and then sat up to watch her scurry around to get dressed. "I told you I don't like to stop at just one of anything."

She grinned, and it suddenly struck him funny that he could joke about his drinking with her. Maybe that was a good sign. Maybe he'd prove Doc wrong, and this relationship would help take him across the finish line with his recovery.

Once fully clothed, she sat at the edge of the mattress and clasped his hand. "Please don't start regretting this as soon as I walk out the door. I know the odds are that this affair will be brief, and we'll probably never be more than long-distance friends. But let's see where it leads, one day at a time."

*Long-distance friends* already sounded wrong. Of too little significance to carry the full weight of his feelings for Gabby. Yet, he'd known her for so short a time, how could he possibly consider them anything more?

"One day at a time . . . my new mantra." He tugged on the ends of her hair, and pulled her in for a final kiss good night. "No matter what happens next, I'll never regret tonight. I'm only sorry you have to leave now."

He stood and followed her to the door, then watched until she disappeared into her dark house. The apartment suddenly seemed cold and empty, like the night he'd lost power.

Questions and judgments began circling his thoughts, threatening to destroy the pleasant buzz still surging through his veins. He shook them off, determined to sustain this sliver of happiness.

Closing his eyes, he recalled Gabby's flushed cheeks and parted lips, then drifted into a deep sleep.

# CHAPTER THIRTEEN

Jackson shook Doc's hand before taking his usual seat on the sofa. It struck him then that the office, which initially had inspired a claustrophobic reaction, now seemed cozy. Too bad his change of attitude did nothing to soothe his queasy stomach this morning.

Ever since he'd first opened his eyes, Jackson had been dreading talking about his family and Gabby. Of course, while still in bed, the lingering perfume of pear-scented lotion and long strands of Gabby's hair on his pillow had put a temporary smile on his face.

Doc's gaze homed in on Jackson's knee, which restlessly bounced. "Edgy?"

Jackson stilled his leg and cracked his knuckles, working up his courage. His dad had taught him to tackle the hardest part of any problem first because that made everything else easier to address. This occasion called for him to follow that good advice, although he didn't look forward to facing Doc's disappointment.

Jackson finally looked up. "I've got a confession."

"Did you drink?" Doc leaned forward, his expression engaged but lacking judgment.

"No." Jackson watched the man's features shift quickly from relief to curiosity. "But I've met someone—a woman. Actually, I met her when I first arrived and, against your advice, I've let things develop."

"In what way?"

"The usual way." Jackson slunk deeper into the sofa. His muscles tensed under Doc's scrutiny, reminding him of the time he and his buddies got busted for painting their senior class graduation year across the stadium parking lot.

Doc remained on the edge of his seat. "Friendship?"

"Sex." Jackson then frowned and changed his answer. "Well, friends first. Then sex—last night."

Doc nodded. His eyes remained fixed on Jackson while a few beats of silent contemplation passed. "The fact that you're mentioning this tells me this was different from the kind of sex you've been having lately."

"Yes."

"In what way?"

"In every way." Gabby offered compassion, understanding, desire, and connection all bundled up into an adorable package. Jackson shifted, as if finding a more comfortable position would magically alleviate his mental discomfort. "In every way better."

"Better because . . . ?" Doc's shrewd gaze never wavered.

"She's a rare person. Brave. I really like her."

"You didn't like the other women you've had sex with since Alison?"

"I didn't *dis*like them. I barely knew them."

"But you barely know this new woman, either." Doc rubbed his chin.

"I know her." Time didn't define the intimacy they shared. "Sometimes it feels like I've known her for years. She gets me."

The minute those words left his mouth, he flushed because he sounded like a teenage boy with a bad crush.

Doc, however, didn't smirk. "How so?"

"Can't explain it." Jackson shrugged. "It's a feeling, like comfort or understanding. It just *is*."

Doc narrowed his eyes, clearly thinking about how to phrase whatever had crossed his mind. "Why do you suppose this 'friendship' developed so quickly?"

"Circumstances pushed us together. I've been helping her until her father recovers."

"So she's dependent on you."

"No." Jackson shook his head. "Gabby can stand on her own, but I want to help."

"And sex is helping?" Doc's eyes twinkled above a goofy grin.

"In a manner of speaking." Jackson laughed.

"Naturally." Doc chuckled. "Although that's not what I meant."

"I know."

"Talk to me about this 'feeling' of connectedness. Why do *you* think it exists?"

Jackson rested his elbows on his knees while staring over Doc's shoulder, thinking. "Openness comes easily to her. When I'm with her, it's like her honesty taps into some hidden part of me. I feel safe sharing stuff with her that I haven't been able to share with others. She's not the kind of girl who'll bail or betray me, either."

"Yet *you* will be 'bailing' in a few weeks."

Jackson stared at his feet while the gloomy reality settled around him, choking him like a room full of smoke.

When he made no reply, Doc cleared his throat. "Jackson, is it possible you've allowed yourself to confide in this woman because you know that it has to end?"

"No." Jackson sat back and crossed his arms.

"Think about it. This girl can't disappoint you because you won't be sticking around long enough to let her. It could be that her temporary status, not some mystical bond, makes her safe."

"No way." When Doc failed to look convinced, Jackson pressed the point. "I'm telling you, I didn't go looking for a confidant—that's *your* job. But as soon as I met her, I knew she was different. I tried to resist, but I can't walk away when being around her makes me happy. We're both adults. We know the facts. I haven't withheld the truth about my problems. But last night we decided to spend what time we have together, and then whatever happens, happens."

"Which brings me to my initial concern. Three or four weeks from now, when you're back in Connecticut working through your business and personal issues, how will you handle missing her and this newfound closeness?"

"People have long-distance friends and relationships." Jackson squirmed on the sofa. "Vermont isn't thousands of miles away."

"For the sake of argument, let's assume you want to and should get involved in a romantic relationship. Choosing a geographically undesirable woman doesn't seem like the best move, does it?"

"What I *want* is for people to stop looking at me like I've got a major drinking problem. I *want* to leave my bitterness here," he said, gesturing around the room, "and return to my family and business, and get on with my life. Gabby's a completely unexpected complication, but I'm not sorry, and I don't want to put the brakes on."

"Even if being with her puts you at higher risk for slipping back into alcohol abuse?"

Jackson wished he could deny it all. The abuse label, the idea of Gabby hurting him, this whole conversation, really. But he'd always understood the risk. Problem now was, he didn't care. "I'm not asking for your permission. I'm only telling you because I'm trying to be honest."

Doc shook his head. "I'd rather see you focus on your other goals. Let's talk about those. Have you given more thought to inviting your family to a group session?"

"Yes. Let's do it. I want to get to the truth of the stuff between David and my dad."

"Oh?" Doc's amused expression warned of an oncoming question. "Not the stuff between David and *you*?"

"Their situation *is* the problem between my brother and me. Whatever happened between those two changed everything. And it's still going on. I feel it, and my gut's rarely wrong. I can't pretend to be a big happy family, or to trust my brother, if they keep this secret."

Doc raised a questioning hand. "Some might argue their secret's none of your business."

"Now you sound like my sister." Jackson crossed his arms. "Anything so bad it forced David to move halfway around the world for eighteen months and have so little contact with Cat and me must have something to do with us. If David wants my trust, then he should give me his."

Doc scribbled something on his notepad as he replied, "I guess we'll see what happens if he and your dad agree to come. Would you like me to contact them, or do you want to handle that?"

"I'll arrange it."

Doc set his pad aside and tipped his head a bit. "And what about Alison?"

Jackson's eyes widened. "What about her?"

"You need closure there, too."

"No chance." Jackson's body grew hot. "I wanted to marry her and raise our baby, but she spat in my face and took it all away without a second thought. How could there be closure? It's over. The baby's gone."

Doc stared at Jackson until he stopped fidgeting. When he finally responded, he did so slowly. "Are you upset because she made the decision without you, or because she didn't want to be a mother and your wife?"

"Both." Jackson fought that old beast—betrayal—from taking over by focusing on his breathing, but his pulse had its own ideas.

"Given her disinterest, she didn't have many alternatives."

Leaning forward, Jackson thrust one hand upward. "Couldn't she at least have considered having the baby and letting me raise it?"

"Do you really think she should've borne the health risks and other adjustments of pregnancy just to make you happy?"

Jackson stood and began pacing. "Not 'just to make *me* happy.' There was a life—a future life—at stake, too. I know it was a lot to ask, but plenty of women who aren't ready to be mothers have the kids and give them up for adoption. If Alison ever cared about me, she could've at least taken a week or two to think about it before she got rid of our child like yesterday's garbage. And I'm not taking a political stance or saying women shouldn't have choices. I simply hate that Alison made *that* choice about *our* child. It's completely personal."

He stopped and stared out the big window. The crystal threw no rainbows around the room today thanks to a flat, gray sky. Gray to match the unexpected burst of sorrow that swamped him.

Doc narrowed his eyes and hesitated. "I can empathize, Jackson. But given your trust issues, maybe the fact that you put your faith in a woman who wasn't who you thought she was is why you can't get over the past."

"No." Jackson frowned, beginning to crumble under the weight of the thirty-minute self-examination. Was Doc right? Was Jackson disgusted with himself instead of Alison?

"It's worth considering, especially given your feelings about your siblings and Hank. In each case, you're hurt because they did something without considering the impact on you, and you perceive that as disloyalty."

"And?" Jackson shrugged, not understanding Doc's point.

"And yet, you don't apply that logic to your own behavior."

"What the hell have I done wrong?" Jackson's chin jerked back.

"Excessive drinking, random sex with women who may have cared more for you than you did them, refusing to let your brother make amends—aren't those all examples of your needs coming ahead of others?"

Jackson's defenses awakened, causing him to twitch. He plopped himself back onto the sofa. "You're twisting it all around."

"Why? Because unlike them *you* had justifiable reasons to be selfish and reckless?" Doc cocked a brow. "Is that it?"

"Hard to say, since they never really shared their reasons." Jackson resented Doc's misguided attempt to force him to shoulder the blame. "Besides, nothing I did hurt them."

"Really? Your drinking obviously caused ongoing concern. Keeping your brother at arm's length upsets him and puts your sister and dad in an uncomfortable situation. And your workplace altercation put your friend's future at risk, right? All that suffering is a direct result of *your* response to disappointment."

Jackson battled Doc's logic, but it bound itself to his thoughts like a song refrain he couldn't shake. Meanwhile, Doc kept staring at him with that damn patient look on his face. A look Jackson needed to escape.

"Listen, Doc, I've got a screamin' headache now." He rose off the sofa. "Let's call it quits a little early. I'll let you know when my family can make it up."

"It's your dime." Doc stood and held out his hand. "I hope you'll give some more thought to what we've discussed. If Gabby means something to you, don't you owe it to her to be at your best before you get involved?"

Jackson wasn't selfish when it came to Gabby. He'd done nothing but help her since he'd arrived. Any risk of pain arising from their new relationship had been assumed by both of them. Too tired to argue the point, he shook Doc's hand and nodded without answering.

Of course Gabby deserved his best, but she didn't seem to mind him a little bit broken, either. All he wanted now was to go to her and have her untangle the ugly knot of anger and confusion that had balled up in his lungs.

Gabby turned off the leaf blower when Jackson's Jeep pulled into the driveway. It'd been sixteen hours since she'd left his bed. Sixteen hours of wondering what he'd been thinking all day, of tamping down the flutters that arose with each recollection of his touch, of plotting their next rendezvous.

"You're home!" The words rushed out from a smile so enormous her cheeks hurt.

Jackson returned the smile, but then his faded, leaving her cold.

He glanced at the blower as he approached her, holding out his hand. "Hey, let me take care of that."

Dumbly, she handed it to him while searching for any sign of the longing she'd battled all day. Didn't he want to throw his arms around her and kiss her until the moon and stars lit the sky?

After an awkward hesitation, he gave her a quick, passionless kiss hello. "How was your day?"

*Really?*

"Awesome." Gabby refused to play games or pretend like nothing had changed between them. If she only had a few weeks with Jackson, she'd be damned if she'd waste one second being nervous or awkward. "I spent most of my day thinking of you, so it flew by."

At least her honesty cracked Jackson's shell and forced a shocked laugh from him. Then his gaze warmed until her insides sizzled. He lowered his voice. "Now that I'm here, what do you plan to do with me?"

Gabby rose on her toes to whisper in his ear. "Naughty, wicked things." Then she playfully withdrew. "But first, dinner. You'll need a lot of energy."

Again he smiled, though his eyes had that haunted look she'd noticed when they'd first met. "Gabby, I told my doctor about us this morning. He thinks it's a bad idea, mostly for me."

"He thinks I'm bad for you?"

"No, it's not you. He's afraid I'll start drinking when it ends."

*When it ends.* Three words she didn't want inside her head or her heart. She'd spent the day spinning scenarios where those words didn't exist. Weekend visits, FaceTime, vacations: these options meant it didn't have to end—at least, not in the next few weeks.

Then again, she hadn't considered how the fallout could affect Jackson. Somehow she'd disregarded the real reason he'd come to Vermont. Perhaps it had been easy to ignore because nothing she'd seen of his behavior resembled anything she recognized as that of an addict.

Faced with his doctor's concern, however, she couldn't be so greedy. "I'd never want to jeopardize your recovery."

He reached for her hand and brought it to his chest. When they stood this close, everything else faded away until her entire world centered on the stubble of his jaw, the heat of his body, the way his touch somehow reached beneath the surface and warmed her heart.

"The funny thing is, I don't feel like I'm 'in recovery' when I'm with you." Jackson brought her hand to his lips. "But some little voice in my head is buzzing around like a damn gnat. I've put a lot on hold to come here and figure stuff out, so it would suck to go home and backslide because I didn't listen to good advice."

Gabby pressed her lips together to try to keep herself from persuading him otherwise. She barely breathed while standing still, waiting, watching, hoping.

Jackson chuckled. "You look cute when you're biting your tongue."

She wrinkled her nose. "I can't think of the right thing to say."

"You don't have to. The thing is," Jackson said while he caressed her cheek, "I've never let someone else tell me how to live, and I don't feel like starting now."

Then he kissed her for real. Finally. She gripped his pullover, but refrained from climbing all over him.

When he eased away, he glanced at the house and said, "Not here, not now."

"Join us for dinner?"

"Sure. I should talk to your dad. I don't want to be disrespectful by running around with you behind his back."

Gabby rolled her eyes. "I'm not sixteen. It's up to me who I do or don't see."

"I know. Still, I don't want to come between you two." Jackson turned on the blower. "Go on inside. I've got this."

"Dinner's at six," she yelled over the din.

Jackson nodded and put on his sunglasses before setting about clearing the rest of the leaves.

Gabby skipped up the porch steps, giddy with hope. She hadn't been unhappy before Jackson arrived in town. Despite the bumps in the road, she loved her dad, her son, and her little business so much, she almost hadn't noticed that something was missing. Or maybe she'd just learned not to expect romance in her situation. But now the most handsome, thoughtful guy she'd ever met chose to take a chance on her.

Somehow she'd find a way to hold on to this hopeful feeling, even if Jackson had to go too soon. This unfamiliar bliss was worth risking everything.

~

Gabby tucked Luc into bed, eager to return to the living room where she'd left her dad and Jackson. Her stomach gurgled, partly from upset and partly from hunger. She'd barely eaten thanks to nervous anticipation of Jackson's talk with her dad and her dad's unusually reserved conduct during dinner.

She kissed Luc's forehead and set *Curious George Goes to the Hospital* on the nightstand. "'Night, buster."

Before she shut off the light, she caught sight of herself in the mirror and flushed, suddenly shy about the fact that she'd put on a dress and lip gloss before dinner. *Subtlety* had never been a word that applied to her. The outfit had earned her a raised brow from her dad and a heated gaze from Jackson, who'd taken particular interest in her bare legs.

By the time she arrived in the living room, the tension-filled silence informed her that Jackson had already started the awkward discussion with her father.

Jackson looked up at her from the sofa, so she took a seat beside him. Then she held his hand so he knew she wouldn't let her dad come between them. Never one to mince words, she asked, "Who died?"

Jackson's lips quirked, but he repressed his smile. Her father, on the other hand, found no humor in her attitude.

"Jackson's trying to convince me that this itch you two want to scratch isn't going to cause any problems." Her dad shook his head. "And I—"

But Gabby cut him off. "I know what you think, Dad."

"Do you?" He glanced at Jackson. "Jackson, I appreciate your honesty, but now I'd like some time alone with my daughter."

Jackson squeezed her hand before he nodded. "Of course. Thanks for hearing me out." Then he looked at Gabby. "I'll speak with you later."

She watched him exit the room, but didn't look at her dad until she heard Jackson close the front door.

Her father stared at her, his gaze soft and sad. "I want every good thing for you. You think I don't want you to fall in love? You think I'm glad you only have one parent you can count on? I've never wanted to hold you back or keep you from growing up, Gabby. But I can't stand to see you suffer. Look at me. *Hear* me. I've been where you are. Why can't you learn from my mistakes instead of repeating them?"

She paused and gave thought to his question . . . his very reasonable question. He'd rushed into love, and when trouble had arrived, he'd believed he could fix it. He'd suffered through his wife's lies. He'd cleaned up her puke, forgiven her stealing their money to buy drugs— but in the end, all he got for all that love was a broken heart. Of course he didn't want to see Gabby end up in his shoes. But Gabby wasn't her dad, and he had to start cutting the cord and letting her live life her way.

"I don't *know* why, Dad. I have to learn for myself. I can handle getting hurt," she finally replied. "What I can't handle is making decisions solely for the sake of avoiding risk." She shrugged. "I need to see these things with Jackson and Mom through so I don't wonder 'what if' for the rest of my life. 'What if' is the worst kind of regret."

Her father's heavy sigh filled the room, but miraculously, he appeared resigned. "Please promise me one thing."

"What?"

His fingertips pressed into the arms of the chair, his expression filled with concern. "Be careful not to give your whole heart too soon . . . to either of them."

"Oh, Dad." Gabby slid off the sofa, kissed her dad's head, and awkwardly hugged him in his chair. "I can't give my whole heart to anyone when you and Luc already have half of it."

For the first time all evening, her dad smiled. "I love you."

"Love you, too."

～

An hour later, Gabby knocked on Jackson's door. Her entire body tingled in anticipation of seeing, touching, kissing him. She practically vibrated while standing outside waiting for the door to open. When it did, her heart leapt.

"Wasn't sure you'd be coming." Jackson tugged her inside.

As soon as he closed the door, he pinned her against it with his body and kissed her hard. Another cascade of goose bumps broke out across her skin, making her shiver.

Jackson's hands roamed her jaw, scalp, and waist while his mouth never broke contact with hers. She met each hot, greedy kiss with equal longing, and yanked at his plaid flannel pajama pants.

She could feel the hard length of his arousal grinding against her stomach. Then his hand slid up her inner thigh and beneath her underpants, making her glad she'd worn the dress. "Jackson!"

He broke the kiss and gazed directly in her eyes as his finger slipped inside her body. She arched her back and pulled at his shirt. His jaw clenched and then he kissed her neck. "I want you now, like this, up against the wall."

"Then take your pants off." Gabby shoved at the waistband to free him.

He reached into his sweatshirt pocket and retrieved a condom. Once he'd torn open the packet and fitted himself, he kissed her again and impatiently groped her breasts. Finally he cupped her butt and lifted her onto her toes. She wrapped one leg around his waist and cried out upon his swift entry, then curled her arms around his neck and held on as each fierce thrust sent shock waves of pleasure to her core.

He filled her with rough, raw desire, groaning in the heat of the moment as their bodies repeatedly bumped against the door. This was a possession, a full-body invasion. The intensity of the coupling excited her, coiling tighter and tighter until she burst apart in his arms. "Oh, Jackson. Yes!"

His mouth crushed hers in a punishing kiss as he drove himself home a few more times before she felt his body shudder.

She began to lower her leg, but he clasped it and held her in place while he caught his breath. He nuzzled her neck, which felt sweet and sexy.

"That was hot." Jackson tipped his head. "I didn't hurt you, did I?"

"No." She kept her arms around his neck as he eased her off his body.

"Sorry for attacking you like some brute, but," he paused, then shrugged, "I couldn't help myself. I kept thinking of your legs in that dress and I got myself a little worked up before you arrived."

"Quite a greeting."

He kissed her nose. "Let me get dressed and take you out."

"What?" she asked over laughter.

"Let's go do something—a movie, coffee, music? I don't want you to think I'm only in this for booty calls."

"What if I'm only in it for booty calls?"

He stilled and his expression transformed from warm and playful to wary. "Are you?"

"No." Then quietly, she added, "But we shouldn't forget this kinda has an expiration date."

"Don't dwell on that." Jackson grabbed both her hands. "Come on, let's do something fun."

"We just did something fun. How 'bout we do that again?"

"Later." He grinned. "Let's get out of here and go someplace."

"I want to stick nearby in case my dad or Luc needs me." She wondered if her obligations would end up boring him before he even left Vermont.

"Okay, then how about we go light up the fire pit, or walk down to the pond and look for satellites?"

The fact he remembered she liked to do that melted her heart and washed away her insecurity. "That sounds nice. It's not too windy tonight, but we should bring a blanket. It's still cold."

"I like it nippy. Makes me feel alive." Jackson turned to grab warmer clothing and tossed her a pair of sweatpants for her bare legs.

She eyed him, head to toe, while dragging his too-big pants over her shoes. "I can promise you, you're very much alive."

He glanced over his shoulder while pulling on a heavy fleece jacket. "And feeling better than I have in a long time, thanks to you."

"Glad to help." She watched him grab the quilt from his bed.

"All set."

As they meandered down the wooded path toward the pond, she noticed the way the moonlight filtered through the leafless branches, creating a web of light. In the clearing, the moonbeams fell across the glassy black water.

Jackson stopped and spread the quilt on the ground, then lay on his back and gestured for her to join him. She nestled beside him, her head pillowed by his shoulder.

Wispy gray clouds passed overhead while they lay watching the sky. Despite the cool temperature, she felt warm and content.

"Is that one?" Jackson asked, pointing at a faint white pinpoint steadily moving among the stars.

"Good eyes for an old man." Gabby poked fun at the age difference, hoping her joke would show him how trivial it was.

"Not that old." He hugged her closer.

"I don't know, is that a gray hair I see?" She pretended to find a silver strand, but then he quickly rolled her onto her back and braced himself over her.

"*Now* my eight years on you make me look old?" He grinned, but Gabby's thoughts oddly went to her mother. Probably because it had been almost as long since she'd seen her mom. How had those years changed the woman she last saw? Would her hair be graying? Would she be fat or thin?

"What's wrong?" Jackson touched her cheek.

She saw concern in his eyes. "Sorry. I just realized how long it's been since I've seen my mom. Will I even recognize her?"

"Sure you will." Jackson stroked her hair. "She'll look different, but she's your mom. You'll know her. I'm sure she feels as nervous as you do. After all, she's the one who screwed up."

"I'm glad you're going with me." She nestled closer. "I don't think I could do it alone."

"I'm happy to go, but I've no doubt you can do anything on your own. You're tougher than most people I've ever known. If my mom had been able to meet you, she'd have liked you straightaway."

WORTH THE RISK

Gabby's eyes watered from the compliment, because although Jackson didn't often speak of his mother, he wore his respect and affection for her on his face. "Thanks for saying that."

"Thanks for reminding me that there are good people in the world."

"Good? Lots of people considered me trashy for a long while." Gabby frowned. "Maybe your family wouldn't be so pleased to meet me."

Jackson's expression turned dark. "I hate that anyone ever made you feel bad about who you are. Trust me, you are . . . you are pretty perfect."

"Apparently all your drinking did mess with your brain." She laughed, but then grimaced. "Sorry, I was kidding. I didn't mean to joke about the drinking . . . gosh, it's not even funny."

"Shush." He grinned and kissed her, apparently not offended by her gaffe.

She melted beneath him, happy to let him go on with his misconception. No need to let reality spoil what little time they had to share.

# CHAPTER FOURTEEN

Gabby tied her hair back into a low ponytail and triple-checked her appearance. She looked tired. Not surprising, considering the fact that she'd spent the past two nights getting little sleep. Between her midnight runs to Jackson and the tossing and turning in anticipation of her "reunion" with her mother, she'd probably clocked less than eight hours of sleep in total.

She glanced at her phone. Thirty-five minutes from now, she'd see her mother. Clutching her stomach, she vowed not to throw up, although maybe it would offer relief at this point. Each time nausea brewed, it renewed her resentment. Her *mom* should be the nervous one, not her. Gabby hadn't done anything wrong. She didn't have to atone for mistakes.

A knock at the door startled her. Jackson, no doubt. Thank God he'd agreed to come. His presence steadied her. She reminded herself not to get used to that kind of security. He'd be leaving soon, and she couldn't afford to fall apart in his absence. The acknowledgement of his inevitable departure forced a sigh.

Her days would soon return to the long, predictable kind she'd grown accustomed to these past years. She couldn't bear to think of how lonely the days—and nights—would feel when Jackson left. It didn't matter that he'd only been in her orbit mere weeks. In that time, she'd come to know him so well.

Not the little details, like the name of his first girlfriend, or his favorite meal, or his dream vacation. But she understood him. Like how she had to wait for him to confide something rather than push him for answers. Or how he went out of his way for other people because it made him feel needed. That, she believed, was the key to Jackson's happiness. He needed to be needed—not that he'd admit it.

She trotted down the stairs, but her father had beaten her to the door. She found him and Jackson in the small entry.

Thankfully, her dad had stopped trying to talk her out of dating Jackson—a small but important victory in her tug-of-war for independence. Of course, today Jackson would be the least of her father's concerns.

She wondered if some small part of him was curious to see his ex-wife. If he had any wistful, secret place in his heart that harbored a drop of love for her and what they'd once shared. But she wouldn't ask. Gabby may have lacked a normal person's sense of boundaries, but even she recognized when something was too private, too personal to invade.

"I made you a plate of leftovers for lunch, so you can stick it in the microwave." She went up on her toes to kiss her dad's cheek, needing to somehow console him. "I'll pick up Luc on my way home, so I'll see you around five, okay?"

She hadn't seen her father look this stoic since the day she'd told him about her pregnancy. At least she could count on his constancy, though. He never raised his voice. Never freaked out, like some parents she'd seen. No. When he got angry or afraid, he turned stony and cold. Like now.

"I'm good." He didn't smile or pinch her cheek or do any of the little things he typically did when saying good-bye. "Jackson, I assume you'll step in if things take a bad turn."

"Try not to worry." Jackson's gaze didn't waver. "Let's all hope for the best."

Gabby smiled, thankful for the small ray of optimism Jackson offered. At least he didn't think her crazy for needing to hear her mom out. Jackson held the door open for Gabby and, after they'd exited the house, grabbed her hand as they strolled to his Jeep.

"How are you?" he asked while opening the passenger door.

She scooted onto the seat and looked at him. "I'll try not to throw up in your car."

"That would be nice, thanks." He grinned. "You know you'll be fine. You're a lot tougher than you give yourself credit for, Gabby."

A minute later, he revved the engine and backed out of the driveway. On the drive to the motel, Gabby started doubting her entire plan. Initially she'd thought meeting privately in her mom's room, away from the prying eyes of nosy neighbors, would be best. But maybe a public setting would've been wiser. At the very least, any awkward pauses—which she expected would occur—wouldn't also be silent.

She placed her hand over her stomach again while she stared out the window at the near-barren trees.

Jackson reached across the console and squeezed one of her hands. She invited that warmth to travel straight to her heart. "I can only guess the hundred questions running through your mind right now. I'm sure your mom is as nervous. So what's your plan? Are you going to ask a bunch of questions, or first listen to what she has to say?"

"I don't know." Gabby worried her lip. "What would you do?"

Jackson chuckled. "I'm not a big talker, so I'd wait and let her go first. But you aren't me. You aren't afraid to ask or answer anything, so maybe you'd rather take control of the meeting right from the start."

"You're right." Gabby smiled. She liked how he considered her to be capable and strong. Not many people in her life thought of her that way. "I like the idea of being in charge."

"See how easy that was?" He squeezed her hand again and smiled. Every time she witnessed one of his genuine smiles, it awed her, like the first time she'd seen the sunrise over the Atlantic the one and only time she'd been to Cape Cod.

"Thanks for coming today. Honestly, this must be so weird for you. You barely know me, and here I am dragging you into this awkward situation." Her cheeks warmed from embarrassment.

"Oh, I think I know you pretty well by now." Jackson shot a wolfish grin her way before returning his eyes to the road. "Besides, maybe watching you will give me some tips on how to deal with my own family."

His tone had been light, but she suspected that statement carried a fair amount of truth.

"You've never shared all the nitty-gritty details with me. I won't pry, but I hope you know you can trust me."

"Let's tackle one family crisis at a time." He didn't smile this time. His eyes remained fixed on the road ahead, so she let it drop.

A few minutes later, she pointed. "Up there, on the right."

Jackson pulled the car into the motel parking lot and killed the engine. He swiveled in his seat. "We can wait until you're ready."

"No use in putting it off. I'm as ready as I'll ever be."

Before she opened the car door, he surprised her by tugging her into a kiss. Unlike a lot of their kisses, which were heated and hungry, this was gentle, yet affecting. Tender. That he'd tried to soothe her made her heart sing.

"Better." He tugged at her ponytail and then they both got out of the car.

"Room 101." She looked to the far left of the motel. "Over there."

They crossed the parking lot together. With each step, her heart stuttered and skipped. Several feet in front of the door, she stopped in her tracks and drew a deep breath. Another. And another. She gripped her waist, feeling almost faint.

"Gabby, we can pull the plug and leave right now if you want. There's no shame in that, you know."

"No. She drove two hours and spent money on this room. I'll never face myself in the mirror if I bail now."

Jackson enveloped her in his warm embrace. For as long as she lived, she knew she'd never forget the security of being in his arms. His body provided a cocoon from all life's troubles. She'd really miss him when he left, which he would, just like her mom.

She eased away, unable to shake her gloomy admission. "You know what? I've changed my mind. I think I should meet her alone. Do you mind waiting in the car or something?"

"Are you sure?"

She nodded. "I don't want to ambush her. If I need you, I'll text."

"Whatever you want." He stood and let her approach the door alone. Seconds after Gabby knocked, her mother opened the door.

Gabby froze while quickly reconciling her mother's current appearance with her memories. Her mom's green eyes weren't as bright, but they also weren't glazed over. Her skin no longer had the sallow look or stench Gabby had hated, although she'd earned more wrinkles with time. She'd put on a little weight, but remained petite, standing there in secondhand clothing, with her light brown hair pulled back into a low ponytail. Her pale eyes widened upon seeing Jackson a few feet away but then they flickered back to Gabby.

"Gabby." She pressed her lips together, eyes watering, hugging herself like a frightened child. "You're all grown up."

Gabby couldn't imagine not seeing Luc for a day, let alone years and years. Her mother had obviously frozen Gabby's image in time, much as Gabby had done with her mom.

"Hi, Mom. You look . . . good." Good may be an exaggeration, but she looked healthier than Gabby remembered. "That's my friend, Jackson. I asked him to come with me, but he's going to wait in his car so we can talk in private."

"Nice to meet you." Jackson waved.

"Hello, I'm Marie." Her mom took a deep breath and returned her focus to Gabby. "I half expected you to bring your father."

Gabby barely registered the words because she'd been studying every detail of her mom's worn face.

They stared at each other another few seconds, and then her mom said, "I'm so glad you came. Please come in."

Gabby had envisioned a reunion for so many years; now it seemed surreal and disjointed, like a hazy dream. She might as well have floated across the threshold. The shabby room, with its standard motel motif, matched her once-attractive mother's dingy appearance.

She kept waiting for a swell of emotion—anger, joy, suspicion, guilt—anything at all. Yet nothing came. It seemed almost as if she were watching it all from a distance. What did it mean, this lack of feeling? Had she buried everything so deep she no longer had access? Or had her nerves hijacked all her other emotions?

Her mom smoothed her hair and straightened her sweater before sitting. Gabby sat opposite her, struggling not to feel self-conscious under the weight of her mom's intense scrutiny. Finally, she decided to take control of the situation, as Jackson had suggested. "Your letter shocked me. All these years I'd figured you'd moved on. I had no idea you'd thought about me or tried to contact me."

"Of course I thought about you." Her mother's voice sounded barely louder than a whisper. "Maybe not at first, when I'd still been so high it numbed everything."

"Then why didn't you ever come back?"

"It's been a long road, most of it not very pretty."

Gabby crossed her arms. "I came to hear about it."

"I know." Her mother closed her eyes, sighing. When she finally opened them, she looked up, as if searching her brain for the information. "The year after I left, I bottomed out. I was homeless, finding shelter in empty buildings, eating other people's garbage. That part is what finally made me realize I needed help. I couldn't believe I'd given up everything, my education, my husband, my baby . . . and that I'd fallen to the point of eating garbage."

Gabby tried to conceal the disgust she felt from the image of her mother Dumpster diving. Her mother trembled, as if shaking off the bad memory. "At that point, I found a free clinic and got clean. Once my head cleared, regret and depression set in. I knew your father would never forgive me, so I was too afraid to just show up. That's why I wrote to you, hoping you might be willing to meet me."

After a brief pause, during which Gabby's mind raced, she asked, "So, you've been clean for six years now, not twenty-two months?"

Her mom's shamed gaze fell to her hands, which were tightly clasped together on the table. "I wish, but no."

Gabby's heart sank. Just like when her mom had still been at home, she'd had good stretches and bad. Would that be Jackson's fate, too? Was he merely in a "good place" today, but six or eight months from now, be doomed to plummet?

Her mother's voice pulled her from her mental ramblings. "I stayed clean for three years. Regularly attended meetings, worked in a little café in Burlington, got out of the shelter and rented a tiny studio. Eventually I met someone and my life finally seemed pretty stable. That's when I'd tried to contact you again. I needed to apologize for so many things, but when my second letter went unanswered, I assumed you were done with me, like your dad. Of course, I never blamed you. I'd failed in the worst way a woman—a mother—can fail. If you leave here knowing nothing else, you have to believe that *I* know I lost everything when I walked away from you."

Gabby couldn't think about apologies or forgiveness now. Not when she needed the rest of the story. "So what happened next?"

Another sigh from her mom braced Gabby for more ugly details. "Within one month's time, I lost my job because the café closed, and then Robert, the man I'd been seeing, left me for another woman." Her mom's gaze turned even sadder and more distant. "I couldn't get out of bed. Everything I'd worked so hard to rebuild disappeared and it seemed pointless to keep going. I know you can't understand it, but that kind of isolation, it makes it so tempting to check out." She clutched a fist by her heart. "I didn't want to be sober, because that gave me too much time to think about how I'd walked away from you and your father. How, no matter what I tried to do to get clean, the world seemed determined to make it impossible. To keep taking things from me, like when I first got sick and couldn't find relief from that pain. It probably all sounds trite to you. I'm glad you're not as weak as I am. That you've never bumped up against utter despair."

Gabby leaned forward, a million questions clogging her throat. Intent on hearing the entire story, she kept quiet. "So what changed?"

"I ended up back on the street, but this time I nearly OD'd. The only reason I'm alive is because the cops happened to raid the abandoned house where I'd collapsed, and called an ambulance."

Gabby blew out the breath she'd been holding, completely unprepared to learn that her mother had nearly died. Her mother could've been dead and she wouldn't have known. Not that she hadn't wondered about that from time to time. But to learn that it nearly had happened! That she might just as easily have gotten a government-issued letter informing her of her mom's death instead of the letter her mom wrote.

How would she have felt? Even now she still couldn't access any feelings about this meeting with her mom. Her brain had taken over, treating the entire reunion from a cerebral perspective. Maybe it was protecting her?

She didn't have to answer that question because her mom continued talking. "Needless to say, that was a wake-up call. I went back to the clinic to wean off the drugs. Got a job as a housekeeper in a B and B near the college. I haven't tried dating, because I'm not sure I could take another rejection." Her mom paused, and Gabby remembered Jackson's doctor's warning against testing a relationship too soon. "I've been drug-free for almost two years now. The only reason I didn't try to contact you this time was because I knew I'd been gone too long to have the right to barge back into your life. But when I ran into the Dresslers and they told me about you and Luc, I couldn't stop myself." Her mom covered her sad smile with her hands. "I can't believe my baby has a baby. I'm a grandmother. I cried for two days, but instead of turning back to drugs, I wrote to you. Your response felt like a miracle, and I'm so grateful."

A miracle? Suddenly a tremendous amount of pressure—of responsibility—about how she handled the rest of this meeting pressed on Gabby's chest. "I'll be honest, Mom. I almost didn't come today. I didn't know what to expect. Would I cry, yell, be relieved or sad? The last thing I expected was to feel nothing, which is kind of what's happening. Everything, even my own body, feels foreign right now. Maybe I'm just overwhelmed and processing everything, and later the feelings will come. But I have to wonder, what do you expect from me?"

"Nothing, Gabby. I'm grateful you came and listened to my story . . . my apology. I'm so sorry. Sorry for all the pain I caused you and your father. Sorry for all the times I let you down or scared you. Sorry I destroyed our family. I honestly wouldn't blame you for hating me. I hate myself, more than you know. But I'm trying, again, to build a decent life. Seeing you today is a reminder of the fact that, at one point in time, I did something right."

Not until she felt the wet warmth of a tear rolling down her cheek did Gabby even know she was crying. Finally, some sign of a heart in her chest. Of the girl who'd soldiered on, hiding the pain and shame she'd felt. She had hated her mom at times, maybe even still did. Yet, she'd worried and wondered and prayed all these years, too. And now they were seated across the table, talking to each other.

Would this one-time visit satisfy Gabby? Should she invite her mom back into any corner of her life? And what of Luc?

"Gabby, I understand why you didn't bring Luc," her mom said, as if reading her mind, "but do you have a picture I could see?"

Luc had a grandmother he might never know—a woman who, once upon a time, had been a happy wife and mother. Snippets of memories started flowing now—sled rides and cocoa, her mom reading *Anne of Green Gables* to her, stretchy-cheese sandwiches and soup when she'd been sick. A vivid image of her mom and dad kissing in front of a Christmas tree popped to the forefront. Then, like a plume of smoke, the bad memories lay over the good. The shingles scabs and complications. Her mom crying in pain. The irritability and desperation—until she found relief. Relief that ultimately swallowed her up and carried her away.

The entire situation filled Gabby with sorrow and bitterness, tightening her throat. Now she sat with her mom—a stranger—who begged to see a photo of her grandson. How could she say no? Gabby blinked back her tears and cleared her throat. "Sure."

She removed her phone from her pocket and scrolled through her photos until she found a recent one that captured a bit of Luc's ornery personality. "This is Luc."

She slid the phone across the table. Her mom picked it up, her eyes fixated on its screen. During the silence that descended, Gabby glanced at the window, wondering what Jackson must be thinking. She looked back at her mom, who quietly studied Luc's face while a tear leaked from the corner of her eye.

Her mom's hands trembled before she burst into sobs. Uncontrollable sobs coughing up seven years of remorse and grief.

"Excuse me." She stood, wiping her eyes, leaving streaks of mascara on her cheeks. "I'm sorry."

Without another word she strode to the bathroom at the back of the room and closed the door. Gabby heard her mom crying and started to tremble. Without thinking, she texted Jackson. Sixty seconds later, he knocked at the door.

"You okay?" Jackson set his hands on her shoulders.

She nodded, dumbly. "She's crying in the bathroom. I showed her a picture of Luc and she broke down."

Jackson stepped inside and closed the door. "What do you want to do?"

"I don't know. Part of me wants to bolt. This is all so much. But I can't leave her alone, crying. If she'd never had the complications from shingles, she would've never needed so many painkillers, and none of this would've happened. She'd never have left, been homeless, or nearly died. Knowing it's not entirely her fault makes me want to forgive her and try to be friends. But then she's also gone back to drugs more than once, and I can't live with that worry again. If I let her back in my life, I will always, always worry. But if I walk away, will that send her back into that dark place, too?" Gabby's head pounded. "Either way I'll worry. I don't know what to do."

Jackson pulled her into a hug, a bit overwhelmed by Gabby's summary of her mom's homelessness and near death. Although he'd never come close to Marie's level of addiction, he hated sharing anything in common with the woman. And seeing her impact on Gabby damn near broke his heart.

Knowing he'd caused his family even a fraction of this kind of worry made him hate himself a little, too. And now he'd dragged Gabby into his life. "I suppose you look at me the same way, always wondering if you'll catch me drinking, or if what you do will cause me to drink?"

"Not really . . . or, at least, not often." Her brows pinched together and she glanced back toward the bathroom. He'd expected that answer, but it still stung.

"Gabby, you don't need to worry about me. I'm under control." He stopped then, because this wasn't the time or place to launch into a discussion about his problem or their "relationship." He wished they could leave and erase the past thirty minutes from her memory.

Gabby's lip trembled. "You don't think she's in there doing drugs now, do you?"

God, he'd be pissed if Marie did that to her daughter again. "She's probably collecting herself. Seeing Luc must've tipped her over the edge."

Gabby's face crumpled. "Do you think this will make her go back to drugs?"

Worse than seeing worry in Gabby's eyes was seeing her guilt, as if she would somehow be to blame if her mother decided to use again.

"I know you think I have some inside track on all addicts just because I have an issue with alcohol, but I honestly can't answer for your mom." He thought of Doc's warning about whether or not he'd be able to cope with loss without cracking a bottle of Scotch. At the time, he'd blown off the remark because he'd been feeling strong. But could he hold up if truly tested? A tremor of doubt slid along his spine. He forced himself to focus on Gabby's needs instead of his thoughts. "All I can say is that, if she does, it's on her, not you."

"Cold comfort." Gabby's head drooped.

"You're putting too much pressure on this meeting. Today is a first step. Maybe it's the last step, or maybe there will be another. You don't need to make any decisions today."

Gabby glanced at Luc's picture. "Even if I might be willing to risk being disappointed, I can't put Luc in that situation. How will I ever know if she's trustworthy enough to meet him?"

"I don't know, but I do know it'll take time." Rebuilding trust. Despite multiple sessions with Doc, he'd still not learned that trick. "Guess you'll have to go with your gut."

"My little buster." She smiled at Luc's image and then tucked the phone back in her pocket. "*His* biggest worry is whether or not he'll get enough pie at the costume party on Saturday."

"Hey, that's one of my biggest worries, too," Jackson joked, hoping to lighten her mood.

He gathered her into a hug. Held her close because she needed comfort. Held her because *he* needed reassurance, too. He selfishly wanted Gabby to give her mom a second chance because, if Gabby could do that, then she wasn't likely to bail on him, either.

"Should I check on her?" Gabby sniffled, her brow knitting.

"Sure." But before Gabby made it to the bathroom door, her mother emerged.

"I'm fine." She opened the door without looking at him and crossed to Gabby. "I'm sorry for the little breakdown. Seeing Luc overwhelmed me. He's so beautiful, my grandson."

"Thanks," Gabby said uncertainly. "He has Dad's eyes."

Jackson's eyes widened, sensing Gabby had intentionally opened that door.

Marie met Gabby's challenge exactly as her daughter might—head-on. "Like you. You both look a lot like your dad. How is he? I'm sure he didn't encourage you to come."

"He doesn't trust you." Gabby failed to mention his stroke.

"I understand."

"The truth is," Gabby began, "I don't know if I do, either."

"I know." Marie's eyes misted again. "If you give me a chance to prove myself, I will." Then she looked at Jackson. "I didn't mean to eavesdrop, but I overheard you two talking. Paper-thin walls." She gestured around the room. "It sounds like you might be a little empathetic to my situation."

"Excuse me?" Jackson's pulse doubled.

"Not with drugs, but alcohol." Marie's sad eyes crinkled with compassion. "You know something about the struggle, but it looks like you're winning your battles, like I've been winning mine lately."

Jackson bit his tongue to prevent a slew of disclaimers and insults from tumbling out. He did *not* empathize with this woman, nor did he enjoy the comparison. But Gabby looked far too fragile and vulnerable to withstand a confrontation between him and her mom. "I'd rather not get into my situation, if you don't mind. I'm only here to support your daughter."

"Thank you for making her feel safe, then. I'd certainly be the last person to judge you, or her for choosing a friend like you."

His insides were turning colder by the minute, but he willed himself to sit on his temper. "I'll always put Gabby first; you can count on that."

Apparently sensing Jackson's barely leashed outrage, Gabby jumped into the discussion. "Mom, I need to go. I need time to digest everything. Give me time to think, and I'll call you with whatever decisions I make about the future."

Her mom sighed, head bowed. "Okay. Just remember, if you give me a chance—like you're giving Jackson—I swear I won't let you down. I'll do anything to have you back in my life, and to meet my grandson."

Jackson shoved his hands in his pockets to keep his fist from driving through the drywall. How dare this woman keep comparing him, a stranger, to her horrible choices and habits? And a little piece of him was not happy that Gabby had let her mom draw such wrong conclusions.

Gabby, however, seemed in another world, her expression solemn. "It'll be a very long time before I'd let you into Luc's life, so please keep realistic expectations."

"Whatever you say, honey." Then she approached Gabby. "Would it be too much to ask for a hug good-bye?"

Jackson noticed a rush of uncertain surprise fill Gabby's eyes before she raised her arms. He guessed she feared any kind of rejection would send Marie back to the streets.

For the first time, Jackson considered that perhaps Jon had been right to discourage this meeting. Now, no matter what happened next, Gabby would be worrying about Marie. By coming today, she'd unwittingly taken on the burden of concern—and maybe even misplaced responsibility—for Marie's welfare. The thought made him sick, especially because he'd encouraged the meeting.

When he projected ahead to what might be another round of heartbreak for this brave young woman he'd been so lucky to meet, his stomach tightened. Then his thoughts turned toward his own family.

All this time he'd been thinking so much about how he'd trust them again, when in reality, they would probably not trust him any easier.

"I'll be in touch in a couple of weeks, Mom. Whatever I decide, I'll let you know." Gabby eased out of the awkward embrace.

"That's all I can ask." Marie inhaled slowly. Her tight smile didn't fool Jackson. He suspected the woman had expected Gabby to be more eager for a reunion.

Marie waved as Gabby and Jackson strode across the parking lot toward his Jeep, and he couldn't have been happier to leave.

Jackson fell silent during the drive to Luc's preschool. Partly because he figured Gabby needed time to think, and partly because Mrs. Bouchard's situation forced him to think about a bunch of stuff he didn't know how to address in his own life.

He'd been so off in space, he didn't know Gabby had been crying until he heard her sniffle. He pulled over and put the car in park. "What can I do?" And then, because physical comfort had always worked for him, he kissed her. "I hate seeing you upset."

"I should be happy, right? After all these years, I actually saw my mom. She apologized. She's sober. There's hope for a future relationship. On the surface, it's all good, but I feel . . . afraid."

For the first time since they'd met, Jackson lied to Gabby. "You've got nothing to fear. You're in control, and anything you choose is okay."

Her faint smile told him she knew it'd been a lie, or at least an exaggeration. Some lies were worthwhile, though. He knew firsthand how fear could change a person, and he didn't want to see Gabby's heart change one bit.

Maybe it was too little, too late. In less than one hour, Marie had already stolen Gabby's peace of mind.

"Hey, you've got lots of time to deal with your mom. Let's think about something more fun, like the party this weekend."

That remark earned him a dimpled smile, and suddenly he knew that, together, they could weather any storm.

# Chapter Fifteen

Jackson smothered a smile when yet another toddler broke down in frustration in the middle of the small maze he and Gabby had constructed from bales of hay. It'd taken him half of yesterday and all morning to help her deck out the yard for this costume party. The maze had been the hardest job, but they'd also carved a bunch of pumpkins, built a spooky scarecrow, and set up a pin-the-heart-on-the-skeleton game she'd found on Pinterest.

Fortunately, the weather cooperated by giving them a sunny, if chilly, day. As he soaked up the simple pleasure of the shindig, he marveled at the shrieks and mess that a dozen young kids could make.

A little boy dressed as Superman darted in front of him, chased by an older girl in a princess costume. Jackson chuckled to himself thinking about how, in a few years, that chase would reverse.

As for his own costume, he'd slicked back his hair and dressed up as Dracula, donning a cheap, black satin cape, fake teeth, and ruby-red lips. The choice had been particularly effective earlier when caving to Luc's pleas to play "monstore" with the kids, all of whom he'd won over pretty easily.

A month ago he would never have envisioned spending his time this way, let alone enjoying it. Satisfaction flooded him, warming the distant, fragile pieces of his heart he'd guarded these past couple of years.

Gabby had parked her dad at the picnic table with one of the other kid's grandmothers, and then proceeded to set out large covered tins of fruit and potato salad. She'd dressed as a Dalmatian and, damn, she looked cute as hell with her little blackened nose and floppy ears.

Her big smile indicated she enjoyed being the hostess. Thankfully the festivities had given her something more pleasant than her mom to think about these past few days. Only twice had she mentioned Marie—both times at night, after they'd made love. He let her talk, offering only support now instead of advice.

Wishing to be near her now, Jackson made his way across the lawn. "Want me to start flipping burgers?"

"Sure." She smiled as she lumbered toward the back door in her costume. "Everyone's having a good time, huh?"

He followed her into the kitchen. Once inside, he snaked his arms around her waist and pulled her against his chest, right where she should be. He bared his false vampire teeth and said, "I vant to suck your blood."

She craned her neck, teasing, "Please do!"

Jackson removed his fangs, tugged her costume aside, and then planted a quick kiss near her collarbone before shoving the vampire teeth back into his mouth. "Later."

"I'll hold you to it." She flashed a saucy look when she turned around.

That look always knocked his knees out from under him. "Give me the burgers before I change my mind about waiting."

"Thanks for helping today." She went to the refrigerator and handed him a tray of premade patties and a large spatula. "This is so much easier with an extra set of hands."

"No place I'd rather be, although I can think of a few better uses for my hands." He winked, then wandered out of the kitchen carrying everything and nearly ran into Noah, who must've just arrived. "Sorry!"

Seemed that Noah decided his uniform could pull double duty as a costume. He eyed Jackson's outfit. "Looks like things are already in full swing."

"Don't worry, these little tykes won't lose steam anytime soon." Jackson smiled, hoping to keep Noah's nose from feeling knocked out of joint by his presence. "Has Luc seen you yet?"

Gabby breezed through the door then. "Oh! I didn't know you came. Maybe you can corral the kids while Jackson cooks and I set up the plates and stuff?"

"Sure." Noah's eyes homed in on the red smudge at the base of Gabby's neck, then his gaze darted to Jackson's ruby lips. A streak of resentment exploded in his eyes, but he quickly snuffed it out. "Anything for our boy."

*Our boy.* Noah hadn't emphasized the words, but Jackson knew them to have been deliberate. Like a lion, Noah had just marked his territory. Jackson, however, had no plans to stand down. Hell, he might feel sorry for Noah if the man had ever tried to be part of his son's life. The fact that Noah walked away from Luc and Gabby proved him unworthy and stupid, which diminished Jackson's pity and guilt.

"By the way, you might want to wipe that red smudge off your neck, Gabby. Wouldn't want folks to get the wrong idea now, would you?" He stared at her as if he enjoyed making her uncomfortable.

Using the back of her hand, she swiped at her neck without showing any sign of remorse or discomfort.

"Jackson, can you get those burgers started, please?" She smiled sweetly, but Jackson guessed she wanted to say something to Noah in private.

"Sure." Jackson walked to the grill, wishing he could hear their conversation over the din of children's laughter and the Halloween music blaring from the speaker.

"Need a hand?" Jon asked, having sneaked up on him from behind.

"Nah, I'm all set. You go relax. I think Gabby had a plan in mind when she sat you beside Carrie's grandmother." Jackson smiled, hoping to dispel some of the awkwardness he'd been feeling with Jon since he'd started seeing Gabby.

"That girl's always been a dreamer." Jon glanced past Jackson toward Gabby and Noah. "Romantic notions are fun for the young, but you and I are old enough to know better."

The unsubtle remark struck several chords. Jackson and Gabby's age gap and the temporary nature of his visit in Vermont might make Jon view this new relationship as a foolish lark. Yet, when Jackson spent time with Gabby, *foolish* didn't describe his state of mind at all. And the age gap seemed less and less important the more he'd come to know her. In some ways, she even seemed more mature than him. She certainly recovered from disappointments a helluva lot faster.

"Dreamers move mountains, Jon." Jackson flipped a row of burgers and avoided making eye contact. "Without dreams, there's no hope. Without hope, there's not much to look forward to, is there?"

"But dreamers also suffer more than realists, because most dreams don't come true." Jon raised one brow.

Jackson couldn't help but admire Jon—a man who loved and protected his family without being demanding or rude. However, Jackson didn't happen to agree with his opinion about dreamers.

"But when the dream *does* come true, it's magic." Jackson grinned. Magic aptly defined the gift of meeting Gabby.

A frustrated grin crept across Jon's face as he shook his head. "So you're a dreamer, too."

Used to be. Not so much anymore. But lately that dormant side of him had sprung back to life.

"I try to avoid labels these days." He managed as honest an answer as possible at that point in his life.

Jon's constipated expression suggested he'd stifled an overwhelming urge to roll his eyes. Then he grew pensive. "Has Gabby spoken with her mother since their meeting?"

Jackson went still, debating how to answer. "Did you ask her?"

"No. Given my disapproval, she's not likely to share anything with me for a while."

"It's not my place to say." Jackson realized Jon wouldn't back off when the man continued to stare at him, silently demanding information. "If it'll ease your mind, as far as I know, they haven't spoken again. Gabby asked for time to think it all through. I haven't pushed her to talk it out because she needs to come to this decision on her own."

Jon tipped his head to study Jackson, but said nothing. Then Luc's calling out "Dada" attuned them to the commotion in the yard.

"Noah's usually been a no-show at these little parties." Jon glanced back at Jackson. "Must sense the competition."

"Too bad it took my presence to make him appreciate his son and Gabby." Jackson piled the cooked burgers onto a clean platter. "Excuse me while I take these to the table."

Jon followed Jackson across the yard to the two picnic tables. Luc broke away from Noah and dashed toward them. "Jackson, come play with me."

"I'm busy helping your mom, buddy." Sensing Noah's gaze burning a hole through his head, he added, "But I bet your daddy would like to play."

Jon acknowledged Noah then held his hand out to Luc. "Luc, come sit with me and eat some dinner."

Noah relinquished Luc to Jon and, with a curt nod at Jackson, wandered away. Chaos took a backseat to hunger, and the other parents helped gather the kids and fix their plates.

Jackson searched for Gabby. By the time he picked her out in the crowd, Noah had already caught up to her. Jackson resisted the impulse to interrupt them. If Noah planned some campaign to win back Gabby, Jackson couldn't afford to get sucked in to each small battle for her attention.

Noah had time on his side—time to prove he'd changed, time to offer help or compliments or whatever else he thought would further his cause.

Jackson's time was running out. His only option was to give Gabby the respect she wanted—to allow her the room she needed to make her own decisions. The only advantage he had over Noah was that, to date, he'd never let her down. She could count on him without question.

The thought of leaving Gabby before they had time to figure out if what they shared was more than a burning infatuation ate at him. Turning away to regain control of his faltering mood, he decided to fix himself a plate. He was heaping potato salad on his plate when the crunching sound of gravel caught his attention.

A small, beat-up Toyota pulled into the driveway and parked askew. Seconds later, Gabby's mom got out of the car.

Jackson watched Gabby's expression shift from shock to panic. Noah's brows shot up, but then he immediately wrapped his arm around Gabby for support. Jackson might've been jealous, but he figured Gabby barely registered Noah's presence, because her gaze remained utterly locked on her mother.

"What's *she* doing here?" Jon's angry voice drifted across Jackson's shoulder before the man himself appeared at his side.

"I have no idea. Noah's got Gabby. You stay here and keep Luc occupied, and I'll go deal with your ex." Jackson didn't wait for Jon's consent. His stride ate up the ground between him and Marie. Her gaze darted across the yard, probably searching for her grandson.

Marie clutched the frame of the open car door, her gaze zooming from the crowd to Jackson to Gabby and back to Jackson. Her befuddled demeanor differed greatly from the calm, remorseful woman she'd presented to Gabby earlier this week. When Jackson drew near, Marie stepped back.

"Marie, if you want a relationship with Gabby, the best thing you can do right now is get back in your car and wait to hear from her like you promised."

"I only want to see my grandson." She craned her neck, steadying herself against the car. Was she that nervous?

"Now isn't the time. Trust me, you haven't done yourself any favors by barging in here uninvited." Jackson gestured toward her car. "You need to go, please."

Jackson stepped toward the front door but she raised her voice. "Stop!"

Suddenly Noah and Gabby were at his side.

"Mom, what are you doing here?" Gabby asked.

"I want to see Luc." Mrs. Bouchard wobbled and Jackson realized that she might be high, or drunk. "Please, Gabby, please let me look at him."

"No, Mom," Gabby said. "You promised to let *me* decide."

Noah's confusion about what was happening didn't stop him from going into cop mode and taking over.

"Come on, Mrs. Bouchard, let's not cause a scene in front of all these kids." Noah flashed her the phony smile Jackson remembered from the diner.

Mrs. Bouchard's eyes narrowed. "Noah Jefferson, don't try to sweet-talk me."

"Trust me, this ain't sweet talk." Noah's smile tightened. "I'm trying real hard not to draw any more attention to this situation than need be. Doesn't seem like you're welcome here."

"Don't you judge me, either." Marie shook her finger at him. "I know all about the way you walked out on your son and my daughter. You're no better than me."

"Mom!" Gabby stepped closer, then her nose wrinkled. Jackson had caught the scent of gin, too. Gabby's voice turned sharp with disgust. "You're not sober!"

"I'm not high. I only had a drink." Mrs. Bouchard's mood deflated and she pulled a puss. "It's your father's fault. I know he's trying to keep you and my grandson from me, so I took a drink to relax."

Jackson winced, recognizing the same justification he'd often used when drinking.

"Please leave, Mom." Gabby glanced around at the guests, whose attention had turned from their meals to the scene unfolding in the driveway.

"Please, baby, let me see Luc for a minute." Marie attempted to step past Gabby, but Jackson blocked her.

"Dad was right." Gabby's voice cracked. "I can't trust you. You couldn't even keep the promise you made me the other day!"

Noah cast a sharp glance at Gabby. "Why did you see her recently?"

Before Gabby answered, Marie's eyes hardened as she pointed at Jackson and croaked, "Why won't you let *me* around my grandson, but you let *him*?"

Gabby's cheeks burned red beneath angry eyes. "It's none of your business who I allow in my son's life."

Marie wobbled again, then looked at Noah, gesturing toward Jackson with her thumb. "Do you know he's got a drinking problem?"

Jackson absorbed the blow without faltering, but his skin crawled under the weight of a dozen eyes or more ogling him. His mind riffled through a series of replies, but Gabby jumped in before he got one out. "Noah, if my mom doesn't leave this minute, arrest her for trespassing."

Noah shot Jackson a hard look before turning his attention to Marie. "I can't let you drive drunk. Get yourself into my squad car now and I'll drive you to your motel so you can sober up. Hand your keys to Jackson and he can follow us."

"I want to see my grandson!" She resisted, backing up.

"Surely you don't want Luc and these kids to see me take you out in cuffs." Noah's voice had gone cold.

Jackson noticed tears in Gabby's eyes and reached out to comfort her. She shrugged away and ran toward the house. Jon cut through his peripheral vision, carrying Luc across the yard to meet up with his daughter. Seconds later, they all disappeared into the back of the house.

"Come on, now. Show's over." Noah gestured toward his squad car. "Time to go."

Marie remained rooted to her spot, her body tremors visible. "Why can he stay, but I can't?"

"Trust me, Mrs. Bouchard, I'll get to the bottom of any trouble where my son is concerned. Don't you worry." Noah shot Jackson another hard-boiled look.

Defiant anger brewed in Jackson, mixed with a touch of alarm. Marie had just opened a can of worms, and Noah now had another reason to meddle in Gabby's and Jackson's lives.

Noah's authoritative voice commanded, "Now hand your keys to Jackson so we can get you out of here without causing more trouble."

"You should've helped me. Now you'll see how it feels to be judged unfit," Marie muttered as she handed Jackson her keys.

Jackson had no doubt Noah would exploit her grossly exaggerated characterization of his situation and plant all kinds of doubts about him in Gabby's mind. Doubts Gabby already nursed on some level.

Ten minutes later, Jackson parked Mrs. Bouchard's car in front of her motel room and waited outside while Noah escorted her to her room. When Noah returned, he pointed at his car. Dread encased Jackson's feet in lead slippers for the duration of the walk to Noah's squad car.

Bracing himself for a slew of sarcasm and an interrogation, he climbed in beside Noah in the front seat.

Surprisingly, Noah didn't speak at all. When they pulled onto the Bouchards' road, he finally said, "I've got some things to take care of now. Tell Gabby I'll be speaking with her soon."

The cool tone of Noah's voice chased a chill up Jackson's spine. The man had been far too controlled for the occasion, which could only mean he'd been formulating some plan. As Jackson guessed the first time they'd met, Noah was slick, and now armed with a boatload of suspicion.

"Maybe you should come say good-bye to Luc. We left in a hurry, and I doubt you want him to think he did something wrong."

"Don't worry about what I should or shouldn't do with *my* son." Noah shot him another cool glance, but put the car in park and killed the engine.

When they rejoined the party, Jon and some of the other parents had the kids engaged in a game of musical chairs. Jackson headed inside to search for Gabby without another word to Noah.

He found her in the kitchen scrubbing the party trays. She glanced over her shoulder when she heard him. "You're back already."

"Yes." He waited, unsure of what to say.

"I can't believe she showed up here." She kept scrubbing, her hands moving at a frenzied pace. "Drunk, no less."

Jackson shrugged. "What can I do to help?"

"I should've listened to my dad and ignored her letter." She placed the last tray on the drying rack and faced him. "What happened today is worse than any regret I might've had from not knowing."

Although she hadn't blamed him for the fiasco, she'd basically inferred that he'd given her shitty advice. He couldn't blame her. Jon had been right, and all Gabby's worst fears had come true. He stood, frozen, unable to make it better.

"Today sucked. I'm sorry your mom showed up, and showed up drunk. Maybe she lied the other day. Maybe she hasn't been as sober as she'd led you to believe. But that's her problem. You can't worry about her or feel responsible for her choices. Damn, I wish I hadn't encouraged you to meet her." Then he reconsidered, because if he'd been learning anything this past month, it was that peace of mind required courage and honesty. "Or maybe you're better off having seen her and talked to her. Now you know for sure your dad is right. Had you not seen her for yourself, you couldn't have been certain."

Gabby heaved a sigh, unwilling to agree, but clearly too upset to argue. "Doesn't matter. All that matters is Luc. I can't keep making selfish decisions without thinking about how the fallout could hurt him."

Jackson didn't particularly like the implication of that statement. Had she lumped him in with her mother now? "You'd never do anything that would hurt your son."

"I think we both know that's not exactly true." She glanced at the ground.

"Are you still talking about your mom, or does that statement include me, too?" He crossed his arms.

Her brow pinched, but she didn't answer. He stood there, heart sinking to his toes, waiting for her to say more, but all she muttered was, "I need to get back outside."

"Guess we'll talk later." He gestured toward the door, but then stayed behind after she went outside.

Rationally, he knew things weren't looking good and he needed to regroup. Normally he'd reach for a bottle now, but he'd be damned if people like Marie and Noah torpedoed his recovery at this point.

Jackson strode through the house and exited through the front door so no one would see him slip away. He left his Jeep by the garage and started walking, with no destination in mind.

∾

Gabby breathed a huge sigh of relief when the last of the guests pulled out of the driveway. The wonderful day she'd planned had ended in near disaster. Fortunately, Luc remained oblivious to everything other than Jackson's disappearance. That mystery had her concerned, too, which she kind of resented.

He'd known she'd already had her mind blown once, so him leaving without a word seemed insensitive. Of course, she'd pushed away any effort he'd made to comfort her, so maybe she owed *him* the apology. In either case, the fact that she and Luc both already missed him underscored how difficult it would be when he returned to Connecticut.

"Luc's tuckered out," her father said. "I think he'll fall asleep as soon as you give him a bath."

Gabby glanced across the living room. Luc had wedged himself into the corner of the sofa to suck his thumb and gaze into space.

"I'm exhausted, too." Then, because she hadn't had a chance to say so sooner, she admitted, "Dad, you were right. Contacting Mom was a huge mistake. I don't know why I couldn't stop myself. I'm sorry I didn't listen to you."

Her dad opened his arms for a hug, which she gladly accepted. Then he shocked her by saying, "I suppose this was one of those things you needed to find out on your own before you could accept the truth. I've always wanted to keep you safe from any more disappointment. But you're an adult now, and you have the right to make these decisions for yourself."

The fact he'd basically echoed Jackson's earlier sentiments struck her as funny. Not that anything about the situation held a trace of humor.

"I'd better bathe Luc before he falls asleep." She eased away from her dad and fetched her son. As they climbed the stairs, she couldn't help but wonder where Jackson had gone and what he was thinking.

Forty minutes later, when a light shining through his window informed her of his return, she decided to find out. Grabbing a fleece, she made her way to the apartment and rapped on its door.

～

"Come in." Jackson drew a deep breath to steel himself for a confrontation. His walk hadn't shaken off his funk, but weariness made him too tired to argue. He remained on the recliner with a book across his lap.

"Hi." Gabby stood near the door, hands clasped together, thumbs twiddling.

"Hi." He didn't smile or tease or make any move to touch her. He wanted to keep her close, but today he'd felt her pulling away, and he wouldn't risk another rejection.

"Where'd you go today?" Although tentative, the question sounded like another accusation in his ears.

"Why? You worried I'm drunk?" He noticed her wince at the bite in his tone.

"No." She crossed the room to him and, in her typical manner, kicked the hornet's nest of his foul mood. "Are you mad at *me?*"

"I'm not mad." He closed the book and set it aside. "I'm hurt."

"Why are *you* hurt?" She crossed her arms, donning a puzzled expression.

Jackson knew she'd had a lousy afternoon, but so had he. "Because you keep lumping me in with your mom."

"No, I don't."

"Yeah, you kinda do, Gabby. You keep asking me what she's thinking or feeling, as if I, with my moderate issue, have anything in common with a full-blown drug addict who left her only child. And you keep suggesting that I'm going to end up hurting you and Luc."

"I don't think you'd hurt us on purpose." She slumped onto the sofa. "But you can't deny we'll miss you when you leave."

"As I'll miss you both. Which is sort of my point, Gabby. You keep thinking about what you and Luc stand to lose, but you never think about how trusting you might end up hurting me."

"How could *I* possibly hurt you?" She looked utterly incredulous with her wide eyes and slack jaw. "When you leave, you'll return to your family and business feeling better than you have in a long time. I can only imagine all the women there who'll be happy for your return. By New Year's, I'll be a blip in the rearview mirror. Meanwhile, I'm stuck here with a toddler and a dead-end kind of life. So excuse me if I don't see us as being equal in the 'whose heart is going to take the bigger hit' contest."

He knew she hadn't meant to insult him, but his heart registered the insult anyway. "If you honestly believe that, then you don't understand me the way I thought you did."

His quiet tone appeared to catch her attention.

Her defensive expression eased into something curious as she sat forward. "Then enlighten me."

When he'd stormed away from the party this afternoon, he'd dumped the costume by the road and walked for ninety minutes thinking through all the decisions that had led him to needing to have this conversation. He'd grappled vanity, doubts, and his fear of vulnerability. Ultimately, he'd vowed not to run away from his feelings.

Although he'd considered all the ways he might articulate the fucked-up mess of emotions that had hijacked his life these past years, it wasn't until this moment that he'd known how to start the conversation.

"Has it never occurred to you that, if my life back home were so great, I wouldn't have ended up here in the first place?"

"No, because you've never shared more than vague details with me." She chewed on her lip. "Why *did* things get so bad this seemed the only option?"

"Because when everyone I loved let me down, I gave up. It always seemed that no matter how much I'd been willing to give, it never mattered. People kept taking more and more without giving much back. So, I pulled away, kept to myself, and started drinking a little bit more each month." Jackson blocked out Doc's recent attempt to get him to see how he might be a little hypocritical with his opinions.

She edged closer, but didn't touch him, as if she sensed that he needed a little distance to finish this conversation. "How, exactly, did people take from you or let you down?"

"All kinds of ways." He rubbed his hands on his thighs to buy time. "My mom was the heart of our family. I thought nothing could be colder or darker than those weeks leading up to her death, but then the permanent, profound loss struck even harder. Even now, that doesn't fade."

He paused, allowing the memory of his mom's smile to linger. "David left the country without any warning three days after my mom's funeral. He and my dad had a falling-out, which neither will tell us about. Whatever caused it had to be major, because David not only moved around the world, but also barely spoke with Cat and me for more than a year. He finally came home, but the distance between us is still there. He and my dad are talking now, but there's tension there, too. David won't share whatever the hell the big secret falling-out was all about. I've tried to overlook it, but the truth is, I can't. I'd always thought we were close, but the way he left me and still won't trust me with the truth makes me doubt everything I thought I knew about us."

"Maybe it's not his secret to share?" Gabby interrupted.

Apparently she shared his sister's opinion, but Jackson disagreed. "Except I'm pretty sure he told his wife. And anyway, there's more to my story. A couple of months after David first left, my then girlfriend got pregnant. I was psyched. I'd always wanted a family, and since mine had starting falling apart, I thought fate had thrown me a bone."

He leaned forward a bit, staring into space. "Maybe it's crazy, but at one point I thought my mom manipulated things from heaven to give me the family I missed. Alison didn't agree. She didn't want to be a mother or my wife, so she aborted our child without considering any options. That's when I really began drinking more regularly. Finally, my sister stole my best employee—and friend—to start up some new business. Honestly, Gabby, I'd about given up on people until I met you."

That admission set off a wave of panic that bunched up in his shoulders, but he forced his way past the emotion before it stopped him from finishing what needed to be said.

"You and the way you greet each day with a smile. The way you never take the easy road, whether it means being a single mom, accepting your mom's abandonment, or facing her down twice this week without falling apart. You inspire me. You give me hope that there are people who are worth the effort. But then, when you imply I'm some hookup who's only out for what I can take for myself, that feels like a bomb going off in my heart. Makes me think my faith in you is misplaced. Like what seems worth the risk of letting you in here," he tapped his chest, "isn't anything special at all. That maybe you're just another Alison in disguise, and I'm still as gullible as I ever was when it comes to people I care about."

Now that he'd spilled his guts, he could barely make eye contact with Gabby. His heart raced, and his skin prickled from overexposure, like he'd been standing next to the sun.

"I'm sorry." Gabby tentatively reached for his hand. "I guess I let my insecurities take over. I do know who you are, Jackson."

His body stiffened at first, determined to reject any overture as pity. But at the moment of contact, he found himself gripping her hand and tugging her onto his lap. She curled against him like a child, resting her head on his shoulder and wrapping one hand around his neck.

He enveloped her in his arms and buried his face in the crook of her neck. They sat intertwined in a silent embrace until his heart returned to its natural rhythm. A warm rush of contentment replaced the shame and discomfort that had consumed him minutes earlier.

"Thank you for sharing all of that." She grinned against his neck. "And for all the flattery. I'm sure I've never 'inspired' anyone else to do much more than roll their eyes."

He kissed the top of her head and looped a chunk of her hair around his finger. "I meant every word. You *do* inspire me. So stop assuming that, the minute I go home, you and Luc will be nothing more than a faint memory. That's not what I see happening at all."

She kissed his cheek. "I'm sure you'll never be a distant memory for me, Jackson."

He tipped her face up to force her to look him in the eye. "Maybe the odds are against us, but if I'm going to get more invested, I need to know that you aren't using me because I'm convenient and helpful."

"No! I'm using you for the great sex." She stared at him—straight-faced—and then grinned. "Sorry, but you walked right into that one."

"Don't be sorry. I'm about to make good on that great sex—right now." He kissed her mouth this time with a playful growl, but then gentled his hold. "I'm glad you came over tonight."

He eased her off his lap and stood, then immediately lifted her and carried her to his bed. His body thrummed with anticipation as he slowly undressed her. He wanted to savor the little moments—the feel of her skin beneath his fingers, the catch of her breath, the sparkle in her eye—hoping she shared his sense of preciousness about the moment.

Once he'd removed her clothes, he quickly discarded his own and crawled on top of her, pinning her hands to the mattress while nuzzling her neck and slowly showering her shoulder and breasts with lingering kisses. As her scent swirled around him, he knew he'd never see or smell a pear again without thinking of her.

She arched in response to each lick of his tongue, seeking him out yet unable to pull him close. "Jackson, let me touch you."

He released her hands and lowered himself so that they were skin to skin. The friction of their bodies created heat until, in the frenzy of caresses and kisses, their skin turned slick.

Jackson's body broke out in goose bumps wherever her fingers traced his skin. For the first time in years, he'd bared his soul. It seemed impossible to feel simultaneously lost and safe, yet the intense intimacy of it all tossed him about like a ship in a storm.

His need for her affection overwhelmed him. If he hadn't been so hungry for her, it might've terrified him. But with each kiss, the fear ebbed, giving way to a deepening sense of belonging. Like invisible ink, the tie between them seemed as if it had been there all along, waiting to be discovered.

He cupped her breasts, then stroked the inside of her thigh until she opened her legs. Her face lit with pleasure, evidenced further by her sexy moan, as his fingers explored her center. Seeing her so utterly undone by him filled him with longing and tenderness.

She opened her eyes and threaded her fingers through his hair. "I want you. Don't wait."

"I won't," he murmured in her ear as he thrust himself inside of her. Once fully seated between her legs, he forced himself to slow down and to hold her gaze. To see her and, more importantly, be seen by her. His heart filled with passion and warmth as their bodies took over and meted out a rhythm that alternated between smooth, slow thrusts and quick, ravenous ones.

He lost all sense of time until they both found their release together and came crashing back down to earth, bodies sweat soaked and intertwined.

Gabby smiled and brushed aside his damp bangs. "I feel much happier now."

Jackson kissed her temple and tucked her against his chest. "Can you stay?"

"Not all night." She lazily traced the lines of his chest with her finger. "Sorry."

"Don't apologize." He closed his eyes, enjoying the quiet and the heat of her little body.

His mind aimlessly meandered but too soon recalled the events of the day. Marie's drunken behavior, Noah's stern glare, Jon's concern, Gabby's devastating disappointment, and Luc's confusion.

He hated to ruin the peaceful moment, but knew they had to address what had happened. "Did Luc have a lot of questions about the commotion today?"

Gabby's muscles tensed beneath his hands. "A little. I panicked and lied. Told him my mom was a stranger who got lost."

"That's not a complete lie. She is a stranger to him, and a virtual one to you. And she is lost. Sadly, she might be hopelessly lost. Besides, most people believe that lies told to protect someone are probably okay."

Repeating David's rationale for keeping *his* secret disturbed Jackson, but he pushed the feeling away. "You're trying to protect your son, who's too young to understand the truth anyway. I'm sure, at some point, you'll be honest with him."

He felt a subtle shift in Gabby's breathing. A heaviness borne of resignation and frustration.

"I never want to hurt him like my mom's hurt me. Truth is, I can't be sure I wouldn't become addicted to medication if I were in excruciating pain every day for months." Gabby sighed. "All this time I've held on to a sliver of hope that she'd conquer the problem and return. That perhaps we could be friends. It sucks to have almost had that dream come true but then turn into a nightmare."

Jackson didn't know what to say about that, so he squeezed her tighter and kissed her head again. How could he offer advice when he hadn't sorted out his own family issues? Issues he could now admit ran both directions because, while he needed honesty from them, they needed him to prove that he wouldn't be reckless. Maybe the best he could offer Gabby was to open up even more about his own situation so she didn't feel so alone in hers.

"I'm inviting my family up here to come to a counseling session." As soon as the words came out, his stomach clenched.

Gabby popped up onto one elbow and looked at him with a pleased grin. "Will I get to meet them?" Then she grimaced. "Sorry, I didn't mean to put you on the spot. This isn't about me . . . I know that. Are you looking forward to their visit, or dreading it?"

"Both." Jackson twirled some of her hair around his finger again and kissed it. "Kind of like lacrosse conditioning. The anticipation sucks and it's hard work, but when you're in it and getting stronger, you feel good."

"You played lacrosse?" she teased. "I bet all the cheerleaders chased you around."

He shrugged and smiled at the memories of his high school and college antics. "Yeah, I can't lie. I had a good time on and off the field."

She slapped his shoulder, and he rolled her onto her back, nipping at her earlobe.

"When do you have to go home?" he asked while feeling his cock stir back to life.

"Hmmm." She stroked his growing erection. "Not just yet."

"Good." He cupped her face and kissed her, giving himself over to her and the lightness she brought to his heart.

# CHAPTER SIXTEEN

"Doug Kilpatrick countered your settlement offer." Oliver fell silent, apparently allowing Jackson a minute to brace himself. "He's demanding one hundred thou—"

"Stop!" Jackson repressed the urge to throw his phone against the wall. "The answer is no."

"Jackson, we must—" Oliver began.

"Don't tell me what I *must* do. You're crazy if you think I'll ever pay that jerk twice his salary after his own shitty behavior got him fired!" The artery at the base of Jackson's neck nearly burst, it throbbed so hard.

David broke in. "No one is suggesting you meet his demand. This is a negotiation. We've got an eighty-eight-thousand-dollar gap between your offer and his. Now we fire back. The question is how much."

"The answer is nothing." Jackson folded one arm across his chest, tucking his hand under his armpit, while he held the phone with the other. Instead of letting the circumstances take control from him, he took control of them. Felt damn good, too.

"No counter?" Oliver asked.

"No. *Nothing*, Oliver . . . as in, pull the original offer, too. See how happy that fucker is to have walked away from three months' salary because he thought he had me over a barrel."

"Jackson, I don't advise you to take that action," Oliver said slowly.

"Understood." Jackson grinned to himself. "Do it anyway."

"Jackson," David began.

"No, David. I'd rather go to court. If a judge or jury thinks he deserves anything, then I'll accept that. I'm *not* willing to be fleeced by him like some coward. My reputation and the quality of my work speak for themselves. If I suffer six months of a downturn, so be it. I know who I am and what I can do. No one, especially not him, can take that away from me."

Jackson heard them conferring on the other end of the line again. Finally, Oliver spoke. "I'll call his lawyer and pull the original offer. I hope you're prepared for what could be an ugly, protracted fight."

"I'm ready." And oddly, Jackson believed it.

"Jackson, hang on the line a second. Oliver is going back to his office to make the call," David said.

"Sure." Jackson waited until Oliver left the office.

"Jackson," David began. "I'm concerned about your decision."

"Don't be. I heard your advice and I take full responsibility for any negative blowback. But it's my business, my reputation, and my call to make."

"Fair enough." David paused. "You sound good, actually. Not angry, just decided."

"I am." Jackson smiled, letting the truth of it flow through him. Not only was Jackson decided about this matter, but he'd also put to bed his doubts about getting involved with Gabby. Since their heart-to-heart a couple of nights ago, he'd allowed himself to embrace his good fate.

"Your doctor must be great. I look forward to meeting him next week."

"He's a good guy. I'm not sure I'd say I look forward to the family session, but I hope it's a step in the right direction."

"As do Vivi and I."

Jackson smiled, as he always did when thinking of Vivi. "How's the pregnancy going?"

"Good. We had another ultrasound last week. I'll send you a copy, if you'd like. I can't believe I'm going to be a father in five months."

David, a father. Jackson knew his brother would be protective, strict, yet gentle, too. Unlike Jackson, who'd been a little rowdy and reckless, David had always been an observer and a peacemaker. He'd prized structure and order, and needed to understand the hows and whys of everything. David couldn't have chosen a more opposite partner than Vivi, but somehow they provided each other a sense of balance.

"It must be an amazing feeling." Jackson meant it, too. Of course, he thought about the baby he might have had. He then thought about Luc, and about his soon-to-be niece or nephew. There were many ways to love a child and be a role model. Alison had stolen something important from him, but now he could see that she hadn't robbed him of every chance for happiness. He'd been doing that to himself.

"So, have you spoken with Dad about the counseling session?" Unease laced David's tone.

"Yes. Why?"

David hesitated before answering. "Nothing."

"Bullshit, David. Whatever he's said to you can't be worse than what he said to me."

"What did he say to you?" David's anger edged his voice as he went into big-brother mode.

"Pretty much what you'd expect. He didn't hide his disappointment, but he's coming, which is enough."

"He can be a son of a bitch."

Jackson's brows rose because David rarely used harsh language or raised his voice. "Given your recent history, I'm shocked you're surprised."

After a pronounced pause, David said, "I suppose part of growing older is learning to accept our parents' flaws—some of which are appalling. Sometimes, though, I wish we could go back to being ignorant and utterly trusting."

Jackson sensed David's musings loomed larger than he cared to discuss. Before he could say anything, David muttered, "Mom always acted happily married, but she sure deserved more love than she got."

David's voice had taken on a gruff quality, as if his throat had tightened. Jackson almost pushed the conversation, sensing suddenly that his mom might have something to do with the big secret. But his hesitation cost him a chance to press his brother.

"Hey, Jackson, I've got to run to another meeting." David's abrupt shift of focus gave Jackson whiplash. "See you next week."

"Bye." Slightly dissatisfied, Jackson set the phone on the counter and refilled his travel coffee mug with an extra-strong Starbucks blend. When he headed out the door, a brisk November day greeted him.

He trotted down the rickety stairs and went to his car. Garbage day in the 'hood. Hoping to set aside the unease the end of his conversation with David had instilled, he unfolded the map of homes Jon managed and mentally retraced the efficient path he'd figured out last week.

Of course, today's duties didn't require much thought, which gave him too much time to dwell on the past. Each of the vacation homes he serviced made him think about his family's second home on Block Island—the years they'd spent taking friends and family there.

When he reflected on his mother's time on the island, he mostly remembered her in the kitchen, or reading a magazine on a deck chair, or, when they got older, mixing a pitcher of sangria and breaking out a deck of cards. His father had only ever come for two or three days at a time, and even then, had usually been preoccupied. He'd never mistreated his wife, but now that Jackson thought of it, he hadn't been affectionate.

His mom probably *had* craved more than she'd received. Had she suffered in silence for her kids' sake? Did his parents' marriage have something to do with the big secret? A sickening feeling took root in Jackson's gut as he neared the dump.

Fortunately, his phone rang before the unease overwhelmed him.

"Yello," he said.

"Jackson, it's me," Hank said. "You got a minute?"

"Sure. I may lose you because I'm driving on some rural roads, but I'll call you back if you drop out."

"Okay. It's about Ray. Well, really the whole crew, but Ray spoke with me. Did you pull your settlement offer?"

Jackson straightened in his seat, knuckles whitening around the steering wheel. In an even tone, he said, "Yep."

"Ray just heard from Doug, who apparently went ballistic today after getting that call. He's gunning for you big time now. It's got the crew nervous. Given your lengthy absence, morale isn't good. I'm concerned they may start looking for other jobs."

Blindsided, Jackson pulled off the road. Each passing hour and conversation transformed his mood to something darker than the gray November clouds overhead.

"Jackson? You still there?"

"I'm here," he snapped. "I need a second to process the fact that my own crew is afraid of that dickwad and doesn't think I have the stones to see this through. That no one trusts me."

He heard Hank's frustrated sigh.

"Everything's not about you, Jackson. They've got families to support. They're concerned about the future in the face of a lawsuit. Secondly, I'm worried, too. I don't want to see you put through the wringer when you're working so hard to find balance. I know you feel like settling is rolling over, but I agree with your lawyers. The smart decision—personally and professionally—is to negotiate an end to this as soon as possible."

Jackson fell silent. A couple of hours ago he'd been certain of his decision to pull the offer, but he hadn't considered the possibility of his crew seeking other employment. If they walked out on him now, he'd be up a creek.

For almost five weeks he'd been focusing almost exclusively on his own peace of mind. He'd left Hank in charge, assuming that everything would be in place when he returned. Now he saw he'd been naïve to think he could compartmentalize his life so neatly. That he could ignore the day-to-day demands of his business without creating questions.

"Hank, gather the crew at the office tomorrow morning for an early conference call."

"A little pep talk from you won't resolve the problem."

"I hear you. I need the day to think about my options. First, I need you to tell me where things stand with each house and what the worst-case scenario would be if Ray and Jim left, for example. Call me with that update as soon as you can, then I'll make some decisions and talk to everyone tomorrow."

He heard Hank's sigh of relief through the phone. "Absolutely."

"Thanks for calling, Hank." Jackson hung up, frowning.

*Dammit.* Hiring Doug had been a misstep from start to finish. He could blame Doug for a majority of the bullshit, but Jackson couldn't escape one cold truth. If he hadn't been burning both ends of the candle, he probably wouldn't have made the mistake of hiring Doug in the first place.

Driving along a sunlit carpet of red and gold leaves lining the mountain road, Jackson considered how life away from the pressure cooker of Fairfield County had shifted his perspective on success and happiness. Gabby helped, too, he amended with a smile.

Soon he'd be thrust back into his old world to face all the problems he'd temporarily left behind, some of which he'd created. Today he could turn to Gabby for comfort, but who would he turn to back home?

~

Gabby was putting away the wheelbarrow after a long day of preparing her gardens for winter when she heard someone pull into the driveway. A grin curled her mouth. Jackson must've finished the dump runs a bit ahead of schedule.

He'd called her earlier to see if her dad could babysit Luc tonight so they could go out to dinner. He wanted to take her to the Chop House at the Equinox Hotel in Manchester Center. She'd never eaten at anyplace that fancy before. Although she wasn't sure she had an appropriate outfit for the occasion, she doubted Jackson would care.

She exited the garage smiling, only to be disappointed to see Noah get out of his car.

"Gabby." He strode toward her, the late-afternoon sun casting shadows over the sharp features of his face.

They hadn't been alone together since he'd asked her for a second chance, nor had they discussed the situation with her mom. She had neither the interest nor time to revisit either of those topics, which required her to think fast and deflect.

"Luc's still at nursery school." She forced herself to keep smiling.

"I know, that's why I've come now." He glanced around. "Jackson's not here, right?"

Although Gabby didn't believe Noah would ever physically hurt her, something about his demeanor opened a pit in her stomach. "Jackson's out taking care of my dad's garbage runs today."

"Good." Noah drew a deep breath. "I want to know what's going on with you and him, and, more importantly, if what your mom said about him is true."

Gabby refused to be bullied by Noah. "A. None of your business. B. Also none of your business."

"I beg to differ. If Jackson's an addict and you're letting him babysit our son, it sure as shit is my business." A determined glint shone in Noah's blue eyes.

The subtle threat burned like lemon juice in a paper cut. "Since when did you ever believe a thing my mom said, Noah?"

"I don't know what to believe, which is why I'm asking you. I've checked around. He's not been to any AA meetings, but he's been seen coming out of Doc Millard's."

"How dare you spy on him! He's done nothing but be kind and generous. Good grief, you barely paid attention to us for three years, now all of a sudden we're your top priority? Please, let's go back to the way things were before you gave a fig about me or Luc."

"Just answer my questions." His flinty eyes locked on hers. "How involved with him are you now?"

How dare he? How *dare* he make her answer to him after he'd paraded around town with a string of women since dumping her? In the heat of the moment, she lashed out. "Jackson is the best thing that's *ever* come my way."

"Oh, Gabs." Noah laughed before he sneered. "Let me tell you, sweetheart, you're just a piece of small-town ass to him. He's on *vacation*, or in rehab. Either way, you'll be dropped the minute he goes home."

"Think whatever you like, Noah. The truth is that you know nothing about him."

"Frankly, Gabs, how much can *you* really know about him and his life? Have you met his family or friends? How do you know he doesn't have some other girl waiting for him back home?"

"Not every one's faithless like you. In any case, Jackson and I are none of your concern."

Noah had the audacity to shake his head in a pitying manner. "Your mom made you so desperate for love that you're willing to put our son in harm's way for a guy you barely know."

She stepped back, his blow having struck her deep inside. When she found her voice, she said, "Maybe, but she didn't make me desperate enough to want you back."

Noah's expression turned menacing. "Two months from now, when Mr. Wonderful hasn't called or visited, we'll see how you feel." His voice had climbed a few decibels at that point. "In the meantime, I don't want him—or your mom—near Luc."

Gabby rolled her eyes. "Honestly, if you weren't so damn annoying right now, you'd be comical."

"I'm not joking, Gabby." Noah's voice cooled, his temper now under control. "I doubt anyone else thinks letting a guy with a drinking problem get involved with Luc shows good judgment. Worse yet, you let your drug addict mom back in your life, where she could have a bad influence on our son."

"*You're* more likely to hurt Luc than Jackson ever will. And I didn't let my mom see Luc, nor will I." Gabby's anger flared to life, resentment brimming over like lava. "What gives you a right to dictate to me? *You*, who's never paid one penny in child support? You, who never showed your face during the first nine months of Luc's life? You, who maybe give your son a total of ten hours per *year* of your time? The only reason you give a lick about Jackson is because your ego's bruised. If you think *this* attitude is winning you any points, you can think again. How about you walk away now, and I'll forget we ever had this ridiculous conversation."

She yanked the garage door closed and stalked past Noah toward the house. She hadn't quite hit the porch when he called out, "You best not make an enemy of me."

Gabby stopped and shot him a cold stare over her shoulder.

He crossed to his car and opened the door. Before he got in, he said, "Contrary to your opinion, I have some say in Luc's life. I'll give you a day or two to come to your senses, but this discussion isn't over."

With that, he hopped in the driver's seat, slammed his door, and took off, leaving her whole body feeling wrung out, like she'd been tossed into the spin cycle of her aging washing machine.

As soon as she entered the house, she bumped into her dad, who'd apparently been watching the whole scene through the window.

"What're you doing?" The deep creases in his forehead showed his bewildered concern. "Why rock the boat with Noah for a guy who's leaving in another week?"

"Oh, come on, Dad. Noah can't do anything. We don't share custody. He's not even named on Luc's birth certificate."

"Gabby, Noah's a town native and beloved by many. He's a cop in good standing in this community. You've openly acknowledged him as Luc's dad. What if he tries to assert his rights? Setting aside the stuff with your mom, is this fling with Jackson worth disturbing our situation with Luc?"

"Noah doesn't want custody. He'd never want to be on the hook for child support. He's throwing a temper tantrum because I turned him down when he asked for a second chance." Gabby crossed her arms.

"Are you willing to roll the dice? The stakes are sky high." After a brief pause, her dad's tone turned softer. "Noah's not the only one around here who can see the potential danger in having Jackson's problem around Luc."

Gabby had grown tired of defending her choices, so she hugged her dad. "You worry too much. I know Noah. He won't do anything, and even if he tried, he can't win with his track record as a dad. But I don't have time to hash this out now. I've got to run and pick up Luc from nursery school."

"This is a train wreck waiting to happen, despite your attitude."

Gabby wrapped her favorite blue scarf around her neck. "I'm realistic. And I'm done letting anyone, including Noah, tell me what I can and can't do. I'm almost twenty-three, for Pete's sake. And I deserve a little romance in my life." She kissed his cheek. "See you later."

As she drove toward the nursery school, however, a slight tremor whisked through her body as adrenaline ebbed. Noah shouldn't have a leg to stand on, but what if she was wrong? What if Noah used her relationship with Jackson against her? Used her own mother against her? She'd learned the hard way that Noah could be a dick, but would he sink so low as to use their son as a pawn?

# CHAPTER SEVENTEEN

The roaring fire gilded the neutral tones of the Chop House's tastefully decorated dining room. Gabby savored another bite of the pistachio crème brûleé she'd ordered. Decadent, like the grand old resort and the handsome man sitting across the table.

Jackson had pulled out all the stops to treat her to a magical night, although occasionally he'd appeared preoccupied. She'd also noticed his gaze linger once or twice on other patrons' glasses of wine or cocktails tonight. Seeing that struggle pass through his eyes had troubled her.

However, at the moment he sported a goofy grin. Unlike his mercurial eyes, those grins always made her smile.

"Why are you staring at me?" She licked her spoon.

"I'm trying to decide if you're prettier in your overalls and ponytail, or with your hair done up like that and those shiny earrings." He smiled, his amber eyes warm and relaxed.

Self-consciously she touched her fake gold hoops. "I hope the former, because this getup isn't something you'll see me in often. Doesn't quite suit yard work."

"I suppose not, although when you come to visit me, pack it and I'll take you to some of my favorite places."

Gabby's heart sped up. Contrary to her father and Noah's warnings, the invitation proved Jackson had every intention of keeping in touch beyond his lease. "I'd love to visit, but what would I do with Luc?"

Jackson shrugged. "Until your dad is well enough to handle him, bring him with you."

The mere idea of her and Luc taking a road trip to see Jackson in his own environment shot a thrill through her until she remembered Noah's threats. Her face must've revealed the dark memory, because Jackson asked, "What's wrong? You don't want to bring Luc?"

"It's not that." She set her spoon down, determined not to let Noah usurp one of the most romantic evenings she'd ever enjoyed. "It's nothing. Let's not spoil our night by dwelling on when you'll be gone."

"I thought we agreed to be honest with each other." Jackson tilted his head, his eyes narrowing. "You know how I feel about trust, Gabby. Please don't keep anything from me."

The sugary dessert she'd inhaled now soured in her stomach. Noah's warning might not only insult Jackson, but also cause him to rescind his invitation. Of course, she couldn't be in a relationship that required her to censor herself. She'd already ridden that merry-go-round with her mom, and look how that turned out.

"Noah and I argued today because of my mom's accusations about your drinking. He's pretending to be concerned about Luc's safety, but I think he's just jealous."

Jackson leaned forward. "So he doesn't want me around Luc?"

"It doesn't matter what he wants." Gabby averted her gaze while folding her napkin and setting it on the table. "He's got no right to get involved."

"I'm no fan of the guy, but he *is* Luc's dad." Jackson's slightly defensive tone caught her off guard. "I think that gives him some rights."

"He's a glorified sperm donor, Jackson. Little more. If it had been up to him, Luc wouldn't exist." She could feel her brows pinching together. Then she remembered Jackson's ex stripped his rights as a father, so she softened her tone. "As far as I'm concerned, Noah gave up his rights when he walked away. He can't waltz in now and pretend to be more important to, or care more deeply for, his son." She clasped

Jackson's hand. "Besides, I know you're not a danger to Luc. That's all that matters."

Jackson's expression grew pensive while he drew a deep breath. "Maybe so, but I can't blame the guy for being worried. He doesn't know me, and now your mom's got him thinking my problem is as bad as hers. Maybe I ought to talk to him."

"No." Gabby shook her head. "Don't dignify his BS with a response. This will blow over as soon as Noah finds a new woman to chase. Trust me, right now he's mad because I turned him down."

"Turned him down?" Jackson drew back.

*Oops.* She'd forgotten that she'd never mentioned Noah's recent plea for a reunion. "The other week he asked for a second chance, but I'm not interested."

"He blames me." Jackson nodded, as if finally fitting together pieces of a puzzle.

"Maybe, but it *isn't* about you. Noah blew any chance he ever had with me a long time ago." She cocked a brow. "That's all on him."

"I'm sure he doesn't see it that way. I'm an obstacle he needs to get rid of." Jackson's heavy sigh loomed between them. "Guess he'll be celebrating when I take off later next week."

"He might." She squeezed his hand. "But I won't."

"Neither will I." He raised her hand to his lips. "That's why I hope you'll visit. I won't be able to get back up here for a while. My business will demand my full attention in the coming months, especially with this damn lawsuit I'm going to have to settle."

"What lawsuit?" An unpleasant jolt of surprise arrested her, having believed he'd shared all of his troubles with her earlier.

Gabby listened while he explained the incident with his former employee; the incident that had led to the intervention that had prompted Jackson's trip to Vermont. The details confirmed her suspicion that he hadn't yet fully accepted the significance of his drinking problem. If he couldn't admit the truth to himself about that, might he also be lying to himself about the depth of his feelings for her?

"You're not asking my opinion, but settling seems like the best way to stay focused on being healthy and moving on."

"Quickest way, but not the best. You weren't there that morning, so you didn't hear Doug's smug voice or see the look on his face." The golden light in Jackson's eyes dimmed as he cracked his knuckles. "Dammit, I can't let him win."

As someone who'd never been too proud to ask for help, shied away from admitting mistakes, or allowed humiliating experiences to destroy her attitude for long, Gabby couldn't relate to Jackson's feelings at all. In fact, they rather annoyed her. "So your ego is more important than your employees' concerns, or your family's? More important than keeping your recovery on track?"

Jackson scowled. "No."

"Great." Gabby smiled. "Then walk away from the fight."

Jackson's mouth fell open, but the waiter arrived with the check, thankfully shutting down the discussion. She didn't want to argue, nor did she want to end the lovely date on a sour note. And ultimately, it was his call, not hers.

Gabby covered a gasp when she watched Jackson toss two hundred dollars on the table. He'd just dropped more money on a two-hour dinner than she'd spend on Luc and her dad this year for Christmas.

Somewhere in the back of her mind she'd known he must be wealthy, but she'd never before considered how it was yet another gulf between them. Would his family consider her—an undereducated, slightly impoverished single mom—a gold digger?

Jackson tucked his wallet away. "Are you still upset because I don't agree with your advice?"

"No." She was glad he didn't know what she'd been thinking. "Although I wish you'd reconsider. Compare the worst-case scenario of each choice. Settling will cost you something you can probably afford and makes you eat a little crow—not so bad. But the worst case of not settling could," she began enumerating her points on each finger, "a, cause you to drink to cope with the stress of the lawsuit, which would b, cut you out of your soon-to-be niece or nephew's life. Not to mention c, how I couldn't stomach seeing you backslide toward alcoholism. Add to that the potential damage to your business and employees and that all seems a lot worse than swallowing a little pride."

She braced for everything except his smile. His gorgeous, dazzling smile. "Not saying I totally agree with that analysis, but sometimes your way of looking at things is pretty smart. Anyone ever tell you that?"

"Never." She chuckled.

"Well, you're wise beyond your years."

Despite the compliment, what she heard was another reference to their age gap. Although he hadn't mentioned her age in a while, she still wondered if some small part of him was bothered by it. As much as she enjoyed this fairy tale she'd been living lately, so many forces worked against it. Forces she didn't know how to control.

When they stood to leave, Jackson draped his arm over her shoulder, kissed her temple, and whispered in her ear, "Let's go someplace more private."

As usual, her entire body hummed in response. Physical contact and anticipation made it easy for her to push aside her doubts and live in the moment. What else could she do?

～

Once alone in his apartment, Jackson's shifting thoughts and moods swirled together. With each passing day, life encroached more and more on his newfound happiness. He'd be gone soon, unable to see Gabby, hold her, make love with her.

When they were alone, a universe unto themselves, time stood still. He'd been no more able to avoid falling for her than he could ignore gravity, but now what? How would he leave her without losing a part of his heart?

He unzipped Gabby's dress while pressing kisses on her shoulder. Her silky garb dropped to the floor before he unfastened her bra and cupped her bare breasts. All evening he'd been fairly mesmerized by the sight of her more sophisticated, stylish appearance. Her twisted knot of hair with curling tendrils brushing her cheeks. The dip in the front of the dress that revealed a hint of her perky cleavage. The high heels that showed off her prettily shaped calves. Throughout dinner, he'd found himself counting the minutes until they could be alone.

Gabby turned to face him, her blue gaze penetrating his with desire. She wrapped her arms around his neck, kissing him as if she needed to taste him to survive. He loved being needed. Loved being her confidant and lover. Loved every single thing about her except for the fact she'd be forever tied to Noah through Luc.

Determined to block out all the negative events of the day, he swept his hands down her back and settled them on her bottom. Cute and petite like everything else about her.

She unbuttoned his shirt and pants, and helped peel him out of his clothing. The sweet scent of pears pulled him further under her spell. He didn't mind being her captive, and for the first time in years, wasn't afraid of his feelings. He trusted her completely.

Skin to skin, awash with surges of possessiveness and lust, Jackson growled a little when holding her dainty form in his arms. "You overwhelm me."

He felt her smile against his neck before she kissed him. "Prove it."

*Gladly.* Without breaking apart, they staggered across the room toward the bed. When they landed on the mattress, Gabby climbed on top of him. In the dim lamplight, she appeared to glow with equal parts pleasure and yearning. She reached up to undo her hair, then shook her head to let her loose curls cascade around her shoulders.

If possible, he grew even harder at the sight. When he sat upright, Gabby pushed him back against the mattress. She attempted a seductive grin, which mostly came across as cute. Her face would likely always look too young and innocent to pull off a sultry appearance. Not that he minded. He loved her doe eyes, deep dimples, and fresh-faced appeal—a perfect reflection of her open, hopeful personality.

"Come here," he coaxed, reaching up to her neck to ease her nearer so he could capture her breasts in his mouth.

When his mouth clamped over one nipple, she moaned and writhed against him in a tantalizing rhythm.

They spent an hour lost in a private, perfect world—kissing, touching, suckling, savoring—until they came together in a sweat-soaked rush of intense lust laced with tenderness.

Lying beside her in the dark, he believed himself to be a starving man who was only sated when Gabby fed him pieces of her soul, as if her absence of bitterness with life's disappointments could seep into him by sheer proximity.

He needed more time with her. In a wild moment, he wondered if his life would be better if he sold everything and moved to Winhall. The stray thought ran counter to thirty years of his father's grooming.

His dad measured success by statistics, with little interest in invisible measures like happiness. According to him, money, power, and respect were the only worthy goals for any man. His mother had never contradicted her husband, but her actions suggested she didn't agree. She'd thrived on the intangibles, like warmth and affection, and had little interest in keeping up with the Joneses.

Jackson recalled David's questioning whether their mom had been happily married. His heart ached a little for having never considered whether or not his mother had enough affection in her life. Jackson doubted he could ever be happy married to someone as cool and driven as his father.

Might Jackson's life be different—more satisfying—had he not been compelled to take on more and more projects because he'd heard his father's voice inside his head, driving him to do and be more? Because he'd been aware of his father's comparing him against David's success, something he'd never honestly cared to match?

He'd never questioned his goals before, but he couldn't ignore the satisfaction he'd felt working here, eating with Gabby, Luc, and Jon, hiking, and reading the books he'd been meaning to get around to but had never found the time for.

"I really like it here." He hadn't meant to say those words aloud.

Gabby kissed his chest. "Will you miss Vermont?"

"Not as much as I'll miss you." He peered down at her. "You've restored my faith in love. I wish I could pack you and Luc in my suitcase and take you home with me."

Although he hadn't directly told her he loved her, the word lay there between them. It seemed impossibly soon to make a declaration, yet he didn't recoil from the idea, either. If anything, he only rebelled at the thought of giving it up.

She laid her head against his chest and he squeezed her tight. A few seconds later, he felt something wet on his skin.

"Are you crying?" He tipped up her chin.

"I'm sorry." She sniffled and forced a small laugh. "I've always known you would go, but now that we're closer to the end of your stay, it's harder."

"If I didn't have so many responsibilities, I'd stay longer."

"Don't apologize." Then she grimaced. "We both knew the situation from the beginning."

"I can't regret it." Jackson smiled at her and pulled her into a kiss, then rested his forehead against hers. "It's not like we won't see each other again."

"But it won't be the same."

"No. It won't." The thought of leaving scared him, and not only because he'd miss her. During the past couple of weeks, he'd barely thought about having a drink. He'd been happy and relaxed.

But after his conversations with David and Hank this morning, his mouth had watered with a hankering for whiskey. Knowing he'd be seeing Gabby had snapped him out of it, but what would happen when she wasn't there at the end of his day? And what did it say about him that he needed her so much?

"I'm only a phone call away." She tried for lightheartedness, but he could hear tightness pinching off her voice. Her resigned tone saddened him. Determined to assuage their sorrow, he clutched her tighter.

"My going home isn't good-bye." He sighed. "And maybe my leaving next week will give Noah a chance to cool down."

Gabby shrugged. "Let's stop talking about this. I should go home soon, and I don't want Noah's name to be the last thing I remember about tonight."

She kissed his neck and brushed her hand down his torso to the inside of his thigh.

"Me either," he said, savoring the goose bumps fanning over his body before he rolled on top of her.

# CHAPTER EIGHTEEN

Gabby hurried out of the nail salon. After working in the Haymans' yard all morning, she needed a quick fix to make her hands more ladylike before she met Jackson's family. Although manicures weren't part of her usual repertoire, she'd bet dollars to donuts Jackson's sister's nails were perfectly polished.

Her own were now a pretty shade of pink, but the pit stop left her barely enough time to race home and change before they arrived. She longed to make a good first impression despite how brief it would be. If his family caught her in her shit-kickers, stained overalls, and braided hair, they'd add her appearance to the pile of other reasons Jackson shouldn't be involved with her.

She turned onto her road, knowing she had forty-five minutes to shower and change. The last thing she expected to see in her driveway was Noah's squad car. They hadn't spoken since he'd tried to use their son to come between her and Jackson several days ago.

"Been waiting for you. Jackson said you'd be home soon," he said while stepping out of his car.

"Sorry, Noah, but I'm running late." She glanced at the garage apartment window to see if Jackson noticed her arrival. "Whatever you want will have to wait."

He withdrew an envelope from the car and waved it in the air. "I think you'll want to make time for this."

The triumphant gleam in his eye made her heart kick unevenly. Unwilling to let him see her squirm, she squared her shoulders, forced a bored sigh, and stuck out her hand. "Fine. What is it?"

"Open it and see." He handed her the envelope, which she promptly opened.

Across the top she read the words *Voluntary Acknowledgement of Parenting Form.* A tingling sensation bloomed at the base of her neck and crept along her spine.

"What's this about, Noah?" Feigning calmness, she employed a meditation tip to slow her breathing and repress alarm. "I've never denied that you're Luc's dad."

"True, but you never put my name on Luc's birth certificate. I get why you didn't when he was born, considering how I reacted to the pregnancy and all. But since we weren't married when Luc was born, the law doesn't recognize me as his father until we file this . . . or I take you to court to establish paternity." He tapped the papers in her hand. "This is cheaper and easier."

Her throbbing heart shimmied up her throat, making it difficult to speak. When her obvious discomfort elicited a knowing grin from Noah, she wanted to toss her purse at his head. Resentment rushed in to crowd out fear.

"Why do we need to do this? I've never denied you the right to spend time with Luc. Even so, you've hardly been an enthusiastic father, especially when it comes to financial support."

Noah, being Noah, didn't even wince at her accusation. If anything, he seemed more eager to spit out whatever spurred this little showdown than to defend himself against her barb. "I did some digging around about Jackson. Did you know that, in addition to his drinking problems, he's also facing legal trouble? Got into a scuffle with an employee. Now I've got evidence that he's a boozer *and* a hothead."

Apparently Noah had used whatever detective skills he had to discover the public records pertaining to Jackson. Getting defensive or fighting him here in the driveway would only cause him to fight harder. Gabby needed to reason with him. To soothe his ego and pride.

"Noah, you've met Jackson. You've seen how kind he's been, to Luc, to my dad, and even to you." Gabby donned her best puppy-dog eyes. "You *know* me and you know I'd never, ever put Luc in harm's way."

"I used to know you, Gabby. Used to know you better than anyone. But I think this guy's got your head turned around. I don't blame you, though. I blame him. He knows women like mysterious men, and he knows you've been stuck at home for a while. Of course he saw you as ripe for the picking. If I'd come to you a year ago, we'd be together and he'd be a nonissue." He dipped his chin and lowered one brow. She forced herself to swallow a scathing rant, knowing one wrong move in this chess game could cost her a lot. "But here we are, and since you didn't seem to take me too seriously before, I thought you needed a little proof of my resolve."

"I doubt this act of yours is actually about Luc's safety, so what's the real end game here? If I sign off on this form to legally establish your place as Luc's dad, then what, Noah?"

"Depends on you. If you agree to keep Jackson and your mom away from my son, then there's no reason for me to go after custody. But if you continue to show bad judgment, well . . ."

In her imagination, Noah's head exploded in a blazing fireball. Damn him to hell and back for bullying her. Contrary to the maturity demonstrated by her prior restraint, she shot back.

"What judge is going to hand you custody of our son?" She laughed, although none of this was funny. "Unlike you, who abandoned Luc, I've given him a stable, loving home for three years. I've provided for him without *any* help from you. I don't drink, smoke, or do anything else that makes me unfit . . . and that includes my relationship with Jackson." Before she could stop herself, she shoved her pointer finger in his face. "You don't have the right to tell me who I can and can't see. Jackson isn't a danger to anyone. He's been more helpful and loving toward Luc than you've ever been. Besides, if you file this," she waved the paper in the air, nostrils flaring, "I'm pretty sure I can start insisting on regular child support from you. Heck, maybe I can even get back support for the three years you've ignored. Come to think of it, that sounds pretty good to me. Where do I sign?"

Noah stood stock-still, eyes narrowed. Before he got back in his car, he leaned in toward Gabby. "Test me, Gabs. I dare ya."

She held her head high while watching his car drive away, then collapsed against her own car. Her entire body trembled as she gave in to the panic that had been coursing through her for the past five minutes despite her bravado.

Swiping the tears from her burning eyes, she waited for the alarm to subside. A quick glance at her reflection in the window painted an ugly picture—messy hair, red-rimmed eyes, worry lines.

Now she no longer wanted to meet Jackson's family. She wouldn't have time to prepare, and she didn't think she could hide her mood. Not from them or Jackson.

She cursed aloud. Noah had obviously talked to someone who knew about all this custody stuff. Noah was a cop, for God's sake. People respected him. She could picture him charming a judge into overlooking his piss-poor parenting to date because he had been young and confused. Hear him painting Jackson as a degenerate and her relationship with him to be depraved. Hear him using her own mother's past to paint an unsavory image of her family. Meeting with her mom had been a mistake, but she couldn't believe Noah had sunk so low as to use it against her, especially when he'd known how her mom's leaving had wrecked her those years ago.

Jackson came out of the apartment and jogged down the steps and over to her. He tipped up her chin. "What did Noah say?"

"Let's not discuss it now. Your family will be here soon. I need to think and calm down before I can talk to you. I'm sorry, Jackson. I can't meet your family like this, either. Maybe I can meet them after your meeting . . . and after I've showered and settled?" She assumed they weren't racing back to Connecticut, but maybe she was wrong.

"I don't know. Things could get a little messy today, so dinner might be tense. I'd rather not subject you to all that." He paused. "Sure you can't talk to me about Noah? I can guess he came loaded with more threats."

She wanted to wail, but wouldn't. Wanted to ignore Noah and flaunt Jackson right under his nose. But if Noah really planned to mess with custody, she had to seriously consider her next steps. A court battle would cost money she and her father didn't have. And even if Noah's chance of getting custody of Luc was slim, was anything—or anyone— worth the risk?

Closing her eyes, she let another tear trickle down her cheek. If she walked away from Jackson now, he'd surely see it as a betrayal. A rejection, just like all the others that sent him into a tailspin. How could she hurt him that way? But how could she share custody, or worse? And did she want to live in fear like that . . . wondering what Noah might do next, or worrying that Jackson would respond to her decisions by drinking? All she knew was that she needed time to think.

"I'm sorry, Jackson. Now's not a good time to talk. Please apologize to your family for me."

He sighed. "Okay. I'll catch up with you at the end of the day, assuming I'm still standing."

Despite his joke, she could hear the underlying tightness in his voice. He'd obviously not only wanted her to meet them, he'd needed her support before he faced down some of his demons.

"You'll be fine." She hugged him like it might be one of their last hugs. "Whatever hurt you're harboring, they're harboring some, too. You've all disappointed each other in some way, and you're all here today out of love. Keep that in mind if tempers flare."

"Easier said than done." He kissed her, and she wanted to cry. "Go on inside and try to relax. We'll figure out how to deal with Noah tonight. Whatever you need to fight him, I'll help you."

"Thanks." Then she hugged him again, wishing she could be sure Jackson could help her defeat Noah. "Good luck."

Once inside, she ran up the steps, clutching the legal mumbo jumbo in her hands and fighting her tears. This morning she'd been optimistic about the future, Jackson, and his family. Then Noah ruined everything, like he always did. She'd thought he could never hurt her again, but she'd been wrong.

Stripping out of her filthy clothes, she stepped into the hot shower and scrubbed her hair clean. As she stood there letting the water sluice off her skin, she had the sinking feeling that her relationship with Jackson had as much likelihood of surviving as the soapsuds circling the drain.

∾

Ten minutes later, Jackson came back to the driveway to greet his father, David, and Cat. "Where's Vivi?"

David hugged him before answering. "I asked her to stay behind. I didn't think the stress would be good for the baby. I hope you understand."

"Of course." Jackson nodded. "Though I was kind of looking forward to seeing her little bump."

"She fought me to come, but I wanted to be able to stay focused on you without having to be concerned about how everything might be affecting her."

"You don't have to explain. I got it." And he did. David would do anything to protect Vivi, just as Jackson would protect Gabby from Noah, or anything else that upset her. "I'll see her next week anyhow."

"My turn." Cat shoved David aside and hugged Jackson. "I'm so glad to see you. Look at you! Did you lose weight?" She smiled and ruffled his hair. "You still need a haircut."

Jackson chuckled and kissed her cheek before he turned to his dad, who'd been studying the Bouchards' home.

"Jackson." His father, impeccably dressed and pressed, with his silvering hair perfectly coiffed, shook his hand. "We stopped to eat on the way, so we're ready to get this over with when you are."

Jackson shrugged. "Fine with me."

David pressed his lips together, clearly annoyed by their dad's clipped attitude. Jackson wondered how unbearable the drive had been, and whether one hundred words had been spoken among the three of them. In any case, Jackson had not only expected his father's attitude, he didn't even mind. Their dad might be rigid, but Jackson knew he loved his children.

His father had always provided for them, given them every opportunity imaginable, offered tons of advice, and while praise came less often than criticism, it did come. In short, their father had been demanding, but he'd also held himself to the same high standards, which seemed fair.

Cat glanced around. "Do we have to race off? I hoped to meet your landlord . . . and his daughter."

Jackson tossed his sister his keys. "Gabby's not free now, so you'll have to wait until later. I thought maybe we'd all have dinner at the Equinox?"

"I have a client dinner at seven thirty, so I can't linger after our meeting. We'll plan a family dinner when you return to Connecticut." His father gestured to his car, unaware that his abruptness ruffled any feathers. "Shall I drive us all?"

When they filed into Doc's office, everyone made his or her preliminary greeting. Once Jackson sat on the sofa, David and Cat flanked him, forcing their father to take the chair next to Doc.

Jackson's nerves had been relatively settled until right then. Although in recent weeks he'd become comfortable in this setting, being here with his family seemed to set him back to square one. Like his very first visit, now pins and needles fanned throughout his limbs. His heartbeat ticked a little faster than normal, and his stomach burned with the sinking sensation that this meeting was a very bad idea.

"It's great to meet you all and attach faces to the names I've heard throughout the past five weeks." Doc rested his notepad on his lap and crossed his ankles. "It's been a pleasure to get to know Jackson. We've butted heads now and then, but I think you all should know he's taken this very seriously. He's committed to his recovery, and to your family."

Cat rested her head on Jackson's shoulder and squeezed his hand. The tender gesture humbled him. It also saddened him to acknowledge that his behavior—his inability to cope with his life—had ultimately forced this meeting.

"If I can interrupt, Doc, I'd like to say one thing," Jackson said.

Doc gestured with his hand while flashing an encouraging smile. "The floor is yours."

"I want to start with an apology." He'd been looking at his dad, but then averted his gaze and cast his eyes to the floor. "For a long time I only focused on my own hurt without seeing that I was also dragging you all through hell with me. Until Doc here started challenging my opinions, I figured it was my life, my right to brood, and none of your damn business. But even his advice didn't make all the difference." He suppressed the grin that always came when thinking of Gabby. He looked up at David. "It took watching someone else struggle with a similar issue in her family for me to really get it. So, from the bottom of my heart, I'm sorry I worried you. I know it'll take time to earn back your trust and respect. I'm feeling more optimistic now. And I'm grateful you all came here today to be part of the process."

"I never lost respect for you, Jackson." David touched Jackson's thigh for emphasis. "I've only been concerned."

"Thanks," Jackson replied.

"If you were listening carefully, you heard Jackson use the word *'trust,'*" Doc said. "Trust is a key element of both his problems and his recovery. The picture of your family I've drawn from our discussions is one that functioned rather well until Mrs. St. James's death. After that, a number of relationships broke down and Jackson coped by turning to alcohol and other destructive behaviors rather than to anyone in the family with whom he'd previously been close."

Doc paused and took a second to make eye contact with the others. "Jackson told me that, during the intervention held at David's, he conveyed some of his feelings of betrayal and abandonment. We've since discussed at length how his impulse to avoid negative feelings by checking out with alcohol needs to change if he's to enjoy a long-term recovery."

David faced Jackson. "I accept some of the blame here. You checked out in your way, but I'd checked out, literally, by leaving. Like you, I got too wrapped up in my own concerns to consider what you or Cat might've needed. I should've been there for you both, and I'm sorry that I wasn't. I promise I'll never bail on you again. If Vivi's taught me anything this past year, it's that we all need to be more open."

Aside from a raised eyebrow, their father made no response. He continued to sit quietly and listen from an emotional distance, as he'd done for as long as Jackson could remember.

"Do you mean that?" Jackson asked David.

"Of course I do," he replied.

Jackson shifted on the sofa, wondering whether coming straight out with his big question so early in the discussion might be a terrible idea. The opening, however, couldn't be more perfect. "I'm glad, because I can't turn to you if I feel like you're withholding stuff. And I can't completely trust you—or Dad—as long as you're keeping this big secret." Jackson glanced over his shoulder at his father, who remained stoic. "Whatever happened, it affected our whole family, so I think Cat and I have the right to know the truth."

David's gaze lingered on their father and then dropped to the floor. "You're asking me to betray someone else's trust to satisfy you. To pass your test, I have to fail it elsewhere." When he finally looked up at him, Jackson felt the weight of David's conflict. "Everything I've done since coming home should be proof of my love. I'm here. I'm not going anywhere. Can't this be enough?"

Jackson glanced at Cat, who tended to be silent during family confrontations, so he hadn't expected otherwise. He returned his attention to David. "Does Vivi know?"

David's eyes widened, having not expected the question. "Why is that relevant?"

"Because if you told Vivi, then you already broke your promise. And if Vivi can know, dammit, so can I." Jackson heard the bite in his voice and took a breath to calm down. "Don't treat me like a baby who can't handle bad news."

"Strictly speaking, I didn't break my promise by telling Vivi. The promise didn't extend to her." Once more David's gaze wandered to their father, whose only response was a heavy sigh. "How is learning the details of my fight with Dad—which had nothing to do with you— necessary to reestablishing our relationship?"

"Because if you can't confide in me, how can I confide in you? We never had secrets before, especially not ones that affected our whole family."

David's eyes glistened. "Even if I were willing to break my word, which I'm not, I know you'd regret it later. If you knew . . . Please let's all leave the past where it belongs."

"Doc," Cat interrupted, "who's right, here? I mean, I'm not sure who to support. Is Jackson's recovery contingent on forcing David to choose?" Then she looked at her dad. "And you're awfully quiet for someone who's equally involved in the big cover-up, whatever it is."

"I'm quiet because my opinion on this whole subject won't be welcomed by anyone." Their father's posture, his tone, his eyes . . . everything screamed annoyance. The opposite of what needed to happen here today.

"Why'd you come, Dad?" Jackson asked, a little wary and angry at the same time. "Honestly, if you're just going to disengage, then why'd you bother at all? You've always been distant, but without Mom around to balance the scales, it feels like the family is broken. Her heart was the sun, and when she died, all the light and warmth vanished from our little universe."

"More revisionist history and fairy tales." His father heaved a weary sigh. David's deadly expression didn't falter even when their dad shot him a quelling glance. "Your mom was a good woman, but she was human. She wasn't perfect. And she'd be the first person to tell you to make your own 'light' in the world instead of relying on hers."

Jackson absorbed that remark, wondering what his mom would say, and if she could see them now. Cat nervously picked at her nails, and David continued to glare, although now his gaze looked unfocused, as if he, too, were lost in a jungle of agitated thought.

Their father leaned forward, clearly agitated. "You want to know what happened, I'll tell you."

"Dad!" David practically reached across the room to stop him. "Don't. It won't help. In fact, it could undo all Jackson's progress. Please!"

"Christ Almighty, David." Their father shook his head. "I can't believe both my sons are so weak willed that they can't handle life's bumps without running off to Asia or drinking themselves into trouble. If your mom hadn't coddled you all, especially you boys, we wouldn't be sitting here now. And yet you all revere her 'warmth,' the *very* trait that made you so fragile."

His father dismissively waved a hand. "Even if we disagree about that, my God, I'm glad she's not around to see all of this! Whatever you all think of me, *she* admired my strength and practicality. She relied on it to keep all of you secure and grounded in reality. She'd be sorely disappointed to see you floundering and blaming others for your inability to handle disappointment." He then pointed a finger at Cat. "Your sister's the only St. James other than me with any grit."

Cat's face paled. "Don't say it like that . . . like I'm insensitive. I have feelings. I can be warm."

Jackson put an arm around his sister and muttered, "Stand down, hedgehog."

She'd never liked that little nickname, but he hoped it would stop her from fighting with their dad. He didn't want to be responsible for any more family rifts. Maybe he should drop the matter.

Before he had a chance to say anything, David erupted.

"Every time I think I've gotten past everything, you say shit like that, and I could almost hate you, Dad." David's sharply edged voice sliced through the air like a fine knife blade.

Jackson's heart thumped heavily in his chest, but Doc held up his hands. "Everyone, let's dial it back. Emotions, or the lack of them, must be shared without fear of reprisal. Let's stay focused on the trust issue without resorting to personal attacks, which won't help anyone."

Their father stood and practically shooed Doc away with a wave of the hand. "No disrespect, doctor, but my kids know this kind of 'session' isn't for me. I may not be jolly and soft, but I do love you three, and want to see each of you back on track with your lives. So, Jackson, if the truth is what will push you along, here it is.

"I cheated on your mom with Janet. It started before your mom got sick. I was about to talk to her about divorcing but then she got hit with that diagnosis. Janet agreed to wait so I could devote myself to your mom's recovery. I'd hoped, for all of you, and because of what she and I once shared, that she'd survive. But when it became clear that she wouldn't, I quietly spent some time with Janet again. Believe it or not, I needed comfort, too.

"About a month before your mom died, David found out and confronted me. Your mother heard us arguing and begged us to keep this from you and your sister. She considered her family her only legacy and worried that, if you all learned the truth, the family would disintegrate after she died." He paused then, running his hand along the side of his head, resigned. "Maybe she was right, considering how David couldn't handle keeping the promise without drawing all kinds of attention to it. And you," he pointed at Jackson, "respond to trouble by crying into a glass of whiskey every night. I think it's time you both man up and accept life and me, warts and all. Now David can rest easy for never having broken his promise to his mother, and you've got the truth you needed to 'feel better.' I'm fine being the bad guy, but none of you have the right to judge because none of you were in *my* marriage. So are we done now? Can everyone please move on with life, finally?"

Jackson's vision blurred, blotting out whatever reaction Cat and David had to their father's outburst. Pain gripped his chest as if his heart were a stiff joint being stretched beyond its limits. His father's words danced before his eyes, arranged out of order such that he couldn't make any sense of them.

Surely he'd heard wrong. Surely his father had *not* betrayed their mother and then married the very woman who'd stolen him while his wife lay dying of cancer. My God. My. Fucking. God!

And then, an utterly inappropriate bout of hysteria bubbled up. Everyone looked at him with surprise when he laughed, but he couldn't stop. "All this time I thought Dad was the only one who hadn't totally let me down. David had left, Cat kinda stole Hank from me, Alison . . . but I believed Dad was exactly who he'd always been. Steady. Strong. *Honest.*" Then, as everything sank in and the delirium wilted, rage sprouted. "Stupid me. I should've known better."

Jackson heard David sigh and, when he glanced over, he watched his brother bow his head.

"David, how'd you let us be nice to Janet? How'd you let her be part of your *wedding*?" Jackson stood and paced. "My God, I'm gonna be sick. I've been *nice* to Janet. She must've gotten a good chuckle out of that, huh, Dad? Out of how she stole Mom's husband and her kids at a time when Mom couldn't even fight back! How can you respect a woman like that, much less love her? How could you do that to Mom, and to all of us? And now, acting like you and Janet were noble to 'wait' for Mom to die? I can't even look at you right now."

He heard a sniffle and his eyes darted to Cat, who'd withdrawn and was crying. David scooted beside her to offer comfort, but the hedgehog elbowed him away.

David glanced at Doc. "Now what? We're all here. The big secret is out, and as I predicted, it's helped no one. Now everything is *worse*."

"Everyone sit down, please," Doc said. "Everything may feel worse, but it is not worse—not forever. Despite the fresh wave of pain for Jackson and Cat, now there's honesty. The stage is set for healthy intimacy. For real healing. Regardless of what you all think of your father's past actions, he confessed. That can't have been easy, knowing how you'd perceive him."

"He's done exactly what our mother asked him *not* to do." David groaned. "After everything I suffered to keep the family together, he's just ripped it all to shreds."

Doc leaned toward David. "Your loyalty to your mother is laudable, David. I can tell you value your word, which I'm sure Jackson understands makes you eminently trustworthy. However, it seems your mom's request was predicated on the misguided hope that keeping the secret would hold the family together. But secrets rarely keep people together, which is why the family frayed. You were on one side of the globe, your sister floundered in a bad relationship, and Jackson slowly poisoned himself. Had your mother foreseen those consequences, she never would've asked you to burden yourself with such a heavy weight. I'm confident of that."

David sank into the cushion, appearing mollified. But Jackson didn't care. Resentment bubbled and popped like hot oil. Disgust for his father's behavior corroded any hope he'd had of a family reconciliation.

Jackson needed to leave. He couldn't remain surrounded by sadness and lies. By betrayal and more loss. He needed to make this all go away. He needed Gabby. "I'm outta here."

As he headed toward the door, Cat jumped up. "Jackson, wait. Where are you going?"

"Away from all of this," Jackson exploded, his arms raised overhead.

"Jackson . . ." David said, but then his voice trailed off, defeated.

"Let him go," Doc said, not looking at Jackson. "Give him time to figure it out."

Jackson stormed through the waiting room and out the front door, onto the street. The sun shone in a cloudless sky, making him squint. Everything hurt, but he couldn't stand there blinking like an idiot.

He jogged a block and then ducked into a bagel shop. He found an open seat in the far corner, where he had a clear view of the street. Drawing several deep breaths, he beat back the hard lump wedged in his chest. No way would he lose his shit here amid the scent of garlic and barley malt in this tiny shop in Vermont, despite the fact that he couldn't think straight. Not when his thoughts played leapfrog—his mom's discovery, David's knowing of it for so long, Janet triumphantly taking over. That last thought made him want to punch something.

He took out his phone and called Gabby, but when she answered, he couldn't speak.

"Jackson?" she repeated. "Are you there? What's wrong?"

"Everything," he managed. "Everything is wrong. I need you. Can you come?"

# CHAPTER NINETEEN

When Gabby pulled into the parking lot of the bagel store, Jackson practically dove into the passenger seat.

"Sorry it took me a while," she said. "Your family showed up as I was leaving. Your brother, in particular, seemed distraught."

"You didn't tell them you were picking me up, did you?"

"No, but I didn't enjoy lying to them."

"Sorry." Jackson winced. "I can't see them now. Especially not my dad."

Gabby had never seen him so discomposed. He'd obviously speared his hair with his hands more than once. His normally bronzed skin had turned ashen. His eyes had lost all traces of the golden sparkle that typically brightened them. His jaw, firm and tight, twitched.

"You won't have to. They left because of your dad's appointment. I did promise to text when I heard from you, so I waited a few minutes and then texted David." She reached for his hand. He clasped it and followed her without another word. "We have to pick up Luc, but then we can go home and talk."

Jackson stared out the window in silence. Gabby spent that time thinking about how telling him about Noah's threats and all her fears would only make his day worse.

How could she do it when Jackson looked on the verge of a nervous breakdown? Thankfully he'd gone to the bagel shop instead of the liquor store, but if she shared her concerns and suggested they take a break while she figured stuff out, would it push him over the edge?

"I'll be right back," she said as she parked in front of the day care center.

"Okay." Jackson didn't move.

When she returned with Luc, her son's face lit up upon seeing Jackson.

"Jackson, look." Luc handed Jackson one of his crafts—a turkey made with a brown paper plate and colorful feathers.

"Wow, buddy, this is awesome. I like the googly eyes." Jackson rolled his own eyes while he shook the plate, making Luc giggle.

Gabby's heart squeezed hard as she backed out of the parking lot and headed home.

"Dat's for you, and deez are for Mama, Pappy, and Dada." Luc kicked his feet in the car seat, carefree and happy like a three-year-old should be.

Gabby noticed Jackson's eyes water. His voice wobbled when he spoke. "Thanks, Luc. I'll bring this with me to Connecticut, so it'll be like you're at the table with me at Thanksgiving."

"Okay," Luc said, unaware that it had been Jackson's gentle way of telling Luc he wouldn't be around by then.

"Should we give him a name?" Jackson asked, still turned around, facing Luc. "Tom?"

"Not Tom!" Luc giggled, like Tom Turkey was the silliest name he'd ever heard. "Fwog!"

"You want me to name him Frog? Frog Turkey?" Jackson asked in a silly voice, then he shook the plate again. "Guess that makes as much sense as these googly eyes."

Luc clapped with another giggle. And then, without hesitation, said, "Mama, I'm hungwee!"

"When we get home, Mommy has to talk to Jackson first. You can show Pappy your crafts and watch TV for a little bit until I can cook."

They arrived at the house and found her dad walking around the driveway, building up his stamina.

"Come over when you're ready," Jackson said to her, then he squatted and tapped Luc's nose. "I love Frog Turkey, Luc. Thanks."

He stood and made his way to the apartment while she took Luc's hand and led him inside, hoping she could get Luc settled quickly.

~

As soon as Gabby entered the apartment, Jackson gathered her in his arms and held her. No kisses, no words, just a bear hug in which he clearly sought comfort rather than offered it.

Her heart ached and she didn't even know what had happened. She did know something had broken his spirit. Something big enough to make him walk out on his family, and maybe big enough to undo everything he'd been working so hard to accept.

Gabby's stomach burned as anxiety and guilt oozed through her veins. Why *did* people usually end up hurting each other? His family, Alison, Noah, her mother, and on and on. She yearned to comfort Jackson, but too soon he'd view her as yet another person who let him down.

"Whatever happened, whatever happens next, you must believe everything will be okay, Jackson. We all heal with time, and every day is another chance to start over and be happy." Gabby stroked his back and head. "Whatever was said in therapy, it seems to me like your family loves you very much."

"Love?" Jackson abruptly released her. "Honestly, I'm beginning to think no one but you knows what the hell that word means."

"What it means? Maybe it's a state of being—of affection, esteem, concern, memories, friendship—just everything you feel about another person all rolled up in your heart."

"You make it sound like some whim. Like there's no obligation or commitment." He eased away, forehead wrinkled. "I don't agree. Love is a choice. An act. A promise you make every day. And love doesn't lie. Love doesn't betray. Love doesn't give up when things get hard."

Gabby swallowed the lump in her throat. The more he spoke, the more certain she became that her decision would deal him a knockout punch. If she'd eaten anything for lunch, she'd surely throw it up now. "Why don't you tell me what happened so I can understand why you're so hurt?"

Jackson paced the room. She stood, waiting for him to speak. When he finally recited the events that unfolded in therapy, the weight of his anguish consumed the room. His continual pacing made her nearly dizzy as she tried to keep up with his words, to understand who'd done what to whom. How could she help him accept all this when she, too, would be handing him news he wouldn't like?

Her deafening thoughts temporarily preoccupied her, keeping her from realizing that he'd finally stopped talking. He'd stopped, period. No pacing. No movement at all. He stood by the window, looking out at nothing in particular.

Given the state of her own mind, she couldn't imagine the chaos inside his. She crossed to him and, from behind, wrapped her arms around his waist and rested her cheek against his back, wishing she could stay like this forever. Wishing Noah would disappear from her life again instead of using her son and lack of resources against her.

Jackson didn't stiffen, but he didn't turn around at first. When he finally did, he kissed her. Not the hungry, passionate kisses he'd showered her with before, nor the tender, loving ones she'd enjoyed so often. These were angry kisses. Kisses meant only to distract himself.

These kisses hurt—not from roughness, but because she could feel all his pain.

He stopped suddenly, his expression filled with misery. Before he could cry in front of her, she reached up around his neck and pulled him into another hug. She knew he was proud and wouldn't want her to see him fall apart. If he cried over her shoulder, he could pretend she didn't know how much he ached.

"I'm sorry," he murmured.

"Don't be." She stroked his hair. "Don't ever be sorry for having a heart, Jackson."

He heaved a sigh in her arms and then eased away. "I don't know what to do with all this." He gestured like he was holding a heavy weight in front of his chest.

"Running from it won't help." Gabby immediately pressed her lips together, wishing she'd have kept quiet and let him talk.

He scrubbed his hands over his face before he sputtered, "I know what my dad did wasn't about me. Yet, he was willing to rip apart our family, so in a way, it was about me. Honestly, I knew he was a cold fucker, but I never thought him devious. And the worst part," his voice cracked, "is knowing my mom went to her grave humiliated and heart-broken. How do I forgive him for that when it makes my stomach hurt this much?"

"I'm so sorry." Gabby hugged herself, unsure of what else she could do or say.

"On top of all those feelings, I hate myself for forcing that secret out into the open. I basically destroyed my mom's last wish and, at the same time, forced all this shit on Cat. I'm so fucking selfish, I can't stand it."

He covered his eyes with one hand and she heard him gulp for air. "All this time David's been protecting us like Mom asked. The only way I can honor her wish now is by not letting this tear the family apart. But God, how can I deal with Janet? I hate her. Hate her! She's as bad as Alison . . ." He swiped a tear from his cheek.

Gabby touched his shoulder. "Talk to David. I'm sure he went through all these emotions, too. He can help you cope. I know he wants to do that, Jackson. And now that you know why he left, maybe you can finally really forgive him, too."

Jackson stared at her. He shrugged with a slight nod of the head, which she took as a good sign. "I suppose. Truthfully, I don't know how to do this sober. God knows I want a drink right now. It'd be so much easier to tune out than to have all this noise in my head. Thank God I have you to keep me from going over the edge."

She froze. His comment hadn't been a surprise, but it bothered her nonetheless. A sense of déjà vu made her angry with him for putting her in this position like her mom had done time and time again. For somehow foisting responsibility for keeping him sober on *her.*

All these weeks he'd done such a good job of hiding his cravings that she'd convinced herself his drinking problem wasn't a real problem. But looking at him now, she knew the truth. His doctor had been right. He wasn't ready. And she didn't have the ability to raise her son, run her business, fight Noah, *and* take on responsibility for seeing Jackson through his recovery. Although painful, he'd confirmed for her the decision she knew she had to make.

"You won't like this, Jackson, but I have to say it." She set her hands on her hips.

"Say what?" he asked, eyes wide.

"Your dad didn't have to confess. He only did it because you said you needed it and could handle it. He did it to help you, so now you have to be as good as your word. They all came up here for you. They're all dealing with the same truths you are. Now it's up to *you* to figure out how to move forward like you promised, without a damn drink, and without counting on me to stop you. You have to learn to forgive, trust, and accept everyone with all their flaws, like they love and accept you with yours."

"Flaws are one thing. These are lies!"

"Not all lies are equal. If David had never found out about the affair, would your mother have told any of you? Would you be so angry with *her* if she kept her marital troubles private? And David didn't lie. He kept a promise. If you choose to see it as a lie, then at least acknowledge it was one meant to protect you." The next thing Gabby said had more than one meaning, not that Jackson would know it. "I'd do any-thing—*anything*—to protect Luc, and I sure hope I don't have to justify every mistake I ever make to him—or anyone—just to prove my love. We're all human. We've all hurt people, intentionally and unintentionally. But it doesn't mean we don't love them. Who made you the judge and jury of people's sins? Leave that to God. Honestly, if you go around expecting perfection, you'll never be happy."

"I don't expect perfection." He grabbed hold of her hands. "All I want is for people to be more like you."

"Me?" Her heart thudded, knowing she was about to tumble off whatever pedestal he'd put her on.

"Yes, you. Honest, kind, and a straight shooter." He gathered her in his arms. "At least with you I don't have to worry about a sucker punch."

Tears filled her eyes before she could stop them. "I'm not so brave."

"Sure you are." He grinned for the first time all afternoon. "Why does that make you cry?"

She bit her lip, her breaths coming in short gulps. "I'm really not so brave. At least, not when it comes to Luc."

"You're awesome with Luc. Look at how you took on motherhood when other choices would've made your life easier." He hugged her tight, his own troubles apparently taking a backseat while he tried to soothe her.

"I love him Jackson. More than anything . . . or anyone."

"Of course you do." He looked at her with such fondness, she wanted to disappear.

"Oh, God, Jackson, I wish we had more time . . . I . . ." She pressed her palm to her forehead, chest tight. "I'm sorry."

"Sorry for what?"

"Noah served me legal papers this morning." She bent at the waist for a second to catch her breath. "He wants to establish paternity."

"So?" Jackson shrugged. "You know he's Luc's dad, right?"

"Yes."

"I'm confused." He tilted his head. "Why is this a big deal?"

"I never put Noah's name on Luc's birth certificate because we weren't married. Legally I didn't have to acknowledge paternity. But now he wants to make it official so he can seek custody."

"No judge is going to take Luc from you, Gabby. But if Noah wants to finally step up for his son and get some kind of regular visitation, isn't that better for Luc in the long run?"

Jackson's blind spot when it came to fathers' rights amazed her.

"You don't get it. This isn't about Luc. It's a power play. Ever since my mom's accusations, he's been sniffing you out. He found out about your lawsuit and now he's labeling you a violent drunk. He talked to a lawyer, and he thinks that between my having you around and my mom's reappearance, I'm putting Luc at risk."

Jackson's expression shifted from comfort to something distant, but she pressed on. "*I* know it's not true. You're wonderful with Luc. But Noah's a native son of Winhall, and a cop that most people like. I was a teen mom with a drug-addict mother—one I stupidly invited back into my life recently. Noah will paint this whole situation to look much different than it is."

Her body sagged. "I'm afraid, Jackson. I'm afraid to risk him convincing a judge I'm unfit. I just can't. Who knows, maybe Noah would even use my dad's stroke to show that the whole situation here is unstable." She looked at Jackson, whose emotions she couldn't discern. "All I know is, if we're not together, he won't press this. You're leaving in a few days anyway, so . . ." She paused, unsure how to finish the thought. How to say it seemed rather pointless, because long-distance relationships were tough even without all of the baggage she and Jackson had between them. "I hate all of this, but I'm too afraid to take a chance. I couldn't live with the worst-case scenario if I fight and lose."

"Have you talked to a lawyer?" Jackson asked.

"Not yet."

He brightened a little. "Don't get all worked up until a lawyer weighs in on Noah's threats. I don't believe any judge would take Luc out of this home. Besides, I'm not violent, nor am I drinking."

"But you *want* to drink." She bit her lip.

"Come again?" His brows rose.

"A little while ago, you said you needed a drink and I'm the only thing that stopped you. What if I hadn't been around? Would you have gone to a bar? That's a lot of pressure on me. I can't be the only thing standing between you and alcohol. It's too much. I've lived that way once, always worrying if I'd trigger a bad impulse. I can't do it again. It's not fair to me, and it's really not fair to Luc."

"Gabby, I didn't mean it literally." Jackson threw out his hands.

"You say that now, but I heard it in your voice and saw it in your eyes. That desperation. Heard the relief in your voice when you said you were glad you had me to stop you. Maybe if I hadn't dealt with my mom all those years I'd feel differently. I don't know. I *do* know I need to give one hundred percent to my son. If I have to worry about you not being able to handle a tough day without drinking, or worry every week about Noah scheming to manipulate Luc because he wants you out of the picture, none of us will be happy."

Jackson stepped back, arms crossed. "What are you saying, exactly?"

"Maybe we should've listened to your doctor. You need more time to get yourself together. To deal with your family and to go a longer period of time without drinking before you get involved with me, or anyone." Her nose tingled as tears clogged her throat. "I think, since you're leaving, we should break things off for now so I can protect Luc, and you can heal the *right* way. Maybe in six months or so we can talk and see . . ."

The only physical reaction she noted was a slight slackening of his jaw. No explosion of anger, thank God. No pleading. No tears.

He turned away again, staring out the window. His shoulders bunched. The air in the room seemed suddenly colder.

"Luc's hungry," he said without turning around. "You should go make him and your dad dinner now."

Not the retort she'd expected.

"Jackson, you're freaking me out a little." She approached him. "Talk to me. What are you thinking?"

He remained closed off. "I'm thinking you should go."

"I'm afraid to leave you. I don't want you to drink."

"I think we've just established that that shouldn't be your concern."

Gabby approached him, worried by the flat tone of his voice and the fact that he wouldn't look at her. "Can we finish this discussion after dinner?"

"Don't think so." He shook his head.

"Tomorrow, then?"

"No."

"Jackson, this isn't easy for me. This is the last thing I *want*." She reached out to touch his arm. "I lo—"

"Don't. Don't say that word. God, I'm so sick of people tossing that word around but not standing behind it." He crossed his arms and looked at his feet, his back still turned. "Please, go."

Gabby swiped the tears from her cheeks and stumbled down the stairs. She glanced up at his window, but didn't see his silhouette watching her. Pinching her runny nose, she darted into her house.

Of the hundred images she had of Jackson, she could only hope her very last one wouldn't be of the stony man she'd just left behind.

# CHAPTER TWENTY

Jackson willed himself not to go to the window. Not to watch her disappear from his life. Not to acknowledge the newest hole in his heart.

He sat at the dining table and set his forehead against the cool, wood tabletop, remembering when she'd promised to stand by him, right here in this room. But when the first test came, she caved. Bailed on him, like others in the past. Didn't even call a lawyer first to figure out whether Noah's threats were credible. Hadn't even asked Jackson for help. Not to mention dumping this on him in the wake of his own lousy day.

The effort he'd put into the past five weeks now seemed an utter waste of time. The day's revelations had demolished whatever strides he'd thought he'd made in therapy and with Gabby.

His head throbbed thanks to the uncompromising thoughts knocking against his skull. The sense of isolation—something he'd thought Gabby had eliminated—clamored the loudest. He sat, alone once more, with no one to talk to.

Of course, he remembered one friend he could call on. One who always made him feel better—or numb, in any case. Ol' Jack Daniel's. A friend he could trust.

Jackson snatched his keys from the counter and stalked out the door. When he pulled into Mulligan's parking lot, his body fairly shook from the adrenaline rush of anticipation. A seductive craving pulled at him despite images of Gabby, Vivi, Cat, David, and Hank temporarily disrupting its grip.

Perspiration dampened his skin, making his shirt stick to him like masking tape. He tightened his hands around the steering wheel until he couldn't fight the urge anymore. For what, or whom, did his sobriety matter now? Everyone probably expected him to end up here again, so he might as well start now.

Jackson got out of the car and strode inside. He hefted himself onto a stool at one corner and, within a minute, Tess sauntered over to him.

"Hello, handsome. Nice to see you again. What can I get you?" She flipped her hair over her shoulder and flashed a flirty smile. "Another root beer?"

He aimed for a polite grin. "Jack on the rocks."

"You got it." She winked.

When she turned away, he added, "Make it a double."

While she fixed his drink, his skin itched. He looked around at the others in the pub. All men. Probably men escaping their troubles, like Jackson.

Tess set the glass in front of him. "Want a snack, too?"

"Nope."

"How 'bout some company?" She leaned forward, the contents of her V-neck shirt on prominent display.

Tess may have been forward, but at least she didn't pretend to be someone she wasn't. Maybe he should take advantage of what she offered as another way to block out his pain, but his heart wanted only one woman. Stupid heart had never served him well. "No, thanks. Kind of need to be alone."

"If you change your mind, gimme a whistle." She touched his hand and then wandered to a customer at the other side of the bar.

Jackson stared at the glass, twisting it in circles, watching the amber liquid slosh against the rim.

He lifted it to his nose and sniffed. Instantly a jumble of hazy memories passed through his mind. With them came unwelcome hints of shame and regret, of a cold so bone-deep it hurt, and of fear. Fear of what might happen if he put his lips to the rim and tasted the bite of alcohol.

The mighty call of numb bliss gripped him, urging him to tip the glass and slide into that place where his feelings didn't claw at his insides. Where reminders that all of his relationships had fallen apart today wouldn't hurt so much.

He continued twisting the glass, his thoughts wandering to his mother, who'd borne her broken heart with dignity and grace. A new wave of shame consumed him for being unable to follow her example.

He rubbed his eyes with his palms. His dad had been right about one thing. His mother wouldn't be proud of his behavior. She'd asked David for that damn promise to keep her family—her legacy—intact. Seeing him torn apart this way would've killed her if the cancer hadn't. *Sorry, Mom*, he thought as he grasped the tumbler once more.

"Well, well. Looky here." Using his phone, Noah snapped a photo of Jackson holding the drink. "Thanks, buddy. I couldn't have asked for better evidence."

"Fuck off." Jackson stared at the full glass of whiskey. What did it matter? Gabby had walked away. Everyone kept pressuring him to cave in to Doug. His family seemed even more lost to him than before.

"Maybe I should buy you that drink to celebrate the fact that Gabby's going to dump you the minute she sees this photo."

"You're too late, so send the photo or don't. Doesn't matter to me."

Noah cocked his head, as if trying to determine whether or not Jackson had just lied to him. "That so?"

Normally Noah's smug attitude would anger Jackson, but other thoughts preoccupied him. He thought about Luc, an innocent victim in his father's schemes. The trusting little boy who'd embraced Jackson completely and healed a little part of his heart. He thought about Vivi and the baby she'd have this spring. Of how much he wanted to be part of that child's life when he or she came into the world. He thought about the child he might've had already, and the children he wanted one day, which would never happen if he didn't learn how to control himself and cope with pain.

The combination of thoughts drove him to shove the whiskey across the bar.

"Thanks, Noah," Jackson said, rising from his stool.

"Thanks?" Noah chuckled.

"Yeah, thanks for following me around and spying on me. For being such an asshole. In a twisted way, you just stopped me from making a big mistake."

Jackson tossed twelve bucks on the bar.

"*I'm* the asshole?" Noah rolled his eyes. "*You're* the one with a drinking problem."

"Yeah, guess I am. But I'm *not* the one who walked out on my pregnant girlfriend. I'm not the one who didn't go to the hospital to witness my son's birth. I'm not the one who has neglected to support my son for three years. And I'm not so desperate and insecure that I'd resort to threats and bullying in order to control a woman I'd already wronged in so many ways." Jackson smiled as smugly as Noah. "That's all on you. Now, if you'll excuse me, I've got some bags to pack."

"Don't let the door hit you on your way out." Noah sat on the stool and motioned for Tess.

Jackson took two steps then stopped and turned around. "Now that I'm leaving, Gabby's going to need lots more help with Luc until her dad's fully recovered. Be a man, for *once*, and step up."

Jackson stalked off and didn't stop until he got to his car. He'd entered the bar at dusk, but now all traces of the sun had vanished. Dried leaves rustled around the parking lot. He inhaled the brisk clean air feeling marginally better about himself for having withstood temptation despite the shittiest day in recent history.

He drove to his apartment thinking about next steps. Things he needed to do to make his mom proud and move on with his life. *Start small,* he thought. Pack, drive home, get some sleep. Those things he could manage, barely, as long as he didn't think about the big stuff.

Once he'd packed his duffle, he thought to leave without saying goodbye. Through the window, he stared at the little house across the way and couldn't budge his feet. He'd known Gabby less than six weeks, but she'd fundamentally changed him. He loved her, even though he'd never said the words. Despite the fact she hadn't been as brave as he'd thought, he couldn't deny his feelings, or pretend not to understand her valid concerns.

It'd be wrong to ask her to live in fear of his sobriety, and to risk her son's security. His cynicism would surely snuff out her light over time, and he'd hate himself for that. It was better this way. Better that he be forced to leave before he did any real damage here.

He tore a sheet of paper from a notepad and dashed off a note, which he left on the table along with the apartment key. Frog Turkey lay there, googly eyes staring at him. Jackson's eyes stung while recalling Luc's elated face and giggle. Although Frog Turkey would be a painful reminder, he couldn't leave him behind.

Jackson took one last look around, memorizing every detail of the room. A room in which he'd learned to hope again. To love again.

Those hopes and his heart may have been bruised today, but tomorrow would be another chance to start over. Even if Gabby hadn't been able to stand by him, she'd taught him that much.

He glanced at his watch. If he took off now, he'd be home by ten. His text pinged. Reluctantly, he looked at it. A wave of sadness crashed over him as he read that Hank's mom, who'd been suffering from early-onset Alzheimer's for years, had passed away this evening. Jackson didn't have to imagine the tremendous pain his friend felt tonight. Perhaps the need to attend the funeral and support Hank was another sign that the time had come for Jackson to leave Vermont.

Resolved about where he needed to go, he texted David and Cat to let them know he was safe and coming home. Then, without any fanfare, he shut off the light and closed the door on what might've been.

~

Gabby opened her puffy eyes wishing it weren't dawn. A restless night had left her drained and confused. She'd watched Jackson's Jeep pull out last evening not long after she'd received Noah's text showing Jackson with a drink in his hand.

She'd wanted to believe Noah Photoshopped it or found an old photo on Instagram, but she'd recognized Mulligan's interior.

By ten, Jackson hadn't yet returned, so she went to the apartment to wait for him. When she'd found his note and realized he'd packed up all his things and gone, the air had left her lungs.

Reaching across to her nightstand now, she picked up his note to torment herself again.

> *Gabby,*
> *Thank you for being a friend when I needed one, and for reminding me that there are still things in life worth fighting for. Although I understand why we can't be more than a fond memory, you will always be in my heart. Take care of yourself and your son, and be happy.*
> *Love, Jackson*
> *P.S. Tell Luc I had to take Frog Turkey on an adventure.*

New tears welled in her eyes as her throat tightened. She pressed the note to her chest and rolled to her side, limbs heavy with grief. Luc's pitter-patter sounded before he entered her room and broke the stillness.

He crawled into her bed. "Mama, why you cwying?"

Gabby swiped her tears. "I had a bad dream. But I'll feel better if you snuggle me, buster."

Luc happily complied by nestling against her. She held him tightly, stroking his hair and breathing in the sweet smell of his skin. Nothing mattered more than him, not even her broken heart.

She'd lay down her life to protect him, so if giving up Jackson was the price she had to pay to keep Luc safe and secure with her and her dad, then that was what she must do. And if Jackson was drinking again, she really needed to say good-bye anyway.

"Mama, can we make cocoa?" Luc pleaded.

"Cocoa sounds perfect. Let's go." Gabby heaved herself from the comfort of her blankets and found her slippers.

Luc scampered ahead, calling out for his pappy. Today seemed like another normal day in his life. Hopefully he wouldn't react badly to Jackson's absence, or at least not for longer than an hour.

When she arrived in the kitchen, her father had already poured Luc a bowl of Cheerios and started the coffee. He was whistling and fixing himself an egg. The great strides he'd made in therapy this past week greatly improved his mood. He expected to be cleared to drive any day. Without Jackson to help, that day couldn't come soon enough.

"The Wilsons are coming up tonight for the weekend, so make sure Jackson turns up the heat and leaves a light on for them on his rounds today." Her dad put bread in the toaster and cracked an egg in the pan.

"Jackson's gone, Dad." She couldn't look at him. "But I'll make sure it's done."

"Jackson's all gone?" Luc's bottom lip pushed out.

"Yes, honey." Gabby sat beside Luc and smoothed Luc's hair. "He had to go home, but he took Frog Turkey with him."

"Why?" Luc asked.

Gabby drew a breath and averted her eyes from him and her dad's quizzing gaze. "He was only here on vacation. He had to go home to his family and his work."

"How long, Mama?" Luc scooped a spoonful of cereal, half of which fell off the spoon and onto the table.

"A long time, I'm afraid." Gabby's voice cracked.

Thankfully, her father didn't ask any questions until Luc finished eating and left the table.

"I thought Jackson would be here the rest of the week," her dad finally said, flipping his egg.

"He changed his mind." She got up from her seat and placed her cup in the dishwasher.

"What happened?"

"Noah." Her voice cracked. "Noah started paperwork to mess with custody. God, if only I'd have listened to you and not responded to Mom's letter, she'd never have come, and Noah wouldn't have suspected anything about Jackson's past."

Of course, Jackson's past might now once again be part of his present. Something she didn't want to believe or share with anyone, including her dad.

"I know I wasn't supportive of your relationship with Jackson, but only because I worried you'd end up hurt. It seemed doomed, for one reason or another." Her dad's eyes turned hard as he buttered his toast. "But damn that Noah Jefferson. He's gone too far. We need to figure out how to prevent him from holding these kinds of threats over your head in the future. Otherwise, he'll start using Luc to make you dance like a puppet until he gets whatever he wants."

"What he wants is a second chance." Gabby frowned. "He claims to want us to be a real family."

Her dad's eyes narrowed, but before he spit out what might've been another string of insults, he held his tongue. Finally he asked, "What do you want?"

"Jackson."

"That's not what I meant." Her father's sigh carried a solemn note. "Once upon a time you did love Noah. Is there any chance you'd rekindle those old feelings?"

"How can you ask that?" Gabby leaned against the counter.

"Because I've been around long enough to know love is never rational. And I also know what I was willing to forgive of your mom for years and years." He tugged her into a hug. "You shouldn't live your whole life alone, or here with me. You deserve to be loved and be happy. Maybe have another child. This is a small town, and there aren't that many single men your age. Noah was young and full of himself, and probably scared back then. I'm not giving him a pass, or condoning this bullshit he's pulling now, but he is Luc's father. If you decide to make a go of something for Luc's sake, I'll support you."

She eased away and handed him his breakfast plate.

"I don't want to be alone, but I'll never settle for someone who abandoned me when I needed him most. For a guy who has slept around so much, he's been with almost every girl I know. No, Dad, I don't much like Noah anymore, let alone love him."

"Fair enough. I only wanted to be sure." He finally sat and cut into his breakfast. "As soon as I eat, I'm going to call a lawyer and see if he even has a leg to stand on."

Her dad had faith in the legal system, but Gabby had seen the news enough to know it got things wrong as often as it got things right. Besides, Noah wouldn't be pressing all of this if the lawyer he talked to didn't think he had any chance.

"Dad, we can barely pay our bills, let alone waste money on lawyers." She raked her hair with her hands.

Between bites, he said, "We can't afford not to spend money to protect Luc and you from Noah's bullshit, Gabby."

"I don't have time to argue, now. I've got to get Luc to day care and then get to work. We can talk later." She kissed her dad's cheek and went to gather Luc.

～

Gabby tucked her phone away after the thirtieth time of staring at the picture of Jackson eyeing his glass of whiskey. She regretted her final two memories of him—the rigid set of his spine when she left the apartment, and the depressing, entranced gaze in the photo. That damn photo had been driving her crazy for almost twenty-four hours.

She couldn't take not knowing what had happened. The fact that Jackson had left without seeing her proved he didn't want to hear from her, and quizzing him about drinking would be the absolute last thing she'd want to do if he were willing to talk to her. With no other option, she swung by Tess's house in the middle of the afternoon.

Her unplanned visit would probably shock her friend almost as much as it surprised Gabby, but she couldn't move on until she had an answer from someone she trusted.

"Gabby?" Tess looked around when she opened the door. "What's up?"

"Long story, Tess," she replied. "Can I come in?"

"Sure." Tess waved her in, and Gabby took a seat on the sofa. "I was making a Thanksgiving list. My mom needs help this year, although you and I both know I'm no cook!"

Gabby smiled, although Thanksgiving held little appeal to her today. "I won't be long. I have a question . . . about Jackson."

Tess sat in a chair and put her feet up on the ottoman. "Why can't you ask him?"

"He's gone, and I doubt he wants to hear from me." Gabby wrinkled her nose.

"Why not?" Tess leaned forward, interested. The girl loved gossip, but Gabby didn't wish to be fodder for the local rumor mill.

"He had to get back to his life, and Noah stirred up some trouble."

"I think Noah wants you back, or at least, that's the word on the street." Tess flashed a conspiratorial smirk.

*Word on the street.* Like or it not, Gabby's life would be discussed by folks with or without her consent.

"I don't care what Noah wants. And I'd rather not get into a whole discussion about everything right now. What I really came to ask is whether Jackson drank last night?" Gabby held her breath.

"He didn't order root beer, if that's what you're asking." Tess raised her brows.

"Noah sent me a photo of Jackson holding a glass of whiskey. Did he drink it?"

"Ah . . . so the root beer wasn't a sweet tooth thing, was it?" Tess tipped her head. Gabby remained silent, unwilling to spill Jackson's secrets.

"Tess, please tell me the truth." Gabby looked at her hands, afraid to hear the answer.

Her friend sat back, sighing. "I can't promise he didn't take a sip, but when he left, the glass was still full."

Gabby exhaled a whoosh of relief. "Thank you. That's what I'd hoped to hear."

"Seems kinda moot now, if he's gone and all." Tess shrugged.

Those words struck like a kick in the gut. "I still can't believe he took off without a word. Of course, right from the start I knew he'd eventually be gone. Maybe this was better . . . not prolonging it? Doesn't feel better, though. Feels unfinished. Empty. At least, it does for me. I suppose he'll be swept back into his normal life soon, which is surely more exciting than anything going on around here."

"Um, *any* place has to be more exciting than this one." Tess laughed, and Gabby couldn't help but agree.

Their small community offered a certain charm and security, but without Jackson, the cold air now just felt bitter. The sun shone too harshly. Ominous-looking leafless trees stood everywhere, like prison guards.

"I should get going. Need to pick up Luc and then make dinner. Ah, the glamorous life I lead."

"At least you had it a little more interesting for a while. That's more than I can say."

"True." Gabby knew she should be grateful for the few weeks she'd spent in Jackson's sturdy arms. Flattered, even, by the fact that he'd wanted their relationship to continue, or at least he had until she'd panicked and cut him out. Regret wrung her gut. She needed fresh air. "See you later."

~

The clock by her bed ticked as Gabby poured her feelings onto the page in front of her.

> *Mom,*
>
> *I opened myself up to you, hoping that we could eventually have some kind of relationship. I'd wanted to believe that you'd finally gotten your habit under control. That you'd honestly wanted a relationship with me.*
>
> *But when you disrespected my express wishes and barged into our party drunk, you proved that my feelings would always come second to yours. Worse, your behavior and exaggerated accusations about Jackson gave Noah ammunition to question my judgment, which has put him in a position to threaten me with a custody battle.*
>
> *Once again, you've cost me a piece of my heart, but you will never get another chance to do that to me. Please do not write, call, or show up. I'm going to put a restraining order in place to make sure you never come near Luc so you can never hurt him as you've hurt me.*
>
> *A part of me will always be sorry for what happened to you, and to our family. I'm also sorry for all the things you've suffered. And I'm sorry that things couldn't have turned out differently for us. You should know, although I'm furious and so sad, I don't hate you. I feel sorry for you.*

*I will pray that you don't end up dead from an overdose someday, but I cannot let myself feel responsible for your choices. And I cannot leave the door to my heart open to you any longer.*

*I will always love the mother I knew until middle school. I wish we could go back and start over from there, but we both know that's impossible. So I must finally say good-bye.*

*Gabby*

Wiping her nose with her sleeve, Gabby folded the note and then licked the envelope and sealed it. She shut off the lamp and then snuggled under her covers. Step one of the advice from the lawyer her dad had spoken with earlier was now in place. Now she had to think about Noah and Luc.

Naturally she thought about Jackson and how he'd staunchly defended fathers' rights. She thought about what Luc might want, despite Noah being far from Father of the Year material, and about what resentment Luc might one day feel if Gabby didn't find some way to cooperate with Noah.

Resigned to the fact she'd always be inextricably tied to Noah, she closed her eyes and began to make a mental list of worst-case scenarios.

# Chapter Twenty-One

Gentlemen, this will be short and sweet. Once you each sign here and here, we will deliver the funds and settle this case." Oliver pushed the documents in front of Jackson and Doug.

Refusing to let Doug see him squirm, Jackson donned a business-like expression while mentally humming the melody of The Rolling Stones' "Satisfaction." Thinking about the thirty-five grand he'd be shelling out made him sick, but he and his ego would survive the hit.

Last month, he'd spent a majority of his three-hour drive home from Vermont thinking about his business, his goals, his life. He'd considered his crew, David and Oliver's advice, and Gabby's opinion about his pride taking precedence over more important issues.

Most importantly, he'd accepted one inescapable truth: he had no one to blame but himself. Had he addressed his issues earlier or in a healthier manner, he wouldn't be in this position today.

Thirty-five grand may be more than he'd ever dreamed this would cost, but it was a lot less than the hundred grand Doug had expected. All in all, he'd write it off as the price for moving forward with his plans. For regaining control of his life and his future.

Oliver handed Doug a pen and said, "Mr. Kilpatrick, as you know, if you speak of any of the incidents related to or leading up to this settlement, including the amount, it will be a breach of the agreement, and Mr. St. James will be entitled to a full refund plus additional damages."

"I know." Doug signed the documents and pushed them away, as did Jackson.

Oliver collected the papers and spoke to Doug and his lawyer. "Gentlemen, if you two would like to remain here until we receive confirmation of the wire transfer, Melissa will bring you coffee." Then he turned to David and Jackson. "Perhaps you two would prefer to wait in David's office?"

Jackson nodded, eager to absent himself from Doug's presence. He couldn't bring himself to shake the man's hand, so he merely nodded at Doug and his lawyer before leaving the conference room.

"Thanks, Oliver." He shook Oliver's hand. "Glad that's finally over."

"Put this behind you now and enjoy your Christmas. Good luck." Oliver smiled, then walked in the opposite direction from David and Jackson.

"Shall we?" David gestured to the hallway on the right.

Jackson followed David down a long, smoky-glass-lined hallway to his swanky office. He took a seat opposite his brother's enormous mahogany desk and stared at the Manhattan skyline through the large window. The leather-and-lemon scent of the Midtown office smelled of money, and his brother looked the picture of success sitting in its midst.

David's career suited him, with its constant brain-crunching demands. His brother thrived when mentally challenged. Unlike their father, however, Jackson knew his brother actually loved his work more than the money or the fancy office or the titles and committee positions.

For as long as he could remember, Jackson had also tried to emulate his father. But now he realized he'd gone about it the wrong way. Instead of pursuing his own values and passions, Jackson had strived to impress his father and prove himself the equal of his brother or sister. Ironically, freedom had been the unexpected silver lining in no longer caring for his father's approval.

David withdrew an envelope from his desk drawer and handed it to Jackson. "Here's that other information you wanted. I hope it helps."

Jackson set the envelope on his lap and looked at his brother. "David, I need something else, too."

"Anything." He waited.

"For the past several weeks, I've been doing a lot of thinking about my life and what I want. What I need. I've decided to sell my business."

"Why?" David leaned forward. "You've worked so hard to build it up. This settlement is intended to make sure you can keep things going."

"I know all that, but I'm going to make some big changes, and I can't do it here."

"What changes?"

"I want to live a different life. A quieter one with less pressure—less everything. I want to start fresh and build something that makes me really happy, and a big business isn't it."

"Where will you go?"

Jackson held up the envelope. "Depends on what this says, in part."

"What about your projects, your employees?"

"There's a competitor in Fairfield, Mosley Construction. He's got a solid little outfit and can absorb my guys and finish my existing projects. He and I have spoken a bit. I need to speak with my existing clients, but I need you to make sure everything is done right and I'm fairly compensated." Jackson crossed his feet. "I'm going to lease my house while it's on the market. Hopefully it'll sell soon and I'll have another bundle of cash to invest."

"So you'll be leaving the area just when we're finally okay." David sighed, resignation weighing heavily in his tone. "How about you and Dad? Any progress there?"

"Not really. I spoke with him briefly to tell him my plans, but it's gonna take some time before I'm able to see Janet and him without feeling shitty." Jackson grunted a laugh. "Any tips?"

"Afraid not. I never could've gotten through everything without Vivi. She's helped me be more forgiving. I try to be worthy of her by taking her advice when it comes to Dad. He's not perfect, and he's made some *terrible* choices, but he also did a lot of things right over the years. I can't erase the good just because the bad is so distasteful."

"I suppose. Maybe acceptance will be my New Year's resolution."

"That's right around the corner." David leaned back in his chair. "Will you stick around for Christmas? I can't believe you're actually thinking of moving away. I'll miss you, and Vivi will be disappointed that you won't be a more involved uncle."

"Don't worry, I'll be involved. The truth is, I want what you have. Well, not all this." Jackson waved around the office. "I want what you have with Vivi. And I want time to enjoy it. Mostly, I want peace. As much as I love you all, I need something and someone of my own. Worst that can happen is my plans fall through, and I start over again. Seems there are lots of second chances out there if you're not afraid to ask."

"Lucky for us."

"It's crazy to think about how much things have changed since Mom died." He glanced at the picture of his mother on David's credenza.

David followed his gaze and smiled. "For the first time in years, I feel like we'll all be okay without her. Cat's finally in a good relationship. I'm about to be a father. And you've put your own demons to rest."

"Speaking of demons, I saw Alison." Jackson sank deeper into the chair.

David's brows rose. "Where?"

"Online. I needed some kind of closure, so I went online and stalked some of her posts to see what her life looks like."

David's expression turned uncharacteristically meddlesome. "What did you glean from your snooping?"

"She's in love . . . with herself. Selfies galore, shopping posts, all bullshit. Not sure how I never saw how self-absorbed she was, but now that I do, I'm glad she's not my wife, and really glad we're not parents together. It would've been a disaster. In a twisted way, she made the right choice for all of us. It hurts to admit that, but given how messed up I've been, I can't honestly say I'd have been a good father. But I will be someday, when everything is right."

"I'm sure of it."

Oliver stepped into David's office. "Funds are transferred. Doug and his lawyer are on their way out. Shall we have lunch?"

"You two go ahead." Jackson stood. "I've got some things to take care of at home this afternoon."

Jackson tucked the envelope beneath his arm and said good-bye.

He bought a coffee at Grand Central and then took a seat on a Metro-North express train to Connecticut. Once settled, he opened the envelope and began reading the information David had pulled together on Vermont's child custody laws.

Gabby helped Luc out of his car booster seat and then walked him up the snowy walkway to Noah's front door for his first ever sleepover with his father. All morning her stomach had been flipping like a gymnast on the balance beam, and she felt as precarious, too. Yet each time doubts surfaced, she looked at her son's face, which beamed with excitement.

Noah, for all his faults, had persisted in his desire to play more of a role in Luc's life even after Gabby had made it clear that she would never, ever take him back.

It had taken Noah a week to admit that Jackson hadn't had that drink. Then it took another week and very strong signals from her lawyer (and, to a lesser extent, his) for him to accept that, even if Jackson were in town and dating Gabby, Noah didn't have sufficient evidence to support a winning claim that Gabby was reckless or unfit. After a few heated arguments, he'd finally agreed to meet with a mediator, and Gabby had successfully avoided shared custody by agreeing to a generous visitation schedule in exchange for a minimal amount of financial support.

She'd taken control of her life and, for the most part, felt better. Her only pang of regret involved Jackson. He crossed her mind on a daily basis, mostly in the quiet moments. She refrained from texting or calling. It'd be easier on him if he never heard from her again. But with Christmas on the horizon, she couldn't help but say a little prayer for his peace of mind and happiness. Hopefully he'd found a way to reconnect with his family instead and not given in to his urge to drink.

Gabby blew out a breath and knocked on the door. Noah opened it with a smile and looked right at Luc. "Hey, little man. You all set for the best night of your life?"

When Noah smiled like that, Gabby recalled how he'd sucked her under his spell at seventeen. He could make someone feel like she was the center of his universe—until she wasn't. Hopefully he wouldn't flake out on Luc the way he'd done with so many women. Then again, Luc would have to learn how to handle life's ups and downs like every kid in the history of the world.

"Here's his blanket, Bingo, and his bag. There's a toothbrush and nighttime pull-up. Sometimes he still wets the bed at night, so I thought I'd pack one for you. He might be nervous here because it's unfamiliar. Don't be surprised if he wakes up at night and cries out or something. If you need any help or anything, call me and I'll come right over. And don't give him chocolate after five or he'll never sleep. And he likes you to read at least three books, and—"

"Relax, Gabs." Noah took the bag from her hands. Although he'd accepted his defeat, he hadn't liked it. For now, he played things cool with her. Hopefully one day they'd be able to both let go of the past and be friends. "I got it covered. Everything will be fine."

Her nose tingled and she blinked back tears. Bending down, she gave Luc a bear hug. "You be good for Daddy, buster. Listen to all the rules, okay?"

"Okay, Mama." He tried to pull away, but she held him tighter.

"Let's do our nighttime kisses now since I won't be here later."

He nodded and then kissed her nose and forehead and she did the same. "I love you, sweet pea. See you tomorrow for lunch, okay?"

"Bye bye, Mama." Luc barely waved before barreling behind Noah's legs and into the house.

She stood frozen on the doorstep. Her throat hurt. "I've never been away from him since the day he was born."

"Enjoy the break." Noah patted her shoulder with an air of condescension. "I swear he'll be fine. I've got pizza and ice cream and Dory. We're all good."

"Okay." She still couldn't move. "I'll see you tomorrow at noon."

"See you tomorrow." Noah closed his door.

Gabby walked to her car and then sat at the wheel and cried. It took a few minutes for her to remember that this was good for Luc. To be grateful that she and Noah had found a compromise. To embrace the idea that she'd have a few nights of freedom each month when she could meet a friend for dinner, or sleep in, or go on a date. Not that there was anyone worth dating, but maybe one day.

The drive home—normally a five-minute ride—seemed to stretch on for an hour. She dreaded going home, having no idea what she'd do with herself all afternoon. Her dad had gone to some Rotary club event, so she'd be alone, rattling around the empty house.

Restlessly, she turned into her driveway and then, stunned by the sight of Jackson's Jeep, almost forgot to hit the brakes. She blinked and checked the Connecticut plates again to make sure her imagination hadn't just played a nasty trick.

When he stepped out of the car holding a bouquet of flowers, tears filled her eyes. No use trying to look pretty. She slid out of the truck cab and waved dumbly. "Hi."

"Hey." Jackson crossed to her and handed her the flowers, his eyes drinking her in. "I was hoping we could talk."

"Sure." She took the bouquet without taking her eyes off his face. So many questions raced through her mind, but all she could think to ask was, "How are you?"

"Better," he said. "Let's go inside. It's freezing out here."

"Okay." They walked toward the house, and again she fumbled for words. "Are you hungry?"

"No." He grinned, and her heart melted.

She walked to the kitchen, feeling self-conscious and awkward, like a preteen on a first date. She busied her hands by trimming the flower stems and putting the bouquet in a vase while Jackson took a seat at the table. With nothing left to do, she poured them both a glass of water and sat down.

In keeping with her default response to nerves, she teased him. "You sure came a long way for a conversation. You know, there's this thing called the phone . . ."

"I've never done anything the easy way, so why start now?" He leaned forward and grasped her hand. "Besides, I wanted to see you, and FaceTime wouldn't cut it."

"I'm glad to see you. You look good . . . healthy." Those words had been stuck in her throat since she'd seen the Jeep. She didn't want to move a muscle, desperate to preserve the moment for as long as possible.

He glanced around the room, appearing to take note of the red-ribboned wreath now hanging on the back door. "I know my arrival puts you in a tough spot with Noah, but I want to talk about that."

"Actually—"

"Hold that thought and listen. I have something . . . a Christmas present of a sort." Jackson pulled out a manila envelope. "I had David do a little research about Noah's rights. *If* I were drinking excessively and he could prove it, he might have some kind of leverage, but that's not the case. I swear I haven't had a drink since August twenty-ninth. That's almost four months ago. So I don't think I'm a serious threat to your custody situation. But beyond that, I know you don't want to live in fear of my needing a drink. Just so you know, Doc thinks one day I could occasionally enjoy a social drink, but I won't if that would cause you anxiety. I don't need it anymore. Honestly, I don't even miss it much these days. What I do miss is you."

Gabby's eyes glanced over the memo that David had written, and she thumbed through printouts of case law. "I can't believe you went to all this trouble. Thank you for caring, Jackson, but with you living so far away and the way you took off, I'm surprised you went through the effort."

Jackson's hopeful smile faded and his expression turned serious. "Last time I saw you was one of the worst days I can remember. A big part of me about gave up. But Noah, of all people, ended up intervening and the whole day became a major turning point for me. The long drive home gave me time to think about everything. As a result, I'm making a lot of changes, and one of them depends on you."

"Me?" Her pulse began to race. "How?"

"Between speaking with Doc all month and reminiscing with David and Cat, I've recalled a bunch of stuff I'd forgotten . . . or not so much forgotten as buried. The bottom line is that I've realized a lot of things I'd put into place weren't actually making me happy. I'd chased after a big bank balance instead of focusing on things that really matter to me.

"Between the crazy project schedule, the terrible choices in women, and the drinking, I'd pretty much turned my back on who I am. But I won't do that anymore. I'm transitioning my current business to another contractor and then I'm moving out of Fairfield County and starting someplace fresh. Someplace inexpensive. And someplace where I think I can be happy."

She'd been holding her breath. "Where?"

"My first choice is here. I know I can be happy with a small remodeling business that leaves me plenty of time for hiking, fishing, reading, and spending time with you and Luc. But if you're afraid of my drinking history and don't want the risk, I'll find another place."

"You want to move to Vermont?" Her heart pumped hard inside her chest.

"I want to be where you are. And I think you know I'm crazy about Luc," Jackson joked, then glanced around. "Where is he, anyway?"

"He's with Noah."

Jackson's eyes widened. "Has he already taken you to court?"

"No." Gabby shook her head. "We came to an agreement. I've got sole custody, but he has regular visitation with Luc. Tonight is Luc's first sleepover there."

"How do you feel about that?" He touched her hand again.

"Terrified." She bit her lip.

He paused, and she could tell that he was quickly assessing his own thoughts.

"I think it's the right thing. David says establishing paternity is important for a lot of things, like survivorship benefits, medical stuff, not to mention Luc's sense of identity." Jackson frowned then, looking disappointed. "So, maybe my being here will make waves when this truce is still fresh. I don't want to cause any trouble for you."

"Noah realizes he can't control my personal life through Luc. The lawyers and mediator warned him the court wouldn't look kindly on that manipulation, either. I think he knows he went too far."

"Oh." Jackson's expression brightened. "Then all I need to know is whether or not you still care about me."

"Do you even need to ask? I fell for you that second day, when you built Luc's swing set, and nothing's changed for me since then."

"But you did want me to take more time. I'm not a patient guy, though, and I don't need time to know how I feel about you. Still, if you need more time . . ."

"I am concerned about the drinking, but I believe you when you say you've got it under control. You've never broken your word to me, which is more than I can claim. Given the way I let you down, are you sure you want to change your whole life for me?"

"I'm not doing it all just for you, but I'm sure I want you to be in the picture."

"I can't believe you're really sitting here saying all this." Finally she let the tears fall.

"Believe it, Gabby, and let me be part of yours and Luc's lives."

She leapt onto his lap. "I was having the worst day until I pulled into the driveway. Now I'm so happy. I might make it through my first night without Luc without falling apart."

Jackson cupped her face and kissed her, and her entire body melded against his. It all seemed like a too-good-to-be-true dream—a really vivid one. She'd spent so many nights remembering and missing these kisses. Yearning to be locked in the safety of his arms again. She could kiss this man forever, but her body cried out for more.

When she unbuttoned the first button of his shirt, he asked, "Where's your father?"

"Rotary club." She kissed him and unbuttoned another one.

"Maybe we should take this reunion to the apartment so we don't give him another stroke if he walks in." He nuzzled her neck.

"Good idea." She rose from his lap and snatched the apartment key from the junk drawer. "Race you."

# EPILOGUE

*May*

Jackson proudly took his place with Cat at the altar, standing beside David, Vivi, and little Graciela—*Gracie*—Marie St. James. David and Vivi had named their daughter after his mother, which she would've loved. His mom had adored Vivi from the first time she'd come for a sleepover in eighth grade, and although she would never meet her firstborn grandchild, Jackson knew she would be her granddaughter's guardian angel.

Jackson laid his hand on Gracie as Vivi held her daughter's head over the baptismal font. Grace wailed when Father Fernando poured water over her head. Jackson covered a smile and then caught Cat grinning, too.

"She's fussy, like me," Cat whispered.

"We're all in trouble," he replied.

David and Vivi were too absorbed by their daughter's distress to pay much attention to Cat and Jackson's joking. He glanced at the pews and spotted Gabby, who was sitting with his father and Janet.

Jackson and his siblings had discussed the whole situation at length back in December and decided to find a way to put the past behind them for their mom's sake. She'd wanted the *whole* family to remain intact, including Dad and Janet, so they were working on accepting the fact that life can be messy and ugly, but blood is blood. Family works shit out and forgives each other.

Jackson needn't have worried about whether Gabby could handle his group. She might be young, but she was a tough survivor who handled his family like a champ.

"Gabby's super cute, Jackson." Cat elbowed him with a grin. "Bonus points for how she seems to be handling Dad and Janet."

"No kidding." He smiled, knowing that Gabby could handle almost anything.

After the christening, the family posed for photos. Jackson cradled Gracie in his arms. She smelled sweet and stared at him with her round, solemn eyes.

"She's always calm with you," Vivi complained. "It's not fair."

"It's 'cause she knows I've got her back." Jackson smiled at his niece, totally entranced by her.

"*I've* got her back, too!" Vivi laughed.

"Maybe I just smell better than you." Jackson wiggled his brows. "Or she likes my deep voice, which is ten times better than all that baby-talk jibber jabber you and David do."

"Gimme!" Cat held out her arms, impatient for her turn. She practically snatched the baby from Jackson, then brushed her nose against Gracie's cheek. "You are the most precious girl in the whole wide world."

"Not the most precious," Hank said as he sidled up beside Cat.

Jackson shook Hank's hand, happy that his sister had ended up with his best friend. Hank would faithfully take care of her, even when she turned into that hedgehog. They'd planned a small wedding for late summer, and had begun looking into surrogacy as an option to Cat's infertility.

Jackson waved Gabby over. His dad and Janet followed her.

Cat leaned in. "You haven't seen Janet since my engagement dinner, huh?"

"Nope."

"You okay?" Cat asked.

Gabby had taught Jackson a lot, the most important lesson being to choose happiness. He knew each step he'd taken this fall had set him on the path toward one day having the family he wanted.

"Mom wanted us to be a family, so I'm going to force myself to be okay." He slid his sister a glance. "If you can manage, so can I."

Gabby shyly approached everyone, all of whom she'd met briefly before the service, but this was her first family event.

"Thanks so much for coming, Gabby." Vivi hugged her. "I'm looking forward to getting to know you better. Jackson's had such wonderful things to say about you and your son. Sit with me at lunch and tell me about this run-down house he's renovating."

"Everyone thought he was crazy to buy it, but he got it dirt cheap, and it's going to be gorgeous when he's finished." Gabby winked at him, and he felt a surge of pride.

"He's always had a good eye for design." Vivi smiled. "We can't wait to visit."

"Any time, V." Jackson wedged himself between the two women and wrapped an arm around Gabby's shoulder. "Now, if you'll excuse us a sec."

He hustled Gabby away from the crowd. "You survived my dad and Janet."

"They were very polite, actually. Only made one remark about my age, but I think Janet meant it as a compliment."

"She *is* always trying to look your age instead of her own," Jackson grumbled.

"Be nice. Let everyone move on and be happy."

"I'm happy." Jackson kissed her. "You happy?"

"Very." She looked at Vivi, David, and Gracie. "You looked pretty comfortable holding your niece."

"Maybe one day we'll give Luc a little brother or sister."

"Please, no more unwed pregnancies for me," Gabby teased. "One's my limit."

"Okay. After a wedding, then." He smiled and kissed her, certain of her place in his life.

"Pretty sure of yourself there for someone who hasn't even asked what I want."

"If you're not interested," he teased, "then I guess I won't ever ask."

Gabby slapped his shoulder. "Don't joke about marriage. That's not nice."

"Who said I was nice?" He tickled her side.

Gabby gave him a sidelong glance, so he let her off the hook. He leaned close and whispered in her ear. "I'm not going to ask you here at the christening in front of my whole family, but I will be asking."

Her smile lit up the church and he almost wished he had the ring in his pocket. "Maybe I should leave you guessing a little while longer. I hate to be so boring and predictable."

"Just keep on being exactly who you are." He hugged her, making a vow right there before the altar. "That's all I'll ever need."

# ACKNOWLEDGMENTS

I have many people to thank for helping me bring the St. James family to all of you, not the least of which include my family and friends for their continued love, encouragement, and support.

Thanks, also, to my agent, Jill Marsal, as well as to my patient editors Chris Werner and Krista Stroever, and the entire Montlake family for believing in me, and working so hard on my behalf.

A special thanks to Angela Lafrenz, a fan and nurse practitioner, who answered all of my questions about stroke victims. To the extent I've made mistakes, they are mine alone! Also, many thanks to Chris Glabach of Vermont Escapes, who graciously described the ins and outs of running a home-caretaking business in the Stratton, Vermont area.

My Beta Babes (Christie, Siri, Katherine, Suzanne, Tami, and Shelley) are the best, always providing invaluable input on various drafts of this manuscript. Also, thanks to Heidi Ulrich for the hours she spent critiquing the story.

And I can't leave out the wonderful members of my CTRWA chapter (especially my MTBs, Jamie Pope, Jamie Schmidt, Jane Haertel, Denise Smoker, Heidi Ulrich, Jen Moncuse, Tracy Costa, Linda Avellar, Katy Lee, and Gail Chianese). Year after year, all of the CTRWA members provide endless hours of support, feedback, and guidance. I love and thank them for it as well.

Finally, and most importantly, thank you, readers (especially those who have been writing to me inquiring about Jackson's story), for making my work worthwhile. With so many available options, I'm honored by your choice to spend your time with me.

AN EXCERPT FROM

# Before I Knew

## (BOOK 1 IN THE CABOTS)

*Editor's Note: This is an uncorrected excerpt and may not reflect the finished book.*

# PROLOGUE

*Two years ago*

O f all the dilemmas Colby Cabot-Baxter had faced in her twenty-eight years, none had tormented her like this one. It didn't help that, unlike many spring mornings in Lake Sandy, Oregon, the sun peeked through the clouds now, causing the fine mist coating the grass to glitter. Normally she'd savor the reprieve from the dank air that settled beneath the skin, but today she would've welcomed its bite.

Although warm inside the car, Colby shivered while frowning at the sun. Through the passenger window, she watched the mourners entering the church. Heads bowed, shoulders hunched, looking as if the weight of their grief might tip them forward.

A fleeting image of Joe's rugged face from days earlier, just before he and her husband, Mark, had set off on a hike, flashed.

She'd grown up trading smiles with Joe across the backyard fence. He'd had a broad smile that showcased the gap between his front teeth. The gap he'd used to squirt water at her sometimes just to be irksome. They'd been buddies—coconspirators, even—sneaking into the tree house their fathers had built in the nearby woods to spy on or torment their older brothers, depending on their moods.

Five years ago, when Joe had welcomed her then-new husband into his circle, Colby had been tickled, especially in light of the cooler reception Mark had received from her brother, Hunter. Of course, now she rather wished Joe hadn't liked Mark so well.

Her eyes misted again, like the dew-covered earth, as her throat tightened.

Mark's movement beside her snapped her back to the decision she couldn't put off any longer.

"Wait." She clutched Mark's forearm as he prepared to open his door. "This is a mistake."

"Joe was my best friend. I need to pay my respects." Mark's crystalline blue eyes widened in defiance beneath thick, straight eyebrows. Innocent-looking eyes that belied his often convoluted thoughts.

"He was my friend, too." She loosened her grip but left her hand resting on his arm. Whatever the weakened state of their marriage, she wouldn't compound his misery by arguing. At least, not today. Gentling her voice, she added, "But maybe we shouldn't add to his family's grief by showing our faces."

Mark's jaw clenched. "You mean *my* face, don't you?"

Reflexively, she shrugged, then wished she hadn't. Mark's eyes dimmed at the silent accusation.

"Mark," she said, her voice barely audible, but then couldn't think of what else to say.

Heavy silence, the kind weighted down by unspoken sentiment, consumed the car. In the trees near the church, she noticed a black-headed grosbeak eating from a bird feeder, acting as if the world hadn't been indelibly altered.

If only that were true.

"You can't blame me more than I blame myself," Mark finally muttered. "You think I don't wish that I would've kept hiking past

Punchbowl Falls without shooting off my mouth? But it's done. I dared, he jumped, and here we are. I can't hide from it, and neither can you. I have to go say good-bye to my friend, Colby, and I'd like your support."

Tears welled in her eyes. Saying good-bye to Joe would be hard enough. But walking into that church to face Joe's parents and his brother, Alec, seemed an impossible task. "My mother warned me against it. She's been neighbors with the Matthewses for thirty years, and even *she* feels awkward about coming."

Alec had even kept Hunter at arm's length yesterday evening at the funeral home, so he surely wouldn't welcome Mark or her today.

"I'm going. You can wait here if you want." He tugged his arm free and opened the door, letting the cool air rush inside.

Colby sighed. She exited the car, squaring her shoulders and lifting her chin. Mark reached for her hand, which she grudgingly offered. Perhaps her subconscious knew that being dragged inside might be the only way she'd cross the threshold.

They'd barely stepped through the door when Alec's unerring gaze fell on Mark. Normally Alec smiled when he saw her, but today his mouth remained fixed in a grim line, and his green eyes mirrored the mossy color of Lake Sandy on a cloudy day. Grief had carved lines into his handsome face, giving more depth to his boyish good looks. His chestnut hair fell across his forehead thanks to the cowlick he could never quite tame.

She wrestled free of Mark's grip when Alec began his approach. Words clogged her throat making it hard to swallow, much less speak. She opened her arms to greet him with a hug, but he brushed past her and walked straight up to Mark.

Alec stood at least two inches taller than her husband. As a teen, he'd been somewhat lanky, but he'd grown into his body as he'd matured. Now he looked powerful, confident, and angry.

"Please leave before my father sees you." Alec's typically soothing voice carried an edge today that scraped against her skin like a rug burn.

"I've apologized to your family." Mark didn't flinch. "You have to forgive me, Alec. You know I loved Joe like a brother."

"Lucky for me *we're* not so close." He spared her a brief glance. "Please take him and go, Colby. You know this isn't right."

When their gazes locked, she noticed a cold, yawning distance in his eyes that had never before existed. The loss of warmth hit her deep in her chest, even though she'd always taken their friendship more or less for granted. "I'm sorry. We don't want to cause you more pain."

She reached for Mark's arm, but he shrugged her off. "I'll sit in the back of the church and slip out early, but I'm staying. Joe would want me here."

"Would he, really?" Alec gritted his teeth. "We wouldn't even be here if it weren't for you."

Colby's heart sank because she saw the flicker of heat in Mark's eyes that warned he was about to do or say something awful. Before she could pull him away, he snarled, "We both know he'd want me here over you. Maybe if it weren't for what you did, he wouldn't have been so eager to go on that hike, or take that dare."

Pain—bitter, brutal anguish—arrested Alec's features. She had no idea what Mark had meant, but apparently Alec did. Colby reached out to comfort him, but retreated when he snapped, "Get. Out. Now."

Other mourners had started to stare at the two men despite the fact that, until Alec's outburst, they'd kept their voices low. Colby heard whispers, saw shaking heads. "Mark, let's go."

She yanked his arm, forcing him to bend to her will just this once. He ripped free of her grip and stalked to the car. Before he opened its door, he punched the roof and bellowed at the sky. By the time she took her seat, Mark's head was in his hands, his shoulders shaking. Sniffling, he then repeatedly banged his forehead against the steering wheel while muttering, "I'm sorry. I'm sorry. I'm sorry."

Colby sat beside her husband in the wake of his palpable suffering and cried.

She cried for all the years Joe would miss. She cried for the unbearable pain she imagined Mr. and Mrs. Matthews enduring. She cried for Alec's tortured history with his brother that may or may not have contributed to Joe's fatal decision. And she cried for the empathy she could not feel for her husband.

For the last bit of love that seemed to have died right along with Joe.

# ABOUT THE AUTHOR

*Photo © 2013 Lora Haskins*

Jamie Beck is a former attorney with a passion for inventing realistic and heartwarming stories about love and redemption, including her popular St. James and Sterling Canyon series. In addition to writing novels, she enjoys dancing around the kitchen while cooking, and hitting the ski slopes in Vermont and Utah. Above all, she is a grateful wife and mother to a very patient, supportive family. Fans can learn more about her on the web at www.jamiebeck.com and on Facebook at www.facebook.com/JamieBeckBooks.